Sydney Bauer has worked as a journalist and TV executive. While Director of Programming for a major Australian network, Sydney was able to indulge a personal passion for US dramas such as *CSI*, *Law and Order* and *24* and meet with revered TV writers such as Steven Bochco.

Also by Sydney Bauer

Undertow
Gospel
Alibi
Matter of Trust

MOVE TO STRIKE

SYDNEY BAUER

PAN
Pan Macmillan Australia

To Brian – my 'Arthur'

First published 2009 in Macmillan by Pan Macmillan Australia Pty Limited
This Pan edition published 2010 by Pan Macmillan Australia Pty Limited
1 Market Street, Sydney

National Library of Australia
Cataloguing-in-Publication data:

Bauer, Sydney.

Move to strike / Sydney Bauer.

978 0 330 42555 1 (pbk.)

A823.4

Typeset in 10/13 pt Birka by Post Pre-press Group, Brisbane, Queensland
Printed in Australia by McPherson's Printing Group.

Papers used by Pan Macmillan Australia Pty Limited are natural, recyclable products made from wood grown in sustainable forests. The manufacturing processes conform to the environmental regulations of the country of origin.

ACKNOWLEDGEMENTS

As always there are so many people to thank.

First up a huge thank you to all at Pan Macmillan – James Fraser, Kylie Mason, Jane Novak and especially my publisher and friend Cate Paterson.

Thanks also to Harvey Klinger.

To my amazing friends in Boston including: Boston Municipal Court's Christopher Connolly and the wonderful Superior Court's Dana Leavitt – one of the smartest, kindest people I have ever had the pleasure of meeting; Jake Wark and the legendary Tom O'Reilly for allowing me to pick their experienced prosecutorial brains; Marcia Izzi and all at the Boston ME's Office for their learned advice and sunny dispositions; the DYS's Mary Sylva and Fred White – who not only taught me all there is to know about juvenile justice in Massachusetts but also showed me the 'rock'. A special thanks to David Yannetti – my real life David Cavanaugh; Kevin Molis – my very own Joe Mannix; and John Sorese, the man I was lucky enough to sit next to on a plane.

To Dr John Donnellan – a brilliant physician, sharp-shooting firearms expert and friend rolled into one.

To my friends and family – a big thank you for your support. And most importantly to Jarrod for steering me through the most difficult of plot twists both in these pages and not, and Claudia, who feeds the squirrels in Boston Common with peanuts and me with hope and inspiration and love.

PROLOGUE

Saturday 10 February

'Remind me why I am here again,' said Boston Police Department's Homicide Unit Chief Joe Mannix as he tugged at the too-tight bow tie around his neck. It was almost eight and pre-dinner drinks had been flowing for well over an hour – the noise level in Boston's impressive Four Seasons Hotel ballroom increasing with every glass of Veuve Clicquot.

'Ah . . . well,' began Joe's good friend, Boston criminal defence attorney David Cavanaugh. 'I'll start with the fact that I spent my entire last weekend shovelling snow from your driveway, and then, let's see, there was that little matter of my helping you push your SUV down said driveway so I could charge it with jumper leads from *my* LandCruiser which saw *your* car purring like a kitten and *my* battery left flatter than the beer at the Idle Hour,' he finished, referring to Joe's less than savoury drinking haunt in South Boston.

'The beer at the Idle tastes just fine,' said Joe. 'And

you should stop complaining. In the very least I was kind enough to give you a lift home.'

'In *your* SUV,' smiled David. 'Which I have no doubt is still purring like a . . .'

'Kitten?' interrupted a now grinning Joe. 'Nah – more like a contented tiger, or a jaguar ready to pounce.'

'There you go,' smiled David as he accepted another beer from a passing waiter.

The room was packed. The close to 4000 square foot high-ceilinged space was now overflowing with 300 men in dinner suits and women in ball gowns who swept in and out of the ornately decorated tables with all the elegance and urgency that networking at high-powered events such as these required.

The annual Massachusetts Law Society St Valentine's Day Ball was a major asterisk on Boston's legal fraternity calendar – the first chance since New Year's to don the finery and make contact with old friends, new acquaintances and, more importantly for many, stroke the egos of those they either needed to impress on one hand, or intended to exploit on the other.

When David's boss, Arthur Wright, of Wallace, Wright and Gertz, begged off the annual do for the second year in a row, and David's pregnant partner Sara announced she was flying south to see her birth mom in Atlanta for the weekend, David had roped his good pal Mannix into playing his 'date' for the evening – figuring that if he was going to suffer mingling with the 'in' crowd for close to four hours, then at the very least his detective friend could repay the previous weekend's disaster by graciously sharing the 'pain'.

'David,' said a voice from behind.

David turned to see his good friend and fellow Boston College Law School grad Tony Bishop move towards him with his arm outstretched. 'Hey, Tony,' said David. 'You remember Joe?'

'Sure,' replied the good-looking Bishop, wearing a designer tux David knew would have cost the blue chip corporate attorney a cool four figures. 'It's good to see you again, Lieutenant. Although, judging by the look on your face, I'm guessing you are here under sufferance.'

'More like torturance,' replied Joe with a smile. 'And if that's not a word it should be – simply to describe how a cop like me feels at a five-star schmooze fest such as this.'

And they laughed.

Fifteen minutes later, dinner was served – a four-course feast which began with an entrée of salmon marinated with lightly smoked wild fennel, followed by roast octopus tartare with avocado, tomato and spring onion, progressing to a wild mushroom crusted filet mignon with truffle jus, and finishing with a dessert of lemon fallen soufflé tart with coconut ice cream.

The room appeared to sparkle inside and out. Four crystal chandeliers hung like diamonds from the silver leaf ceiling complementing the fairy lights strung on the now leafless trees outside the windows. The imported silk drapes had been pulled back to reveal the snow-drenched expanse of the sculptured Public Gardens and beyond.

'You've done it now,' said Tony Bishop, pointing to an anxious-faced woman who was arguing with a hotel employee about some sort of problem with the seating.

'Jesus, Tony,' said David, taking another sip of his European beer. 'They put me and Joe on a table with Roger Katz for Christ's sake.' The ambitious Suffolk County Assistant District Attorney was an old opponent and egotistical ass who both David and Joe were more than comfortable despising.

'True,' said Tony. 'But switching name cards is more than just a little juvenile, DC,' he smiled, still referring to David by his college nickname after all these years.

'Having said that,' Tony continued, 'I've just noticed that Amanda Carmichael is sitting across from Katz which gets me to thinking that maybe *I* should have been the one screwing with the seating allocations from the get-go. That woman is smart, driven and . . .'

'Not bad to look at either,' said David, who knew that every red-blooded male in the ballroom had checked out the twenty-something ADA Carmichael, whose normally well-secured long blonde hair now fell loose down her pale, bare-skinned back.

'You think?' smiled Tony, who had always had the ability to not only target, but more often than not leave, with the best looking woman in the room. 'I hear she broke up with that high-powered ass from the Attorney General's Office.'

'I hear that ass talked Scaturro into promoting her to Katz's second-in-charge in Scaturro's absence,' offered David, referring to the current Suffolk County District Attorney Loretta Scaturro who, late last year, had taken extended leave to look after her Alzheimer's stricken mother.

'A girl's gotta do what a girl's gotta do,' smiled Tony.

'As long as she does it with you, am I right, Bishop?' said David.

Tony grinned. 'I'll be on my way to pay my respects then,' he said, using a napkin to wipe his mouth before rising from his cream silk chair to head towards the other side of the room.

'At least he's consistent,' said David, returning his attention to Joe.

'Regular as sunshine in August.'

'Hello,' said a soft voice, and David turned to see a thin, pale-skinned woman now perching in Tony's vacated seat beside him.

'It's Stephanie,' she said with a smile, obviously realising David had failed to recognise her. 'Stephanie Tyler from . . .'

'College,' finished David, taking her hand – surprised by the narrowness of her face, the coldness of her grip and the whisper-like texture of her voice. 'My God, Stephanie, you look . . .' He wanted to say fantastic but in all honesty the woman before him appeared a smaller, meeker shadow of the vibrant, boisterous girl he remembered from law school. But then he saw the spark in her bright blue eyes, and the memories came rushing back.

'Gosh it's good to see you,' he said – and he meant it. 'This is my friend Lieutenant Joe Mannix. Joe's a cop who works homicide so be careful what you tell him.'

Joe reached across the table to shake her hand. 'Pleasure,' he said.

'Nice to see the force present at one of these do's, Lieutenant.'

'I owed dateless David here a favour,' explained Joe.

'Ah. You *are* a good friend then,' she smiled.

'Not that good,' said Joe. 'I'm heading to the bar, if I'm not back in ten you can send out a search party.'

'You bail on me and I'll kill you, Mannix.'

'And you see the irony in that, don't you?'

'I guess I do.'

David moved his chair so that he might face his old friend.

'You look good, David,' Stephanie said. 'How long has it been – thirteen years, fourteen?'

'More like seventeen,' he said. 'In fact the last time I saw you I think we were trying to work out a way to explain to your father how we had commandeered his cruiser, broken the steering equipment, flooded the motor with gasoline and . . .'

'Failed to check the fuel gauge so that we . . .'

'Ran out of gas about fifteen minutes into our clandestine trip,' he finished with a laugh.

'We made you swim back. Do you remember?' she smiled.

'Do I ever – a good mile to the jetty with an empty petrol tin strapped to my back. I remember getting about a quarter of the way and looking back to see you and Tony and Karin laughing yourselves senseless on the top deck.'

'We got seriously drunk,' she laughed.

'And I got the nastiest head cold I'd had in years.'

This was fun, David thought, as his mind cast back to a time when he and his first wife Karin double-dated with Stephanie Tyler and Tony Bishop. Karin was David's first love – his teenage pre-med-student sweetheart who he married at nineteen and divorced at twenty-three after she fell in love with a bigwig Washington surgeon by the name of Professor Stuart Montgomery. And Tony Bishop – the same tall, dark and handsome attorney who was currently sweet-talking Amanda Carmichael mere feet away, was Stephanie's ex – the two of them genuinely in love, at least at the time.

'Tony was just here,' said David, thinking aloud. 'Did you . . .?'

'Yes, I noticed,' she said, gesturing at the obviously preoccupied Bishop. 'Hasn't lost his touch then?' she joked.

'Tony always knew a beautiful woman when he saw one, Stephanie.'

'I'll take that as a compliment then,' she said.

'Please do.' He smiled.

'I was so sorry to hear about your father,' he said, referring to Malcolm Tyler, sole owner of one of the most successful, independently owned wineries in the country. David had read that Tyler, a single father to his only child Stephanie, had died in an unfortunate boating accident some time late last year.

'Thank you,' she said, taking a breath. 'At least he died doing what he loved best.'

David nodded, noticing her wide blue eyes fill momentarily with the slightest tinge of sorrow.

'So tell me,' she said. 'What have you been up to? Not that I haven't been following your successes – the Martin Trial, Montgomery and the Matheson thing last year.'

'I'm about to become a father,' he said, feeling the need to tell his old friend the most important new development in his life. 'My partner Sara is a couple of months pregnant – she's in Atlanta for the weekend. You two would get on like a house on fire, Stephanie. She works with me at our firm and, well . . . things are good.'

'Oh that's just wonderful,' she said. 'Parenthood is the best, David. I know. I've done it twice.'

'Your kids must be all grown up now,' he said, recalling that Stephanie married and had children not long after she left college.

'Chelsea just turned sixteen and J.T. is thirteen.'

'Unbelievable,' said David.

'Time flies,' she said, her eyes glistening once again – perhaps with a sense of sorrow at the momentum life had forced upon her.

'And your work?' asked David then, sensing a change of subject was in order. 'The last thing I heard you accepted some big job at Cunningham, Eather and Groves. Not that you didn't have a million offers out of college, with your grades and . . .'

'I was in corporate development,' she interrupted him. 'Oh it was terrific, David, interesting, demanding – a real challenge. But I was only there a year when I met Jeffrey and got married and had kids and . . . long story short, now I run a small practice from home, servicing local businesses and the like.'

David got the sense that Stephanie Tyler was almost ashamed of her lack of career advancement – ashamed or regretful, or maybe just resolved.

'My husband works long hours, you see,' she said, as if in justification. 'And he travels to and from the west coast – he's in television.'

'I know.' David smiled. 'When Tony heard you married the famous Doctor Jeff,' he said, referring to Stephanie's husband, the popular TV talk show psychologist Doctor Jeffrey Logan, 'he didn't eat for a week.'

'Or until the next eligible bachelorette came along,' she said, and smiled.

'Fair point,' laughed David.

'In the very least he's . . .'

'. . . *consistent*,' they said together – and then laughed.

David looked at her, her long neck thrown back in that familiar joviality – her deep, enthusiastic, slightly guttural laugh filling him with memories from not so much *happier*, but definitely *easier* times. People's lives didn't always end up as you expected, he thought.

If anyone had asked him years ago who would have been the most likely of their BC graduate year to conquer the world, he would have named this bright-eyed, auburn-haired, sharp-minded woman hands down.

But here she was before him, looking small and fragile and meek – and while David could totally understand her decision to give up her career for family, respect it even, he wondered why she, of all people, appeared so defeated by the choices she had made.

'Anyway,' she said, taking his hand once again and this time squeezing it slightly in a gesture that told him how pleased she was to have run into him, 'I had better find Jeffrey. Despite the fact that I am the lawyer in the family I am afraid he is the one who scored us a seat on the head table – and my absence, while perhaps not missed, will be duly noted.'

'It's been great to see you, Stephanie,' said David. 'In fact, Sara and I, we would love to have you over some time to . . .'

'Catch up?' She smiled. 'Of course,' she added, but her head was already shaking in the negative.

'We'll see each other soon then,' he said as she got up to leave. 'We'll keep in touch.'

PART ONE

1

Friday 11 May
Three months later

'Who's in charge here?' asked Lieutenant Joe Mannix as he lifted the yellow crime tape that cut off half of the narrow street so that he and his fellow Boston homicide detective Frank McKay could duck under and push forward towards the house.

'O'Donnell,' shouted the rookie, a kid named Reno who was sharp and ready to please. 'We secured the scene as soon as we could,' he continued to yell above the din. 'But the media picked it up on the wires. They noted the address. Were here before we could even . . .'

'*Reno*,' yelled another cop, Reno's partner, an older officer named Schiff. 'The animals are encroaching,' he said, lifting one arm to shield his eyes from the TV lights and the other to point at the barrage of five, six, maybe more 'live transmission' vans now blocking the well-preserved roadway and making it close to impossible for police and other 'official' vehicles to get either in or out.

'I need you over here. I need . . . Oh, sorry, Lieutenant,'

said Schiff, recognising Joe. 'I didn't see you there. These lights are enough to . . .'

'Lieutenant, Detective,' interrupted a third police officer from behind. It was Sergeant Patrick O'Donnell, the most senior uniform on site.

'O'Donnell,' said Joe and Frank as they all shook hands.

'We've secured the scene,' said O'Donnell, now falling into step with the two detectives, turning back the way he had come. 'The crime lab guys are already at work. Parked their vans out back.'

'There's a back?' asked Joe.

'Yeah,' answered O'Donnell as they reached the house. 'A narrow garage at the rear.'

'Schiff,' said O'Donnell, turning to the older of the two officers moving with them. 'I need you to keep those people back.' He gestured at the 'audience' with his thumb. 'The ME's technicians can't fit their truck around the back entrance. We are going to have to bring the body out front and I don't want these people gawking . . . *Oh shit*,' said O'Donnell, now noticing the hubbub from above. 'Helicopters,' he said, craning his neck to look beyond the roof. 'Our job is hard enough without all these parasites breathing down our necks.'

'Who the hell is this guy?' snuffled Frank McKay at last, as Schiff and Reno waved off and made their way back down the footpath. Frank had a heavy chest cold and O'Donnell instinctively moved a foot away so as not to catch his breath.

'Sorry,' he said. 'I'm on leave as of Monday and the missus will kill me if I'm sneezing my way through

Florida. We're taking the grandkids on vacation – me at Disney World, if you can believe that.'

O'Donnell took a breath. It was an old cop coping mechanism Joe knew, reminding anyone in earshot that life went on beyond the gruesome catastrophes of their profession. O'Donnell was a little shaken, Joe sensed, which meant this one must be worse than the usual. Not that the usual was ever actually anything near usual in your average guy's stretch of the imagination.

'Jeffrey Logan,' said O'Donnell, back on the beat, answering Frank's original question. 'As in Doctor Jeff, TV psychologist extraordinaire.'

'The relationship guru with the talk show?' said Frank. 'Jesus, my wife loves that guy.'

'I thought the vic was a female?' said Joe, getting them back on track as they took the sandstone front steps of the three-storey Beacon Hill brownstone two at a time. The crime scene traffic was thick and fast, the echo of police radios beeping and scratching beyond the front entranceway.

'Sorry,' said O'Donnell. 'She is. She's the doc's wife. One Stephanie Tyler. She's an attorney – works from home.'

'A lawyer,' said Mannix, the name ringing a bell.

'Yeah, graduated magna cum laude of BC if the certificate on her office wall is anything to go by.'

And then he remembered.

They pushed into the hallway.

'So what's the story?' asked Joe, trying to visualise the small-framed redhead he had met briefly a mere three months ago. His eyes danced over the expensively decorated rooms around him: the original artwork on the walls, the antique rugs under their feet, the European furniture, subtle lighting, heavy drapes and flower-filled vases.

O'Donnell flipped open his notepad. 'Stephanie Tyler, thirty-eight. COD single gunshot wound to the chest. The weapon was a Mark V DGR, the calibre a .460 Weatherby Magnum.'

'DGR?' asked Frank.

'Dangerous game rifle,' replied O'Donnell.

'So not for rabbits,' said Frank.

'Not unless they have a trunk and a pair of long ivory tusks to go with it.'

O'Donnell, Mannix and McKay put their backs to the hallway wall, allowing two crime scene guys to shuffle past with a nod. Joe noticed the looks on their faces. This one *was* bad, he could smell it.

'This way,' said O'Donnell, leading them towards the back of the house. 'Vic was shot at the kitchen table while drinking a Shiraz and reading an old issue of *Vanity Fair*. The wine was one of her family's, by the way. Tyler was the heir to the Rockwell Winery fortune.' O'Donnell let this little fact hang, not attaching it to anything as yet, most likely because he was not too sure where, or even if, it might fit.

'Shot came from just inside the kitchen door. Point blank. Bang!' he said, kicking a louvred door open with his foot as they left the house through a side passageway and headed south once again.

'Jesus, O'Donnell,' said Mannix. 'What's with the merry maze?'

'We need to approach from the side. The evidence

guys are all over the blood spatter patterns near the back of the kitchen.'

'Okay,' said Joe, as they rounded the back courtyard which led down to a terraced entertaining area. Big by anyone's standards, but huge for a home in historic Beacon Hill – four mill-plus price tag or not.

'Where's the family?' asked Frank.

O'Donnell shook his head. 'That's why I took you round the side way,' he said, lifting his leg over a crouched crime scene worker huddled over a metallic case carrying fingerprint lifting powders and brushes. 'This one, I swear, it has to be seen to be believed.'

They reached the side bi-fold doors and stepped into the kitchen. The image before Joe and Frank nearly blew them away. The back wall of the room was covered in blood and other bodily chunks. The pool of blood on the floor was massive – Joe guessed over four litres – and was now congealing on the tasteful limestone floor. The kitchen benches were covered in spatter, the shiny stainless steel sink now patterned with deep red tracks of fluid that had hit and slithered down its squeaky clean sides. There was even a hole the size of a melon through the under-sink cupboard where a bullet had obviously passed before smashing through the double-brick wall behind.

'Jesus,' said Joe.

'It gets worse,' said O'Donnell, gesturing towards the middle of the room.

Within seconds Joe could see he was right. The victim, Stephanie Tyler, was sitting on a white wicker chair, her entire body arched backwards so that her pale thin arms draped awkwardly over the sides of her chair.

From behind, it looked like she had been pulverised, the hole between what would have been her shoulder blades at least the size of a soccer ball. The blast must have hit her in the chest from the front and had enough force to shoot her chair backwards at least four feet into the middle of the room.

'What the hell kind of calibre are we talking here, O'Donnell?' asked Joe, blinking his eyes at a photographer's flash before refocusing on the police sergeant before him.

'Not that I'm any expert, but Schiff, who knows a thing or two about this shit, tells me the .460 Weatherby is the most powerful calibre in the world. It, and the fancy customised rifles that fire it, are designed for those rich assholes who take pleasure in jumping a plane to Africa and facing off against charging elephants from less than a hundred feet away. The recoil on the bastard is something fierce.'

Joe nodded, taking the information in.

'Where's the family?' asked Frank again.

O'Donnell shook his head once more. 'I told you this one was a doozy,' he replied, before directing them around a cooking island and into the kitchen proper.

'They haven't moved since we arrived,' he said. 'Doctor Jeff and his two kids refused to do so until he spoke to a detective of rank. To be honest, it has suited us fine, given their lack of movement is preserving the crime scene. Still, when you check this out you will wonder why the hell a father would . . .'

And then they saw it. Three people sitting at the kitchen table – evening out the fourth who had been shot across the room like a rocket.

Across from the mom, at the far end of the table, in front of the kitchen door, sat a young boy of no more than thirteen. His eyes were closed tight, his baggy white long-sleeved T-shirt singed at the shoulder and patterned with tiny spots of his mother's blood.

Next to him, on his right, sat his father, the famous one – straight-backed, eyes unblinking, staring ahead at nothing in particular. He looked remarkably polished compared to the boy, his shirt crisp, his hair neat, his hands in his lap and his chest withdrawn as if afraid to be tainted by the spatters that had settled on the table before him.

Across from him sat the daughter – a pretty ginger-haired teenager who, Joe guessed, would have been about sixteen. She, like her father, appeared relatively 'clean', but was set apart from the other two, simply because she was the only one crying.

'*Jesus*,' said Frank.

'I know,' said O'Donnell, before approaching the table from the left. 'Doctor Logan,' he called out in a voice which suggested the doctor was hard of hearing. 'These are two detectives. Lieutenant Mannix here is the commander of the Homicide Unit at Boston PD. As high as you can go on the ladder of – well, what he does.'

O'Donnell was about to say the 'ladder of death' which is how they referred to the hierarchy in BP homicide. But under the circumstances he had decided not to state the obvious.

'Doctor Logan,' said Joe, approaching the table without compromising the crime scene now mapped out by laser lights before him, his eyes flicking back towards the dent in the white kitchen door, his foot stepping over a hat stand that had obviously been knocked over by the blast.

'I'm Lieutenant Joe Mannix and this is Detective Frank McKay.'

Logan finally looked up from the table and nodded. 'I want to call a public defender,' he said, his voice low and even.

'You want to get up from the table and talk, Doctor?' asked Joe, taking another small step forward, wondering how long it would take to get a public defender on the scene at 9.45pm on a Friday night. 'It might be more appropriate if your children were taken somewhere other than . . .'

'No, I told them to sit here. I wanted us to stay together, as a family, at least until . . . I want someone to get my business partner,' said Logan, obviously linking two separate thoughts together. 'Her name is Katherine de Castro. She will be waiting out front. I called her after I dialled 911. She will look after the children.'

'Get de Castro,' said Joe to O'Donnell, making sure that Logan heard the instruction. Something told him he needed to play this one cool, step by step, inch by inch. The doc looked ready to blow and there were still two extremely traumatised kids in the room.

'Please, Doctor, you need to get up from the table so our tech guys can finish their job. Your children may need to be treated for shock.'

'I know,' said the handsome olive-skinned, pepper-haired man, before nodding at his two kids, a strange look of what Joe took to be pride in his large brown eyes. 'They have been very brave,' he added, using his legs to push the chair backwards and finally getting to his feet – and gesturing with his hands for his two children to do the same.

Joe's eyes shot to the son, the younger sibling with the telltale spatter covering his upper body. His eyes were still shut, a smear of blood he had wiped across his otherwise clean face now gluing his eyelashes together. Joe turned to Frank.

'Ring Cavanaugh,' he whispered, having made the decision. 'Get him here now.'

The paramedics moved in, and Joe pulled one of them aside quickly, issuing a short command before turning back to Logan.

'I'll have a defence attorney here within the half-hour, Doctor Logan,' he said. 'And while it is within your rights to remain silent until you have representation present, I have to advise you that it is also in your best interest to provide us with any relevant information regarding the incidents which led to your wife's death as quickly as possible.'

Joe looked up to see Boston Medical Examiner Gus Svenson enter through the now open bi-fold doors. Joe met Gus's eye and caught the brief expression of horror on his face, before the professional Swede nodded his head towards the victim. Joe nodded back, indicating that he was clear to get to work.

'I know this is difficult,' said Joe, returning his attention to the good looking TV star before him, noticing that his face was still thick with make-up from the afternoon's filming. 'But any information you can provide us now . . . anything you can . . .'

'I killed her,' he said, softly at first before repeating

it with gusto once again. 'I killed her. I shot my wife.' It was like a declaration. A statement of fact. 'It was an accident. My children were not involved,' he added as if needing to make a point.

'Doctor,' began Joe, shooting a quick glance at McKay. 'I . . .'

'I'll make a brief confession giving you the basic details, Lieutenant. But that's all I am willing to share until my attorney arrives,' interrupted Logan who, in that moment, turned to look at his dead wife once again before losing his footing and shuffling backwards to lean on the kitchen counter behind him. 'Is Ms de Castro here? I . . .'

Joe called for a paramedic who rushed forward.

'Don't worry, Doctor. We'll find her,' said Joe. 'In the meantime, why don't you take a load off until your attorney arrives. You talk with him and then he'll talk with us and then, we'll sort this out, all calm and civilised like – one way or another.'

2

'I don't believe this,' smiled Sara Davis, her face glowing in the muted candlelight. She was at the head of the white-clothed table when they brought out the cake – an old-fashioned ice-cream extravaganza in the shape of Cinderella's glass slippers, no less. 'You didn't!' she said, her aqua eyes looking across at her boyfriend and fellow attorney David Cavanaugh.

'Well I never,' said their office secretary and surrogate 'mother', the Irish-born Nora Kelly.

'Is someone going to fill me in on the joke here?' smiled their boss, mentor and friend Arthur Wright who rounded out their group of four. 'Or are we about to be joined by a five-year-old with a Disney fetish?'

'No,' laughed Sara, who had opted for the cosy North End Italian eatery Il Ristorante for her thirty-second birthday dinner. This was the first place David had taken her four years ago – a working dinner following his taking on the case to defend Sara's then boss, African–American civil rights attorney Rayna Martin, in a controversial murder trial. And it had been a special place for them ever since.

'It's just that . . .' she began, shaking her head at David.

'No,' interrupted David. 'We have to sing first, and then you have to blow out the candles, and then you have to make a wish, and then I will attempt to explain to Arthur and Nora why the thirty-two-year-old love of my life, an educated attorney no less, has a serious shoe fetish and once admitted to me that she had coveted Cinderella's glass slippers since she was two.'

'Not two,' she protested. 'I was three, maybe even four.'

'Well that explains it then,' grinned Arthur, lifting his wine in salute.

David looked across at her, as the restaurant owner, a cheerful elderly Italian named Milo, pulled out his violin so that he might play 'Happy Birthday' as Sara blew out the candles.

She was so strong, so beautiful, David thought as she threw her hands up in victory at having managed to blow out all thirty-two candles with one breath, a stray chestnut curl landing over her pale blue eyes, her complexion shining with happiness and health.

He did not know how she had managed it – how she had become the person that she was, so willing to accept life's shortcomings for what they were, and take on the causes she believed in – no matter what the cost. True, she was the product of a loving home, having been adopted as a baby by a white couple from Cambridge who later gave her a younger brother by the name of Jake – but she had always bore the slight insecurity that came from knowing her African–American birth mother was only seventeen when she slept with her nameless white biological father, one of many men her mother had 'been with' in order to survive.

'Strawberry,' she said, beaming up at Milo. 'My favourite.'

'Lucia lived on it during her five pregnancies,' smiled Milo, his Mediterranean accent still strong despite having lived in Boston for half of his sixty-two years.

'Does that mean I have no excuse after the baby is born?' she said, resting her hands on her belly.

'No, Signorina,' said Milo. 'It just means you and young David here get busy with the next one as soon as young Milo here is born.' He smiled, gesturing at Sara's swollen middle.

'Milo?' said Arthur. 'I thought you were naming the boy after me.'

'Boy?' said Nora in protest. 'No, Arthur. The little one is a girl who looks just like her mother. And we can all thank the Lord for that.'

'True,' said David with a grin; he and his beloved sixty-something PA shared a history of friendly sparring. 'Because if it was a boy, like me, his extremely high intelligence would have been repeatedly overshadowed by his incredible good looks. I hear Brad Pitt has to battle with that particular stumbling block 24/7.'

'God save us,' said Nora.

Sara smiled and pointed to David's cell phone which was muted but now vibrating on the table. 'It's okay,' she said, taking a big scoop of ice cream from her pale pink dessert. 'Pick it up. It might be Jake or my parents.'

'Or Angelina Jolie wanting to know where the hell I am.'

3

It was cold, the spring chill crisp in the late night air. David took off his scarf and wrapped it around Sara's neck as they jumped out of his LandCruiser, his silence a result of the shock at Joe's news and his frustration at not being able to persuade Sara to get a lift home with Arthur and Nora, his suggestion met by outright refusal from his stubborn partner who was clearly tiring of his growing tendency to treat her with kid gloves.

'I'm pregnant, David, not terminally ill,' she said as they made their way in and out of the haphazardly parked traffic towards the house. 'And besides, if you knew this woman I . . . I just want to be there in case you . . .'

'I'm fine, Sara,' he said, reaching for her hand and squeezing it. 'I hadn't seen her for years until we ran into each other a few months ago. But you are nearly six months pregnant, and from what Frank says,' he hesitated, his breath billowing fluorescent clouds of condensation into the over-lit yard. 'Stephanie was – I mean the crime scene is . . .'

'Which is why I'm staying,' she said, as they instinctively lowered their heads and quickened their pace past the bevy of media personnel, hoping they would not be recognised.

'I know,' he said, squeezing her hand once more before dropping it to guide her past a barricade on the far left-hand boundary of the house. He was recognised in seconds – his name called and then repeated by media representatives who were now grabbing cameras and shouting out questions and no doubt praying for some sort of official comment on the 'goings-on' inside.

David had earned himself quite a reputation over the past few years – taking on various seemingly unwinnable high-profile cases such as the Martin matter, *Montgomery vs the US*, and more recently, the *Commonwealth vs James Matheson*, in which David and Sara defended a young Ivy League student accused of killing his corporate heir girlfriend. And so his arrival at this scene – a setting the media were obviously hoping would provide the backdrop for the 'celebrity crime of the year' – was no doubt viewed as a welcome addition by the camera- and microphone-toting minions now jostling behind the yellow and black police barricades.

'David Cavanaugh and Sara Davis, here to see Lieutenant Joe Mannix,' called David to a uniform manning the front entryway, lifting his voice above the hubbub.

'Go ahead, Mr Cavanaugh,' said Reno, stealing a glance at Sara, his eyes automatically darting downwards to the mound beneath her overcoat. 'The lieutenant is expecting you.'

'I knew it,' said David as they entered the house. 'Even the rookie thinks this is a bad idea.'

'Oh for Christ's sake,' Sara said as another policeman led them towards the back of the house, the crowded hallway now covered in plastic, the lights casting odd shadows throughout the twisting corridor, the air tinged with the scent of alcohol. 'Just how bad can it be?'

But she stopped as they entered the bi-fold doors and took in the scene before them – the once-attractive woman, flattened against the back of her stylish kitchen chair, her skin now drained of colour, her middle barely held together by two bloody folds of ribcage on either side of her chest.

'David, I am so sorry,' she said, touching his elbow before collecting herself and waving at a now approaching Joe who had obviously seen them enter.

But David did not hear her. All he saw was the horror of the tragedy before him – the brutal onslaught of violence that had taken a life with so much promise, and ripped it from existence with hostility, with cruelty, with disrespect. And in that moment he felt an all-encompassing need to run to her – to take her hand and feel for a pulse and do something, *anything* to try to bring her back, which was ridiculous of course, considering the scene before him.

'I didn't mean to ruin your birthday,' said Joe as he reached them, talking to Sara but stopping right in front of David as if trying to protect him from the view of the victim, at least for a second or two. 'And I'm sorry, man,' he added, meeting David's eye. 'I know you two were friends.'

David nodded.

'Frank said the husband confessed,' replied Sara, now flicking her eyes towards David before refocusing on Joe, aware that David knew she was trying to snap him out of the shock of what lay before them, by forcing him to concentrate on the task at hand. 'Said it was an accident – that he shot her by mistake.'

'That's what he says,' said Joe.

'Where is he?' David asked. 'And does he want to talk?'

'In the living room,' replied Joe, leading them back outside the house and towards the path down the far western boundary. 'And I'm not sure how much he wants to say besides reiterating what he told us earlier.'

'And the kids?' asked David, having been briefed by Frank in the initial phone call about the two children's status.

'They're in the boy's bedroom. They're with the doctor's business partner, a TV exec by the name of Katherine de Castro. She is sitting all nervous like at the boy's desk while the two kids are straight-backed and silent like two petrified statues on the kid's bed.'

David and Sara nodded.

'Okay,' said Joe as they moved inside the house once again and reached the living room door. 'For what it's worth, I'm going to give you a brief snapshot of how I see this – but keep in mind the evidence guys have yet to do their analysis, and Svenson is waiting for them to finish up before he gets a decent look at the vic . . . Sorry, I mean, Ms Tyler,' he added, looking at David.

David nodded back, acknowledging Joe's efforts to show Stephanie the respect of personalisation. He and Sara both knew that until the ME arrived, no one moved the body – and when the ME got the go-ahead, he would do a 'minimal' examination so as not to upset the crime scene. Then it was back to the morgue, where the autopsy would be carried out either tomorrow or the next day, or considering it was Friday night, some time early next week, depending on Svenson's 'back-up'.

'The dad,' Mannix went on, 'the TV guy, says he was cleaning his hunting rifle in the garage and needed some extra rags from under the kitchen sink. Says he forgot the piece was loaded, kicked the kitchen door open with his right foot and accidentally lost his footing. Says he lunged into the kitchen and shot his missus, who was sitting down with a wine and a magazine.'

'The murder weapon was a hunting rifle?' asked David.

'The mean kind,' Joe confirmed with a nod. 'The one used to pop big game animals.'

'The guy shoots game?' asked Sara.

'No – at least he says he hasn't had a chance to try it yet. Says the gun was a present from his wife.'

David immediately found this strange, given the Stephanie he once knew was a vocal advocate against cruelty towards animals.

'Says he has never shot with anything bigger than a two wood,' Joe went on. 'In his whole entire life.'

'Until tonight,' said David.

'Until tonight,' repeated Joe.

'So how do you see this?' asked David as another crime tech walked by.

'The guy is lying. His theory just doesn't add up. He was too clean. That rifle is a spatter gun, and the only traces of blood on him were transferred. There was no gunpowder residue on his hands.'

'Did he have time to shower?' interrupted David.

'He didn't shower,' said Joe. 'Still had make-up on from the TV thing earlier in the day.'

'So?' said David, taking it all in.

'So the dad is clean and his son is covered in a thousand miniature droplets.'

'Of his mother's blood?' asked Sara.

'Like he just ran through a sprinkler.'

'You think the father is covering for the kid?' David asked.

Joe nodded. 'I'm sure of it. The kid's eyebrows are knotted with his mother's blood. His hands were clean but that was probably because of the length of his T-shirt sleeves and the way he was holding the rifle. Up high,' said Joe, mimicking an old rifleman's pose. 'Like this. The burn mark on the shirt is probably a result of the blast literally smouldering the fabric at the point where it made contact with the gun – and if the crime lab guys find trace powder residue on it, that, and the blood, will pretty much confirm the kid as the shooter.'

'Which means he'll be arrested within days,' said David.

'It is just a matter of time,' said Joe.

'Are you taking him in for questioning?' asked Sara.

'No. Frank and I had a go at him earlier but he's terribly distressed, practically catatonic. I've called for a psyche consult but . . . the thing is, with the father's confession, until we can prove the good doctor *didn't* kill his wife then our hands are somewhat tied.'

'Because officially you already have the perp in

hand,' finished Sara. 'And no legal reason, at least until the evidence is analysed, to pursue any other possible perpetrators.'

Joe nodded again.

'One last thing before we go in,' said David at last. 'Does this guy know Stephanie and I have a history? Because if he does, he might not want me to . . . In fact, *I* am not sure I want to . . .'

'I understand,' said Joe. 'I know the wife was a friend and I don't want to put you in a position where you feel obliged to defend her killer. But if the kid is disturbed, maybe she would want someone like you helping him out. He was her son, after all – and in the very least it might be worth trying to get a handle on the truth before you decide which way you want to go.'

David nodded.

'As for the father,' Joe went on, 'if his reception is a little chilly it's because he originally asked for a public defender. And if you want to give him a heads up about your history with his wife then, by all means, start with a clean slate.'

'But why would he ask for someone from the PDO when he must have legal contacts all over this city?' asked Sara. 'I mean, he works for a big-time network, his wife was an attorney, they must have legal representatives looking after their substantial assets.'

'I have no idea,' admitted Joe. 'But if I was to hazard a guess, I'd say that maybe it's because he doesn't want an experienced attorney anywhere near his defence.'

'You think he wants a rookie so that he can lose?' asked David.

'Or win,' said Joe. 'Depending on how you look at it.'

There was a pause.

'So long story short,' said David after a time, feeling more than a little uncomfortable with the impending task at hand, 'we have to go in there and offer my old friend's famous husband decent representation for accidentally committing a murder he appears to have had nothing to do with, so that he can have a fair chance at saving himself, so that we can set *him* free and make way for the ADA to drag Stephanie's youngest kid into juvenile court for shooting her point-blank with a big game rifle.'

'That about sums it up,' said Joe.

'Unbelievable,' said Sara.

'Welcome to my world,' finished Joe.

4

The first call went straight to message bank. She heard it ring, but ignored it. Not like her at all, but her sometime 'companion' and blue chip lawyer was, well, 'down there' at the time, and she allowed herself a few moments of pleasure before returning the favour and partaking in at least fifteen minutes of some seriously good sex before rolling off to check who the caller happened to be.

Suffolk County Assistant District Attorney Amanda Carmichael was a woman on the rise. Everything about her was hot right now and she knew it. The current DA, a respected prosecutor named Loretta Scaturro, had finally resigned a few weeks ago after the Massachusetts Attorney-General got sick of extending her endless months of compassionate leave. And the AG, a legal dinosaur named Pat Sweeney, was backing his sunshine boy – Amanda's boss and acting asshole DA Roger Katz – for the upcoming elections in November, a move which would see Amanda officially second-in-charge of the busiest district attorney's office in Massachusetts at the ripe old age of twenty-nine. It was a record, she knew, but then Amanda was an old hand at breaking records, the fact that she had managed to drag out Tony's explosive orgasm for the past quarter hour being testament to the fact.

'*Shit!*' she said, as she listened to the voice mail on her cell. She expected it to be one of the junior morons checking in for the night but it was Katz's PA, a useless blob named Shelley. With Katz in DC attending the National District Attorney's Association Metro Conference, a seminar he practically greased himself to get to despite having to offload three cases to some useless plebs who had more experience treating acne than they did attending court, Shelley had taken it upon herself to call 'the most senior ADA in the county' or in other words, Amanda, who was currently 'the man', or more pointedly, 'the woman', now running the Goddamned show.

'*Jesus*,' she said as she bounded out of bed, finding her lace knickers and bra at the far end of Tony's tastefully decorated Copley Square penthouse bedroom.

'What is it?' he asked, now rising on his elbows, still high from the rush, Amanda knew – his cheeks flushed, his penis size still challenging that of an aroused Clydesdale horse.

'Work,' she said, not wanting to give too much away. Tony was a corporate lawyer with absolutely no interest in coveting her job. But Amanda was born suspicious – the only child of a US Supreme Court judge who taught her never to share a single crumb with anyone with the letters JD after their name.

'Let someone else get it, babe,' he said, obviously hungry for more.

'Katz is away,' she said, putting on her high-heeled pumps, knowing her profile against the moonlit window was probably driving Bishop insane. 'I'm it,' she added, slipping on her white silk blouse and navy pencil skirt.

'Yes, you are,' smiled Tony. 'And this must be something big if you are so hot to trot.'

'Tony, every case is of equal importance to the District Attorney's Office, and as a representative of the people I . . .'

'. . . have a sixth sense on how to cherry-pick the good ones,' finished Tony, 'which this one obviously is.'

Amanda could not help but smile. She had to admit, she liked Bishop, probably because they had so much in common – a shared narcissistic perspective of their 'noble' profession, a knack of how to manipulate the system for their own personal gain.

She threw on her jacket – the top half of a $700 Armani cool wool suit.

'Turn on the TV and you might catch it,' she said, checking herself in the bureau mirror as she twisted her hair into a conservative French roll. She applied a natural shade of lipstick before assessing herself once again, grabbing her Balenciaga handbag and heading for the door.

'You're a piece of work, you know that, Carmichael?' Bishop smiled.

'Just doing my job, Counsellor.' She smiled. 'Just doing my job.'

*

It was an episode about mixed signals, David recalled. A whole hour devoted to Doctor Jeff trying to teach some incredibly wholesome looking couples how to 'read' their partner more effectively. The doctor told them how miscommunication was a 'universal phenomenon', and more importantly, just how these fine people could address it. And the couples soaked up his wisdom with enthusiasm, with the utmost of gratitude and respect.

Lisa had forced him to watch it. His younger Massachusetts General nursing sister had been going through a difficult time with one of her many transient boyfriends and asked if he would make her a cocoa and sit down and veg for a while. Which he did, and while it definitely wasn't his personal cup of tea, he could remember thinking that this almost too good looking Doctor Jeff certainly had the knack.

'Doctor,' said David at last, after two minutes of absolute silence. Logan had said he needed to think. He was confused, distraught, angry even when David and Sara entered the living room. He recognised them from their previous high-profile trials and immediately protested that they had been asked to represent him.

David had been honest from the outset – he had told him that he and his wife were once friends, and that while they had not been in contact for many years, he had been pleased to see her at the Law Society ball some three months ago.

'I asked for a public defender,' the doctor had responded after a pause, surprising David somewhat by making no reference whatsoever to David's past association with his wife.

'You asked for a criminal defence attorney, Doctor, and that's exactly what we are. If you have an issue with my knowing your wife then . . .'

'This was an accident, Mr Cavanaugh.' Logan had stood then, and started to pace the room. 'Why would I have an issue?'

'Fair enough,' David had answered. 'So if it's a matter of payment then I am sure we can work something out.' But David had been sure that Logan's objections had nothing to do with the money. 'The thing is,' David had continued, 'it is now late Friday night and your arraignment will be set for Monday. You have the weekend to get us up to speed so that you have adequate representation in court. Now, if after that time you want to go with someone from the public defender's office then that's fine. But under the circumstances, I suggest you allow us to get you through this all-important first stage. For your sake, and for that of your children.'

And that was when Jeffrey Logan had gone silent, lifting a single finger as if indicating he needed a moment to think.

So here they sat, David staring at the man who seemed all too capable of helping others make decisions, without any inkling of how to make one for himself.

'All right,' said the doctor at last, moving back to his plush single sofa chair to take a sip of water from a plastic cup one of the paramedics had supplied for him about a half an hour ago. 'I'll repeat to you what I told the police and you may represent me at the arraignment. But beyond that I . . .'

'We understand,' said David as the doctor left his

statement hanging. 'We can take this one step at a time. The police are waiting to take you into custody so I am afraid there is little we can do tonight bar hear the original statement you gave to the detectives, and then, tomorrow, we'll have some fresh questions, discuss things in greater detail, build a strategy for Monday.'

Truth be told, David was more than keen to learn exactly what had gone down in this house mere hours before – but he knew better than to press, at least for now.

'All right,' said Logan, now taking a breath. 'But you are not going to like it – the statement, I mean. I shot your old college friend, Mr Cavanaugh, in an accident that shall haunt me forever – and *you too* I would suggest, given the scene we were all just exposed to.'

In that moment, as Logan met David's eye, a look of probing curiosity on his face, David sensed the famous psychologist was looking for a reaction from him – some sort of emotional response to having just seen his former friend blitzed by a bullet powerful enough to take out the biggest animals on the planet.

'Accidents happen,' said David, the only thing he could think of to say.

'Not as often as you would think,' said Logan. 'But, yes, in this case . . .' He paused. 'Bottom line, Mr Cavanaugh, Miss Davis,' he continued after a beat, 'and I cannot stress this enough – your role in this matter is an easy one. For I killed my wife, and when it comes down to it, there is nothing for you to defend.'

'Why don't you let us be the judge of that, Doctor,' said Sara, perhaps reading David's discomfort, instinctively stepping in. 'No matter what, we're here to help.'

With a half smile that suggested gratitude, or in the very least some sort of satisfaction at having established his point, Logan replied, 'I know you are,' while shaking his head in disagreement at the very same time.

Just as Stephanie did, thought David, when he'd suggested they catch up a mere three months ago. Mixed signals, they were more common than you think.

Half an hour later, David and Sara watched as their client was handcuffed and led from the building – the ever-present press finally getting a return on their five-hour investment. David and Sara walked behind the doctor as he was led to a waiting police car – as much to provide 'support' as to make sure their client did not decide to repeat his '*I did it*' mantra to every local and national media outlet in the country.

The voyeurs – hundreds of people who, for some reason, had nothing better to do on a Friday night than roll up to play 'extras' in the real-life drama starring the most popular shrink on TV – went crazy. It was a circus, backlit by floodlights, filmed by the cameras as hundreds of flashbulbs popped like fireworks on the fourth of July.

And that was when they saw her, bounding up the road. Amanda Carmichael was already making comments to the press, providing sound bites she knew would headline the morning shows. She hadn't even been properly briefed and already she was taking command of what she knew would be the highest profile case of the year. David looked around for Joe, hoping his detective friend could rein her in. But it was too late. With Logan ensconced in the now departing police car, Carmichael had everyone's attention.

'Jesus,' said Sara, eyeing the ADA with distaste. 'First Katz and now . . . this.' She gestured at the stunning-looking prosecutor before them.

David looked at the ADA, as she cleared her throat and called for quiet so that she might make the first official statement in the Stephanie Tyler murder case. In that second, as David's head still reeled from the death of his friend, the scene of her family and the somewhat unnerving behaviour of her husband, Carmichael met David's eye and gave him the slightest of smiles. And then, on top of everything else, he remembered the last time they spoke . . . and the proposition she had made.

5

Katherine de Castro was exhausted. She had been up for most of the night. The police had finally allowed her to take the two Logan children back to her apartment at midnight (given they had no other immediate family and there was nowhere else for them to go) and she spent the rest of the night wondering what the hell to do with them.

J.T. had said nothing since the 'accident' but he obviously felt the need to stick as close to his older sister as possible, for when de Castro had gone to check on him, around 2am, she'd found he had left the living room couch to set up camp on the floor next to Chelsea's bed in de Castro's rarely used spare room – his body taut, his jaw clenched, his eyes wide, staring at the ceiling.

And wanting desperately to help, but having no real maternal instinct to draw upon, she'd gotten a blanket and put it over him before slipping quietly out of the room, and back into her own king-sized bed down the hall.

How had it come to this? she asked herself now, as she tightened the blue silk robe around her and poured another strong black coffee from her Italian percolator. She was perched on the edge of one of her designer stools, the early morning sun making its way into her stylish brownstone kitchen, wondering how in the hell she, Katherine de Castro, the forty-year-old, over-achieving, Stanford business grad, '*Premiere Magazine* Female Media Executive of the Year', had ended up trying to 'comfort' two grieving teenagers who had just seen their mother blown to bits.

She could not focus. Any moment now they would be calling and she did not know what to say. The personal assistant to the network's powerful CEO had rung at 7.15am – just over an hour ago – to tell her that CBC's head honcho, one Allen Greenburg, had requested a transcontinental conference call at 8.30am Eastern Standard Time – a communication that would involve Greenburg, the President of CBC News, Bob Prescott, the President of Network Entertainment, Nancy Schaffer, and the network's Vice President and General Counsel, a smarmy little weasel by the name of Walter Goth.

She had had no time to prepare. She had smoked ten cigarettes in the past sixty minutes and still wasn't sure how the hell she should handle this. She thought they would give her the morning at least, considering they were in LA and she was three hours ahead. But then again, she also knew that when Allen Greenburg requested a 5.30am conference call, his loyal staff jumped. And if she was to survive, if she were to have any hope of saving what she and Jeffrey had built from scratch, she would have to jump with the best of them – higher, faster and without the slightest hint of hesitation.

The timing could not have been worse. First of all, they were in the middle of the all-important May sweeps. November, February and May were the three months when the networks pulled out their big guns – when they and their affiliates ran seasonal campaigns aimed at huge ratings in order to maximise advertising revenue. The May sweeps represented their last chance in the viewing calendar to impress existing and potential advertisers so that they might set ridiculous fifteen- and thirty-second spot rates and those all-important program sponsorships for the following season, before the industry lumbered into the long, slow summer where re-runs were ripe and audiences were at their lowest.

Secondly, Katherine and Doctor Jeff were just about to sign a new three-year contract with CBC – a deal which would see *The Doctor Jeff Show* through to its seventeenth season and earn Jeffrey, and herself, somewhere in the ball park of $25 million per year.

The deal included tie-ins for specials and other promotional opportunities used to showcase the Doctor's website, books and DVDs, and coincided with another major agreement with Imperial Productions for the syndication of three earlier series of the show – assuring affiliate and cable stations across the country would be running and re-running episodes of the high-rating show at one time or another twenty-four hours a day.

These agreements alone, topped with international distribution deals with over thirty-five countries worldwide, would earn Katherine and her famous psychologist partner thousands of dollars every time the muted tones of their familiar opening credits rolled up on the screen. They would be making money while they slept, and lining their bank accounts in twenty different currencies as Jeff consolidated his role as international counsellor extraordinaire, and their program became the most watched relationship talk show on the whole Goddamned planet.

And so what to do?

She had to decide.

She was not stupid. She knew exactly what had gone down in that painstakingly neat mansion in Beacon Hill less than twenty-four hours ago. She saw J.T. before the crime people took his clothes into evidence and there was no doubt in her mind – nor, she garnered, anyone else's at the scene – exactly who had murdered Stephanie Tyler, accident or not.

Now running out of time, she tried to think logically. She decided there were three major points to consider in her now urgent deliberations.

First up, as much as she hated to admit it, the survival of the show – and their careers, their future – was her number one priority. She felt for the boy and knew that he needed help, but that might have to wait until she and Jeffrey could set things straight. Once his father was freed, they could deal with J.T.'s 'issues' and hopefully help the boy sort out whatever was going on in that psychotic little mind of his.

Secondly, she needed Jeffrey out of prison ASAP. She was no lawyer but she was sure that if he somehow managed to pull off his 'it was a tragic accident' theory in order to protect his son, he was most likely looking at a charge of involuntary manslaughter which more often than not carried a jail time of anything from three to ten years (she had Googled it at 4am). There had to be a way to limit, if not eradicate, the prison time, and she intended to explore this with Jeffrey's lawyers as soon as she had the chance.

Finally, she knew that, above all else, she had to protect Jeffrey's reputation. If Jeffrey was freed, absolved, exonerated, that would be one thing – but unless the real truth behind J.T.'s actions was revealed, the damage could be more damaging than ever. Jeffrey was a relationship expert for God's sake. He counselled people on *how to bring up their kids* – nurture them, protect them, give them as solid a fucking grounding as possible so that they might lead fruitful, productive and independent lives. He spoke of parent/child relationships, he advised how important it was to swap aggression for understanding, he won the fucking 'Father of the Year Award' two years ago – and now his son had popped his own mom without so much as a peep.

So while Jeffrey had told her not to speak of it, while he had stressed it was a private family matter *never* to be shared – she could not help but think that it was not only in her best interests to tell, but it was her *responsibility*. For Stephanie was gone after all, the problem solved . . . at least from one perspective.

And so, as the phone rang, its shrill tone cutting a swathe across the silence in her stylish Back Bay apartment, she took a breath and ran her hands through her long dark hair. She closed her eyes and exhaled with force as she decided, then and there, that the 'truth' was the only way to go. She would request to speak to Greenburg privately, and allude to him that circumstances were not as dire as they first appeared, and he needed to trust her until she had an opportunity to speak with Jeffrey's lawyers.

And then she would speak to Cavanaugh, and then he would understand, and then they would carve out a course of action so that the world would know the truth, and all would be forgiven.

6

'I told you,' said Jeffrey Logan, his athletic frame now swimming in the too big, red prison jumpsuit. 'I was cleaning it. It was new. I'd never cleaned a gun before. I wasn't sure what I was doing.'

It was now almost noon. David and Sara had arrived at Boston's Nashua Street Suffolk County Jail – a huge modern construction on the Charles River across from Bunker Bridge which housed close to seven hundred temporary detainees awaiting trial – at eight. And they had been sitting in the close confines of a whitewashed interview room on the building's sixth, or 'homicide', floor and grilling their client ever since.

David was trying desperately to put the image of his good friend Stephanie behind him, as he knew, above all else, that his immediate responsibility was, ironically, to the man who had confessed to her murder. But it was clear from the outset that Logan's story was full of inconsistencies, and so David and Sara had decided that their priority was showing Logan that just because he said he was responsible for the crime, it 'did not make it so'.

'Look, Doctor,' said David.

'Please call me Jeffrey,' said Logan, who despite appearing tired, David had to admit, still had that familiar TV sparkle in his eyes.

'Jeffrey,' David began again. 'We hear what you are saying, but establishing the facts is the only way we can help you. Our problem is that your story doesn't quite fit together. The details are there, but right now they are hanging like mismatched pieces of a jigsaw.'

'I . . . I don't know what else I can tell you,' Logan replied, shaking his head.

David took a breath. 'All I am saying is that this whole gun thing doesn't ring true – and the problem is, Jeffrey, if *we* can't see it, chances are a judge, or a jury, won't see it either.'

'But surely I am making it easy for them,' protested Logan. 'And for you and your co-counsel too.' Logan gestured at Sara. 'I would imagine you spend most of your time trying to convince your clients *not* to exaggerate circumstances to assure their freedom, and now you have me, who simply asks that you corroborate my guilt.'

David had to admit he was right.

'I understand your reasoning, Jeffrey, but with all due respect, just because you say something happened, it doesn't mean others will believe you.'

'But that's where you're wrong, David,' said Logan. 'In case you haven't noticed I have built an entire career on being believed. People live by my every word. They make decisions based solely on my advice. It's like . . . I am Doctor Jeff!' he said then – an exclamation, not a statement. 'And with the risk of sounding completely supercilious, if I say something happened – then that alone makes it so.'

There was silence as David swallowed the knot in his throat. In all honesty he had never met anyone like Jeffrey Logan before; the man *was* arrogant, superior – but in a strangely appealing way. And the fact that he was, at least on the face of it, making one of the most selfless acts a human being could make, certainly counted for something.

'Look,' said Sara, trying to fill the increasingly awkward silence. 'We are not trying to make this difficult for you, Jeffrey, but David is right when he says the facts are all skewiff. For example, why would you be cleaning a brand new rifle that had never been used before? And why, given you had never hunted before, was it loaded? And why did you decide to clean it at a time when, you admit, you had no plans to go on a hunting trip at any time in the near or distant future? And why did you . . .?'

'Maybe I wanted to clean the gun so my wife knew that I appreciated her gift,' Logan interrupted again. 'The whole idea of hunting may not be something I have ever embraced, but that doesn't mean I didn't want my wife to see how much I valued her generosity. Perhaps I figured, if I took it to the kitchen, if she saw I was taking care of what must have cost her a small fortune, then she would know how much I . . .' And then he hesitated, as his brain perhaps tracked ahead to how his supposed expression of gratitude had eventually played out.

'You said you wanted some fresh rags from the kitchen,' said David, taking Sara's lead, getting them back on track. 'But a police search confirmed your garage was stocked with fresh rags and there were no similar cloths in the kitchen.'

'I mustn't have seen the ones in the garage,' said Logan, taking a breath now, shifting in his worn plastic chair which scratched in protest across the dirty concrete floor.

'Where do you normally keep your gun, Jeffrey?' asked David, not missing a beat.

'In the hall cabinet. Under lock and key.'

'And the key?'

'Like I told you, in the upstairs drawer.'

'In your bedroom.'

'Yes.'

'Beside your bed.'

'Yes.'

'In a drawer that remained unlocked.'

'*Yes*.'

'Did anyone else in the household know where this key was kept?' asked Sara.

'No,' said Logan, tapping his prison issue flip-flops on the cold grey floor. 'My wife knew but my son . . . I mean my *children*,' he corrected himself, shaking his head as if in self-admonishment, 'they did not know where it was kept.'

David looked at Sara. Logan was lying again – and this time, not very well.

'What time did you get home last night?' asked Sara. She was tag teaming it now.

'Ah . . . seven-thirty, eight, I am not sure.'

'It was eight-sixteen,' continued Sara. 'A neighbour saw you turn into your drive.'

'Well, it might have been . . .'

'But Stephanie was shot at eight-twenty,' said David. 'Which means that you must have gotten out of your car, taken your briefcase to the study, run upstairs to the bedroom, retrieved the cabinet key, run downstairs to the hallway, taken out the gun, gone to the garage, looked for the cleaning rags, found none, walked back to the other end of the house to the kitchen and accidentally shot your wife – all in the space of no more than four minutes.'

'Then I suppose I am . . . a fast walker,' said Logan.

'Did you re-lock the cabinet?' asked David, this new question stopping their client dead.

Logan looked at them then, his foot frozen mid tap, his brow contorted in a knot of confusion, his head shaking rapidly as if trying to clear the fog.

'I'm sorry?' he managed.

'Did you re-lock the cabinet – in the hallway, where the gun was kept?'

'Ah . . . no. There was no need, I was going to put the gun back so . . .'

'Then why did the police find it locked?' asked Sara. 'And why was the key found back upstairs in the bedroom drawer?'

'I must have . . .'

'Walked, quickly, we know,' finished David, not meaning to be harsh but determined to show his client just how unbelievable his story was.

Logan looked at him then, and David could have sworn that in that second his lips had clenched in anger.

But then they quivered, and David realised that he had misread the doctor's sorrow for resentment – sorrow at his own predicament and the predicament of his son.

'The thing is, Doctor,' said Sara, 'the gun, the cabinet, the timing of the whole thing – the fact that there was no blood on your clothing, no residue on your hands . . .? We don't mean to be unsympathetic, but we needed you to see just how implausible this whole thing is. We understand your motives are selfless, but your story . . . it is so full of holes, so desperate in its irrationality, that in many ways it only goes to consolidate your teenage son's guilt.'

So, she had said it – plain and clear.

Logan lifted his head, his eyes burning with what could be fear, frustration, perhaps even irritation at Sara speaking of it before he had the chance to utter it himself.

'Please,' he began, his voice much softer than the expression on his face. 'You must understand that this is the *only* solution, for if you don't, all is lost. Not one life, but two – my wife's and that of my son. What happens to me is now inconsequential. I had my chance in life – at a family, at parenthood, and somewhere along the line I forgot what matters the most. So now I have a chance to make amends – a sick and twisted opportunity that I must hold on to, no matter what the cost.'

'This isn't going to work,' said David at last.

'Probably not,' said Logan. 'But if I do not try, I will *never* forgive myself.'

David nodded before glancing at Sara. 'Okay, Jeffrey. Let's see if we can't get you indicted.'

7

She was up on a chair when they entered her office, wearing her 'weekend' clothes – snug-fitting tailored pants and a polo top, her hair out and parted to one side, the bulk of it fixed behind her diamond-studded ears.

'Detective, Lieutenant,' she said as they moved into the room.

Joe and Frank had originally gone to her office down the hall but, upon finding it not only empty but stripped of books, paperwork and personal belongings, they had wandered back to the Acting District Attorney, Roger 'The Kat' Katz's office – the bigger one next to the DA's.

'You moving in?' asked Joe, noticing Frank – a somewhat prudish, happily married father of two, trying to look anywhere but at Amanda Carmichael's perfectly formed butt.

'Yes,' she said, twisting to look at them, and Joe knew this was all part of her 'game' – her top shifting to reveal her toned stomach, her expression a mixture of efficiency and innocence. 'Roger is in DC for the next couple of weeks and it seemed silly to delay the move considering DA Scaturro is not coming back,' she added, pointing to the hastily packed boxes in the corner of the room.

'I'll get Roger's PA to move his things into the DA's space on Monday. It'll give her something to do besides file those too long acrylic nails of hers.'

Truth be told, from what Joe knew of Amanda Carmichael's reputation, he was more than just a little suspicious of the motives of the BU-educated show pony with the Supreme Court dad and the Country Club mom. She was smart, that was for sure, and ambitious, but he had also heard stories of her arrogance, her intolerance, and her general belief that she knew better than everybody else.

However, she was new at this 2IC gig, and so Joe was willing to cut her some slack, and the fact that she had the balls to shove Katz's belongings into dirty cardboard boxes had gained her some points in Joe's estimations – considering Joe deemed Roger Katz to be one of the lowest assholes on the ladder of legal depravity.

'So,' said Carmichael, hopping down from her chair and pushing it behind her desk. 'Take a seat, gentlemen,' she said gesturing at the two leather-covered visitors' chairs on the opposite side of her desk. 'I appreciate your coming in on a Saturday,' she said, taking a pair of designer reading glasses from her top drawer and placing them on the tip of her perfectly shaped nose. 'But as you can appreciate, this is one of the biggest cases we will be prosecuting this year. The press have been calling all morning, the story is headlining every major news bulletin in the country and this is only the beginning. This is a big deal, gentlemen, and we are in the thick of it.'

Frank was rolling his eyes, Joe could sense it. Carmichael was revelling in the attention and was obviously hungry for more. The fact that she gave a statement to the press late last night without consulting Joe was evidence enough of her desire to 'own' this thing from the beginning, and that action alone was enough to make Joe suspicious of her motives – new kid on the block, or not.

'You shouldn't have given a statement until we briefed you,' said Joe, not one to beat around the bush.

'Detective McKay briefed me on my cell, Lieutenant,' she argued.

'I gave you a basic run-down,' said Frank, opening his mouth for the first time.

'Which was very comprehensive,' said Carmichael. 'The media were hungry. They had been awaiting an official statement for hours. I made sure they were satisfied so that they did not distort the truth from the outset. I gave them a brief statement relating to Mrs Logan's . . .'

'Tyler,' interrupted Joe then.

'Excuse me?' said Carmichael.

'Stephanie Tyler. The victim went by her maiden name.' He was not sure why he needed to make a point of it; maybe because he met Tyler and found her gracious, maybe because he knew cops too often forgot to give their victims the courtesy of the correct acknowledgement, or maybe because he sensed Carmichael couldn't give a fuck what the woman was called – just that she was prosecuting this Goddamned headliner of a case.

'Right,' said Carmichael, making no attempt to hide her displeasure at the correction. 'Well, as I was saying, I gave a brief statement relating to Ms *Tyler's* death and confirmed that Doctor Logan was being taken in for questioning. It was a consolatory gesture so that the media did not go away disappointed. Nothing more, nothing less.'

'With all due respect, Miss Carmichael,' said Joe, now leaning forward in his seat. 'We were running a murder scene. And satisfying the press's insatiable appetites was not exactly a priority.'

'Ah, but that's where you're wrong, Lieutenant,' she said, her long slender finger waving in a gesture that reeked of superiority. 'Satisfying the media is *key* to any major prosecution – especially one involving a fellow media identity.'

Carmichael sat back in her seat then, a satisfied smile on her high-cheekboned face, and in that moment, Joe actually missed the previous asshole who used to pontificate from the seat which the incredibly stunning blonde now occupied before him. At least he could tell The Kat to go fuck himself when he treated Joe and his fellow cops like inferior subordinates. This one was going to be harder to tackle.

'So tell me, Lieutenant,' Carmichael went on unfazed. 'What have you got?'

And so Joe and Frank spent the next half-hour summarising their findings – findings that were yet to be backed up by the solid technical evidence reports soon to be provided by their experienced forensic analysts. Basically, they explained that no matter which way you looked at it, Doctor Jeffrey Logan was not good for the kill. His son, however, was another matter altogether.

'Long story short, we think the dad is covering for the kid,' said Joe. 'The BPA alone points singularly at the boy,' he said, referring to the bloodstain pattern analysis carried out at the scene and currently being confirmed by Boston PD's respected Crime Lab Unit technicians. 'And there was a burn from the blast on the right shoulder of his T-shirt, and chances are, despite the fact the .460 Weatherby blows the powder out and forward with a hell of a force, that we'll find trace powder residue on the shirt as well.'

'The thing is, Miss Carmichael,' said Frank. 'Under normal circumstances we would have arrested the kid last night. But when his father confessed, we knew we didn't have a leg to stand on until the crime lab stuff came in.'

'Which is when exactly?' said the obviously displeased ADA.

'Mid-week at best,' said Joe.

'*After the arraignment?*' said Carmichael, now removing her glasses and shaking her head. And in that moment Joe was sure the spectacles were just a prop, a theatrical accessory she used to give herself an air of authority in court.

'It's not good enough,' she said. 'This arraignment will be viewed, recorded, picked to pieces by every major media outlet in the country. You cannot expect me to go in there and argue for this man's incarceration if we know he is as innocent as a . . .'

'You don't have any choice,' interrupted Joe. 'You have to play this one straight – and then, when the evidence comes in, we can arrest the son and hand him over to the juvenile court.'

'The juvenile court?' she said, incredulous.

'The boy is only thirteen.'

'Shit,' she said, making no attempt to hide her disappointment. Massachusetts was one of the few states in the US which had passed a law stating that a person as young as fourteen charged with murder would be tried as an adult in the Superior Court. Such a person, if found guilty of first-degree murder, could be sentenced to life without parole in state prison; if found guilty of second-degree murder, they could be sentenced to life with parole eligibility after a lengthy fifteen years.

'When is he fourteen?' she asked.

'That's a moot point, Ms Carmichael, and you know it,' said Joe. The woman was really starting to piss him off. 'Thirteen is thirteen, no matter how you look at it.'

'And how is Cavanaugh going to approach this?' she asked, obviously knowing that Joe and David were friends. 'In fact, come to think of it, how did a lawyer of Cavanaugh's calibre become involved in the first place?'

She knew the answer; this was just another dig at Joe.

'From what I am told,' Carmichael went on, 'Doctor Logan asked for a public defender, which, under the circumstances might have worked better for us considering . . .'

'Doctor Logan asked for a lawyer and we got him

one,' said Joe, refusing to explain further simply because he was not answerable to the twenty-nine-year-old upstart before him. 'And considering the doctor confessed, my guess is Cavanaugh will play Monday's arraignment as straight as he can – stress that this was an accident, argue for bail.'

'Jesus,' said Carmichael. 'What is this – a fucking kangaroo court where everyone avoids the truth?'

'No, ma'am,' said Frank. 'It's called due process, it's part of the fifth and fourteenth amendments. It's about safeguarding the rights of every individual – even those who have the guts to lie to protect their kids.'

'You actually *admire* this man, Detective McKay?' asked Carmichael, incredulous, her big blue eyes now narrowing in contempt.

'I got two teenage kids, Ms Carmichael,' replied Frank, with determination. 'Let's just say, I can see where he is coming from.'

'Christ,' said Carmichael. 'Well, cue the fucking violins.'

They were silent then, Joe deciding there was no point in arguing further. *This one was dangerous,* he told himself. *Dangerous and smart and ambitious to boot.*

'Is that it?' asked Joe at last.

'Apparently so,' said Carmichael. 'At least as far as you two are concerned.'

'I'm sorry, Miss Carmichael,' began Joe, not sure what the ADA was insinuating. 'But . . .'

'Just tell me the minute the crime lab stuff is in,' she interrupted, now rising from her chair and moving around the desk to dismiss them. She headed straight for the entrance of her brand new office, strutting across the room like a Goddamned diva. And then she stumbled into one of Katz's hastily packed boxes, tripping herself up so that she had to grab at a side table to regain her balance.

'*Shit*,' she said, as she regathered her composure and stood beside the door.

'Better watch your step, Miss Carmichael,' said Joe, as he and Frank turned to leave. 'As the Chinese say, you keep looking at the mountains you're gonna fall into the molehills.'

'I've never taken a fall in my life, Lieutenant,' she countered.

'Well then, maybe you're due, Miss Carmichael, maybe you're due.'

8

'Are you sure you're okay?' asked David for the umpteenth time. They had just entered one of their favourite eateries, a popular breakfast and lunch café at the northern end of the harbour known as Myrtle McGee's.

'I'm fine,' Sara said. 'It was just a little slip, David,' she added, referring to her 'slide' down the wide stone front stairs of Suffolk County Jail barely half an hour earlier. They had been harassed by a barrage of media the moment they left the building, and Sara had been caught in the crossfire.

'What's up, lass?' asked a concerned-looking Mick McGee, hurrying around his counter to meet them at the door. Mick was Myrtle's proprietor, a large, red-faced Irishman with a number two crew cut revealing a shock of bright orange spikes. He was also a good friend – and as such, now obviously concerned about the lack of colour in Sara's pasty complexion.

'Nothing!' she said, managing a smile in protest as

Mick and David helped her to a corner booth. 'I'm fine. It was my fault. I caught my heel in a crack and . . .'

'Don't listen to her, Mick,' said David. 'The press holed us up on the front steps of County, practically barrelled her down the stairs.'

Mick shook his head. 'Barbarians,' he said, never one to hold back on an opinion. 'Not to worry,' he said, helping Sara into her seat. 'I'll get you a . . .'

'Coffee, strong, black,' interrupted Sara.

'Juice, combo, orange,' countered Mick. 'You need a little sugar is all – and I'll add some wheat grass for protein.'

'Thanks, Mick,' said Sara, knowing there was no point in arguing, as Mick rushed back to his lime green counter and set about 'fixing things' the only way he knew how.

'Not another word,' said Sara, as David reached across the table to take her hand. 'It was just a fall, David. If I thought it was anything more I'd be at the doctor's in a shot. You *know* that.' She smiled. 'Besides, you keep sweeping me off my feet like you did on the front steps of County and people are going to assume we are trying out for the lead roles in the next live action version of *Cinderella*.'

'You and Cinderella,' he said, squeezing her hand with a smile.

'Hey, stop complaining. I could have had a Snow White fetish and then I'd be demanding seven little people come share our cosy two-bedder.'

'This your way of telling me you're carrying septuplets?' asked David with a smile.

'Over my dead body,' she laughed.

*

Half an hour, two roasted chicken sandwiches, one coffee and an extra large juice later, David and Sara were back to discussing their case. They didn't have much time. They had promised their client that they would look in on his two children later in the afternoon and had called ahead to Logan's business partner, Katherine de Castro, to make sure she would be at home. She was, and she would be, she had assured them with enthusiasm, and they set up the visit for three.

'I know he has hired us to represent him,' Sara began, referring to their client, 'but in all honesty, part of me thinks we should be talking to the ADA. Logan didn't kill her and I am not sure what it says about us – basically sharing in his lie and endorsing his confession by representing him in court.'

'I know,' said David. 'But we have no other option. Carmichael will be going through the motions just like us – charging Jeffrey with involuntary manslaughter, and then waiting for the forensics to come in so that she can arrest J.T. and hand him over to juvie.'

'She isn't going to like that,' said Sara.

'She won't have any choice.'

'And you?' asked Sara after a pause. 'Is that going to be enough for you?'

David knew this discussion was coming – and he loved her for bringing it up.

'I'm not sure,' he replied. 'It's just that this whole case comes with so many questions it is hard to know where I should stand. Stephanie was so generous, so selfless, so full of ideas and opinions and dreams. And for her life to end the way it did – at the hand of her only son . . . part of me needs to know what went down, Sara, and not just for Stephanie, but for me.'

Sara nodded. 'It's like you knew her at "A", and she ended up at "C" and "B" is . . .'

'A sixteen-year mystery I owe it to her to understand.'

'Stephanie didn't ask you to do this, David.'

'She didn't have to.'

The look of understanding on Sara's face said it all.

'So we start by supporting the lie, and after that, well . . . we see what we can do about unveiling the truth.'

'Something like that.'

'It's not like we haven't come at things backwards before,' she said, reaching across the table to kiss him.

'Really?' he said, managing a smile at last. 'And I thought all our cases were a piece of cake.'

'That's because you work with me,' she said.

9

Caroline Croft stretched back in her red leather ergonomic chair and took in a long, cool breath. Her perfectly coiffed blonde hair was freshly combed and cut in the standard newscaster's style, her arched stockinged feet now crossed and resting on the glass-topped office desk before her. Her husband, Bernard Jefferson, the executive producer of their high-rated *Newsline* program was now watching and listening anxiously from across the room. He had a bet with her that she wouldn't be able to pull this off, knowing the thrill of competition would make her all the more determined.

'I *want* this, Allen,' she said into the phone, her smooth 'anchorwoman' voice now tinged with the slightest hint of frustration. 'Boston is my city. Stephanie was my *friend.* I've known the family for years, even attended Chelsea's high school graduation.'

'The daughter is sixteen, Caroline,' said the network CEO who was now on speaker. 'She won't graduate high school until . . .'

'Well, I went to something with square hats, Allen – and what the fuck does it matter? May I remind you *Newsline* is the number one current affairs magazine program in the country. We make *60 Minutes* look like two and half hours of total indigestible crap and you know it.'

Bernard was cringing by this stage, obviously concerned his fearless wife with the big TV profile and the even bigger balls had overstepped her mark. Allen Greenburg was one of the most powerful media execs in the country, and Jefferson obviously doubted even Greenburg's mother had the guts to speak to him like this.

'Bob Prescott wants it to go to his news teams,' said Greenburg, referring to his President of News. 'He says he can stretch any interview over days – chop it up for a late night bulletin, leave the softer stuff for the morning programs, milk the exclusive for maximum return.'

'Bullshit,' Caroline said. 'Prescott is an idiot and you know it. He wouldn't know a decent story if he fell over it, which isn't such a stretch given the last time he attended an industry awards ceremony the man drank three bottles of red and had to send his deputy up to accept the award – for the network's exclusive on the latest treatments for alcohol abuse, no less.'

When Greenburg fell silent, Caroline knew she had hit a nerve and took it as her cue to move in for the kill.

'Have you spoken to de Castro?' she asked, her dislike for Logan's 'partner' barely disguised in the sharpness of her tone.

The silence continued – and Caroline's instincts told her Greenburg knew something he was not sharing.

'Come on, Allen, we all bat for the same team. If Katherine needs our help in making sure any interview is treated with respect and sensitivity . . .'

'Katherine just needs a little time . . . to square things up with Jeffrey's lawyers. She is meeting with them this afternoon and she promised me she'd call and talk interview as soon as things were locked down.'

'Well, that's great,' said Croft, her mind now adjusting to this latest news. She and Cavanaugh had a history and not all of it was rosy. 'But you can tell Katherine I am happy to talk to Cavanaugh direct. I know him, Allen, and I have his trust. Besides, I have always felt Katherine was a little threatened by my success – and I don't want any ill feeling on her part resulting in the network losing the best chance it has to send this interview into the May sweeps ratings stratosphere.'

But Greenburg wasn't biting – at least not yet.

'Look,' she said at last, knowing she had only one chance to get the CEO's green light. 'I really don't need your permission to chase a story, Allen, but I am calling out of respect, for you and for the network. You give me the go-ahead and I promise you I will deliver one of the best two hours of news journalism this country has ever seen.'

'You think you can fill a two-hour?' asked a now interested Greenburg, questioning her ability to provide an extra hour to her one-hour Friday night news magazine program, while no doubt counting the potential prime time share in his head.

'I'll fill three if you fucking let me,' returned Croft.

And then, further silence.

'It's already the twelfth of May,' offered Greenburg

after a time. 'You have to deliver before the end of the month.'

'Don't worry, Allen,' said Croft, looking across at her husband with a smile. 'You think I'd waste this gem out of sweeps?' she asked. 'This Friday or Friday week at the latest. The exclusive is all yours, Allen, all you have to do is . . .'

'Okay,' said the network chief. 'I'll talk to de Castro. You have my blessing, Caroline, but I promise you, if you fail to deliver . . .'

'Have I ever let you down before?' she asked, the honey now returning to her previous stinging tone.

Greenburg did not reply.

'No, I didn't think so.'

10

Deputy Raul Delgado had seen many things in his years as a security guard at Boston's county jails. He had been with the Sheriff's Department for nearly thirty-five years, having started his career as a junior corrections officer at the now defunct Charles Street Jail (which, ironically, had been transformed into some fancy four star hotel) before moving to Nashua Street back in 1990 when the new and improved Suffolk County facility opened its double glass doors to some of the meanest sons-of-bitches in the city.

But nothing – *nothing* – had prepared Delgado for the scene he was witnessing this afternoon as Asian Boyz head honcho Damien Chi, one of the meanest street gang leaders in the city, embraced the new white guy like he was his long-lost brother, before quietly starting to cry.

'What the hell is going on here?' said Delgado's fellow sixth floor deputy, a cold-hearted whippersnapper by the name of Snipe. Snipe, like Delgado, had seen Chi and his cronies approach the new guy and, like Delgado, he had assumed there was trouble afoot.

'Nothing,' said the new inmate, the famous one with the chiselled jaw. 'Mr Chi just asked me for some advice and I gave it to him. He was just showing me his appreciation, Deputy, and I am happy that I could be of some help.'

Delgado looked at a teary Chi who, to his surprise, nodded in accord.

'All right then,' said Delgado, whose wife swore by the advice dished out by the man now standing before him – and given the events of the last few minutes, he could certainly understand why. 'No harm done now. Get back to your cells.'

'Of course,' said Logan graciously, before gesturing a nod of encouragement towards the silent Chi. 'I want you to think about what I said, Mr Chi, and if you like, I can assist you in sharing your misgivings with your friends. I am glad I could be of help, and like I said – if there is anything else I can do . . .'

Chi nodded, and Delgado had to pinch himself on the back of his leg, just to prove this was not some merry fucking fairy tale in the lunatic land of louts.

Flip, *slide*, *turn*, thought Jeffrey Logan, as he relaxed back on his grey blanketed bunk. It was that easy.

Jeffrey Logan had learned years ago that whenever you were confronted by an antagonist set on rebuke, you simply flipped the balance of power by preying on the protagonist's weaknesses, slid your agenda under the confused aggressor's radar, and turned what could have been a potentially negative experience into one where you came out in front. He had in fact found that it was these unexpected potential altercations that often acted as catalysts to acquiring some previously unanticipated 'gift' – his first meeting with his wife being the ultimate example.

That is not to say that this most recent situation had not been a precarious one, he considered, as he shifted on the less-than-comfortable bed. The man called 'Chi' had been angry – very much so, and Chi's obvious role as 'shepherd' meant his equally as pissed off 'sheep' had approached Logan with the intent to do damage – and then some. What was worse was that it took Logan a minute or two to work out the source of Chi's resentment – for he had not, in a million years, expected to come face to face with an inmate who had been the subject of one of his shows.

'You're a mother-fucking asshole,' had been Chi's opening line. 'But now you stuck in my hole, motherfucker, with nowhere to fucking run.'

'I am sorry Mr . . . ah . . .?'

'My name is Chi, and I rule the Asian Boyz, you bitch, and you mess with my mother's head you meddling son-of-a . . .'

Then it had come back to him. Chi, mother, the Asian Boyz – that was it! The show had been titled 'Move On' and had focused on parents of children who had 'lost their way' by becoming drug addicts or prostitutes – or, in Chi's case, leader of the notorious Asian–American street gang known as the Asian Boyz.

Now, Jeffrey Logan had to admit, if he were to consider Chi's choice from a purely entrepreneurial point of view he might have even championed the young man's ingenuity, given Chi swapped his legitimate job at the local chicken shop for a position at the top of an organisation that was turning over millions of dollars a year (in what Logan's researchers had discovered was professional theft, arms dealing, drug running, prostitution and, more recently, skilful intimidation and then extortion of those foolish enough to express a willingness to testify against an Asian Boy at trial). But 'Move On' was not so much about what Chi had gained but, more poignantly, what his widowed mother had *lost* – a 'beautiful, intelligent, loving young boy' who, despite his being given 'every opportunity to lead a good and decent life', had chosen evil over goodness, darkness over light.

'You told my mother to disown me,' Chi had said. 'And after she go on your show she not take my calls or answer her door.

'And since that day I vow I will return the favour, you stinking white mother-fucker son-of-a-whore. I gonna make it so your momma doesn't recognise you!' And then Chi and his plebian puppets laughed, and Logan could not help but smile at the 'height' before their fall.

Flip.

'Come here,' Logan had whispered.

'What?'

'Come here,' he had repeated, this time using his right pointer finger to beckon Chi close. And Chi, not one to appear scared of a skinny, middle-aged white man who stood at least a foot shorter than himself, had moved forward and bent in low as if humouring his prey before moving in for the kill.

'You listen to me, you Goddamned idiot.' Logan had gone in strong. 'We did not screen the whole program, you ignorant son-of-a-bitch. There was more. Your mother told me about your sexual dysfunction, about how you had been born impotent and how she reasoned your lack of sexual prowess had been the trigger for your radical "change of lifestyle". So, my good friend, my advice to you would be to shut the hell up and listen to exactly what I need from you.'

Slide.

'I want you to leave me the fuck alone,' he had said, while maintaining a fixed smile on his face. 'But by the same token, if I ever need a favour, I want you to return it, no questions asked. And if you do not agree to these terms, Mr Chi, I shall call in my chips and get my producers to re-run the entire episode in full.'

Chi had held his breath and Logan had known he had him.

'So, now that I assume we are in agreement,' he said, placing his hand on Chi's shoulder as if in consolation, 'I want you to step back, you stupid Chinese prick, and then start the fuck crying – so I can explain away this incident to those nosey deputies approaching stage left. Are we on the same page, Mr Chi?' Logan had asked then, as he took a slight step to the side.

Chi had nodded.

Turn.

It was that easy.

Just as it had been with her.

'You're lying,' said the gorgeous red-haired woman with the striking blue eyes and the killer figure in the expensive navy blue suit. She had agreed that he could buy her a third drink, a vodka martini no less.

'Lying?' said a young Doctor Jeffrey Logan, still basking in the glow of the six-figure deal he and his partner had just signed with America's number one TV network, and the early, record-breaking ratings of his first few shows.

'I asked you what your parents did and you told me your father was in accounting and your mother in the arts. But I could tell by your eyes that you were lying, and if there is one thing I cannot stand, Doctor Logan, it is a liar, TV show superstar or not.'

There was something about her forthrightness that aroused him – no doubt the fact that it was screaming out to be curbed.

'It wasn't a lie,' he said, lying freely about the lie not being a lie. 'My father was a freelance financial advisor. And my mother reached the top of her field in artistic expressionism.'

'Artistic expressionism?' she said. 'Well, I would believe you, if I knew exactly what the hell that was.'

He had noticed her the minute he had walked into the bar, correctly picking her as one of the lawyers attending another conference in the similarly sized meeting hall downstairs. Logan was in Miami to speak at the Annual American Psychological Association Symposium, and the high-cheekboned red head next to him was doing likewise at her own legal shindig below.

'Your profile says you were born in Nevada,' she went on, picking up the conference brochure he had handed her minutes earlier and turning to the section where his biography and the accompanying B&W publicity shot was given full page pride of place.

This harping on his origins was both grating and

stimulating at the very same time – the unique combination, which always made him stir.

'That's right,' he said, accepting the martini and scotch on the rocks from the pristinely dressed barman before handing him a twenty and suggesting he 'keep the change'.

'Vegas,' she said.

'Excuse me?'

'Vegas, you were brought up in Las Vegas.'

'Well . . .' he began, knowing his bio did not specify his actual city of origin. Logan had always been irritated by the fact that his parents had chosen to rear him in the City of Sin. It did not exactly scream 'credibility', at least not in his chosen line of work.

'Honestly, Jeffrey,' she said, referring to him by his first name for the first time, her Boston brogue making her sound like one of those outspoken Kennedy daughters – all breeding and class but with an edge of congenital bravado. 'If anything, you should be proud of your home town. Vegas has guts – it's full of colour and adventure and . . .'

'Debauchery,' he finished, his eyes never leaving her own.

And then she laughed, a deep alluring chortle, throwing back her long pale neck, allowing her thick red hair to fall lusciously across her shoulders.

'I'm sorry,' she said. 'It's been a long day – during which I sat through endless sessions on corporate trust and communication issues. We even did the role playing thing – had to break off into little groups and try to guess when a fellow delegate was lying.'

'Which is why you suspected I was lying about my parents.'

'Something like that.' She smiled, taking a long slow drink of her martini.

'My mother danced nights in the casinos while my father made ends meet by working days doing the books for a local Vegas car dealer,' Logan admitted, knowing he had her, and it would not matter in the end.

'And you are ashamed of them?' she asked, the slightest furrow in her brow.

'They are not around to be ashamed of. They died in a car accident when I was a teenager.'

He saw it then, the embarrassment in her eyes, the mortification at her own insensitivity, the regret at having 'judged him too soon'.

'I am so sorry,' she said. 'I have had too much to drink, and as a result, have been uncharacteristically rude.'

'Apology accepted,' he said, offering his right hand for her to shake as if they were agreeing to some sort of deal.

'Thank you,' she replied, her hand still firmly in his grip.

'Are you doing anything after this?' he asked after a pause, his agenda now firmly in place.

'Not really,' she said. 'Are you?'

'Yes. I am taking you out to dinner.'

'Well then.' She smiled. 'I most gratefully accept.'

'In spite of the fact that my mother was a whore and my father a sap.'

'No, Jeffrey,' she said. 'Because of it.'

11

There was an old saying about Boston's wealthy Beacon Hill and neighbouring Back Bay – something that went along the lines of: 'Only real Americans lived on Beacon Hill and Back Bay – and they were Unitarians and medics and members of the Somerset Club with blood lines that dated back to the earliest of brave and adventurous settlers.' And it was still true today, to a point, with Back Bay second only to Beacon Hill as the most expensive suburb in the city – its historic townhouses fetching around a cool three mill and the super-chic shopping strips of Newbury and Boylston streets screaming upmarket fashion with prices to match.

The fact that the suburb was once literally a 'back bay' for Boston – a tidal waterway that was eventually filled following the construction of the old mill dam – did nothing to diminish its historical superiority as the earliest of New England architects took great care to line its streets with uniform and well-integrated three- and four-storey brownstones, stylish late nineteenth-century constructions which still stood firm today.

So, as David and Sara climbed the stairs of Katherine de Costa's well-preserved residence, giving the now standard 'no comment' to the handful of press who had been camped out front all morning, they had a feeling the décor inside would match the successful TV executive's elegant address. And they were not disappointed when the attractive de Castro opened her door and led them into her stylish designer abode.

'Wow,' said Sara, who was a big fan of minimalist chic. 'Your home is beautiful, Ms de Castro.'

'It's Katherine, and thank you,' said their host, an exotically beautiful Latin–American with long dark hair and golden skin. She was dressed in all black – the only hint of colour was the myriad brightly hued bangles that trailed up her slender right arm. They gave the otherwise conservatively dressed woman a hint of ingenuity – a creativity she no doubt called upon when executive-producing what this morning's *Tribune* had described as one of the 'most entertaining talk shows on TV'.

'I decorated it myself,' de Castro went on. 'With some sound advice from some very talented designers.' She smiled as she led them up a set of stairs and towards the back of the house. 'I spent a weekend with Francois Lecoure who gave me a tip or two,' she added, referring to the famous French interior guru who Sara later explained to David was a designing legend with his own program on one of those popular cable channels. 'He even helped me source some special pieces from

Europe, such as the white leather lounge from Milano and the complementary hand-woven Belgian rug.'

'They're amazing,' said Sara.

'Yes,' smiled de Castro, gesturing for them to take a seat on the lounge. 'But not at all child friendly, I'm afraid.'

'So that's why I grew up in a house where every carpet, rug and piece of furniture was black or grey or brown,' smiled David, not sure as to how else to enter this conversation.

'Your mother sounds like a very sensible woman,' said de Castro, as she poured them a cup of tea from the gold-rimmed pot before her.

'Let's just say that with three kids causing constant havoc, she had no choice but to forego style for practicality.'

A few more minutes of chitchat and a round of deli-fresh cinnamon cookies later, David had to admit he was getting a little curious about the whereabouts of Stephanie's children. De Castro had been right; this was not exactly a 'young-person-friendly' residence, and he was wondering where Chelsea and J.T. Logan might be hiding.

'Chelsea and her brother are upstairs in the sitting room,' de Castro said, as if reading his mind. 'Watching some music video special on someone or other unplugged. They have been remarkably good . . . considering.' She stopped there, as if not sure how to continue.

'Ms de Castro,' David began. He did not want to offend the obviously intelligent and hospitable woman before them, but truth be told, all this politeness and pleasant conversation was starting to frustrate him. He knew de Castro was Logan's friend but he also got the sense that she might tend to look at things more practically than emotionally which, at this point in time, could be exactly what they needed.

'We understand you and Doctor Logan are friends – and we can assure you that, as his attorneys, we only have his best interests at heart.'

De Castro nodded, a perfunctory gesture which suggested she knew this was coming.

'But you were there last night, Ms de Castro, and I think we are safe in assuming that you realise your partner's actions were, well, extremely altruistic to say the least.'

'David,' she replied, placing her tea cup on its saucer before looking him directly in the eye. 'Allow me to begin by getting one thing straight. I have known Jeffrey for a very long time, and while I am dedicated to helping him as much as possible, I also – as do you – see things as they *are* rather than the way that I wish them to be.

'I am a selfish woman by nature, David. You do not become as successful as I have in the industry that I work in being otherwise. In fact, I spent the better part of the morning on the telephone to the network CEO trying to salvage our professional future, and I am not ashamed to admit it.

'But this morning, much to my surprise,' de Castro went on, leaning forward to rest her elbows on her knees, her bracelets jingling as they fell down towards her wrist, 'I discovered that I am not the hardened executive I thought myself to be. For while I could have, and probably *should* have, described to my bosses the situation as I knew it, I found myself supporting Jeffrey's version of events to a T.'

'You told them your business partner killed his wife?' asked Sara.

'Accidentally – yes, I did.'

'Risking the possibility the network might drop him from their stable?'

'Drop us – yes,' she said, turning her attention to David. 'But before you go labelling me a Good Samaritan I must warn you that my decision was not entirely gallant. For I told the CEO that I wanted to discuss something with you and Miss Davis here first, before I spoke of the other matter – a matter which Jeffrey has specifically asked me to keep in the strictest of confidence.'

David looked at Sara, wondering where in the hell this might be going.

'I am sorry Ms de Castro, you are going to have to . . .'

'Of course,' she interrupted. 'Forgive me. But if I am to explain I shall need your patience. You see, things are not as simple as they seem. In many ways it is much safer for me to stick to Jeffrey's account of what happened, for despite what you might expect would be the fallout from him killing his wife, in many ways it is the best scenario for him professionally.'

'I don't understand,' said Sara. 'How can Jeffrey's killing his wife not have a negative effect on his reputation?'

But de Castro was already shaking her head. 'Because an accident is an accident,' she said. 'And as strange as it may seem, once the dust settles, the sympathy sparked by such a tragedy may even see a rise in his popularity.'

'You think the American public will embrace Jeffrey Logan for what he is supposed to have done?' asked David, incredulous.

'I think it is better than the alternative.'

'Or rather,' said David, 'the truth.'

De Castro looked at him, before finally nodding.

'You are right,' she said. 'If Jeffrey – a man who has built his entire career on his ability to advise families on how to hold it all together – is exposed as the father of a child who . . .'

'Blew his mother to bits,' interrupted David. He could not hold it in. All this talk of how Stephanie's murder would affect 'poor Jeffrey' was slowly making him sick to his stomach. 'Yes, I can see how that would rankle.'

There was silence as David took a breath before going on.

'Here's the thing, Katherine,' he began, leaning forward in his seat. 'First up, Stephanie used to be a friend of mine, and a good one, so forgive me if equating her murder with ratings points doesn't exactly sit right where I am coming from.

'Secondly, whether you support Jeffrey's version of events or not, it isn't going to change the sequence of the inevitable. The forensics will not adjust themselves to suit Jeffrey's image concerns, and I am afraid the good doctor is going to have to live with that, professional reputation or not.

'Finally,' he took a breath. 'If there is something you have to tell us, if you have *any* information that has some bearing on this case, then you need to share it and you need to share it now. Because if you don't, I can guarantee you, the ADA will find it and take great pleasure in using it against us.'

Katherine de Castro said nothing, just ran her left hand up her right arm so that her bangles chimed against one another in sequence.

'I am sorry,' she said softly. 'It is just that for so many years my job has been to pre-empt problems and shut them down before the public gets even an inkling that they exist. But in this case, once the truth is out, once the media are made aware of what really happened and more to the point *why* then . . .'

'What?' David could not believe his ears. He shot a glance at Sara. '*Why?* Not just *what* really happened but *why*?' he repeated. 'You think J.T. Logan shot his mother deliberately and you think you know why?'

'Oh yes,' she said, her brow now furrowed as if suggesting there was never any argument to the contrary. 'But please don't think that his actions in any way make me feel ill of him – for in all honesty, if I were in his position, I would have picked up that rifle myself.'

12

'You look like crap,' said Amanda Carmichael, as she pushed forward into Tony Bishop's apartment – the bed still unmade, the smell of stale coffee emanating from the small yet surprisingly spacious German-designed kitchen. 'You haven't seen her for years, Tony. She was an old college fling – and one of many, I'm sure.'

Amanda Carmichael hadn't planned to see Tony Bishop this afternoon – in fact she had intended to spend the entire day at her office, preparing for Monday's all-important arraignment. But every now and again a twist of fate provided you with the possibility of an advantage over your opponent, and if that was what this fortunate coincidence was, she intended to make the most of it.

'I know it was a long time ago,' said Tony. 'But Stephanie was something special. She had this incredible sense of optimism, this insatiable zest for life.'

'She was great in bed, was that it?' asked Amanda –

and then, perhaps sensing she should tone it down a little, moved towards him with her arms outstretched.

'I'm sorry,' she said, not wanting to deter him from sharing his thoughts with her. 'I hear she had a lot of promise in her day – until she got married and had kids.'

'Yeah,' said Tony then, taking her hand and leading her towards the kitchen. 'It's funny how people end up, you know. I mean, we used to joke how she'd be running the country by her fortieth birthday.'

'Maybe she wanted the easy life. Maybe marrying the successful TV star was all part of the plan.'

'No,' he said, tipping the old coffee into the sink before switching on the machine to make a fresh batch. 'She wasn't like that. First up, she was filthy rich – her dad owned . . .'

'Rockwell Wineries,' she finished. 'I know.'

'And secondly, Stephanie was definitely not one to live vicariously through anyone else.'

Amanda nodded, taking it all in. 'When was the last time you saw her?'

'God, I don't know, which is kind of ironic given our firm handles her family's business affairs.'

'But you have nothing to do with her account.'

'No. Charles Harrison looks after the winery stuff,' he said, referring to one of Williams, Coolidge and Harrison's senior partners. 'And our media division handles the doctor's interests so . . .'

'Didn't she accompany her husband to the Law Society ball in February?'

'Apparently, but I didn't see her. I was on a table with some of my own clients and Cavanaugh who . . .' His face showed the slightest trace of a smile at the memory.

'Who what?' she asked, her brow furrowing.

'Well, he switched seats because . . .' he began.

'He didn't want to sit on our table,' she finished.

'It wasn't you, it was Katz.'

'It's okay, Tony. If I recall correctly, you did a bit of seat switching of your own that night.' She smiled. 'And besides, Cavanaugh and I aren't exactly pitching for the same team.'

He nodded.

'Kind of strange, isn't it?' she added, as if the thought had only just occurred to her.

'What's strange?' he asked, moving to the refrigerator to collect the milk.

'That he is defending the man who killed his old friend.'

'It was an accident,' Tony said, stopping in the middle of pouring her a long strong black, her raised eyebrows allowing him to read the uncertainty on her face. 'Hold on a minute. Are you saying there is a chance the TV guy . . .?'

'No, of course not,' she said, taking her coffee before turning her back on him and moving towards the open plan living room beyond. 'Did you ever meet her kids?' she followed up after a pause.

'No,' he said, joining her on the living room sofa. 'Well, actually I did meet them once.'

'Really? When?' she asked with interest.

'I was in New Zealand on a skiing trip and . . . that must have been the last time I saw her. I ran into her at Auckland airport. Her little girl was a toddler and the baby boy brand new.'

'She gave birth to her son in Auckland?'

'Yeah. She wasn't that long out of college. She'd taken that big corporate job and then bailed on it as soon as she met the husband. She would only have been twenty-six, twenty-seven . . .

'Anyway, I was in the lounge with a couple of work buddies. One of them had family in the South Island so we took advantage of the early winter and headed for Mount Hutt. Stephanie walked in with a toddler in one arm and a newborn in the other. Her husband was on his cell phone so we were never properly introduced.'

'And this was in the New Zealand winter?' she probed a little further.

'Just before, if my memory is correct, about this time of year. Her husband was launching his show there or something, so she flew down with the other kid and I guess the baby came while she was there.'

'Kind of odd, isn't it?' she queried, the steam of her coffee lifting around her flawless face. 'Making such a long trip when you are so close to the end of a pregnancy?'

'I guess,' said Tony with a shrug. 'Maybe the kid came early.'

Amanda nodded. 'So was she pleased to see you?'

'Sure,' said Tony. 'Although I remember thinking she looked kind of harried. You know – skinny, tired. But then she'd just given birth to a kid in a foreign country so . . .'

'I guess that's what happens when you make the mistake of swapping the conference room for the nursery,' Amanda replied, and then, sensing by his expression that she might have gone too far added, 'I mean at such an early age.'

Tony nodded. 'Do you ever think about it?' he asked her. 'You know, what it would be like to pack it all in, make a commitment to someone, have a couple of kids?'

'Ah . . .' she began, wondering why Stephanie Tyler's death had her mercenary blue chip attorney boyfriend talking like a bona fide metrosexual sap. 'Not yet.'

'But some day maybe?' he asked, taking her hand.

And in that moment she knew he was falling in love with her, and simultaneously realised how stupid she would be – at least at this point – to rock the status quo.

'Some day, Tony. Maybe. Sure.'

13

'The woman was a tyrant,' said Katherine de Castro – plain and simple, just like that.

David knew she could read the surprise on his face, the complete and utter disbelief.

'I know how this sounds to you, David,' she went on. 'I spoke to Jeffrey on the telephone around lunch-time – it is J.T.'s birthday, you see, and he was allowed to make one call to wish him a happy day and . . . anyway . . .' She stopped there, as if the irony of this statement required a mandatory pause in its wake.

'I told Jeffrey I wanted to tell you about it and he warned me that your past association with his wife would make it extremely difficult for you to believe. But then I suggested that not telling you would be worse, that we were way past the platitudes, that unless we acted now, this whole sorry mess would come crashing down upon us, destroying several lives in the process, including Chelsea's and J.T.'s.'

'So Jeffrey gave you the go-ahead to explain this to us?' asked Sara.

'Not in so many words, but . . .' Katherine took a breath. 'You have to understand that, at least at this point, it is essential to Jeffrey that we stick to his story – for any suggestion of impropriety on Stephanie's part simply provides the District Attorney's office with the one thing against J.T. that they do not have, even after the forensics report comes in.'

'A motive,' said David.

'In one.'

'So you are saying that Stephanie was . . .' Even speaking of it was difficult.

'Abusing J.T., yes,' she said with determination, 'and Chelsea, and Jeffrey too to a certain extent. She was a mistress of emotional manipulation, David – the worst kind of bully. She ran that household like a dictator, wielding her delicate fist with skill – berating and criticising and belittling and threatening and using that brilliant but sadistic mind of hers to control her children with the purest of psychological fear. So much so, that J.T. took it upon himself to liberate the family the only way he knew how.'

David felt the anger well up inside him. He was in shock – at the audacity, the ridiculousness of it all.

'I'm sorry, Katherine,' he said. 'But there is no way the girl who I once knew . . .'

'But that's just the point, isn't it,' interrupted de Castro. 'You knew the *girl*, David – the girl who grew into a woman determined to quash the spirit of others in order to take control.'

'No,' he argued. 'I knew the person. I knew her *soul*.'

'You saw what she wanted you to see. The research on people like Stephanie is really quite comprehensive. These sociopaths are masters at creating personas to hide the extent of their narcissistic obsession with dominance.

'Until recently I too knew nothing of what was really going on behind the doors of that meticulously kept mansion in Beacon Hill. Jeffrey went to great pains to keep their "situation" quiet. It was only a month or so ago that he finally broke down and told me the extent of what he and his children had had to endure. He was at the end of his tether, you see, and had finally decided to ask her for a divorce.'

'I'm sorry, Katherine,' said Sara. 'But if Stephanie was as terrible as you claim, why didn't the doctor get out sooner? Why would he leave his two kids in a household where they were subject to such vehement maltreatment?'

'Because he knew if he spoke out no one would believe him, because he was trapped by his valued reputation as a man who championed a stance of zero tolerance against all forms of physical and emotional abuse, because he was ashamed of how far he had let things go – and, most importantly, because he was terrified of how Stephanie might react if he finally got the courage to fight.'

'So he let his children live in a home you describe as a virtual prison?' David was not convinced.

'He was concerned she would go for custody – and given his demanding job and Stephanie's "on paper" reputation as a dedicated stay-at-home mom, he knew she had every chance of winning.'

'But we're not talking about toddlers here, Katherine,' Sara pushed on. 'Chelsea and J.T. are teenagers and surely, if they took their father's side, if they told the authorities of this alleged cruelty . . .'

'Not everybody has the white picket fence upbringing I am sure your parents afforded you, Sara. As Jeffrey explained, those living in the company of a skilled emotional abuser are so diminished they simply cannot see a way out.'

'Well, if you are right,' said David, 'J.T. gave it a pretty good shot.' And the irony of his words lay heavy in the silence that followed.

'All right,' said de Castro, rising from her chair to move towards the kitchen and take a bottle of white wine from the refrigerator and an opener from a stainless steel drawer. She progressed to the cupboard to retrieve three crystal glasses before returning to her sofa and extracting the cork.

'Forgive me,' she said, pouring her own glass first before filling the other two without bothering to ask if they wanted any. 'But it's getting late, and I'm tired, and the stories I have to tell are far from pleasant. I understand you need proof – and so I shall provide it. But as I explained earlier, I am not one to undertake anything without a favourable quid pro quo.'

'What is it you want, Katherine?' asked David at last.

'I want you to promise that when J.T. is arrested, you and Sara will agree to represent him.'

'And is this request also coming from Jeffrey?' asked David, tiring of this little game of Chinese whispers.

'No.' She shook her head. 'This is my little addition

to the contract. The boy needs your help and I am hoping you will agree to provide it.'

'It's not that easy, Katherine. For starters we don't work in the juvenile court system – and secondly . . .'

'Well, I want you to agree to assisting his juvenile specialist attorneys – to help this boy who has never known anything bar humiliation and shame and fear.'

David shook his head, before looking to Sara who raised her eyebrows ever so slightly in an expression that said, '*Perhaps we should at least hear what this woman has to say*.'

'All right, Katherine,' said David at last. 'We will listen, but I can promise you that from where I stand, the chances of your convincing me Stephanie was the monster you describe are somewhere between zero and zilch.'

'Then I apologise in advance,' de Castro began, pausing to take a long slow drink of her wine, 'for destroying your view of a friend you once obviously cherished.'

De Castro began with the gun. She started slowly, proffering questions as she went. Asking why the wife of a celebrated pacifist – a man who was an outspoken advocate for tighter gun laws – would have given her husband a high-powered big game rifle for his birthday. She explained that Doctor Jeff's hobbies were limited to golfing and jogging – and that his show was sponsored by Hallmark, one of the most outspoken anti-gun companies in the country.

'It all started with the handbag,' she said. 'Jeffrey told me Stephanie wanted one for her birthday.

And not just any tote, she requested a Devi Kroell alligator clutch made from alligators with scales of similar sizes – a rarity, I believe, which I suppose, given Stephanie's covetous nature, made it all that more appealing.

'Anyway,' she went on, taking another sip of her wine, 'Jeffrey did his best to locate one, but as his wife's birthday approached, he ran out of time to organise it. He failed to put her name on the waiting list which was, apparently, several hundred strong. You have to remember these bags, which cost a cool thirty thousand each, are made from rare Asian reptiles and do not grow on trees.'

Sara nodded.

'So,' she continued, 'knowing he could not "deliver", Jeffrey got the next best thing. He bought her a forty thousand dollar Nancy Gonzalez Porousus bag made from uncommon ring lizard skin. He presented it to her at a party – a big one attended by all her friends – and when she opened it, and studied it, the slightest furrow formed in her brow, before she adjusted her expression to one more appropriate to her surroundings, and offered her husband a grateful and passionate kiss.'

'She liked the alternative?' asked Sara.

'God, no,' said de Castro. 'Jeffrey told me she hated it. It was not what she had asked for, but she knew better than to let loose in front of an audience. And so she waited – an entire six months – before she returned the favour by giving him a two-foot weapon powerful enough to kill a Goddamned rhinoceros.

'She presented it to him while he was at dinner with

the family. Determined to show the kids what an unsatisfactory partner their father had turned out to be.'

'Her apparent point being . . .?' asked a still disbelieving David.

'That Jeffrey had failed her,' said de Castro. 'She served dinner and gave him the gun and then turned to him to say something along the lines of: "Next time I ask for an alligator skin purse, you can go and shoot the fucker yourself".'

'Oh, come on,' said David. 'You don't expect us to believe . . .'

'. . . and she said this while pointing the rifle directly at her thirteen-year-old son's forehead.'

David was floored. He simply did not know what to say.

'Katherine,' said Sara then. 'How do you know this? I mean, maybe Doctor Logan was . . .'

'Because I saw the whole thing on video,' interrupted de Castro. 'Jeffrey had taken to recording her, you see – for evidence in the divorce proceedings, so that he might win custody after all.'

David sat there, still in shock, the icy chill in his spine now spreading upwards towards his chest. He could not believe what she was saying. This was just not the Stephanie he knew.

'Do you have a copy of this video?' he asked.

'No, but Jeffrey has one – locked away somewhere safe.'

'And are there other videos – other pieces of similar evidence which show Stephanie to be the woman her husband described?'

'I think so,' she offered. 'Although I am not sure what

form they take. I know that Jeffrey only just started collecting such evidence. I know he only asked for the divorce a little less than a week ago.'

'Then why the hell didn't he give this tape to the police?' asked David. 'Why is he playing martyr when he could present such evidence and show his son killed out of desperation?'

'I suppose he was thinking on his feet,' she replied. 'Perhaps he sensed J.T. could not weather the storm of a public arrest. Perhaps he believed his "accident" theory might be enough to protect his two children from the media circus the truth would inevitably create. Jeffrey may be ambitious, he may have worked damned hard to get where he is, but there is no way he would manipulate his son's act of vengeance to score a few extra ratings points.'

'So that video you speak of isn't being held for some big exclusive exposé on national TV.' David was thinking ahead, his mind jumping to and from every scenario he could think of to explain what Katherine de Castro was describing.

'Absolutely not – in fact, if Jeffrey has his way, it will never see the light of day.'

'I'm sorry, Katherine. I am still finding it hard to believe that . . .'

'That what?' interrupted an obviously frustrated de Castro. 'That the recording exists or that Jeffrey has no plans for using it?'

David realised he was stuck – for if he did not believe in one he could not argue against the other.

'Both,' he said at last.

'Then perhaps you will just have to see it for yourself.'

14

Las Vegas, Nevada

Deirdre McCall lengthened her torso, lowered her arms and turned her feet out as she stopped to survey the wide-eyed students before her. She was tired, stiff, her neck protesting at such a long Saturday's work, but she did not show it – no, she stood tall and graceful, her slim body defying the spread of 'late middle age', her legs still toned, her skin supple, despite what life had dealt her and the heavy price she'd paid for refusing to *ever let go*.

She closed her eyes, slowly, deliberately, and imagined a different group before her – Roxy on her right and Gigi on her left, Marilyn diagonally in front and Cindy far stage left. They were doing the stardust number – the one with the pink flamingo headdresses, the crystal knickers and the long cords of fake diamonds wrapped around their bodies just so. And their smooth skin shimmered with every move, their pert breasts barely flinching as they kicked and spun and glided across the stage in heels so high they seemed to defy gravity. And she counted off the steps – one, two, three – and relished in the memory of the show-stopping finale and the inevitable deafening applause.

'Miss Deirdre.'

She heard the words, but refused, at least for this moment, to recognise their owner as she willed the memory to its wonderful conclusion. And she saw his face then at the back of the crowded room – the tall, skinny 'unlikely' one who had caught her eye and, despite all the advances, all the offers and proposals from movie stars and business tycoons and other men of means, had stolen her heart with the genuineness of his smile. And they were happy, and life was good, until their twosome became a threesome and their whole pretty picture got shot to Goddamned . . .

'*Miss Deirdre!*' called Susie Bonkowski – the blue-eyed, buck-teethed brunette in the second row. 'Are we almost done? It's after four and our moms are waiting.'

'Yes, yes of course,' recovered McCall, smiling at the attentive seven-year-olds before her while wondering which ones would make it, which ones would not, and which ones would think they had, only to find out that life had pulled a swift one on them after all.

'You may go,' she said as she curtseyed to her class. 'Good afternoon, children.'

'Good afternoon, Miss Deirdre, and thank you, Miss Deirdre,' they replied – a singsongy response in appreciation.

And then the pitter-patter of their ballet slipper-shod feet, the music of their after-class laughter, the cumulative whoosh of their quick excited breaths filled the room only to dissipate quickly, painfully, as they opened the door and the outside world sucked them from her once again.

She grabbed her wrap and changed her shoes and bolted the double hall doors behind her, deciding to walk the fifteen blocks home rather than wait for the bus – stretching her journey from a pathetic twenty minutes to a decent, time-consuming forty-three.

After she opened the door to her second-storey apartment, she did what she always did when she came home for the night. She moved straight through the entryway and into the living area towards the treated pine coffee table where she picked up the remote and filled the room with noise before the loneliness of the present and the memories of the past took their shot at embracing her with all the cold determination they could muster.

And she left the TV on as she took her shower and defrosted her dinner and settled in for the long dark hours of nothingness. She watched the dramas and the late night news, taking a bizarre form of comfort in knowing there were other lonely souls, other unwitting victims of life out there suffering, just like her.

And then she saw it. The headline story. And it all came back to her – just like that. There had been a murder – in a fancy brownstone, in a fancy suburb, in a fancy city some thousands of miles away. The TV celebrity was being taken away in handcuffs, his murdered wife removed like a clump of meat under a bright blue tarpaulin, the kids sheltered by some good-looking friend, the Barbie Doll District Attorney facing the cameras with some all-important information to divulge.

Deirdre tried to concentrate – to listen, *carefully*, and take it all in – which was hard considering her brain was not exactly firing on all cylinders.

'*Accident*', the serious-looking reporter kept saying – and then she heard other words like '*rifle*' and '*famous*' and '*tragedy*' and '*children*' and '*shock revelation*' and other similar phrases.

Despite the fact that her hearing was not at its optimum, and regardless of the fact that close to a quarter of her brain had been removed almost eighteen years ago after the accident that took her husband's life, and notwithstanding the fact that she was on her fourth glass of chardonnay, Deirdre McCall knew, then and there, that the twenty-nine inch scene before her, distanced by geography and economy and every other thing to do with her lower middle-class life, was not so disconnected after all.

'Dear God,' she said, not noticing that her empty plastic glass had slipped from her sofa and made its way silently to the floor.

'He's doing it again,' she whispered, nodding her head in inevitability. 'He's doing it all over again.'

15

When Chelsea Logan was seven, her father gave her an ink blot test. It was one of those standard things you saw on TV – dark blobs on white cardboard, negatives of things only *you* were supposed to define. She found it uncomfortable, distressing even, as she had no idea which answer was correct. She rattled off her feigned perceptions one after the other, at a speed that was bordering on ridiculous – a house, a sailing boat, two people playing tennis, a bicycle, a palm tree, when in reality all she saw in the blots was ghost after ghost after ghost.

And that is how she felt right now, as if her brain was firing images at her, defying her to make sense of them – to *work this out*! They were like determined shadows whispering in her ear, taunting her with the knowledge that failing was not an option, that as of two nights ago, she was her brother's only protector, and if she failed to 'perform', the truth would be redefined and their desperate little 'plan' would take a catastrophic turn for the worst.

'Do you think he got the letter?' asked a soft-voiced J.T., who had spent a second night on the floor next to her bed.

'Not yet. It's Sunday,' she replied, staring at the ceiling. 'He'll get it tomorrow.'

'I don't think he'll get it when he gets it.'

'Even if he does,' said Chelsea, knowing she should in the very least be *trying* to stay upbeat for the sake of her little brother, but not sure as to how this could be done, 'I am worried that . . . well . . . considering what Katherine plans to show him, we have to be prepared for the possibility that it won't make any difference.'

Chelsea had heard the entire conversation held in Katherine de Castro's living room the afternoon before. She had been perched on the bottom of the staircase, listening to the lawyers listening to Katherine as she repeated the story Chelsea's father had told his business partner mere weeks before.

They had met David and Sara who were nothing but kind and understanding, which made Chelsea think that perhaps she should consider straying from the plan after all and trust them enough to . . .

'David Cavanaugh was meant to be on our side,' interrupted J.T., as if reading her mind.

'And maybe he still is,' said Chelsea. 'If everything else fails, J.T., we may have to contemplate . . . telling him the truth,' she said, needing to broach the possibility.

'*No*,' he reacted without hesitation. 'Maybe before, but now he is working for Father, and you know that no matter what we say, Father has a way of . . .'

'I know,' she said, angry at herself for being a leader with no idea how to lead.

'We are losing control,' said J.T. after a time.

Chelsea did not argue because she knew it was true. They were losing – or had already lost – any semblance of control over a situation they naively assumed they could manage. And now she realised just how foolish they had been for thinking they had the power to alter the universe they had existed in since birth.

'Don't worry, J.T.,' she said, wanting desperately to offer him some words of comfort. 'We haven't lived like we have for all these years without learning a thing or two.'

'But I won't be around to help you,' he replied – and she knew that he knew that she knew.

After a long pause she spoke. 'Then you must trust me to finish what we started.' She draped her hand over the edge of her bed so that her brother might grasp it from below. 'I won't let her down, J.T., I promise. No matter what, one way or another, I will find a way to see this through.'

It was Sunday and it was late, and Sara and David were tired. They had met with Arthur and filled him in, and after several long hours of working on tomorrow's arraignment, David had taken a call from Katherine de Castro who explained that the video was in a safety deposit box that she could not access on the weekend. And so with nothing more to do until tomorrow – and after realising they were going home to an apartment low on food and, more importantly from Sara's perspective, strong Arabica coffee, they decided to do a grocery shop before heading back for a quiet night in.

'Brazilian coffee,' said Sara as she dragged her feet

in feigned exhaustion through the Huntington Avenue entrance of the well-stocked Shaw's in Copley. 'I need some pure Brazilian coffee now!'

Despite their heavy day, David sought comfort in the banality of steering a shaky-wheeled trolley around a busy supermarket – and could tell that Sara felt the same. She took his hand and squeezed it as they moved past the fruit and vegetable section, stocking up on everything from organic Granny Smith apples to fresh, imported kiwi fruit.

'I thought you were going strictly decaf,' said David, as they rounded the coffee section and Sara moved ahead looking for the finest mountain grown beans that she could find.

'And I thought you had agreed it was more than okay for me to enjoy at least one small shot of genuine caffeine per day.' She looked back at him with a smile.

'I think you are over-exhausted and I do not have the energy to argue with you,' he said, smiling in return.

'And I think you are a very perceptive man,' she said, moving backwards to kiss him squarely on the cheek.

Just then they were interrupted by a shout from behind, a man's voice calling David by a nickname only his family and his oldest college buddies still used.

'DC,' said Tony Bishop, as he moved up the aisle towards them, his arm outstretched. 'It's good to see you, man. I heard you didn't make it this morning either?' he added, referring to their weekly round of alumni rugby. 'I was a no-show too – and Negley has already left a message on my home machine ragging us both out for bailing. But, well, given the news – about Stephanie . . . I still can't believe it, DC.'

'I know,' said David, taking Tony's hand and patting him on the shoulder. 'It was a shock to me too.'

'She was always so full of life, you know?' Tony said, genuine sorrow in his eyes. 'She was the unstoppable one – the girl who was meant to . . .' And then he hesitated, Sara stepping forward to fill the void.

'It's good to see you, Tony,' she said, reaching out to take his hand. 'And I am sorry for your loss – David told me you and Stephanie were close.'

'We were,' he said, taking Sara's hand with gratitude. 'In fact once we were more than close. You know, I always wondered if things would have been different if we might have . . .'

'Well, hello there,' interrupted another voice from behind, this one softer, smoother, with a certain tone that said '*fancy meeting you here*'. Amanda Carmichael was striding up the aisle towards them, a bottle of imported mineral water in her pale, slender hand. 'It's good to see you again, Counsellor,' she said, shifting the bottle to her left hand so that she might extend her arm towards David. 'And you must be Sara Davis.' She smiled, nodding at Sara. 'It's a pleasure to meet you at last.'

Tony draped his arm around the shoulder of the beautiful blonde prosecutor before them, and Sara's jaw dropped.

'Of course,' said Tony. 'You guys know each other?'

'We do,' said Amanda. 'In fact, I've been an admirer of David's for years,' she said, her eyes flicking briefly towards Sara. 'Professionally, I mean. In fact, due to the unfortunate nature of our professional responsibilities, we have a date in court tomorrow. How terrible that we should be pitted against each other in a case such as this, David. Tony has told me so many wonderful things about Stephanie Tyler – and I can only imagine how difficult it must be for you to be representing her killer.'

David said nothing – too floored to even begin to respond.

'Amanda . . .' began Tony.

'No,' said David then. 'Amanda is right. But as my client explained in his statement, his wife's death was an accident and the Stephanie I knew would want me doing everything I could to make sure the father of her kids was home to look after them.'

'From what I saw, at least one of those kids seems extremely capable of fending for himself.' It was a surprising statement – almost shocking in its frankness.

'Guys,' said Tony then.

'I'm sorry, Tony,' smiled Amanda. 'You're right, this is no time to be talking shop,' she said, lifting her arms at her surroundings. 'No pun intended.'

There was an awkward pause, with none of them saying anything until . . .

'You live around here, Miss Carmichael?' asked Sara.

'No.' She shook her head. 'I have an apartment on the waterfront,' she added, casually dropping the fact that she resided in one of the most sought after locations in the city. Condos on Boston's popular harbourside piers went for anything between one and six million and David guessed Amanda Carmichael's, given her family connections and money, would not be one of the 'cheaper' varieties.

'But Tony has offered to cook me dinner and

considering I use my oven for extra storage . . .' She smiled.

'Anyway,' said Sara, after a second uncomfortable silence, 'we really just dropped in to find me this special blend of Brazilian coffee.'

'Oh, really?' said Amanda, her eyes darting quickly to Sara's stomach. 'Is that allowed? I mean . . . super!'

But Sara had interpreted her comment for what it was, and David knew it.

'If you're after a good, strong blend,' said Tony, lightening the mood, 'I know just the brand. It's in the South American section – about five aisles down and . . . Here,' he said, scooping up her hand, 'I'll show you.'

Before anyone had a chance to respond, Tony and Sara were gone.

'So how is your client holding up?' asked Amanda Carmichael at last, taking the slightest of steps towards him.

'As well as can be expected,' said David. 'Like I said before, it was an accident, Amanda.'

'You seem to specialise in those, don't you?' she responded.

'The Martin trial was three years ago,' he said, referring to the high-profile case in which he defended a respected African–American attorney. Rayna Martin had been wrongly accused of killing Christina Haynes, the white teenage daughter of a powerful US senator – a man set on manipulating justice to paint his daughter's accidental death as murder.

'That wasn't the accident I was referring to,' countered Amanda, and David could not believe what he was hearing.

'Oh, come on, David,' she said, reading the anger on his face. 'A good Catholic boy like you? If you were serious about this girl you would have married her months ago.'

'Jesus Christ, Amanda, that's none of your business,' he said, his back now flush against shelves packed with baby food.

'Can you honestly stand here and tell me that she is the one for you?' she asked, moving forward an inch. 'I mean she's very pretty but . . .' she paused. 'Besides, if you are so in love with Sara, then why did you come on to me at the Law Society ball last February?'

'What?' said David, incredulous. 'I did not come on to you,' he said, feeling his brow break out in a sweat. 'If you recall, as soon as Tony went to get you a drink, you walked right on up to me and asked me if I wanted to . . .'

'Fuck – yes,' she replied. 'And didn't you?'

'No! Jesus, Amanda, you have got to get a grip. You're dating one of my best friends, for Christ's sake.'

'Tony's a distraction,' she said.

And David felt a pang of regret for his friend who he sensed was falling for the beautiful prosecutor before him.

'And I'm not interested,' he countered.

'Then why are you pressed up against me?' she said.

'Because you have left me nowhere to go,' he said.

'Hmm.' She smiled. 'And I normally reserve that little manoeuvre for work.' She took a step back and David knew this was all part of her sick little game – unnerving the opposition before she was about to face them in court.

'It was nice to see you, Counsellor,' she said then, turning her back on him as she headed off in the opposite direction down the aisle. 'And you better be careful.' She smiled, gesturing at the teetering tower of baby food tins behind him. 'You are about to trigger an avalanche, so consider yourself warned.'

16

The Boston Municipal Courthouse, better known as the Edward W. Brooke Courthouse is a tall impressive structure situated on a triangular block on the corner of New Chardon and Merimac streets in Boston's busy Government Center. The architectural masterpiece, completed in the late nineties and named for the first African–American elected and re-elected to the US Senate, is made almost entirely out of Deer Isle stone, its pale glowing colour adding an aura of brightness to its already impressive façade, its main entrance rising tall and rectangular above the busy pedestrians below, its glass front doors flanked by two flags – one for country and one for state.

David and Sara arrived early, knowing arraignments were usually scheduled at nine. They moved into the wide open lobby – its four-storey atrium flooding the massive space with bright morning sunlight – and headed towards the courtrooms on level three.

'Is Joe coming?' asked Sara, as they headed for the stairs.

'He said he'd try,' answered David. 'Although, according to what he said on Saturday, he doesn't expect any surprises. The ADA is hamstrung until the forensics come in.'

'I don't trust her,' said Sara.

David knew this was an understatement on her part.

'Neither do I. But what can she do? Our client confessed. She has to play this out by the letter of the law.

'Arthur,' said David, waving at their boss who moved to join them at the top of the stairs.

'Our client has arrived and we're first on the docket,' Arthur told them quickly, the corridors now filled with legal workers and star-struck voyeurs who were obviously busting to get a 'good seat' at the celebrity arraignment of the year. 'Joe's inside, back row far left.'

David nodded.

'And we pulled Judge Kessler,' continued Arthur, raising his eyebrows. 'So keep it short and sweet.'

Judge Marion Kessler, an old Municipal Court warhorse, had been serving on the bench for as long as David could remember. The woman was a short, round bulldog of discontentment, with a keen mind and a sharp temper. She was known equally for her intolerance for hyperbole and her distaste of anyone set on wasting the court's precious time.

'I thought she'd been elevated to the Superior Court,' said David, who had heard Kessler's application to the Judicial Nominating Committee had been approved and passed on to the governor who had successfully submitted Kessler's name to the Governor's Council which just recently, after a public hearing, had voted to elevate Kessler to the 'meatier' Superior Court.

'She has,' said Arthur. 'Which is why we can thank our lucky stars this case will most likely stop here,' he added, referring to their assumption that, eventually, the charges against Jeffrey Logan would be dropped.

Ten minutes later they were inside the green-carpeted courtroom, the rather small rectangular room being nowhere near big enough to hold the masses now squeezing through the back doors.

David, Sara and Arthur took their seat at the minimalist cherrywood desk on the left-hand side of the room, the complementary table to their right still empty bar two fresh-faced Commonwealth attorneys who had obviously been called upon to haul Amanda Carmichael's notes and set up her desk.

To the far right of the room, in a space normally reserved for the jury, sat a select number of the press – including David's friend and *Boston Tribune* Deputy Editor Marc Rigotti, who acknowledged David with a nod, and the extremely well-dressed Caroline Croft, frontwoman of CBC's popular *Newsline* program.

David had locked horns with Croft before and knew her to be one of the cleverest journalists in the business. She was also shrewd and manipulative and would stop at nothing to trump all other news programs with the most sought-after exclusives of the day.

'Croft has left five messages on my cell,' said David, leaning into Arthur's ear.

'I wouldn't have expected anything less,' said Arthur, who looked particularly uncomfortable in a button-down shirt and tie. 'My advice is to treat her like a fish on a hook,' he whispered. 'We have something she wants, namely the power to negotiate the most controversial celebrity interview of the year. Keep her at bay until we need her – and then we can reel her in, under our conditions.'

'You think Logan talking might help his son's cause?' asked David.

'I think we should leave all our options open. Remember, in all likelihood, after this week this case will be out of our hands, but if in the end we agree we want to help Logan score a few points for his son then . . .'

'No harm, no foul,' finished David.

'Exactly.'

Moments later, David turned to greet Katherine de Castro who, together with the two Logan children, was being ushered in the back door by their office secretary, Nora Kelly, and a watchful security guard.

Sara had arranged for the reliable Nora and the prearranged guard to meet de Castro's car and help the children past the fray. Both David and Sara were still not sure they had made the right decision by recommending to de Castro that the children attend the arraignment, but in the end they decided it was better for the court, the people and the ever-present media, to see the family standing as one in the aftermath of the tragedy that took their wife and mother. When Logan entered the court from a secure side entrance and saw his two children standing there waiting to support him, and when every man and woman in the room saw the smile that spread across his face, David knew that Logan's loyal fans' hearts would go out to their 'hero' and be rooting for him unswervingly.

Finally, mere seconds before the clerk moved to the front of the room to announce the judge's arrival, Amanda Carmichael entered from the back and strode up the middle aisle with purpose. David did not so much hear her entrance as sense it as every head in the courtroom – male and female – turned to watch the striking attorney move confidently towards her desk. She was like a force of beauty, her long blonde hair in a fashionable chignon, her fitted but conservative beige designer suit moving just so as she shifted her weight from her left foot to her right. And in that moment David sensed she had something up her sleeve after all. Something that would give this impatient young prosecutor the 'wow factor' she had been craving for. And there was nothing David could do about it but wait.

'All rise,' said the clerk, as Judge Marion Kessler pushed into the room, her thick, short legs making surprisingly long strides towards the rectangular bench before her, her shoulder-length grey-black hair set in its usual immovable wave, her broad face flushed with the importance of it all.

'Good morning, everyone,' said Kessler, surveying the crowd before her. 'Dear God!' she responded to the size of the 'audience'. 'Am I running a courtroom or a TV studio? This is an arraignment, people – not a side show. There will be no bells and whistles this morning, just the reading of a charge and the tit-for-tat between defence and the Commonwealth regarding the possibility of bail.'

Kessler was right. In fact arraignments had a threefold purpose – the reading of the charge effectively putting the defendant on notice that he stood accused, the establishment of assignment of counsel and, as Kessler had noted, the hotly contested issue of bail.

'Not boring enough for you?' asked Kessler, as she shook her head. 'All right, but a word of warning, one peep from the masses, one sigh or giggle or cough or burp and I'll call for a closed court which will no doubt seriously dishearten you all. Miss Carmichael,' said Kessler without taking a breath. 'You represent the people in this matter?'

'Yes, Your Honour,' said Carmichael, rising slightly from her seat before taking it again.

'And Mr Cavanaugh?'

'We act for the defendant, Your Honour,' confirmed David. 'Doctor Jeffrey Phillip Logan.'

'Right.' Kessler nodded. 'And the charge, Miss Carmichael?'

'Was set at involuntary manslaughter, Your Honour, following a confession from the defendant, but given new information made available to the District Attorney's Office over the weekend, we have decided to drop said charge altogether.'

That did it. The crowd wasn't to be disappointed after all. Noise erupted in the tiny room – the intakes of breath, the outlet of sighs and, finally, the dawning that their dear Doctor Jeff was about to be set free! In fact, within seconds of Amanda Carmichael's shocking revelation, the audience started clapping, cheering, *yelping* for joy – until the room actually did appear like one of the doctor's live shows in process.

'*Order!*' yelled Kessler, her big, strong voice emanating from her chest and echoing off the whitewashed walls. '*Order!*' she screamed again, this time using her gavel as punctuation.

'Members of the gallery, I take great offence at your disrespect for the decorum required by this court. In fact, the next person to offer any expression of gaiety shall be accompanied from this room and to my chambers where I shall deal with them personally at the conclusion of these proceedings,' she bellowed. '*Do I make myself clear?*' It was a rhetorical question, answered by the crowd's almost instantaneous silence. This was too good to miss – and they knew it.

And in that moment, just as David turned to his client expecting to catch an instinctive expression of relief on his face, he witnessed a complete change to a look of pure horror. Finally, David knew exactly what Carmichael was up to.

'Miss Carmichael,' boomed Kessler, continuing to rule with volume, 'you had better explain yourself – and fast. As you might have heard, I am not a big fan of those who manipulate our hallowed system of justice for self-gratification, and while I am sure you would not dare to attempt such brazen egotistical manoeuvring, I feel the court is owed an explanation – quick smart.'

'I understand, Your Honour,' said Carmichael, now rising to move around her desk towards the middle of the room. 'And I am the last one to want to slow things down – which is why the District Attorney's Office has decided that this particular prosecution, now officially two days old, is two days too long in our opinion.

'The confession was a sham in the first place, Your Honour,' Carmichael went on, her voice calm and even.

'And I can assure you the lead investigators in this matter agree. Doctor Logan did not kill his wife, Your Honour, and I will not be party to any charade which says that he did.'

At that moment a woman in the back row let out an involuntary 'hear, hear' in support of the ADA's proclamation of Doctor Logan's innocence, and was promptly removed from the room. Judge Kessler was not one for making idle threats – and now all present were aware of it.

'You need to explain yourself, Miss Carmichael,' said Kessler, now returning her attention to the ADA taking centre stage before her.

'Your Honour,' Carmichael said, 'on the weekend I held an extensive meeting with Boston Police's Homicide Unit Commander, Lieutenant Joe Mannix, and his fellow investigator in this case, Detective Frank McKay.'

'Jesus,' said David, whispering in Arthur's ear. 'She's going after the boy and she is going to use Joe to do it.'

'The lieutenant and his deputy made it clear to me, in no uncertain terms, that they did not believe Doctor Logan committed the crime for which he has confessed, and they assured me,' Carmichael continued, 'that as soon as the physical evidence had been analysed, the doctor would be quantifiably cleared of the charge and free to return home to his family – or . . . what remains of it.'

At first this last comment sounded like a jibe at the defendant, but David knew better. Carmichael wasn't talking about the loss of Stephanie Tyler, but the impending incarceration of her son.

'Is the lieutenant here?' asked Kessler.

'Ah . . .' said Carmichael, looking around the room.

'I'm here, Judge,' said a stony-faced Joe from where he was standing at the back of the room.

'Come here, then,' said Kessler, using her right pointer finger to beckon Joe towards the front of the room.

David saw Joe shake his head almost imperceptively. His hands curled into fists.

'What is this all about, Lieutenant?' asked the judge as Joe finally stopped in front of her. 'Is what Miss Carmichael claims true? Did you tell her the man being arraigned here this morning was innocent?'

'I told her the evidence would be in on Wednesday,' said Joe, not giving Carmichael an inch.

'He said,' interrupted Carmichael, 'and I quote, Your Honour, "No matter which way you looked at it, Doctor Jeffrey Logan is not good for the kill." And Detective McKay seconded the lieutenant's astute opinions by telling me that if it were not for Doctor Logan's confession, the man would never have been arrested in the first place.'

'Is that true, Lieutenant?' asked Kessler of a now red-faced Joe.

'Well . . . yes . . . but . . .'

'Your Honour!' said David, feeling the need to say something but not sure how in the hell he should proceed. He could not object because Carmichael was basically giving his client a 'get out of jail free' card. But as the victim's friend, he did not want to sit mute and effectively allow this incredibly ambitious young woman to railroad Stephanie's young son into a good ten years of imprisonment – at least until he was aware of the facts.

'This is highly unusual, and while I commend

Miss Carmichael's dedication to speedy justice, she knows that Lieutenant Mannix and Detective McKay were only doing their jobs when they suggested she wait until the evidence report was filed. With all due respect, I would suggest we ask for an adjournment until Wednesday, when this evidence can be examined by the prosecution, the defence and yourself as the current presiding judge in this matter.'

David was trying to buy the boy – and himself – some time, but he was not sure this was going to work.

'You don't want me to send your client home, Mr Cavanaugh?' asked a wide-eyed Kessler.

'Of course we do, Your Honour, but . . .'

'And is Doctor Logan here paying you by the day?'

'No,' stressed David. 'That's not it, Your Honour.'

'Well then, sit down for God's sake and let Miss Carmichael here do your job for you.'

Amanda Carmichael met David's eye and gave him the slightest of smiles.

'Miss Carmichael,' said Kessler, returning her attention to the now victorious ADA, 'I am assuming, given you are willing to let Doctor Logan go, that you have another course of action in mind.'

'Yes, Your Honour. The District Attorney's Office calls for the arrest of Jeffrey Tyler Logan in the matter of the death of his mother Stephanie Tyler.'

The hysteria broke out again as the previously jubilant crowd drew breath in one almighty expression of shock. At least two members of the media were on their feet trying to get a look at the young boy's expression, while David's client swivelled and reached for the young man's hand behind him.

'*Enough!*' boomed Kessler, rising from her seat and raising her two short but substantial arms in protest.

David used his left arm to steer his client back towards the front of the room as Katherine de Castro pulled young J.T. close. David then stole a glance at Caroline Croft in the now animated press gallery – and saw that she was smiling.

'Lieutenant Mannix,' said Kessler, slowing her voice as if needing to ask this question correctly. 'Does the evidence, collected by the police and crime scene specialists at the Logan home last Friday night the eleventh of May, suggest Doctor Jeffrey Logan to be the perpetrator of this crime?'

'Judge,' began a furious Joe, 'like I said before, the analysis is due in on Wednesday and we . . .'

'Answer the question, Lieutenant,' demanded Kessler.

Joe took a breath before stealing a glare at the smirking ADA beside him. 'No, Your Honour. No, it does not.'

'And would you have taken the young boy in question into custody on Friday evening if Doctor Logan had not confessed?' asked Kessler.

'Probably, Your Honour,' confirmed Joe, hamstrung.

An openly emotional Doctor Logan began to cry.

'So what are you suggesting, Miss Carmichael?' asked Kessler. 'That the boy be arrested and held in juvenile detention until he can be arraigned and then tried in the Juvenile Court upstairs?' The Edward W. Brooke Courthouse also served as a home for Boston's Juvenile Court.

'No, Your Honour,' returned Carmichael, taking a step towards the bench. 'Considering the heinous nature of the crime and the fact that the District Attorney's Office can prove premeditation, the Commonwealth wishes to express its intention to try J.T. Logan as an adult in the Superior Court of Massachusetts.'

The crowd erupted again as Doctor Logan got to his feet. '*No!*' he cried, before turning to look at his now completely confused son. 'This is crazy,' he said, twisting back to David, the entire gallery watching as his eyes filled with tears.

'Your Honour.' David was on his feet. 'This is nothing short of preposterous. The boy is a juvenile. Miss Carmichael has no grounds to suggest . . .'

'The *boy*,' interrupted Carmichael, striding back to her desk to pick up two sheets of paper, 'according to his teachers at the respected Curtis Academy, is intelligent beyond his years.' She began to read from the information in front of her. 'His reading age is sixteen; his ability in mathematics suggests that of a seventeen-year-old brain. He is working on a science curriculum two years above his fellow junior high classmates and his IQ is over 140.' Carmichael waved the papers in the air. 'This is one extremely intelligent young man, Your Honour. He is so clever in fact, that he murdered his mother in cold blood and then managed to convince his father to go to prison in his stead.'

'Your Honour,' said David, moving to the front of the room to join his opposition in front of the podium, Joe having moved off to the side – where he stood across from Sara and Arthur and the semi-hysterical Doctor Logan as if needing to show where his loyalties lay.

'Regardless of how smart this boy is, regardless of how hard he works at school to achieve such results, the law states that children under the age of fourteen be tried in the juvenile court system, and J.T. Logan was . . .'

'Fourteen when he killed his mother,' said Carmichael, staring David directly in the eye.

'He turned fourteen on Saturday,' said David, squaring off directly against his opponent.

'He was born in the early hours of the twelfth of May,' she countered.

'Which makes his birthday last *Saturday.*'

'No,' said Carmichael. '*No, it does not.*'

It was as if the entire room had disappeared, as if all David could see before him was the pure determination in the young woman's face. And then he realised that Amanda Carmichael, with the perfect face and the even more perfect body, was not so beautiful after all but rather poisoned by a dire desperation to win. David had refused her advances and now would pay the ultimate price for saying 'no' to a girl who had never lost once in her life. Amanda had found a way to pull this off – he could see it in her eyes.

'Your Honour,' said Carmichael at last, breaking free from David's gaze to face the judge once again. 'The legal definition of one's birthday specifies the exact anniversary of one's time of birth – or more pointedly, the number of exact years, to the second, a person has spent independent of their mother's womb on this planet. And this Commonwealth has always adhered to the case law in place at the specific time of the offence.

'J.T. Logan was born at 12.13am on May the twelfth,' she went on with confidence, 'in Auckland, New

Zealand – which was exactly 8.13am May the eleventh Boston time.

'The young man turned fourteen last Friday morning, Judge,' she said. 'Just before a quarter past eight – twelve hours before he walked into the kitchen and shot his mother to death.'

17

'It's a technicality,' said a frustrated David, the first to push through the front door of their Congress Street offices in Boston's busy Downtown Crossing.

'It's a travesty,' said Nora, following Sara into Arthur's office.

'She can't get away with this,' said Sara, third into the room.

'She can,' said Arthur, bringing up the rear. 'And she just did.'

The group was beyond furious – hot, bothered and anxious to discard suitcases, jackets and ties which were being tossed onto Arthur's couch with abandon. It was almost midday and the world was spinning. J.T. Logan had been formally arrested, charged and arraigned, right there before their very eyes in the adult Boston Municipal Court.

Kessler had been swayed by Amanda Carmichael's ridiculous *'the kid was fourteen not thirteen when he shot his mother'* argument and Arthur suspected the judge had some selfish motives of her own in that regard. He knew that Kessler was chomping at the bit to make her mark in the respected Superior Court, and suspected she would be doing everything she could to make sure she was assigned this media magnet bonanza when it went to trial.

'Carmichael and Kessler are two of a kind,' said Arthur, tugging at the top buttons of his rarely worn shirt. 'Both are determined to get their hands on this one.'

'What?' said Sara, who had kicked off her shoes and was already headed to Arthur's corner fridge for four cans of soda. 'So they team up to play schoolyard bullies and strip this kid of any semblance of dignity that he might . . .?'

'No, it's worse than that,' interrupted David. 'By trying J.T. as an adult they have taken this way beyond the schoolyard. If he is convicted he could be sentenced to life, without parole – no future, no hope.'

They stopped then – noting David's seeming loyalty to the young teenage boy. Yesterday afternoon, after their discussion with Katherine de Castro, David and Sara had spent a good half-hour just 'hanging out' with the kids. And David had to admit that he felt for J.T. instantly, sensing the fear in his quietness and the unmistakable sadness in his eyes.

'All right, I know we haven't seen the video,' he said, 'but this is Stephanie's kid we are talking about here, and I can't help but think that despite the fact that she was the victim in this whole bloody mess, that she would want me to help him.

'Years ago,' he began, taking a seat on Arthur's sofa,

'not long after we graduated, Stephanie told me that she felt responsible for her mother's death. Stephanie was only ten at the time, and with her dad away on business, she had been trying to talk her mom into taking her down to their place at the Cape for Christmas. Anyway, her mom eventually conceded, but a week of intermittent snow followed by days of rain meant the ice on the motorway was thick and slippery.

'Long story short,' David continued after a breath, 'they were almost at the Cape when her mother lost control taking a hairpin bend, crashing into a ditch and dying instantly at the wheel of their family SUV. And Stephanie told me all those years later, that despite her guilt, she knew her mother was still watching over her – furious at her for feeling responsible, angry that she couldn't get over blaming herself for being a determined ten-year-old kid.'

'I understand what you're saying, David,' said Arthur after a pause. 'But that was an accident and this was . . .'

'We don't know what this was yet, Arthur,' interrupted David. 'But my point is . . . Stephanie once told me that when she had kids, she would do anything, *everything* to make sure they knew that her love for them was unconditional – that she would give her life for them in a second, without a single hesitation or regret.'

There was silence, until David looked at Sara, almost predicting what she was going to say.

'You have to be sure you want to do this, David,' she said, taking a seat next to him and looking him directly in the eye. 'Because in defending her son, you will be destroying the reputation of the very person you feel indebted to help. Stephanie is dead, David – and perhaps justifiably so. And if we take this on, if you agree to do this, your job will be to prove her death was reasonable beyond a shadow of a doubt. So unless you feel you are up to this, unless you are willing to crucify your old friend's character in front of an audience of millions, we cannot agree to represent him, because to do so without such a commitment would be unfair to J.T. and, perhaps, cost him *his* life as well.'

David looked at her, before turning his eyes to Arthur and finally to Nora whose knowing nods had never set him wrong.

'I spoke to Logan immediately following J.T.'s arraignment,' he said. 'He will have the video to us within the hour.'

Sara nodded. 'So let's watch it and see what we think,' she said, taking his hand and squeezing it. 'And then you can make the decision for us.'

18

Marc Rigotti was on deadline. The *Boston Tribune* deputy editor had spent the entire weekend working on a Doctor Jeffrey Logan profile piece and now, after the startling revelations in this morning's arraignment, had put aside his feature article to concentrate on a major news story for tomorrow's front page. His editor, a newsprint dinosaur named Ed Wiseman, had been by his office twice, pacing around his desk like an expectant father. Ed was like that – had an inexhaustible passion for his job and considered every one of his potential front-page headliners as 'babies' just waiting to see the light of day.

Briiiinng. The shrill of his desk telephone cut across his stream of consciousness. Rigotti jumped in his seat before deciding the call should be ignored – until none of the editorial assistants deigned to pick it up, forcing him to give in to its incessant buzzing and grab at the receiver in frustration.

'Rigotti,' he barked, his tone loaded with irritation.

'Mr Rigotti,' said the voice, the man's reply also tinged with a degree of intolerance. 'My name is Carleton Blackmore, General Manager of Hunting Rifles Inc. Las Vegas, Nevada.'

Jesus, thought Rigotti, one of those random gun nuts, the last thing he needed.

'Ah . . . right, well, I'm sorry, Mr Blackmore. I'm actually on deadline and . . .'

'Slandering another honest American enterprise, no doubt.'

'Excuse me?' Now this Blackmore was starting to piss him off.

'I know people like you, Mr Rigotti, journalists set on destroying honest businesses with your inaccuracies and lies. Yes, we sell firearms, sir, but our rifles are for hunting and everyone who buys one is skilled in the art of using them.'

'I'm sorry, Mr Blackmore.' Despite himself, Rigotti was intrigued. 'I don't understand.'

'Stephanie Tyler's murder,' explained Blackmore. 'I read your report, sir. You claimed in your article that the gun in question – one of *ours* I might add – was rumoured to have been purchased by the dead woman as a present to her husband.'

Rigotti had had access to the police report in which Logan had explained how he had come to own the gun. He had even been provided details on its appearance, make and model – information he had included in his original post-murder report.

'But we do not operate that way, Mr Rigotti,' Blackmore went on. 'We have a very select clientele and Mrs Tyler would not have been able to purchase that particular weapon – a custom-made Mark V – nor the specified cartridges, the powerful .460 Weatherby magnums – from us without proof of firearms training. In short, your story is a load of rubbish, sir, and makes us appear . . .'

'How do you know the rifle was one of yours?' asked Rigotti, grabbing a pencil from his drawer and dragging a notepad from across his desk.

'Because of what you described, sir – the Mark V Deluxe's aesthetics. I am personally aware of the weapon you spoke of, Mr Rigotti, because all of our rifles are a one of a kind.'

'But how is that possible?'

'We engrave each one individually, Mr Rigotti. We name them.'

'You give your guns *names*?' said Rigotti, incredulous.

'Yes, sir. You said the rifle in question was engraved with the lettering BH. I believe you said the letters were on the lower left-hand corner of the stock.'

'I thought that was part of the make and model number.'

'No, sir,' contradicted Blackmore. 'The BH refers to its name – "Ben Hur". I remember Ben personally – the Claro walnut stock, the rosewood forend tip and pistol grip cap with maplewood spacers and diamond inlay. Beautiful weapon, sir, one of our best.'

Jesus, thought Rigotti, trying to dismiss the ridiculousness of the whole concept of naming a Goddamned gun to concentrate on the task at hand. *If Blackmore is right, then I have just stumbled onto something bigger than the rifle's namesake.*

'Hold up, Mr Blackmore. Forgive me for my

ignorance but if this weapon was purchased in Nevada, wouldn't the state have a record of . . .'

'Our laws are a lot different to yours, Mr Rigotti,' interrupted Blackmore. 'Clark County – minus Boulder City I might add – is the only county which requires registration of a gun and that law applies to handguns only. All other counties have no registration of any guns whatsoever.'

Which was a whole other story in itself, thought Rigotti, before waiting for Blackmore to continue.

'A person must hold a Nevada hunting licence to hunt game animals in this state but there are no laws about carrying a gun over the border – and if Ben Hur is in Massachusetts, sir, then I would suggest he was most likely stolen from his original owner and driven into your fine eastern enclave unnoticed.

'Of course, I know you folks like to slap a law on anything more threatening than a water pistol,' the opinionated Blackmore continued, referring to the fact that Massachusetts had some of the most stringent gun laws in the nation. 'But any non-resident can transport rifles and shotguns into or through Massachusetts if the guns are unloaded, cased and locked in the trunk of a vehicle. And they can physically possess an operable rifle or shotgun while hunting with a Massachusetts licence.'

Rigotti would check this later – but memory and intuition told him Blackmore was more than likely right, and if that was the case then . . .

'Do you know the identity of the original owner, Mr Blackmore?'

'Well of course I do, sir. Haven't you been listening?

We are an extremely efficient operation, Mr Rigotti – a family business that likes to get to know our customers so that we might service their needs with care and proficiency.

'In fact, the purchaser in question is an old client, sir. We may not see him as often as we would like, but I know he can still split a hair with a pistol from a good one hundred feet away, and shoot a Goddamned mountain lion smack between the eyes without . . .'

Lovely, thought Rigotti before interrupting, 'And that purchaser is . . .?'

'Not the deceased ex-lawyer and not her TV star husband, that's for sure. Ben Hur's owner is a local man, Mr Rigotti, a skilled marksman by the name of Jason Nagle who is a respected businessman in his own right.'

'What does Mr Nagle do, Mr Blackmore?'

'Well, I am not exactly sure, but I know he runs his own company, and that his appreciation of a fine weapon – regardless of its cost – is evidence of his financial stability and excellent Goddamned taste.'

'I see,' said Rigotti, his mind now racing a hundred miles an hour. 'And this Mr Nagle, did he leave his contact details?'

'Well, of course he did, Mr Rigotti. Like I said we . . .'

'Yes, yes,' said Rigotti, not wanting the man to lose momentum. 'I'm sorry. I can see you run a very respectable business, Mr Blackmore, and obviously I want to correct my paper's mistake by clarifying the information you have so kindly provided. I'd like to speak to Mr Nagle. And if you could give me his telephone number, Mr Blackmore, I would be happy to make sure the *Tribune* made amends by . . .'

'I am afraid I cannot do that, sir – at least not without Mr Nagle's permission. But given you seem conducive to making amends, I may deign to make contact with him and ask him if he is good enough to give you a call.'

'Are you sure you can't give me his details, Mr Blackmore? Because I am happy to save you the trouble and call him direct.' It was worth a shot.

'No, sir,' said an adamant Blackmore. 'I am afraid that would be both highly inappropriate and bordering on illegal given all of our contracts of sale come with a privacy clause. But I shall get back to you as soon as possible, as long as Mr Nagle is willing.'

Seconds later Blackmore was gone and Rigotti was ten minutes behind in his deadline. But for once, Wiseman would have to wait. Something else was brewing – something big, Rigotti could feel it.

19

The first thing David noticed was the strange green light that permeated the scene before him, casting shadows on the three 'players' now sitting at the far end of a dining room table and making them appear anaemic, lifeless, dead. He knew some videos gave off a bile-coloured tinge, as if someone had placed a film of emerald cellophane over the camera lens, but this was more like the inhabitants of the thirty-two inch screen had been lit with the sickly hue on purpose – as if the illumination befitted the drama, which in the end, he supposed, it did.

They were in Arthur's office – David, Sara, Nora and Arthur, and further away from the TV which Nora had placed on Arthur's desk, Doctor Jeffrey Logan and Katherine de Castro were seated in a second row of wooden guest chairs Nora had commandeered from David and Sara's offices. They were silent – just like the trio on the screen before them – the only noise emanating from the 'home-made' production being the occasional chink of silverware against china. The inhabitants were sitting with their heads down, as if determined to concentrate on their meals, as if hesitant to lift their heads until . . .

'J.T.,' said a voice out of frame, a voice David recognised immediately, despite its lack of any trace of the happy intonation his memory had impressed upon him.

'Yes, Mother,' replied the boy, his chin rising slightly towards the unseen figure stage right.

'Did you finish your biology project?' asked Stephanie, still beyond the camera's eye. She must have been serving from a side table, thought David, or perhaps collecting some napkins from a drawer.

'Yes, Mother.'

'And the DNA bases – are you sure they were in the right order?'

'Yes,' replied the boy, his eyes seeming to flick towards the front of the room before looking 'off-screen' towards his mother once again. 'Adenine in yellow, thymine in green, guanine in red and cytosine in orange.'

'And the adenine attaches to the thymine while the . . .'

'Guanine connects with the cytosine,' finished J.T. robotically.

'I know. Are you trying to lecture me?' she asked, her words paced as if in rhythm, the syllables broken up as if she wanted to sound them out individually for effect. 'I was dux of my high school, you know, and could have just as easily chosen medicine over law – if I had so desired.'

'I'm sorry, Mother,' replied the boy, his voice still a

monotone drawl but now with an edge of . . . sadness. 'I did not mean to . . .'

'Stephanie, really,' said the man at the head of the table at last. Doctor Jeffrey Logan was still wearing his 'work clothes' – a crisp blue shirt teamed with a subtle but expensive gold-striped tie. The on-screen Logan placed his knife on the table, while using his left hand to gesture rather animatedly in the air.

'Is this really necessary? It is my birthday, for Christ's sake. I have no doubt J.T. has done a stellar job as always,' he said, pointing the fork towards his son who sat to his right with his shoulders hunched, his hands now forming fists around his glinting silver cutlery.

'Just for once do you think you could sit down and behave civilly? Just tonight could you try to . . .?'

'I took it apart,' she said then, finally entering the picture.

David found himself gasping. Her skin was so pale – her complexion so insipid – that he almost did not recognise her.

'What?' asked J.T., his eyes flicking forwards again, his question not so much one of surprise but acceptance.

'I took it apart,' she confirmed.

She was in the shot proper now, her right hand resting on the back of a so far silent Chelsea Logan's chair. Chelsea had not moved an inch since this family 'sideshow' began. Her head was still down, her eyes set determinedly upon the centre of the table before her.

'I was not sure of one of your connections so I took it apart,' said Stephanie, talking to her son but staring directly at her husband as if defying him to argue, her hands clenching, her long neck contorting in strands.

'Jesus, Stephanie,' said Logan, before rising from his seat to confront her. 'The boy is just a child. He works so hard. It will take him hours to rebuild it.'

There was silence, and the Logan on the TV screen looked towards his son who, or so it appeared, could not think of anything else to say. And then, in what appeared to be an extremely out-of-context gesture, Logan sat back down and reached across the table for the silver gravy boat before him. Chelsea appeared to be following his hand with her eyes, as if mesmerised by the inappropriateness of his action.

'J.T. is sorry,' said Chelsea, her voice an unexpected bark. 'He's sorry, Mom . . . and he will build it again, won't you?'

'Yes,' said the boy. David could have sworn he was crying.

When Stephanie then looked at her son, David found himself leaning forward onto the edge of his chair, needing desperately to read the emotion in her face. But the lighting was too severe, the shadows too deep, and within seconds Stephanie Tyler had left the frame again.

'Here,' she said, after a time, re-entering the picture to hand her husband a long package wrapped in brown paper and string.

Logan took it, slowly, deliberately, turning it over in his hands. 'What is it?'

'It's your fucking birthday present, you ingrate,' she said, the first time David had heard her answer with any sense of 'spirit' – causing his heart to rise and sink at the very same time.

On the video Jeffrey Logan untied the string and removed the paper, fold by fold, to reveal the long, deadly weapon that would eventually take the life of the pale, thin woman beside him.

'What is it?' he asked again.

'It's your fucking birthday present, you ingrate . . . I mean,' she hesitated, as if annoyed at herself for using the same sentence twice. 'It's a Goddamned walking stick . . . no . . .' She faltered again. 'It's a Goddamned umbrella. What the hell do you think it is?'

'Stephanie,' said Logan, looking at the weapon with disgust, his right hand moving over its grip, his left palm running along the base towards the trigger. 'You know how I feel about guns.'

'And you're not getting it, Jeffrey.' And then, just like J.T. had done previously, her eyes flicked to the front of the room, before she turned back to her husband again.

'*Hear everything, listen please*,' she said, deliberating on every word. '*Maybe even* . . .' she paused, '. . . *decipher the conundrum*.'

Logan looked at her in genuine confusion.

'I may know how you *feel* about guns, but I also know how I *felt* about a certain reptile-skin handbag,' she said, the retort sounding both ridiculous and (considering the preposterousness of the situation before them), appropriate at the same time.

'So the next time I ask you for an alligator accessory you can, in the very least, go shoot the fucker yourself.'

And then she shocked everyone in the room – both in the past and in the present – by plunging towards her husband, snatching the gun and swivelling it quickly, sharply, a full ninety degrees to her left.

'Do you understand me?' she said, as her only son, thirteen-year-old J.T. Logan, looked up to stare down the barrel of the very same weapon he would use against her mere weeks down the track.

'Oh, Mom!' said Chelsea, her own tears now cutting swathes down her pale lime green face.

'Enough, Stephanie,' said Logan, shooting a glance at his daughter before returning his gaze to his wife. '*Please!*' he said, until she finally lowered the gun. 'I understand. I am sorry.'

'No, you don't,' she snapped. 'No, you don't,' she said again and this time with determination. 'But I promise you, one day, that you will.'

And then the screen went fuzzy with that crackly grey haze that signified the 'show' had finally come to an end.

David hung his head in his hands before, after what seemed like a very long time, rose to his feet and turned to the man behind him. 'Your son needs an attorney, Doctor, and a good one at that.'

He could feel Sara's gaze upon him.

'You'll do it then?' asked de Castro, also rising to meet David's eye.

'Yes,' said David, answering her but looking directly at Doctor Jeff. 'For after seeing that tape, I could not live with myself if I didn't.'

20

'Well, this is totally ass about face,' said Detective Frank McKay, leaning on the fingerprint counter in Boston Police Headquarters' booking section, looking across at J.T. Logan who was having his photograph taken across the other side of the room.

'You mean the kid being arraigned before he is processed,' said Joe Mannix, sliding sideways to avoid the now overpowering smell from Frank's 'leaking at the edges' lunch.

'I mean the whole fucking charade,' said McKay. 'Jesus, Chief, the kid is barely out of diapers. Look at him,' he said, gesturing at the terrified looking boy now blinking at the flare of the photographer's flash. 'He looks like he could barely hold a baseball bat let alone fire a big-game hunting rifle.'

Frank was right. J.T. Logan was small for his age – a skinny, awkward-looking kid whose good looks were marred by his obvious lack of confidence. Joe had noticed it the first time he saw him – in that oversized T-shirt with the blood spatter swallowing his narrow olive-skinned face. It was almost like the boy was ashamed to take up the small space in the universe that he did, like he was embarrassed to even be here, like he had done the world a disservice the minute that he was born.

'The kid isn't much older than Joe Junior,' said Frank then, referring to Joe's oldest son.

'Not much,' said Joe, the thought having occurred to him at least once over the past few days. 'Why can't I help but think that this whole thing has gotten away from us, Frank?'

'Because it has, Chief,' said McKay. 'Which means we just gotta take it back.'

Frank was right and Joe knew it, but at this stage, given they had not even had a chance to question the boy who was now giving his full name, address and other personal details to the booking officer, he had no idea as to how this might be achieved. He knew Cavanaugh had stepped up in court, largely because he was livid at Carmichael's blatant manipulation of the judiciary process, but he did not know if his attorney friend would be willing to take this any further, given his relationship with the kid's mother and the way that she had died.

'You want a soda, kid?' asked Joe as the officer went to lead J.T. back towards a juvenile holding cell. The boy had just been digitally fingerprinted – a new ink-free process which detected oils on the offender's hands – and would be held in a juvenile cell until the Sheriff's Department organised his transfer to the maximum security juvenile detention unit in Plymouth.

By law, juveniles in the state of Massachusetts were not to be held 'behind bars', which meant the juvenile cells – set apart from their adult counterparts, also by law – had what Joe considered to be much more intimidating solid doors, with small glass windows at adult eye level. Another example of bureaucracy gone insane, thought Joe, another example of laws being made for the hell of it, without any regard for the individuals involved.

'It's okay, Officer Blunt,' said Joe to the heavy-set policeman now holding J.T. by the elbow. 'We'll watch him until the sheriff's van arrives.'

Blunt nodded, before leading the kid to where Joe and Frank were sitting next to a drink machine in a far corner.

'My attorney told me not to talk to anyone,' said J.T., looking up at Joe, his voice still a high-pitched squeak – months, maybe even years, away from breaking.

'That's okay,' said Joe. 'We can just sit if you like. While you down a Coke and we take a load off.'

J.T. nodded.

'How's the shoulder?' asked Joe, a random question.

'What shoulder?' asked J.T. as he took a seat across from Joe, a look of genuine confusion in his wide brown eyes.

'Your right one. I thought you hurt it.'

'No. The policeman didn't pull me when he brought me here, if that is what you are asking.'

'It was, and that's good to know, kid,' said Joe.

J.T. nodded again, before accepting the Coke from Frank.

'What about your ears?' asked Joe after a pause.

'They're sore,' said the boy.

'Are they still ringing?' asked Joe, probing that little bit further.

'A little.'

And Joe nodded as they all took a sip of their sodas.

'You love your mom, son?' asked Joe – another question, completely out of the blue.

'Yes, sir,' said J.T. without drama or hesitation.

'Me too, kid,' said Joe just as evenly. 'Me too.'

'It's a fake,' said David the moment he had shut the door behind their two obviously satisfied visitors. The others simply stood there, saying nothing – three of the people David respected most in this world, staring at him in blatant disbelief.

'It's a *fake,*' he said again, as if to make sure they had heard him the first time. 'It was a set-up, a forgery, a scam.'

'David,' said Arthur, 'Doctor Logan may be on TV, but I doubt he has the skills to mastermind such advanced technological wizardry. Stephanie Tyler was your friend, and as such it is understandable that you . . .'

'No,' said David, his heart racing. He could feel the adrenaline pumping as he paced around the room. 'The recording itself is for real – but its content is a load of sick and twisted lies.' The three of them stared at him some more. 'It was scripted, directed, acted, crafted, manufactured, contrived.'

'Hold on a minute,' said Sara, striding across the office to meet him. 'You think that the entire Logan family agreed to play themselves in the dysfunctional family video from hell?'

'I think at least three of them were forced to take roles they hated themselves for playing.'

'Dear God,' said Nora.

'That's right, Nora,' he said, moving towards his beloved older secretary. Nora Kelly was like a second mother to him, and as matriarch of their small but tight office 'family', he felt an all-encompassing need to make her understand.

'I know Stephanie was a good mother, she would have loved her kids more than life itself. She must have known her children were in danger – and so she agreed to . . .'

'She held a gun at her teenage son's head,' argued Arthur, his voice now raising a notch.

'Because he was holding a gun on them.'

There was silence, the only sound in the room the thickness of David's breath.

'You saw a gun?' asked Sara.

'Well . . .' David hesitated, shaking his head. 'Maybe not a gun specifically, but there was something on that table that scared the hell out of them – something powerful enough to keep them all in line.'

'You think Logan has been terrorising his family?' said Arthur.

'I think Logan killed his wife.'

'But J.T., the evidence . . .'

'Things are not always as they seem, Arthur.'

'Like the video,' said Nora.

'Like the video,' David repeated. 'Which does not tell us everything, but in the very least, gives us somewhere to start.'

'So that's why you said you would represent him,' said Sara.

'That – and because his mother asked me to.'

'She *what?*' began a completely confused Sara before stealing a glance at Arthur. 'David . . . how on earth . . . when did she . . .?'

'Just then, in that video,' replied David. 'She asked me to help her, Sara – and no matter what it takes, that is exactly what I am going to do.'

Seconds later they were interrupted by the simultaneous ring of two telephones in outer offices – one on Nora's general office number and a second on David's direct line. David moved across the room quickly to pick up his own call from Arthur's extension, while Nora moved just as swiftly from Arthur's office to answer the main line from her own front reception desk. Both Sara and Arthur stood stationary as they watched David and Nora listening, barely responding to the callers on the other end of their phones, before hanging up simultaneously to move back into the centre of Arthur's office. Nora took the first opportunity to report.

'J.T. Logan is out of processing,' she said, her strong Irish accent giving the statement an almost profound rhythm of importance. 'Detective McKay wants you to call him back immediately if you would like to see the boy before he is transported to Plymouth for the night.'

'Call him back and tell him no,' said David.

'*No?*' said Sara. 'But I thought you just said . . .?'

'That was Marc Rigotti,' said David. 'J.T. will have to wait until morning, because Marc says he needs to see us – fast.'

'The Logan case?' asked Arthur.

David nodded. 'It seems Stephanie never bought that kick-ass rifle after all.'

21

The following morning

Tony Bishop rose from his black leather ergonomic chair and moved towards the window. It truly was beautiful, he thought, as he looked out across the eastern side of the city and the royal blue harbour beyond. It was barely after eight but the sun was already burning with a vengeance, bouncing off the cobalt blue water now being sliced at random by boats big and small as they went about their 'business', promising a respite from what had been an unusually cool spring, and warming the pedestrians whose pace always slowed on mornings such as this, as if they needed to soak in every last ray before they hit the confines of their tiny, rectangular, artificially lit workspaces.

Tony had always thought it odd that he could watch people, from up here on the thirty-fifth floor of his circular Financial District commercial high-rise building, but that they could not watch him back. He could see them walking – men and women, solo and in pairs, young and old, tall and short, fat and thin, collar and tie, hat and overalls, trainers and suits and the odd commuter in a compulsory company uniform which no doubt bore some square-shaped shrunken logo embroidered just so on the left breast pocket, suggesting to the world that 'my name is not important but the people who pay me are'.

Tony knew he was one of the 'others' – one of the elite minority who got to look down without the inconvenience of reciprocation, and he had to admit it felt good. True, he only felt the sun on his back a couple of days a week; true, he spent double the time in his office than he did in his space-age Tempur bed; true, he was servicing clients who cared more about the bottom line than they did about world starvation – but in the end it was all a matter of give and take, and in all honesty, the compensation was more than enough to ease the pain. At least it was most of the time, but perhaps not all of the time, as was proven a bare two minutes later when an unexpected visitor came to his door and he felt the first twinge of bona fide professional discomfort.

'Tony,' said junior attorney Harry Harrison from the Family Corporation Management Division way down on the twenty-ninth floor. Harrison had tapped on his door like a bird before sliding into his office sideways, with one foot pointed in and the other staking its claim on his seemingly much anticipated retreat.

'I just wanted to get your take on this – on what I should *do*, I mean,' Harrison began, his weight shifting slowly from one awkwardly placed foot to the other. 'It's about the Logans, or Stephanie Tyler to be exact. It seems when I was on vacation last week, she called and left a message – last Friday, the morning of the day that she died and well, she said that, ah . . . that she needed to see me urgently . . . that she wanted to change her will.'

And that was when the twinge turned into a pang – both professional and personal.

'What did she want to change?' asked Tony, maintaining his composure as he moved around his desk to walk towards the nervous young attorney before him. 'Specifically, I mean,' he added, knowing Harrison was not one to cut to the chase.

'Well, she wanted to remove him as a beneficiary,' Harrison said quickly, a 'cut' if ever there was one.

'Remove who?' asked Tony.

'Her husband,' Harrison returned. 'But the police have the original. They requested it as a matter of procedure early yesterday – the old one where her entire estate goes to Doctor Logan, the one before the changes.'

'But you said there were no changes,' said Tony.

'No,' said Harrison, half-nodding, half-shaking his balding, pointed head. 'What I mean to say is, I didn't make the changes physically because I was away. But I have her instructions on my voice mail. And they are *very* clear.'

Tony nodded, his brain now ticking over at a million miles a minute.

'You still have the message?'

'Yes.'

'And the husband, Jeffrey Logan, he is your client too. Am I right?'

'Yes,' said Harrison. 'I represent the family's interests and our media division looks after the doctor's business interests.'

Tony's firm, Williams, Coolidge and Harrison,

had many divisions, including a growing Media Department. Tony worked in corporate under Gareth Coolidge; the media division was litigation/defamation expert Henry Williams' domain; and Charles Harrison covered the family division, which was probably why his 'thick as a brick', prematurely balding nephew was currently standing in front of Tony.

'Jesus,' said Tony, thinking aloud.

'Yes, sir,' said Harrison.

'Have you told anyone else about this, Harry?' asked Tony after a beat.

'My uncle is still in the Berkshires,' he said. 'In fact, you are the most senior attorney here at present, Tony, with Mr Williams in Los Angeles and Mr Coolidge still recovering from his knee replacement surgery.' It was true, Tony was king of the castle right now – a position he had been savouring just moments ago – but one that now felt decidedly . . .

'So, no,' finished Harrison, interrupting Tony's thoughts, his back foot sliding an inch or two backwards, towards his intended route of escape. 'I haven't told anybody but you.'

'Okay,' said Tony, after a pause, seeking some solace in the fact that, in the very least, the information was 'contained', which would allow him some much-needed time to think. Tony was totally aware of all that was going down in the Logan case – a case he had a fourfold interest in considering his past relationship with Stephanie, the fact that the family were long-term clients, the complication that his best friend was now defending her murderer, and Tony's girlfriend was head prosecutor for the Commonwealth.

And despite his personal feelings, he knew that above all else, this new information created a conflict of interest of the highest order, considering their first client – Stephanie, the one who gave Harrison the instructions – was dead, and their second client – Logan – was the subject of Stephanie's 'evidentially significant' request. Even though Stephanie was gone, both she and her husband deserved the respect and confidentiality guaranteed by the firm's legal and professional responsibility. And the fact that she used to be his girlfriend, the fact that Tony once believed he could well spend the rest of his life with her, was well . . .

'Tony?' said Harry Harrison, obviously eager for a response.

'Leave it with me,' said Tony, moving quickly behind his desk, knowing Harrison would be out the door faster than the roadrunner in one of those old Wile E. Coyote cartoons. But Harrison did not move, and in that moment, as Tony collapsed onto his smooth leather chair, he knew that the worst was yet to come.

Harrison told him the rest of it and Tony felt that nasty little pang become a stab, starting somewhere near his breastbone and finishing way back in his chest. And when Harrison finally made like the roadrunner, Tony closed his eyes as he asked himself, *What to do?* He took a long slow breath and wished for some magical solution that would both satisfy him professionally and personally and avoid offending any of the myriad personalities involved.

No, he reasoned with himself, *there is no perfect solution. Someone is going to get burned.*

He opened his eyes and reached across his desk top, lifting the hand piece of his modern, metallic, multi-functional office phone before he had a chance to change his mind. And then he began punching in the direct line which he had committed to memory a mere few months ago.

'Hi,' he said, just as the woman picked up and answered the call promptly and abruptly, giving only her last name in greeting.

'I'm sorry, Tony, but I'm really busy. I am going to have to call you . . .'

'No, *I'm* sorry, Amanda, but this is urgent. Whatever you are doing you need to drop it – because we need to talk.'

22

Not long after a relieved Harry Harrison had hightailed it from Tony Bishop's office, leaving Bishop with an almighty minefield to negotiate, David Cavanaugh was doing some serious mental navigation of his own. He waited for his good friend Joe Mannix to arrive at a greasy Roxbury Diner known as Lenny's and wondered what in the hell he was going to say.

Joe wasn't the problem – David trusted him 100 per cent – but their respective jobs were a different matter altogether. For while David had a professional responsibility to his fourteen-year-old client, Joe had similar obligations to the District Attorney's Office, or more specifically, to an ambitious ADA by the name of Amanda Carmichael.

'Hey,' said Joe, prompting a deep-in-thought David to look up and half-stand so that he might shake his good friend's hand.

'Hey. I didn't hear you come in,' replied David, as Joe took a seat on the red vinyl bench across from him.

'It's broken,' said Joe.

'What?'

'The bell over Lenny's door.'

'Lenny has a bell?'

'Doesn't every dodgy corner diner in this country have a bell over its gingham-curtained door?'

David smiled. 'You know that that checked material over the door is called gingham?'

'McKay told me,' said Joe.

'Well that explains it.'

A few minutes of chitchat, a double order of Lenny's too-salty bacon and eggs, and two bottomless mugs of hot black coffee later, Joe was the one who cut to the chase.

'You didn't have to do this, you know,' he said as he signalled for a refill from a white-haired waitress named Pearl.

'Do what?' asked a genuinely confused David.

'Meet me here – at my end of town, at this shit hole excuse for a restaurant just to explain.'

Now David was completely confused. 'What do you mean?'

'Come on, David. You hate this joint. You normally want to catch up at Myrtle's where, in the very least, we know the eggs come from chickens and the meat comes from a pig.

'You're dropping the kid,' Joe continued when David didn't respond. 'And I get it. You were friends with his mom and no matter what went down, you've made the decision that it's best for all concerned that you step down.'

'You think I'm bailing on the kid?' asked David. 'You think I came down here to explain why I . . .'

'Well, didn't you?' interrupted Joe.

'No, Joe. No, I didn't.'

'So you're still on board then?' said Joe, and David could not help but hear the relief in his detective friend's voice. 'Because when Frank called Nora yesterday, and when he got the message you didn't want to come down to see the Logan boy after he was processed, and considering the boy is kinda lost right now, well . . .' Joe hesitated, it was not his place as head of Boston Homicide to offer opinions on who defended who, but in this case David sensed Joe was feeling more than a little angry at how the kid had been railroaded.

'It's okay, Joe. I'm still in,' said David.

Joe nodded.

'But there's a but,' said David, after a pause.

'Isn't there always?'

David could not help but smile. 'It's just that, before you go championing my decision to help the kid, I have to warn you that my motives for asking you here are not entirely selfless.'

Joe looked up from his breakfast. 'So the indigestion I am about to suffer won't be put down purely to the eggs.'

'I'm afraid not.'

'And why am I not surprised?'

David began at the beginning – with Logan's hole-a-minute story, Katherine de Castro's accusations, the contents of that all-revealing video tape and the doctor's confirmation of his wife's 'relentless emotional abuse'. He took Joe through the tape in detail, describing the dialogue and movements minute by minute, before stepping back from the obvious to explain what he had *read between the lines* and deducted from, as Sara had called it, the 'family home movie from hell'.

'First up, the lighting is totally off,' he began.

'How do you mean?' asked Joe, the first question he had asked in minutes.

'It's green, a sort of surreal artificial colour, like someone had lit it that way on purpose.'

'Come on, David,' said Joe, shaking his head. 'You and I both know that the lighting doesn't mean jack.'

'True, at least not on its own. But when you watch this thing, you can tell that Stephanie, J.T. and Chelsea . . . it's as if they are all reciting from a script. Their speech is stilted as if learned, their mannerisms are taut, controlled and jerky, and Logan plays it up big time, his arms sweeping in gestures that verge on melodrama, his intonation rising and falling at all the appropriate moments.'

'Like I said, David,' said Joe once again, 'while I need to see this little DIY production for myself, from what you are describing, it is not enough to . . .'

'Their eyes keep flicking,' said David, needing to push on. 'As if there are prompt cards set at the other end of the table. J.T. keeps looking up before he says anything, and at one point, where Stephanie appears to have forgotten her lines, she looks back and forward while repeating the same sentence twice.

'And Chelsea just sits there like a robot. In fact, the only time she actually reacts is when her father re-takes his seat and reaches for something in the middle of the table.'

'And what is he reaching for?' asked Joe.

'A gravy boat.'

'A gravy boat!' repeated Joe. 'David . . .'

'What I mean to say is, it *looks* like a gravy boat but,' David needed Joe to see it, '. . . but I don't think it is a gravy boat or any other piece of expensive silver dinnerware. I think it's a gun or some other form of weapon, because when he reaches towards it, Chelsea reacts immediately. It is like a reminder to them all that their lives are in danger every time they overstep the line.'

'You think this man was terrorising his family to such an extent that he could totally control their behaviour?'

'I think he was, and still is, trying to portray Stephanie as the tyrant, in order to hide the fact that he is the oppressor himself.'

'So he can get away with killing her,' said Joe.

'And setting up his son in his stead. I know all the evidence points to the kid, Joe, but . . .'

'Not all of it,' said Joe.

And there it was – a small grain of hope. David knew he would be asking Joe to cross the line by discussing any new piece of evidence without consulting with the ADA, unless it was just one of Joe's hunches, which to David, was just as good.

'You want to explain?' he asked.

'It's not enough to get excited about, David. It's something small, an inconsistency and nowhere near enough to help you salvage your kid's case in court.'

'You found something.'

'More like a lack of something, and it's been bugging me for most of the day.'

Joe explained about J.T.'s ear problems, but his lack

of shoulder pain. Early this morning Joe had called the doctor who examined J.T. on his admission to Plymouth and confirmed that while the kid did have some inflammation in both ears and his hearing was slightly off, he had no burn or bruising or pain on or in his right shoulder where he would have rested the rifle – the recoil of which was enough to singe his big white T-shirt without making a mark on his skin.

'I called a uniform named Schiff,' said Joe. 'The guy is a gun enthusiast who knows a thing or two about the rifle in question. He said the hearing thing is consistent with the almighty bang that accompanies the .460 magnum's explosion. It's been known to burst eardrums – make them bleed.

'He also said the .460 will launch a 500 grain bullet at 2700 feet per second from a twenty-six inch barrelled rifle with 8100 foot-pounds of muzzle energy. And that means the recoil is a bastard – issuing over 100 foot-pounds of force. It's been known to dislocate shoulders, David – and that's when fired by a grown man, let alone a scrawny fourteen-year-old boy.'

David said nothing, taking it all in. 'You don't think J.T. fired that gun.'

'I'm not saying that, David, because if I did there would be no way to explain the state of his ears and all the other pieces of evidence that will soon confirm him as the shooter – the blood spatter, powder residue, fingerprints . . . It's something, but it's nowhere near enough – at least not on its own.'

David paused, wondering how far he should go. He knew that by telling his friend about the video tape that he had already stretched the envelope by providing him with information David knew he would not pass on to the ADA – at least not yet. But if he continued sharing his speculations, if he persisted with this desire to 'have Joe on board', he knew he would be ultimately asking his detective friend to choose – between what he *should* do and, given their friendship, what he *couldn't*. But in the end this was all about trust and David had to believe that Joe would rather know than not, even if it meant placing him in that awkward position between 'by the book' and 'under the radar' – that familiar no-man's-land they had both dragged each other to before.

'There's more,' he said.

'Besides the video, you mean?' asked Joe, meeting David's eye.

'Marc Rigotti is meeting me here in about half an hour. If you want to . . . you can hang around.'

'Jesus, David, what in the hell have you got brewing?'

'I am not sure yet, Joe, which is why Marc and I figured we'd discuss it before we involved you.' He looked up to see the frustration on his detective friend's face.

'Look,' said David, 'I know I am asking a lot here, so before we get to Rigotti, before you write off my ravings as a misplaced loyalty to an old college friend, there is one more thing in that video that I need to share.'

Joe sighed. 'Okay, David. What in the hell else did you see?'

'Not see, Joe – *hear*. After Stephanie gave Logan the gun, after he unwrapped it, and she made some comment about him being an ungrateful son-of-a-bitch, she glanced at the camera and she slowed down and she said clearly, deliberately: "*Hear everything, listen please. Maybe even, decipher the conundrum.*" '

But Joe could not see it, and in all honesty, given it had taken Sara and Arthur several run-throughs to catch it, David was not surprised.

'It's an odd thing to say, David. But from what you are describing, this whole video scenario sounds a little beyond the ordinary so . . .'

David did not comment – just turned to his briefcase beside him and pulled out a creased legal pad and pencil before writing the two sentences vertically, turning the pad upside down and pushing it towards his friend with determination.

'*Hear*
everything,
listen
please.
Maybe
even,
Decipher the
Conundrum.'

Joe picked up the paper in his hands, bringing it close to his face so that David could no longer read his expression. Then David saw his fingers flex and he knew, as Joe lowered the pad again, that he had seen it, and that David could well be right after all.

'The first letter of each word except for the "the",' said Joe then. '***Help me DC***. She was asking for your help.'

David nodded as Joe shook his head.

'I hate you, David Cavanaugh.'

'I know that, Joe. I know.'

23

'Jeffrey,' said Katherine de Castro, opening the door in her nightgown, her arms automatically clutching at the blue silk tie to secure it around her middle. 'I thought you were going to see J.T.'

'I am. But I just wanted to . . .' Logan began with smile. 'Can I come in?'

'Of course,' she said, moving aside before craning her neck to see if the reporters were still standing sentry outside.

'I thought I might miss them if I came early,' he said.

'Looks like you were right,' she replied. 'Ah . . .' she said after a somewhat awkward pause. 'Can I offer you some coffee or . . .?'

'No.' Logan shook his head, his handsome face appearing incredibly fresh considering what he had been through over the past few days. 'I can't stay long. Like I said, I am anxious to see J.T. But, before I went, I just wanted to . . . well . . .'

Logan fished into his suit pocket to retrieve a small

turquoise box. De Castro recognised the packaging immediately – it was from Tiffany's, a gift that always said 'substantial' despite its miniature size.

'What's this?' she asked.

'A token of my appreciation, for standing by me, for supporting my children. Here,' he said, prompting her to take the box. 'Please, open it up.'

Which she did – to find the most beautiful sterling silver necklace with two tiny locks hanging from its links.

'I figure we play the best tick-tack-toe in town,' he said, referring to the tiny cross inside one locket and the equally as small 'nought' in the other. 'I even had it engraved. The little "X" with a "J", the nought with a "K".'

'I,' said de Castro, momentarily confused. 'Jeffrey this is too much. You really didn't have to . . .'

'It was the least I could do.' He smiled. 'You are a great friend, Katherine,' he said, taking her hand. 'I don't know what I would have done if you had not been there for me and my kids.'

'Don't be silly,' she said, politely retrieving her hand. 'You've been through so much, Jeffrey. And your kids are a delight.'

There was silence, as it struck de Castro just how bizarre this was, the two of them fawning over a piece of jewellery, while J.T. Logan was locked up in some high-security jail.

'Cavanaugh will make this right,' said Logan, as if reading her mind. 'And then we can all get back to being a family again.'

De Castro nodded, simply because she could not think of anything else to say.

'I'll call you this afternoon then,' said Logan, turning back towards the front door. 'And honestly, Katherine, thanks so much again.'

'Ah . . . my pleasure,' she managed. 'And thank you, Jeffrey. Thank you.'

What was that all about? a still confused Katherine de Castro asked herself as she closed the door behind her unexpected guest and made her way back down her thickly carpeted hallway, heading directly for the kitchen where she had left her now lukewarm coffee on her white stone bench. She poured herself a fresh mug and headed for the living room, dropping onto her ridiculously comfortable sofa and feeling anything but at ease.

He was just being kind, she told herself. *It was a token of gratitude.* And it was true they were a great professional team – or, as Jeffrey had put it, savvy negotiators of the corporate 'tick-tack-toe'. But no matter how much she tried to convince herself, no matter how appreciative Jeffrey had appeared to be, she could not help but wonder if he knew that when Tiffany designed that delicate necklace – with those two little symbols inside those newly engraved sterling silver lockets – that they did not intend them to be perceived as noughts and crosses, but as hugs and kisses – like one lover would give another, a symbol of commitment and affection and . . . love.

She shrugged off the ridiculousness of it all, folding herself back into the couch and shutting her eyes. She had not slept well these past couple of days and felt the wave of exhaustion wash over her. And then her mind trailed back – to that night in Vegas all those years ago, to when a young Jeffrey Logan first came into her life, to how she had pulled him from obscurity and built him into one of the most successful TV identities the world had ever known . . .

'I'll see you at dinner then,' she told her fellow TV executives, begging off to escape to her Bellagio Hotel suite to quickly shower and change.

She was in Vegas for the annual NATPE conference – a conference organised by the National Association of Television Programming Executives to review the latest, and ideally predict the next, trends in international television programming. She was working at the time for a production company which specialised in information and lifestyle programming and, despite the fact that her presence at the respected conference was paid for by her current employers, did not feel guilty about using the opportunity to do a little research on her own behalf. For everyone used conferences such as these to network, send out feelers, negotiate a move, or simply consolidate their current position, depending on the job that they had and how much they were being paid to do it.

The talk was about talk – or more specifically the American people's seemingly insatiable appetite for more and more of it. Oprah had become an international phenomenon, the more down-market alternatives were springing up like mushrooms and already making huge money in syndication, and there was a general consensus that there was a gap in the market for a more upmarket relationship advice program, and accompanying rumours as to who would come up with it first.

What was needed, or so everyone seemed to agree, was a show that appealed to both men and women; a program that broke down age barriers but had a core audience of the sweet eighteen to thirty-nine cash-rich demographic; a one-hour, highly marketable package that sent advertisers, and as a result networks, into a flurry of excitement as it won its way into the hearts of America and brought in money by the bucket loads. Half of America was in therapy for God's sake, and the other half loved talking about their neighbours who were – so the hole was there and somebody just needed to fill it.

Katherine knew she wasn't alone – she knew that every decent exec worth his or her salt was currently searching for TV's answer to the family counsellor from heaven. But no one, at least at the time, had been able to come up with the right person to sell the premise. For the front person was the make or break of this so-called ratings bonanza sure-thing. You pick the wrong presenter, you lose viewer confidence and before you know it, you are wallowing in ratings hell and bumped for a 'mid-term replacement'.

Maybe it was luck that brought him to her attention – luck or the fact that she was running late for the closing night conference dinner and happened to ladder the last pair of stockings in her hotel room drawer. She called down for the concierge to bring her another pair and sat on her too soft hotel suite bed to wait for them to arrive. She flicked on the TV, surfed around the channels, only to land on an incredibly cheap, poorly produced, terribly lit, unbelievably tacky, almost shameless sales pitch from a local psychologist – a guy named Jeff Logan who was spruiking his own downtown practice like a car salesman would flog the latest in four-door sedans.

But there was something about him – his George Clooney looks, his deep dark eyes, his chiselled jaw and confident smile that made Katherine dive across the bed for the hotel pen and pad on the bedside table.

The stockings arrived but Katherine never made it to the dinner. Instead she ended up meeting this man named Logan for a late drink at Caesar's Palace – and by one o'clock in the morning, they had formulated a pitch that Katherine intended to take back to LA within the week.

Two months later Logan and de Castro had signed a six-figure deal with CBC – and the rest, as they say, was history. There had been bumps along the way – including Jeffrey's determination to move the show from LA to Boston. Jeffrey had met Stephanie not long after their first show went to air – and while Katherine understood his desire to relocate to his quickly pregnant wife's home town, she also knew that Jeffrey wanted a 'city of his own'. He argued that Oprah's stronghold on Chicago was one of the reasons for her success, and Katherine agreed that moving to a location such as Boston would add a special flavour of individuality to the new program that was already performing 'way above expectations'.

It worked of course, the program making the most of Boston's unique intellectual flavour while not alienating itself from the masses. Within the first year, thanks to Katherine's clever eye and business acumen, and Jeffrey's outstanding talent in front of the camera, the show had become one of the most successful talk shows in US television history – and Doctor Jeffrey Logan, ex-Vegas small-time shrink, a bona fide celebrity.

*

He was like a chameleon, she thought as she opened her eyes and looked down at her coffee to see that it had started to grow cold – *the way he had been able to shape and adapt himself.* The man she met that night at Caesar's was just a local show pony who spent his days in his two by four home practice, his nights gambling away his measly earnings at the various casinos, and every piece of spare change on cigarettes and frozen dinners.

But the moment the opportunity presented itself, Jeffrey took control. He closed his practice, went cold turkey on the cigarettes, quit hitting the casinos, bought a new suit, sharpened his presentation techniques and basically blew away everyone who met him. He became the darling of the network, married a rich and attractive professional, fathered two good-looking kids, and basically led the life of Riley. *Until now,* thought Katherine, *until now.*

Was he losing control? No, that wasn't it – in fact on the contrary, last night in Arthur Wright's office, this morning at her front door, he seemed more than on top of his game. She understood how difficult this must be for him and she acknowledged how the events of the past week were enough to send even the most adaptable of personalities into an emotional and intellectual tail spin – but why did she sense he had something up his sleeve, why did she see that hint of resolve in his eye and why did she feel that this time, whatever he was planning, she wasn't part of the deal.

24

'Jesus,' said Joe once the reporter had finished his story. David and Joe had stopped with the coffees almost a half-hour ago, but Rigotti was downing the black mud like he was feeding a habit – which he probably was.

'I'm sorry, Mannix,' said Rigotti. 'I get that you have the hump with us not calling you last night. But just like you, I have a job to do and my boss wanted me to run this by the lawyers before I . . .'

'Come off it, Rigotti. David already told me I am a late starter on this little coffee date. You were planning to research and run this story without giving a heads up to the police.'

Rigotti, who was an old friend, shrugged. 'Well, you do tend to put a dampener on things, Mannix.'

'That's me,' said Joe, 'a regular wet blanket.' He looked at David, obviously equally as displeased with his defence attorney friend.

'Come on, Joe,' said David, 'we're here now right,

and in all honesty, as the story stands, there is not that much to tell. This Blackmore refuses to supply Marc with Jason Nagle's details. He says he has left a message on the mystery guy's cell phone and is waiting for him to respond.'

'But . . .' Joe began.

'I know what you are going to say, Joe.' David cut him off. 'That the guy in Maine who allegedly sold the gun to Stephanie identified her as the buyer.'

This was true. Calvin Garretson of Garretson Rifles in Bangor, Maine, had told police that Stephanie originally ordered the Mark V rifle over the internet – but had travelled to the Pine State to pick it up rather than having it transferred to a Massachusetts gun dealer where, by law, she would have had to supply evidence of identification in order to collect it.

'There was no alleged about it,' countered Joe. 'Garretson was shown several pictures of Stephanie Tyler. She used her own American Express *and* email address *and* Firearms Identification Card to verify her identity.'

'But he also said his gun shop's surveillance camera was down at the time,' argued David. 'Which means there is no solid proof that Stephanie was the one who walked into that shop.'

'The guy has no reason to lie, David,' said Joe.

David met Joe's eye, the silence deafening.

'Okay, look,' said Rigotti, feeling the need to calm things down a little. 'Whatever the guy in Maine claims, as long as Mannix is now in the loop, I can't see the harm in his putting out a few feelers as to the identity of this Jason Nagle. Maybe if we find him, he can discount his ownership of the murder weapon and we can rule out Blackmore's crazy story as just that – another fanciful tale from a man who names his rifles after B-grade movie heroes.

'Of course,' Rigotti continued, looking at Joe, 'I would suggest you do this on the quiet, Lieutenant, considering the high-profile nature of this case and . . .'

'The fact that you don't want anyone else trumping your precious exclusive,' finished Joe.

Rigotti shrugged. 'So shoot me.'

Joe was still shaking his head. 'Here's the thing, Rigotti, you may be a mate and God knows I have walked the line between moral and professional responsibility in the past, but you and I both know, that when it comes to investigating the origin of a murder weapon, there is no "we" no matter which way you look at it.

'I might agree to make some enquiries as to the identity of this Nagle, even deign to fill you in with whatever information I deem appropriate, but we are talking about a serious criminal investigation here, and the last thing I need is an overzealous reporter rattling some supposed sharpshooter's cage while I am trying to get to the truth.'

Rigotti went to open his mouth, until David shot him a look which said, '*not a good idea*'.

'Even if we discount Garretson's statement,' Joe went on, 'and even if this Nagle exists, finding him may not be easy. My guess is you have already scanned the Nevada white pages and Googled his name ad nauseam only to come up empty.'

Rigotti shrugged again, before giving the slightest of nods.

'And then there is the matter of the lack of a

gun-related paper trail,' said Joe. 'Buying a gun in Massachusetts is a hell of a lot different from purchasing one in Nevada. Here we require licences and keep gun sale records and have consumer safety standards and undergo background checks on purchasers and enforce gun sale waiting periods. But in the Silver State none of those requirements exist.'

'You don't even need a permit?' asked David who, despite what he had heard about the liberal gun laws in other parts of the country, was taken aback by the seemingly 'open slather' attitude to firearms in the 'All For Our Country' state.

'Not unless your weapon is concealed,' said Joe. 'Which means this Nagle, if he even exists, could be very difficult to find.'

'Then why don't you just put the heavy on Blackmore to produce his details?' said Rigotti, asking the obvious.

'Because . . .' Joe began, 'in the incredibly slim chance that he is involved with the Logan case somehow, Blackmore could simply ring this Jason Nagle and . . .'

'Tip him off,' said David, relieved that they had not lost Joe altogether.

Joe reached into his pocket to retrieve a twenty, an indication that this meeting was over, at least for the time being.

'Let me start by rechecking Tyler's gun purchase details. I'll talk to Calvin Garretson again, go over the paperwork, confirm his ID.'

David nodded as Joe rose from his seat. 'Thanks, Joe,' he said.

'Don't thank me yet,' said Joe, his face now contorted in an expression of discomfort as his hand ran across his stomach. 'Shit, Cavanaugh,' he said. 'I knew I shouldn't have ordered the eggs.'

25

Nora Kelly was in an exceptionally contemplative mood. Not in the negative sense – in fact on the contrary. She was feeling more than a little upbeat about the issues she was considering this morning in the quiet of the deserted office around her. All said, the sixty-something widow was extremely pleased with her lot, and while her expression of such contentment may often have been corralled by her prim and proper demeanour, she had to admit that her life, despite setting her on roads unexpected, had turned out to be one filled with direction and purpose and love.

Of course there were those who might argue that her work was her life, a situation that spoke of narrowness and loneliness and regret. But in Nora's case, working with a man who she respected, and two young people she had grown to love as her own, meant that coming to work every day was like spending time with her family – and helping them brought her great pleasure and gratification and pride. They had never once refused to include her. She was invited, or more to the point expected, to sit in on important discussions regarding their cases at hand. They asked her opinion, sought her advice, and never once dismissed her observations as being in any way inferior to their own.

While Nora had never been the emotional type, preferring to disguise her affection in wit, she hoped that her determination to ease their load – a resolve now strengthened by the impending birth of Sara's baby (a child she already thought of as her surrogate grandchild) – was evidence of how much they meant to her and, hopefully, what she meant to them in return. So, as she opened the mail and separated it into piles, she pondered on the Logan case and how she might be able to assist. This one was going to be demanding in more ways than one given David's relationship with the poor deceased mother and the situation befallen her two troubled children. And while she could not think of any specific task she might undertake to relieve the burden at present, she promised herself that she would do everything she could to support her co-workers at this extremely busy time. For she had always believed that, despite arguments to the contrary, the law was designed to bring people together – not tear them apart.

The first thing that unnerved Sara after Chelsea Logan answered the front door of her family's Beacon Hill mansion, was the haste at which she closed it once again. Silence, nothing . . . until ten seconds later when Chelsea, her wide blue eyes now set with an expression of pure guardedness and perhaps the slightest trace of anticipation, opened the door for a second time.

'I'm sorry,' she offered. 'I had to turn off the alarm.' Which made no sense whatsoever given Chelsea was already inside the house and would have been setting off motion sensors left, right and centre of her very own accord.

But Sara did not draw attention to this, realising that if they were right about her father, the kid had to be living in a constant state of trepidation.

'Father is not home,' Chelsea said then, still hugging the side of the door.

'I know,' replied Sara.

It had been Sara's idea to try to catch Chelsea alone. Jeffrey Logan had told them last night that he would be heading down to Plymouth to visit J.T., and while that created its own problems – problems David had a plan to subvert at least temporarily – Sara suggested she should try to 'corner' Chelsea, and hopefully learn more about exactly what went on behind the blue painted door the girl now seemed determined to cling on to.

'Can I come in?' asked Sara.

'I . . . oh,' Chelsea began, her eyes hitting the floor, until she jerked her head up again as if a new idea had entered her previously cautious mind. 'Of course. I'm sorry, Miss Davis.'

'It's Sara,' smiled Sara, attempting to break the ice. 'And I would kill for a coffee if that's okay. I told David I would ration myself to one a day,' she added, gesturing at her stomach. 'But maybe I could sneak an early one in here, before heading back to the office.'

Chelsea smiled, taking Sara's hand with such enthusiasm that she practically dragged her into the hallway.

'Coffee it is, come on into the kitchen,' she said, after turning quickly to punch a set of numbers into the flashing home security system.

'Sit down,' said Chelsea, as she pushed through the dented, white painted louvred door – the same one that just days before had been showered with her own mother's blood.

Less than four days after her first gruelling visit Sara noted that the Logan kitchen was now sparkling clean, the only traces of what had been being the strong smell of lemon antiseptic in the air, the absent under-sink doors and the missing sixth white wicker chair that once sat at the head of the table.

'Milk?' asked Chelsea.

'Yes, thanks,' said Sara, now removing her jacket to place it on a cleared kitchen bench top. 'So, you are on your own, then?' asked Sara, needing to check if they were indeed alone. 'I thought Ms de Castro might be keeping you company.'

'No,' said Chelsea, as she returned the milk to the refrigerator. 'My father was going to visit her before he went to see J.T. He bought her a necklace, from Tiffany's – a thank you for helping us out. He even had it engraved, one locket with a "J", the other with a "K".'

But then Chelsea, who seemed determined to regurgitate this little story, did the strangest thing. She left the room quickly, without warning, returning seconds later with a computer printed receipt.

'See, it is one of those silver ones with tiny lockets hanging off of it.'

'It's nice,' said Sara, looking at the picture of the necklace on the receipt and not knowing what else to say.

'Then you should keep the print-out,' she said almost too quickly. 'In case you want to get one for yourself.'

'Ah . . . thanks, Chelsea, but your dad might need this for . . .'

'It's a copy of a copy,' she forced the issue. 'Please . . .'

So Sara put the receipt in her handbag and the girl relaxed her shoulders – just an inch.

Sara was at a loss. When Chelsea Logan had answered the door she had sensed an immediate chill in her cool blue eyes, but now she was seeing something else – a desperation to be acknowledged, a stifled cry for help.

But something told Sara that this fact-finding mission was not going to be as easy as she had initially hoped, for even though the teenager was alone, her obvious anxiety told Sara that her words, her actions, were still being controlled – either out of habit, or by something more concrete.

'Please, sit down,' said Chelsea after a time, carrying Sara's coffee with one hand and signalling at that now infamous kitchen table with the other. 'I made it pretty milky, in case you were worried about the strength,' she said.

Sara smiled. 'Thanks,' she said, before taking her seat at the door end of the table, thinking Chelsea would probably be more comfortable as far away from the other end as possible. But then she was proved wrong yet again. For in that moment Chelsea Logan not only headed for her mother's end of the table – the space where the sixth chair once rested – she pulled a chair from the side and dragged it *round* to her mother's former position, so that she might stare directly across at Sara, just as Stephanie Tyler was reported to have done last Friday night when her son allegedly entered the room with his father's rifle.

'I'll try to move the hat stand for you if you like,' she said, gesturing at the chipped red oak stand two feet away from Sara in the right kitchen corner.

'Oh no . . . it's fine,' said Sara.

'Silly really, having a hat stand in the kitchen,' Chelsea offered. 'But Mother would put her yellow sunhat on it and it would stand there in the corner looking like a person all on its own. It actually belongs in the hallway. But it's so darned heavy. I don't have the strength to move it alone so . . .'

'Ah,' said Sara then. 'Do you want me to . . .?'

'Help me? Goodness no,' said Chelsea. 'I kind of like it where it is. You just sit and enjoy your coffee.'

Sara nodded, taking a sip of her brew.

'Too milky?' Chelsea asked.

'No, it's fine,' managed Sara. 'Different to what I am used to, but that can't be a bad thing.'

'Different is good. Mother used to tell us that. "*We all live with the objective of being happy; our lives are all different and yet the same*."'

'She was right.' Sara smiled. 'In fact, I think I've heard that quote before.'

'Anne Frank,' said Chelsea. 'She spent two years in an attic with her family and four other people. A prisoner in her own home.'

Sara met Chelsea's eye, hoping the girl would go on, but when she didn't elaborate Sara found herself unable to hold her question in any longer.

'Chelsea, are you okay? I mean, this past week, it must have been so hard on you, on J.T., and . . .' She stopped there, on purpose, hoping Chelsea would note the lack of reference to her father.

'Not just us. Hardest on someone else too, don't you think?'

'You mean your . . .'

'Mother, of course,' she interrupted, as if determined to get it out. 'Considering . . .'

Sara nodded. 'My point is that . . .'

But Chelsea interrupted again. 'I take my SATs in a few weeks' time,' she said.

'Ah . . .' said Sara with a sigh, sensing that Chelsea needed more time. 'That's early, isn't it? I mean, your dad says you only just turned sixteen.'

'I am a year ahead,' she said. 'I am going to study law, like my mother. I want to do pre-law at Harvard and then transfer to Princeton or Yale or Columbia.'

'But why transfer?' asked Sara, broaching the obvious question, and in that moment sensing that it was exactly what Chelsea was hoping she would do. 'I mean, Harvard has one of the best law schools in the world.'

'I am waiting for J.T. to catch up with me, so we can transfer interstate together. He wants to be an architect and all three universities have excellent post grad schools so . . .'

'You could leave home together.'

'*Exactly*,' she said.

And with that, Sara decided it was time for another try.

'Chelsea, I want you to know that if you need someone to talk to . . . It is just us two right now, and as your brother's attorney, anything you tell me in regards to this case is privileged.

'What I am trying to say is that sometimes things are not as they seem. Sometimes we feel obliged to take a certain path simply because someone else has forced us to do so. But that doesn't have to be the case, Chelsea – for you, or for J.T.

'I know you are scared. But in the end you and your brother, you really need to trust us. David was a friend of your mom's,' she said, hoping this might make a difference. 'They went to college together and he says she was . . .'

The teenage girl stared directly at her, the tears now trailing slowly down her smooth, pale cheeks. And then she shook her head as if what Sara was proposing was impossible, before taking a breath to say, 'Can you stand up?'

'*What?*' asked Sara, but she could see the urgency in the young girl's eyes, the silent but desperate plea that Sara do as she asked.

Sara stood, and looked down at the girl, just as Stephanie's killer had done. And in that moment Sara knew she was trying to tell her something – to *show* her exactly what had gone down.

But she could not see it . . . she could not *SEE IT* and Chelsea was unable to tell her – unable or too terrified, and Sara sensed the latter was more likely the case.

'I can't reach it,' said Chelsea then, still sitting but extending her hand towards Sara's belly. 'I wanted to feel if your baby was kicking.'

'Chelsea, I wish . . . I could . . .'

'No,' said Chelsea, the tears now splattering on the table before her. 'That's okay. He can hear us though, can't he? Your baby, I mean, even though he isn't really here yet, he can hear what we are saying and when you think of it that way, there are really three of us in this room.'

Sara nodded, the magnitude of it hitting her square in the face.

'Yes,' she said. 'I understand, Chelsea. Three.'

26

'You are going to have to do something about that,' said child psychologist Barbara Wong-McGregor as she met David at the front door of the Plymouth Juvenile Detention Unit, shaking David's outstretched palm with one hand and shoving a copy of this morning's *Boston Tribune* into his chest with the other.

'It's nice to meet you,' said David in reply, more than a little taken aback by the woman's direct approach to an introduction. 'And thanks for meeting me on such short notice.'

Not long after Rigotti had left them, and David had explained to Joe that he was on his way to Plymouth to see J.T. Logan, Joe had made a call to an old friend by the name of Barbara Wong-McGregor. She was a respected child psychologist and, according to Joe, one of the best juvenile shrinks in the business. After a minute of to-ing and fro-ing on his cell – including some talk about Joe owing Wong-McGregor big time – the respected expert agreed to meet David in the detention unit's lobby in a little over an hour so that she might give him an early assessment of his client and some idea of what the hell might be going on in his traumatised head.

'I read the paper, Ms Wong-McGregor,' said David, guessing the 'call a spade a spade' expert was talking about this morning's report. 'And to be honest, as hard as it is to believe, it is pretty much a fair representation of what went down in court yesterday.'

'It's Barbara,' she said, shaking her head before turning her back on him to head towards the front security desk behind them. 'And I am not talking about the main story but the break-out piece on page five, the one that leads with a header stating: "Furious, Fourteen and Armed". The press is already throwing your kid in the basket with the likes of the Columbine killers, and that is no good for anyone, least of all your client.'

David began to see why Joe spoke so highly of this woman after all.

'That kind of stuff labels our kid as a loon from the get-go.' David had never heard a child psychologist refer to a 'patient' as a 'loon' before, but he guessed there was a first time for everything.

'And,' Barbara went on, 'it pollutes our jury pool before we even have a chance to get started.'

Our . . . we . . . the woman was already on board – and despite her rather odd demeanour, David had to admit he was grateful. 'We don't want him labelled as having serious psychotic tendencies,' said David then.

Barbara nodded. 'The jury think he's crazy, they'll be sympathetic but they'll convict,' she said, raising her left hand. 'The jury think he's a victim, they'll be sympathetic but they'll acquit,' she added, now raising the other. 'You see the difference?'

'I . . . sure,' said David, realising Wong-McGregor had not only listened to Joe's very brief description of the case, but also read between the lines.

'Right.' She nodded as she accepted her security pass from the desk personnel as if she did this every morning, which she probably did. 'Thanks, Walter,' she said to the guard who also handed David his own red-coloured pass before moving around the desk to escort them into the building proper.

'So, we agree you are going to have to make a concerted effort to control the way the kid is portrayed in the media,' she said, as if needing confirmation.

'I . . . yes,' said David, sensing that this was a 'yes' or 'no' question if ever there was one.

'Great,' she said, before her previously serious face broke into one of the biggest smiles David had ever seen. 'Now that that is sorted, we can go and see our kid.'

Twenty minutes later they were sitting in a too-small, windowless interview room in the juvenile detention unit's maximum-security fifth floor. The only thing to break the monotony of the grey-painted walls was the slightly darker door at the far right-hand corner of the room.

Barbara Wong-McGregor dragged the spare seat to the side, while David sat across from his client who was now wearing a maroon Department of Youth Services detention facility jumpsuit, his hands crossed on the metal table before him, his legs parallel to those of the aluminium table which, like the ones on his chair, had been securely bolted to the floor.

'When I came home from school I went straight to my room,' said J.T. Logan who, after several anxious enquiries as to the welfare of his sister ('*Have you seen her?*', '*Is she back at home with Father?*', '*Is she okay?*'), had settled back quietly.

'I did like I always did,' he said, focusing on the small recorder Barbara had asked David to allow her to use as part of her initial assessment analysis. 'Practised my violin until 4.26.39, did my trig homework until 5.01.05, my English until 5.40.29, then biology, history and geography.'

After David had taken Barbara into his confidence regarding their suspicions on the abusive environment of the Logan family home, the child psychologist had warned that, before they even attempt any enquiries relating to J.T.'s home, they must ease him with the security of 'fact' – or in other words, questions that called for a direct reporting of events rather than expressions of his emotional well-being or neglect.

'*Kids like this live by the motto of "trust no one"*,' she had said. '*And direct assumptions or accusations are only going to scare him. Don't forget there is a lot to be learned from J.T.'s responses – and whether we perceive them to be "false" or, more to the point, "coached".*'

So David had begun at the beginning – asking J.T. to tell them about his day from the moment he woke up last Friday morning to the moment the police arrived at his Beacon Hill home later that night. The boy answered clearly and respectfully, describing his movements in detail, sticking to a strict chronological order without any vacillation or delay.

'J.T.,' said Barbara, who had remained silent until now, 'you said you did violin until 4.26.39, trig until 5.01.05, English until 5.40.29. Just out of interest,' she asked, 'why not break your study periods into more obvious time brackets – like four-thirty 'til five, or five 'til six?'

J.T., looked at her as if the question was one he had never considered, the space of olive skin between his two brown eyebrows folding in a crease of uncertainty. 'Because that is how we always did it,' he offered. 'Me and Chelsea, I mean. The times would be changed regularly – to keep us on our toes.'

'And would there be checks that you kept to the prearranged time allocations?' asked Barbara, intrigued by this unusual behaviour, but savvy enough to ask the question as if it were the most natural one in the world.

'No,' said J.T., as though he found the question odd. 'There was no need. We always kept to them. Why would we not?'

Barbara smiled and sat back in her seat, a signal David took for him to move on.

Moments later J.T., who had explained the children did not normally eat dinner until their father returned home from work, finally reached the moments leading up to the shooting – the period of time in which he allegedly went to his parents' bedroom to retrieve the library cabinet key, proceeded downstairs to unlock said cabinet, went to the garage to get the bullets to load into the rifle, and then returned to the kitchen to shoot a hole in his mother bigger than the size of a baseball.

But the boy just stopped. He remembered finishing his geography assignment at 8.17.56pm, and he remembered going downstairs to the kitchen as he believed he had heard his father's car turn into the drive minutes earlier, but he did not recall getting the key, or the gun, or the bullets . . . J.T.'s version of accounts jumped straight from the geography assignment to the moment where he pointed the rifle at his mother – a time lapse of what must have been a good five minutes. David knew it should have taken him at least that amount of time to collect the key, unlock the cabinet, take out the gun, re-lock the cabinet, return the key to the upstairs drawer, go to the garage, load the gun and then make his way to the kitchen – which also meant he would have had to have left his room at 8.15pm at the latest, breaking his precious 'down-to-the-second' routine.

'Okay,' said David, a look from Barbara warning him that he had to stay on track. 'So you remember leaving your room and going downstairs to the kitchen.'

'Yes,' said J.T. without flinching. 'I left my room, went downstairs, opened the kitchen door and saw mother sitting at the end of the table. She was reading *Vanity Fair* and drinking a glass of wine and when I came in she looked up at me and said, "No".'

Barbara frowned; she had obviously noted the boy's inclination to 'regurgitate', rather than 'tell' the story.

'She said "No",' reaffirmed David.

'Yes,' replied J.T., his voice a monotone. 'She said "No".'

'And then you . . .?' prompted David.

'And then I shot her,' he said.

'And do you know why you did that J.T.?' asked Barbara, as David took a breath.

'Because that was my intent,' J.T. said with just the slightest of hesitation.

'You wanted to shoot her,' stated Barbara.

'It wasn't about what I wanted.' His eyes flicked to David. 'It was about what I *intended*.'

'But she was your mother, J.T. Why would you *intend* to kill her?' asked Barbara, using J.T.'s wording.

'Because parents are in charge of their children,' he answered.

'You killed her because she was in charge of you?' offered Barbara.

'No,' said J.T., the crease in his forehead now back with a vengeance. 'I killed her because she *wasn't*.'

David nodded.

'Did she say anything else?' asked Barbara after a time. 'Did she scream or call out or cry?'

'No.' J.T. shook his head. And then, as if a new thought had occurred to him, he turned his head slightly, answering Barbara, but looking directly at David.

'But it all happened so quickly. I had the gun in front of me. It has a fully adjustable trigger that has been precisely adjusted for sear engagement. The trigger lies to the rear of the alloy floorplate trigger guard. The cocking indicator showed the rifle to be cocked. The one-piece forged bolt was straight. The length of pull was set at thirteen-and-a-half inches.' The boy's voice was no longer a monotone, but almost animated in his urgency to explain.

'How do you know all this, J.T.?' asked David. 'Do

you have an interest in guns? Have you played with your father's rifle before?'

'No to the last two questions,' he said. 'And I know this because I *studied* it.'

'When? When did you study the gun?'

'Last Tuesday between 11.06am and 12.24pm.'

'You learnt about it at school?' asked Barbara, now pulling her chair closer to the table.

'No,' said J.T. 'I was home sick.'

David nodded. This last statement was a major setback for the defence, for Amanda Carmichael could argue that J.T. Logan had been planning the murder for at least four days in advance. And as David had no doubt that Jeffrey Logan intended to push the '*my son killed my wife because she was abusing him*' argument, claiming the boy shot his mother after he overheard his father's intention to divorce, he also knew that the savvy ADA would blow this theory out of the stratosphere as soon as the sequence of events was established. For Logan had sworn he had asked his wife for a divorce the night before Stephanie's murder – even speculated that J.T. had overheard his request and thus acted in a state of panic. But now J.T. was claiming he had been studying the gun's features some four days before, which meant Carmichael could argue J.T. was not a weak and defenceless victim in fear for his well-being, but a calculating and intelligent perpetrator who took great pains to end his mother's life with purpose and efficiency.

Exactly the argument Logan was hoping for, David thought to himself, *reasonable, rational, defined.*

'Okay,' said David after a pause, sliding his chair

forward so that he might rest his elbows on the table in front of him. 'So what happened next, J.T. – after you shot your mom?'

'Well, then Chelsea came running. She came into the kitchen. She screamed.'

'And your father?' began Barbara.

'He grabbed me and held me tight, buried my head in his chest. Then he pulled us both from the kitchen and into the hall. And then he called 911.'

'And then?' asked David.

'And then he called Katherine. And Chelsea kept screaming.'

'At you?'

'No, not at me,' he said.

David nodded once again.

'And then?' asked Barbara.

'Then Father pulled me back and looked at my shirt. He said we should get cleaned up. And he pulled me towards the bathroom. But then the police were outside and Father said there was no time, so he ran to the front door and unlocked it and then he told us we all had to go back into the kitchen and sit down – and close our eyes and not say anything.'

David glanced towards Barbara once again.

'Do you know why he told you to do that, J.T?' asked the psychologist.

'Not at the time. But I do now,' said J.T. 'He did it so that he could be arrested.'

'Over you,' said David.

'*Before* me – yes.'

While the boy obviously took the initial question the wrong way – thinking Barbara was referring to the bathroom issue – David was almost glad J.T. had misread her intent. For his answer told David this boy knew exactly what his father had been up to. In all likelihood Logan had suggested J.T. at least feign an attempt to clean himself up so that Logan's 'selfless confession' theory would ring true. But David sensed the boy was more than clever enough to read his father's motives – and probably had been for a very long time.

'I'm sorry, J.T.,' said Barbara then. 'What I meant was, why did your father get you to go back into the kitchen?'

J.T. took a breath before looking at David once again. 'Because he was home,' he said matter-of-factly. 'And that is what we always did at 8.27.55pm Monday through Friday, excluding holidays of course. It was dinner time. And we all knew better than to be late.'

27

'Wow,' said David to Barbara Wong-McGregor.

It was a little after midday and a senior guard had just knocked on the door to inform them that their time was up. J.T. had been told to accompany the guard to the dining hall for lunch – which he did, after shaking Barbara's and then David's hand with a grip that suggested he was either trying to be very 'grown up' or just incredibly afraid as to what lay ahead of him. David figured it was more than likely a combination of the two and found himself holding onto the boy's small palm until the guard physically tugged at the kid's elbow and pulled him from the room.

'Wow is right,' said Barbara, shaking her head as she took the seat previously occupied by David's fourteen-year-old client.

'I know you said we had to take it slow, Barbara,' said an openly anxious David, 'but that was . . . well, one of the most frustrating interviews I have ever undertaken. I couldn't help but feel the kid wanted to tell us about his father, and maybe if we had asked him the question directly he might have . . .'

'No,' said Barbara. 'The kid is shitting himself, David. He can only cope with so much right now. Did you notice the fervour with which he asked about his sister's welfare? The kid is sitting in a maximum-security juvenile detention facility and is more concerned about his sister's well-being than his own.'

'Which just goes to show how desperate his situation is – J.T. is worried what will happen to Chelsea if he spills the beans on his dad. Which means Logan has both kids exactly where he wants them – terrified, separated and well and truly under his control.'

David had been anticipating an argument, but was relieved he did not get one. Barbara believed him, and that was something in itself.

'Okay,' she said after a pause. 'I see what you are saying. We have two kids to consider here. But no evidence to prove either of them is under any threat from their father. And from what Mannix told me, you have evidence that points the finger at the wife as the abuser and . . . Jesus, what a fucking mess.'

'Worse still,' said David, 'Jeffrey Logan is a national hero for Christ's sake. So not only do we have zero evidence against him, but we are fighting a man who has just added a new sheen to his halo by publicly attempting to take the rap for his kid.'

'That was very clever of him,' Barbara replied.

'He's a psychologist, Barbara.'

'So am I, David, but this whole scenario – you have to hand it to him. If what we are thinking is true, well, there is no way I could have come up with it.'

'That doesn't help us,' he countered.

'No,' she said after a pause. 'I guess not.'

David leant back in the uncomfortable vinyl chair, his entire body slumped in defeat.

'Look,' said Barbara, determined to find something positive in what they had discovered this morning. 'It may not have sounded like it, but believe it or not, the kid actually gave us lots to go on.'

'He told us he shot his mom.'

'Yes,' she said. 'But you have to look beyond what he said and start looking at the world through that poor kid's eyes. He doesn't see things the way you and I do, David. His perspective is skewed, distorted. He sees things in pieces and spends his life trying to make sense of them, trying to put them back together.' Her eyes shifted around the room as if she was looking for a way to explain it to him.

'Stand up for a second,' she said. 'Come over here.'

But David just lifted his head, wondering what the hell this small windowless room could tell them. 'What is it?' he asked.

'Just stand *up*,' she said, now having moved around the table, her hands making frantic upwards motions as if to say, '*don't ask, just do!*'.

And so David got to his feet, and Barbara grabbed his left shirt sleeve and began pulling him towards the two-way mirror behind them.

'What do you see?'

'Excuse me?' David asked, wondering why, given all that he had to do, he was currently standing in a cold interview room corner looking at his own reflection.

'What do you *see*?' she repeated, pointing, insisting that he focus.

'I see me,' he said. 'One seriously pissed off attorney who has no idea as how to help his client.'

'Jesus Christ,' she said then. 'Enough with the self-pity already.' And then she dragged him towards the other end of the mirror, where the right-hand corner had been splintered by, David guessed, some frustrated teenager set on slamming the invisible voyeurs on the other side of the glass.

'Now what do you see?' she asked then.

'The same thing,' he said, looking at his tired, stubble-covered face – now dissected and distorted by the cracks in the mirror before him.

'No,' she said. 'Look beyond what you know is there, David. See how the splits in the glass dissect your image, break you down – your nose here, your left ear slightly elevated, your eyes off-centre, your features disjointed, off kilter, out of whack.'

Despite himself, David was beginning to see it. 'I don't make sense,' he said then. 'It looks as if someone has taken a hammer to what I am or what I believe I should be, so that I am left with nothing but . . .'

'A whole lot of sharp, jagged pieces of what you might have been. Nothing fits, David – can't you see? This is how his father has left J.T. And if I am right, I don't think he has ever been given the chance at looking at himself in any other way.

'He has been shattered, David, a new crack forcing its way into his already disjointed perspective every time his father chooses to apply the pressure. We may not yet know exactly what went down in that kitchen last Friday night but to me at least, one thing is obvious: J.T. Logan is at breaking point, David. He is a sheet of glass ready to shatter. He needs our help but we have to be careful how we give it. And we have to be . . .'

'Quick,' said David, reading her mind.

'Yes,' she said.

'Before the kid loses his grip forever and decides he is not worth picking up the pieces for, after all.'

Seconds later a bang on the outside door startled them both, and they turned to see a white-shirted security officer poke his head around the door.

'Are you Mr Cavanaugh?' he asked.

'Yeah,' said David.

'The famous dad is in reception. Says he wants to see you pronto.'

David nodded before turning back to Barbara. 'I asked Joe to call in a few favours down at DYS,' he whispered. 'They must have done what he asked – told Logan his son would not be available for visitors today.'

'You can't keep him away from his son forever,' said Barbara.

'I know. But in the very least, like you said, we need time to earn J.T.'s trust.'

'Mr Cavanaugh?' said the guard, still standing at the door.

'Okay, I know, sorry,' said David, now moving back to the table to collect his things. 'Is Doctor Logan ah . . .'

'About as pissed as a bobcat with a toothache,' said the guard.

'Want to meet America's "Martha Stewart" of relationship improvements?' asked David of Barbara.

'Sure.' She smiled. 'Maybe we could compare notes.'

28

One, two, three.

Access, devise, move.

Amanda Carmichael had learned a long time ago that there was definitely merit in preparation. She had seen so many careers go down the gurgler because the loser in question played his or her hand without first considering the cards that they held before them.

Tony Bishop had just dealt her a hand full of aces. No doubt about that. But strategising exactly as to how to use such advantages was key to maximising her success. From where Amanda had always sat, it wasn't just about winning the game, but also about how you won it, and in this case she planned on something spectacular.

Mannix and McKay had been right, she did like courting the media. Not that she would ever admit it. She liked the whole idea of being in front of the cameras. She was aware of her assets and saw no reason why she should not use them for her own advancement. In fact, a role in the spotlight had been her initial career preference when she entered college – one that she had moved on from but never lost sight of in the hope that she might one day be able to use her current role as 'respected attorney' to gain the national notoriety she craved. And given this morning's double whammy of good news, it appeared that, in all likelihood, she had every chance of doing just that.

After graduating from Groton at the top of her class, the exclusive boarding school providing her with an excellent education and a portal to any university of her choosing, Amanda decided on sticking close to home and enrolled in the equally as highly regarded Wellesley College for women.

Wellesley was one of those historic places that encouraged its scholars to act with independence and forethought. It described its students, including alumni like Hillary Rodham Clinton, as young women with 'high personal, intellectual and professional expectations' – all of which fit an enthusiastic Amanda Wyndham Carmichael to a T.

Amanda's father may have been born and bred in the working class suburbs of South Boston – where he worked weekends in his father's drugstore while studying law and eventually proving that a boy with brains and ambition could defy all the odds and become one of the most respected law-makers in the country. But her mother, Alicia Wyndham Carmichael, was a Wellesley girl through and through, with an estate that ran for acres, a country club membership that began at conception, and a general air of grace that was bred, not taught – found not in one's burgeoning bank account, but decidedly in one's genes.

And so Amanda Carmichael had settled on a degree in media arts and sciences with the full intention of then attending Columbia's famous graduate school of journalism. Her plan was to begin her career as a TV news reporter and then do some serious fast-tracking to become one of those reputable network anchorwomen – a sort of Katie Couric minus the cheese, with a salary and profile to match.

She enjoyed the course, for the first semester or two, until she discovered that, as much as she liked the idea of becoming a national icon, she had a greater desire to *make* the news rather than just report it. She was born to be a doer, not an observer and as such, by the end of her first year, had transferred out of media and into political science and legal studies where she revelled in courses such as courts, politics and law.

Having graduated Wellesley with distinction, she took up a place at Boston University School of Law – following in the footsteps of her father who, *sans* an Ivy League law degree, had gone on to 'conquer the world'.

'A J.D. is a J.D.,' her Supreme Court Judge father used to tell her, referring to the abbreviation of *Juris Doctor* – the US's reference to a professional degree in law. 'It is not where it came from, but what you do with it that counts.'

And he was right, Amanda knew, as she sat back in her olive green leather chair and surveyed the perfectly arranged surrounds of her slightly larger than average Government Center office. Amanda Carmichael, twenty-nine, beautiful and with an IQ of 142, may have looked like her mother but she thought like her dad – clearly, calmly, always assessing the information at hand, devising the best way to deal with it and timing any move with precision.

Tony Bishop may be good in bed but, as it turned out, he was also an incredibly fruitful source of information. Amanda knew how much it would have pained him to divulge such 'news' – knowing full well that his old college buddy would be on the receiving end of the wallop she would inevitably deliver thanks to Tony's willingness to 'share'. But in all honesty, as much as Tony amused her, she had other less altruistic priorities and not enough time to give a damn.

Prosecutors were not hired to be fair, they were hired to win. Her father had taught her that little nugget of wisdom too. 'Laws were made to be kept, not to be negotiated,' he used to say. 'Speculating on a defendant's innocence is not your job – but proving their guilt is.' And so, with that incredibly sound piece of advice now forefront in her mind, Amanda closed her eyes and allowed the elation, the excitement, the pure unadulterated joy that accompanied Tony's 'news' to wash over her, just once, before she set her mind to the task.

Just as her father had taught her, she needed to follow the three-step strategy of 'accessing' the information, 'devising' a plan to use such information in an effort to reach set goals and then, and only then, 'moving' with a determination so swift and so strong that it smacked her opposing counsel straight in his '*I do not want to fuck you*' ruggedly handsome face.

She needed to verify the change-of-will recording, confirm the second, even more spectacular piece of information with the company involved, and then, she needed to plan quietly and thoroughly before timing the move that would slam this case onto the front page of every newspaper in the country – and her professional success with it.

Moments later, just as Amanda Carmichael was picking up her phone to arrange a meeting at Tony Bishop's office, and as David and Barbara Wong-McGregor were taking the lift to the ground floor of Plymouth Juvenile Detection Unit, and Marc Rigotti was making his umpteenth call to Carleton Blackmore, General Manager of Hunting Rifles Inc., Nora Kelly was undertaking a small but rewarding task of her own, trying to connect one lonely old soul with another.

She had no idea why the clipping and accompanying (and seemingly unrelated) brochure had arrived at their offices. The envelope had been made out simply to the firm's street address with no name called to attention. It was a local stamp, mailed last Friday and, considering it had no return information, Nora figured she might as well use the interesting little article for good.

'Ms McCall?' she said as the phone picked up almost immediately. She could hear music in the background – mixed with sounds of laughter, joviality, life.

'This is Deirdre McCall,' returned the voice.

'I am sorry, Ms McCall, you do not know me, but my name is Nora Kelly. I am a legal secretary from Boston and I am ringing to ask your advice.'

Then . . . silence, not a single word.

'I, ah . . .' Nora went on. 'You see I received a copy of an article in the *Las Vegas Weekly*. It was a lovely piece written last year about your dancing school and it mentioned that you taught people of all ages – little ones to, well, people more my age.'

'Mrs Kelly,' began McCall, 'is this some sort of trick, because if it is, I know nothing about anything. I have never even been to Boston, let alone know anyone who lives there.'

'Oh no, dear,' said Nora, concerned she had frightened the poor woman. 'I am sorry. I am not explaining myself. You see, I work for a small law firm which once represented a lovely elderly gentleman by the name of Hector Gabbitt. Without going into too much detail, Mr Gabbitt is a gentle man who lost his wife to . . . well . . .' Nora hesitated. She did not know how to summarise Gabbitt's situation as an elderly gent whose wife had tried to frame him for murder. 'He has moved to Las Vegas, Ms McCall, but as he has no children nor friends in the local area, I thought that maybe if he joined your class for the over-fifties that . . .'

'You are ringing to enrol a friend in my "Follies for over-fifties"?'

'Yes. That's right.'

'Then why isn't this Mr Gabbitt calling me himself?' she asked.

Nora could not help but be somewhat taken aback by the obvious suspicion in McCall's tone.

'Well, it is not the type of thing Mr Gabbitt would do without a . . . ah . . . a little push. He is a little shy, you see?'

There was more silence. 'How did you get the article, Mrs Kelly?' asked McCall at last. 'And where did you get my number?'

'It was sent to me – I mean to us, at our firm –

obviously by mistake. And then I called directories and . . . In fact, you didn't send the article, did you, Ms McCall? Goodness me, of course you did, you simply addressed it incorrectly. I am so sorry, how rude of me.' Now Nora understood the woman's somewhat curt responses. Deirdre McCall had obviously sent the article and brochure – on a holiday resort in Cape Cod – to a relative in Boston . . . but no, that could not be right. The letter was postmarked locally and the woman just said she knew no one back east so . . .

'I am sorry, Mrs Kelly, but the class is full,' McCall said then, and Nora could have sworn she heard a trace of what sounded like fear in the woman's voice.

'Oh . . . I . . .'

'And please,' said McCall, '*please* . . . do not call me here again.'

The first thing David noticed when he and Barbara Wong-McGregor rounded the corridor and re-entered the entrance area of Plymouth Juvenile Detection Center, was the look of pure anger on Doctor Jeffrey Logan's face. The man was beside himself, his entire body knotted in a fit of controlled fury – his knuckles white, his jaw clenched, his brown eyes burning with barely contained rage.

'What the hell is going on?' he said, bounding towards them. 'I want to see my son.'

'Jeffrey,' said David, his arms already up in a 'slow-down' motion. 'I'm sorry, but the morning got away with us and I believe there was some glitch in J.T.'s processing yesterday meaning he has to be . . .'

'Glitch?' said Logan. 'What glitch?' he added,

lowering his voice. The man had obviously noticed the small group of spectators in the lobby now staring his way – and he had an image to protect so . . . he took a breath and managed to relax his shoulders.

'I'm sorry. It's just that I am very worried about him, David,' he said, his eyes flicking towards Barbara Wong-McGregor with the slightest trace of recognition. 'What did he tell you? Does he remember what happened? He has not wanted to talk about it so I was afraid he might have blocked it out or . . . I am dreadfully concerned about his emotional and psychological welfare. He needs me, David. I think I should be sitting in on any interviews you conduct in the future so that I might . . .'

'Doctor Logan,' interrupted Barbara with her hand outstretched. 'My name is Barbara Wong-McGregor and I specialise in the psychological evaluation of juvenile offenders.'

If Barbara had intended to hit a nerve she got what she wanted. The implications of having an independent psychologist probe into J.T.'s head were written all over Jeffrey Logan's face.

'I know who you are,' said Logan, lowering his voice even further. 'And as much as I respect the fact that you have a job to do, Ms Wong-McGregor, J.T. is only fourteen and as the person legally responsible for him, I have not agreed to having him examined by . . .'

'I am afraid, as much as I understand your desire to protect your son, Doctor Logan, that it is really not your call. J.T. has been charged with murder and will be tried as an adult in the Superior Court. The court will require a psych assessment whether you agree to one or not, and as much as I respect your obvious experience in the business, this one is really beyond your control.'

Logan was speechless, his eyes darting to David in an expression that said, '*You work for me – now earn your fucking money and put this woman in her place*'.

But David was at the ready. 'I am afraid Barbara is right, Jeffrey. But if it is any consolation, I can assure you that Barbara is the best. If anyone can give us a true indication of J.T.'s motives psychologically, then I can promise you Barbara is it.'

There was silence, as David met Logan's eye, almost hearing the cogs of his brain turning over in double time as he tried desperately to find a way out.

'I see,' said Logan. 'I am sorry. Forgive me, Ms Wong-McGregor. I know you by reputation, of course,' he said, now offering his hand to Barbara who hesitated, only slightly, before taking it in her own.

'And I you,' she replied with an appropriate smile on her face.

'Thank you,' he said. 'For helping us.'

'No problem,' said Barbara. But if Logan was expecting any postscript of sympathy for his situation, it was not forthcoming.

'I'm sorry, Jeffrey,' said David then, looking at his watch. 'But I have to head back to the office.'

Logan nodded. 'But when can I see J.T.?'

'I'll give you a call,' said David, already moving towards the door. 'Get you in as soon as possible.'

And then, as they were almost at the door, Logan called after them, 'Caroline Croft has been calling me on the hour, David. She's been onto Katherine too, via the network CEO, and we are both under a lot of pressure to . . .'

David stopped in his tracks, knowing that this at least was the truth. Croft had been calling David's offices just as regularly, her eyes set on the 'prize' of the first post-murder interview – a Doctor Jeffrey Logan exclusive.

'Just stay away from her, Jeffrey,' said David. 'I know Croft, and as much as I admire her tenacity, her motives are almost always one hundred per cent self-ish. We need to discuss the way we are going to handle the media as a whole – but until that is done, you and Katherine have to hold off and sit tight.'

Logan nodded. 'I can't hide forever, David,' he said, just as David reached the door.

'No, Jeffrey,' said David, without even breaking his stride. 'You're right. You can't.'

29

It was only mid-May but the evening was already thick with a humidity that suggested spring had given up early, making way for a summer of bright blue mornings, long, hot days and cool nights that brought a fresh salty breeze to chase the mugginess away. They were in Arthur's office, the windows yanked up to their horizontal constraints, the last few rays of sun now thick with particles of floating dust, the atmosphere in the room one of focus, determination, intent.

David had asked Barbara to cancel her appointments for the rest of the day – and despite her ensuing speech about how she could barely afford to squeeze lunch into her already overcrowded schedule, she had eventually agreed to give him an hour back at his office to go through J.T.'s interview in a little more detail. But when she arrived to hear Sara's account of her morning with the obviously terrified Chelsea, the dedicated child psychologist pulled out her cell phone and asked her assistant to *blow everyone off until at least midday tomorrow*, leaving David and his team extremely grateful for her commitment and Barbara immersed in what she described as one of the most 'complex abuse cases she had ever had the misfortune to be involved with'.

'You're sure you were being recorded?' asked Barbara of Sara, the four of them now sitting around the coffee table in Arthur's office, their eyes set on the ink-covered whiteboard before them.

'Yes,' said Sara, getting to her feet to approach the board to point at the list of notes she had written under the half of the board headed with the name 'Chelsea'. 'She practically told me as much, which is why our entire conversation was held in some form of one-way code, with Chelsea trying desperately to feed me clues and me being too stupid to . . .'

'Don't, Sara,' said David, just as Nora re-entered the room with a fresh round of coffees. 'She didn't exactly make it easy for us. I mean the universities and Anne Frank references are easy, considering the kids are obviously prisoners in their own home and desperate to escape as a twosome – but the Tiffany necklace, the hat stand . . .? Maybe she was just blurting out things that made her think of her mother, or her father's lack of respect for her.'

But Barbara was not convinced. 'No, David. I think Sara's right. From what she says, Chelsea is one very smart girl. I think everything on the list here holds some degree of significance, including her explaining how she turned off the alarm at the front door and activated it again after Sara was in the house. And then there is her taking a seat at the end of the table . . . her asking to feel Sara's baby.'

'But what does it all mean?' asked David, scanning the list for the umpteenth time – *1. Alarm, 2. Necklace, 3. Sitting in mother's chair, 4. Reference to the hat stand, 5. Anne Frank, 6. Universities, 7. Reaching to feel Sara's baby, 8. Asking if unborn child could hear/Chelsea suggesting three sets of ears were in the room.*

'Well, the question about the child's hearing was Sara's tip-off that they were being recorded,' said Arthur, sliding slightly to his right so that Nora might perch on the arm of the sofa. 'And I think David is right about Anne Frank and the universities.'

Barbara nodded. 'I agree – with the reference to the interstate colleges telling us she sees herself as a surrogate parent to her little brother.'

'And the alarm?' asked Sara.

They all thought on this a while. 'What if Doctor Logan's house was equipped with one to keep people *in* instead of the other way around?' suggested Nora. 'I know office blocks have coded security systems that require certain employees punch in codes to mark their coming and goings, perhaps Doctor Logan . . .?'

'That's it!' said David. 'Logan wanted to make sure Chelsea didn't go out while he was seeing de Castro and J.T. He has installed some form of system which makes Chelsea accountable for her movements, which is why the moment she opened the door to Sara, she had to re-shut it quickly and reset the code so the alarm did not go off.

'Nora,' he went on, looking at his savvy personal secretary with a smile, 'do you think you could ring Joe and see if he can find out what sort of security system the Logans have installed? It is bound to be linked to their telephone line so he might even be able to get the info from his telephony company.'

'Of course, lad,' said Nora, already on her feet and leaving the room.

'I'm slipping her my card before I leave,' said Barbara when Nora was out of earshot. 'She ever gets tired of you lot, then I'll employ her in a heartbeat.'

'Not a chance,' said David, stealing a glance at Arthur. And Arthur smiled.

'Okay,' said Sara, still pacing near the whiteboard and rubbing the small of her back as she moved. 'What about the hat stand in the kitchen?'

'No idea,' said Barbara. 'This one feels like the odd man out and could well mean nothing. Perhaps she is just missing her mother – and expressing how things would have to change now that she is gone.'

But Sara frowned. 'I see what you mean, but she seemed to make such a point of it.'

'We need to think on that one a little longer,' said Arthur.

They all nodded.

'Do you think she mentioned the necklace because she was angry that her father was giving Katherine de Castro a gift?' continued Arthur after a beat.

'No,' said Sara. 'There was no anger there. I actually get the sense Chelsea likes de Castro.'

'I agree,' said David. 'Both kids seem comfortable in her company. She has been kind to them and I honestly don't think de Castro has any idea what the hell her bastard business partner is up to.'

'Do you think there is a chance that this de Castro and Logan could be romantically involved?' asked Barbara.

David looked to Sara who was already shaking her head.

'I just don't see it,' said Sara. 'De Castro is kind of a loner and Logan is . . . well, he strikes me as the type who likes to possess a woman.'

'But his late wife,' countered Barbara, turning towards David. 'You described her as a strong, independent woman. There are men who target "A" type personalities with the specific desire to quash their individuality. It is part of their MO. They actually get off on watching a strong, beautiful woman wither.'

David could feel the blood rising in his temples, realising that was exactly what had happened to his once free-spirited friend. He leaned across the coffee table, wanting, *willing* himself to see something that might give them a shred of evidence that what they were speculating on was true. He picked up the necklace receipt and studied it word for word, seeing nothing but the obvious until . . .

'Well, I'll be,' he said at last.

'What, David?' asked Sara, moving around the coffee table to look over David's shoulder. 'What do you see?'

'This was never about the necklace, Sara – but more about the receipt.'

'I don't understand,' said Barbara.

'This record of purchase,' said David, holding up the computer print-out in his hand. 'It says Logan ordered this necklace and had it engraved over a week ago, or more specifically, three days before his wife's murder.'

'Then there is no way it was bought as a thank you gift,' said Sara. 'Unless he knew what was going to happen in advance.'

Arthur nodded. 'It appears the man has a new target in his sights.'

'My God,' said Barbara. 'This is worse than I thought.'

A little over an hour later they decided to call it a night, Barbara explaining her brain was fried and suggesting she take the night to go through J.T.'s interview tape before sharing her views on it in the morning. And despite his growing determination to unravel the intricate maze of deception Jeffrey Logan had constructed, David was grateful for the break.

'I called Joe while you were in the shower,' he said, after he and Sara had gotten home, heated up some leftovers for dinner and washed the day's troubles from their skin. He shifted himself on their living room sofa, and lifted the back of her old college T-shirt so that he might rub some massage oil into her back.

'Ouch!' said Sara, arching at his touch.

'Sorry,' he said, shaking his head, feeling guilty for drawing her into this case in the first place. 'You shouldn't be working so late. You need to rest.'

'Don't start, David,' she said, determined to dismiss him. 'I'm fine. What did Joe say?'

David knew there was no point in arguing. 'I briefed him on your conversation with Chelsea – and Barbara's take on it all. I told him we'd be going over J.T.'s interview tomorrow.'

'Any news on the gun guy?'

'No. Joe called the Nevada DMV to do a check on the name Jason Nagle, and put the name through some federal and state crime lab computers, but came up blank.'

'And the Logans' alarm system?' she asked.

'Joe said he has seen alarms like the one Nora described before. He said he remembers something about them being used on a trial basis in some police community in Vermont – something about parolees and curfews and keeping inmates at home between certain hours and so forth.'

'Will the telephony company have a record of it?'

'Not necessarily, especially if Logan does the monitoring himself.'

Sara nodded, her shoulders shifting as she thought of the next question on her list. 'Why doesn't Joe just ring this Blackmore and put pressure on him to release Nagle's details?' she asked after a moment.

'Because he doesn't want Blackmore to tip off Nagle to our suspicions.'

'But this Nagle could well have nothing to do with this case – bar the fact he may have sold his gun to Logan or . . . I mean, it is not like the guy knew what he was going to do with it.'

'True, but if it is the same rifle, and this Blackmore keeps swearing to Rigotti that it is, we need to find out how it got registered under Stephanie's name – and ended up in Massachusetts with a purchase permit that originated in Maine. Joe contacted the Bangor-based company again, by the way, and they are triple-checking their documentation in relation to the purchase.'

Sara nodded again. 'Can Joe sit in on Barbara's briefing tomorrow morning?' she asked.

'No, he says he is expecting Martinelli to front with the forensics report first thing,' said David, referring to Boston PD's Crime Lab Unit chief, Dan Martinelli.

'God, I almost forgot,' said Sara. 'The analysis is due in tomorrow – along with the autopsy report and . . . this case is barely four days old and already I feel like we've been working on it for centuries.'

'That's because you're overdoing it.'

'No,' Sara replied calmly. 'It's because Stephanie meant something to you and in a way this case started the day that you met her and she became your friend.'

David wrapped his arms around her, pulling her tight, grateful for her willingness to understand.

'You do know though, David,' she said, twisting in his arms so that she might look him in the eye, 'that this can't go on forever.'

'What do you mean?'

'What I mean is . . .' she hesitated, as if deciding how to word what she was about to say. 'At some point, we are going to have to acknowledge that it was most likely J.T. who pulled that trigger.'

David had filled his workmates in on Joe's information regarding the boy's shoulder – but like Joe, they all agreed that it was not enough.

'I am not saying that if he did shoot his mom that Logan didn't put him up to it, but tomorrow's reports will be damaging and we are going to have to come up with a defence that will give him his best chance to . . .'

David realised what she was trying to say, and as much as he did not want to hear it, he knew that she was right. Sooner or later they were going to have to weigh up the time it was already taking to try to lay blame on the father against the time they needed to prepare a decent defence for his son. The forensics were indisputable and in the end they may be forced to forgo the wild goose chases so that they might prioritise J.T.'s chance at survival.

'You think if we can't nail Logan that we will be forced to go with self-defence?' And he could tell by the look in Sara's pale blue eyes that she understood how hard this was for him.

'Yes.' She nodded. 'Logan is a very clever man, David, and *if* it comes to the point where we decide we don't have what it takes to prove our suspicions, we are going to have to do whatever we can to reduce J.T.'s sentence – to get him some *help*.'

'You're saying we may need to concede that he was the victim of emotional abuse – and killed his mother out of . . .'

'Fear . . . a need to escape,' she finished for him. 'Yes.'

'And we would use Logan's tape.'

'I am sorry, David.'

He nodded.

'It's the last of our last resorts,' she stressed, reaching up to place her hands on his face. 'And I am sure that we can do this, David – that *you* can bring him down. But in the end you are going to have to decide what Stephanie would have wanted you to do. And, without having even met her, my best guess is, that's to do whatever it takes . . . to save her son.'

30

Moments later, not more than two miles across town, an exhausted Tony Bishop was packing up for the night, contemplating the meeting with his ADA girlfriend tomorrow morning and what it might mean for everyone concerned. They had not made plans to see each other tonight which, under the circumstances, was probably for the best given they were in the middle of a 'situation' that could have huge implications for Tony in more ways than one.

He knew he had done the right thing by calling her, and after thinking of little else all afternoon, was relieved by the knowledge that, despite the fact that he could not discuss any of this with his good friend David Cavanaugh, in many ways the turn of events might eventually work in DC's favour, given he had stopped representing the father and was currently acting on behalf of the son. And this, in the very least, eased Tony's concerns somewhat, given David was the type of guy who never put his job before their friendship, a loyal mate who, no matter what, had always tried to . . .

But then the telephone rang, causing a contemplative Tony to jump, and wonder who the hell would be calling at a little after nine at night.

'Bishop,' said Tony.

'Mr Bishop, my name is Doctor Jeffrey Logan.'

And in that moment Tony knew that this was not going to be so easy after all.

'Do you have a moment?' the doctor asked, his tone all matter-of-fact.

'I . . . well . . .'

'Good, because you see this is in regard to my two children – and I need your urgent advice.'

31

'Twenty thousand dollars,' said Detective Frank McKay, as he took a seat on the couch across from the desk in Lieutenant Joe Mannix's glass-walled Boston Police Headquarters office. Joe's office was bigger than most at the modern One Schroeder Plaza complex in Boston's central Roxbury. The décor was lean and functional and consisted of one two-seater couch, two visitors' chairs, a couple of gunmetal grey filing cabinets and a birch laminate desk which Joe often used to perch on whenever a visitor wandered into his 'high traffic' hub.

'What?' asked Mannix, not knowing where the hell this one was going.

'Twenty thousand dollars, Chief,' repeated Frank, who leaned towards the corner of Joe's desk to hand his boss a coffee. 'I heard on the news that was what someone was willing to pay for Gerry Cheevers' mask.'

Gerry Cheevers, Boston Bruins, 1960s . . . Joe vaguely remembered the story about the hockey goalie's mask – and the way he used to paint fake black stitches on it every time he got hit by a puck. His point was to show how effectively the record-making goalie had defended for his team, taking hit after hit before allowing a single shot to make it past his posts.

'This going somewhere, Frank?' asked Joe, knowing exactly what Frank was doing – retrieving some ridiculously obscure fact from his 'encyclopedia of trivia' mind so as to ease the anxiety and bide the time until the autopsy notes from the ME's office and those all-important forensic and physical evidence reports from their own Crime Lab Unit finally came in.

Frank's ponderings drove Joe crazy, but he also knew that at the basis of every odd anecdote and sweeping generalisation there was always a message, an understanding, an ounce of wisdom that, more often than not, Joe found strangely comforting.

'That twenty grand,' Joe went on. 'Are you suggesting it is a bargain, or a rip-off or . . .?'

'Not sure, Chief,' said Frank, and Joe wondered if there *was* a point to this one after all. 'But they showed a picture of the mask – which Cheevers refuses to sell, by the way, given it has pride of place on his grandson's bedroom wall – and by the time Cheevers retired it was covered in these stitches, see, like the puck had found every available place to smack one on his kisser.'

'Then I guess he was lucky he wore that mask, Frank.'

'Sure,' said Frank, who was now dropping the fourth satchel of sugar into his extra milky coffee. 'And even luckier that as an NHL goalie, the mask did not look crazy out of place.'

Joe nodded, thinking that he finally knew where this one might be going.

'The thing is, Chief,' Frank went on, 'that unlike hockey goalies, for most people – people like Jeffrey Logan, say – the masks they wear cannot be so obvious. Oh, they're there all right, covering their real faces which are scheming and plotting underneath the façade, but the good news is, because their masks are invisible they leave themselves vulnerable to . . .'

'A potential smack in the kisser,' finished Joe.

'As long as someone is clever enough to find his mark.'

Joe nodded as they sat in silence for a while.

'Think we can do that, Frank?' Joe asked after a time.

'I think the bastard is so arrogant that there's a chance he won't see us coming.'

'Then I have tabs on the slapshot that nails him, Frank.'

'Unless I smack the punk first.'

Seconds later, Joe saw Dan Martinelli enter from the far end of the room. Martinelli was the head of Boston PD's Crime Lab Unit and one of the most respected forensics experts in the city. Joe knew for a fact that headhunters for the FBI's famous lab in Quantico had tried to poach him several times, but Martinelli was as loyal as he was talented, and for that, Joe was grateful.

'Hey,' said Joe, rising from his desk to greet the short, stocky Italian–American.

'Chief,' said Martinelli. 'Frank,' he added, as he entered the office proper and shook Frank's hand. 'Well, here it is,' he said, holding up the report and cutting straight to the chase. 'The detail is in the paperwork but if you want a quick run-down I'd be happy to . . .'

'Please,' said Joe, signalling for Martinelli to take a seat. 'Tell us what you got?'

And the answer was – a lot. Martinelli started with the BPA or bloodstain pattern analysis.

'All in all we studied three major types of bloodstains,' Martinelli began. 'Passive – meaning the blood that had dripped on the floor underneath the victim, transferred – referring to the stains incurred when one bloody surface came in contact with a secondary surface, and projected – referring to the bloodstains created when the victim was subjected to the force of the rifle's ammunition.'

That was Martinelli, thought Joe, *Mr Efficiency to a T*.

'DNA tests on the passive stains confirmed them as blood belonging to the victim – type O negative with stain patterns consistent with drainage from the open gunshot wound. Basically Ms Tyler's entire blood volume – about four litres or so – exited the body via the nine-inch wide exit hole, which is not unusual given her mediastinum or central chest cavity, which carries all the major blood vessels, was virtually destroyed by the path of the bullet.

'Transferred stains were minimal, but we did find some on Doctor Jeffrey Logan's shirt and upper trousers, indicating they were a result of contact with another item of fabric. The pattern suggests that some of the stains on the original fabric had not yet dried and as such were transferred onto the secondary fabric.'

'The original fabric being J.T. Logan's T-shirt,' interrupted Frank.

'Exactly,' confirmed Martinelli. 'At some point the father must have come in contact with the boy, perhaps grabbed him and pulled him from the room.'

Joe nodded, knowing Martinelli was confirming everything they originally assumed.

'As for those projected stains . . .' Martinelli took a breath as if this part of the report was the most difficult to communicate. 'Obviously, given the nature of the weapon used, our analysis shows they were HVIS or high velocity impact spatter.'

Joe and Frank knew that, contrary to what the name suggested, low, medium and high impact spatter do not refer to the velocity of the blood droplets as they flew through the air, but to the amount of energy transferred onto the blood to create the stains. In other words, Martinelli was confirming that the myriad stains across the kitchen behind Stephanie Logan and the lesser degree of spatter in front of her – on J.T.'s shirt, the kitchen table, chairs and so forth – were the result of an extremely fast and powerful force impacting on the victim, in this case a bullet travelling at 2650 feet per second and generating nearly 8100 foot-pounds of energy.

'The stains behind the victim were extensive, the result of the "explosive" nature of the weaponry which produced a one-inch wound on entry and a nine-inch exit wound at the rear.

'The spatter patterns in front of the victim were much smaller – around a millimetre in diameter, giving them that mist-like appearance,' Martinelli went on. 'They were mostly tear-shaped, which helped us determine the point of origin and angle of impact.'

Once again Joe and Frank referred to their knowledge of blood spatter flight characteristics. Most people didn't realise that even in flight, blood maintains a spherical shape – a result of surface tension which binds the molecules together. And so, the tear shapes created on impact helped forensic experts to calculate exactly the angle at which the force was released – in this case, the position, height and angle of the gun as it released the bullet that entered Stephanie Tyler in the middle of her chest.

'Basically,' Martinelli went on, 'we measured the length and width of the ellipse-shaped stains using viewing loops and BPA software. The point of convergence was already known considering the scrape marks made by Ms Tyler's chair on the tiled kitchen floor, so that gave us a free ride on determining exactly where the weapon was placed and the angle at which it was directed.'

'Which was?' asked Joe, knowing Martinelli would confirm it came from the area just inside the kitchen door where J.T. Logan had allegedly entered the room to shoot his mother from point-blank range.

'A foot inside the kitchen door from a height of five feet three inches above floor level at a downward angle of thirty degrees.'

Joe nodded. 'And the singe marks on the kid's T-shirt?' he asked.

'Consistent with the marks that would be produced when firing a high-powered rifle loaded with .460 Weatherbies from the right shoulder.'

Joe stole a glance at Frank. There was no point in bringing up the lack of J.T.'s shoulder markings given

Martinelli's job was purely to report what he had found – not analyse what he hadn't.

'And the residue?' Joe continued.

'Trace elements on the T-shirt, but not on the boy's hands. The residue on the shirt suggests the sleeves were in immediate contact with the gun, which isn't such a stretch considering the sleeves were way too long for the kid in the first place.'

Joe looked at Frank once again – this was all going exactly to play. 'Anything else?' he asked.

'That's pretty much it – all the data is in here,' Martinelli said, throwing Joe the report. 'The house was full of prints but most of them belonged to the family. There was some blood spatter but no prints on the gun-bar the single pointer finger on the trigger – which means the kid probably wiped it after taking it from the cabinet and again after shooting his mom. The absence of excessive prints can be explained by the fact he was wearing that oversized T-shirt. He could have kept his hands inside the sleeves, which would also explain the residue findings on said shirt.

'Ballistics confirmed the bullet in a tree in the rear of the victim's backyard was the same one fired from the rifle – which means it travelled a good fifty feet through human flesh and a double brick wall before it came to rest in a particularly sturdy oak.'

There was silence, as this fact alone gave them cause to pause.

'Gus' report should take care of all the other stuff,' finished Martinelli, referring to Boston Medical Examiner Gus Svenson's impending autopsy report. 'He'll have results on the victim's toxicology, biopsies, blood tests and basically give confirmation of the cause of death.'

'One of Gus' easier conundrums,' commented Frank.

'If it walks like a duck, and talks like a duck . . .' said Martinelli as he stood to leave.

'Thanks, Dan,' said Joe.

'No need to thank me, Joe, it's you poor suckers I feel sorry for now. You get to distribute this info to the masses and watch them feed on it for the next three months.' And Martinelli shook his head as Joe walked him towards the door.

'FYI, ADA Carmichael called about an hour ago,' Martinelli added. 'Wants this info ASAP,' he said, pointing to the report in Joe's hand. 'Told me to keep my day free – expects to get a grand jury hearing some time this afternoon.'

Amanda Carmichael – Joe was still seriously pissed at the grandstanding ADA for her performance at Monday's arraignment. Even if she was right about J.T. Logan being the shooter, the fact that she used Joe – and Frank – to score herself some early points in front of the judge had not gone down well with either detective. While the cops were there to help the DA's Office build cases again offenders, the DA's Office usually reciprocated by discussing the appropriate course of action. It was a matter of respect. But Amanda Carmichael had jumped the gun and held her own personal advancement party without giving Joe or Frank as much as a heads up – and it was not something Joe would forget.

And so, given Carmichael's obvious desire for speedy justice, it was no surprise she had gone directly to Martinelli for his help in securing a grand jury indictment.

Truth be told, she probably would not need Joe's testimony in any case, considering the irrefutable evidence in the forensics analysis report. Today was a little earlier than Joe had expected, but once again, it did not surprise him. The woman was on the fast track to personal glory; she'd have her precious indictment before the day was out and with it the official go-ahead to take this case to trial – in an adult court, with a guaranteed audience of millions.

'One thing's for sure, I'm gonna think twice before I rag on my teenage kids again,' said Martinelli. Dan Martinelli, like Joe, was a father to four boys – three of whom were now in their teens.

'Nine times outta ten it's the lack of raggin' that gets you into trouble, Dan,' said Joe, slapping Martinelli on the shoulder as they reached the door.

'You're right,' said Martinelli. 'But there's always that exception to the rule, isn't there? God save us all.'

32

'What's wrong, mother?' asked the boy, his mouth slightly agape, his large brown eyes widening like two round orbs of innocence. 'Who was that on the phone? You seem . . . upset?'

'I . . .' his mother began. But the rage she had felt mere seconds before was already surrendering to the more powerful emotion of fear. Her thirteen-year-old son had her in the palm of his hand. He controlled her every emotion and response. And he knew it.

'It's your father. He's sick,' she said, unable to hold his gaze. And she knew he took this as a sign of her acquiescence, her inability to hold her ground.

'What's wrong with him?' the boy asked – his permanent accessory slung over his shoulder, the rifle sitting silent and ominous, immediately within his reach.

'He collapsed. They called an ambulance. He was rushed to the ER. They had to pump his stomach. They said it was something called "Warfarin". Said it is an anti-cogalient . . .'

'Anticoagulant,' corrected the boy, but the mother chose to ignore him.

'Said if they had not stopped him from ingesting it that his brain would have haemorrhaged and his blood wouldn't have been able to clot and . . .'

'Warfarin . . .?' said the boy, a look of pure curiosity on his face.

'Rat poison,' said the mother through gritted teeth.

The boy lifted a finger as if to say, 'Well now, that's where I've read that chemical name before!'

'He collapsed in the middle of that job interview,' she said, her breath catching as she felt the anger rise once again. 'The one he'd been counting on to help us pay the . . .'

'The one he got all dressed up for this morning?' asked the boy, a look of mock pity on his perfectly formed face. 'In that ugly old grey suit?'

'Yes,' she said, and she could feel the sweat sting at her underarms, as her heart raced and her stomach knotted and her eyes began to swim with tears. 'The man who was interviewing him called 911, told the paramedics he suspected he was on drugs.'

'Talk about blowing an interview,' smiled the boy. 'I mean, my number-crunching dweeb of a father a drug addict? How ridiculous is that?'

And in that moment she met his eyes again and for once – for ONCE *– managed to stare him down, her eyelashes not moving as her son was forced to blink.*

'Where are you going?' he said then, as she moved past him – in the widest arc she could manage given the narrowness of their house – towards the living room. He pulled the rifle from his shoulder and started turning it over in his hands.

'The hospital, of course,' she said, grabbing her handbag from the sofa, before running her chipped manicured fingers through her strawberry blonde hair. 'They refuse to release him until somebody signs him out.'

'So, I'll be making my own dinner then,' said the boy.

'I expect you'll be doing whatever you please.'

The boy laughed. 'Well, you're right again, Mother. I'd say I most certainly will.'

Deirdre McCall closed her eyes as her hands gripped the sides of the toilet seat beneath her, the memory finally fading from her brain. She was in the dance hall cubicles, ensconced in the far stall of the old but clean ladies' room that had a pair of scratched pink ballet shoes painted delicately on the outside of the door. She could hear the children at the basin outside, perhaps wondering who had been in the end lavatory for so long, and she had even resorted to lifting her feet and balancing them on the back of the old wooden door in front of her, in case anyone decided to bend over in curiosity and sneak a peak or two.

It was as she had feared. After the woman named Kelly had called, Deirdre had asked her 'understudy' to take her class while she ran to the local newspaper vendor for a copy of *USA Today*. She had read the story about the teenage son being arrested, noted the name of his attorney, gone to a payphone, called directories, and was connected to the Boston-based firm of Wright, Wallace and Gertz forthwith. She had answered – the Kelly woman, her accent unmistakable – and Deirdre remained silent, gripping the dirty silver receiver so tightly that her hand had begun to turn blue, only moving when an impatient old lady began banging on the booth's smudged plastic door, a look of pure intolerance on her sour, creviced face.

Of course she had no way of telling exactly how Mrs Kelly had got the information. The article she spoke of was organised by the dancing school headmistress without her permission – a sort of sixty-fifth birthday present which left Deirdre in the awkward (dangerous) position of not being able to say 'no'. But the story had run over a year ago and she honestly believed that *he* had not seen it, that *she* was safe – that her successful, TV star son still believed that his poor sap of a mother was dead, buried . . . gone. And so she had been forced to make a decision – a decision to which, despite what her current location and physical stature might suggest, she was determined to hold firm!

Sometime last night, when the moon was high and the temperature unbearable, she had realised that, as pathetic as it may seem, she was actually 'happy' being who she was, and doing what she did, and seeing the joy on the faces of those who conquered a step thanks to Miss McCall's caring and learned instructions. Somehow, she had managed to build a new life independently of the man she once loved and the boy she once bore – finding peace in the knowledge that the intensity of the devotion she received from the former, was (almost) enough to balance the wretchedness the latter had caused.

So she had promised herself that she would not, under *any* circumstances, allow her son to intimidate her again. Thirty years ago she had failed to stand up to him and her weakness had cost her dear husband his life. But that was before she understood that boys like her son would never be stopped unless someone had the guts to confront them. Which, if it came down to it, she was willing to do – when eventually the time came.

And so, as she finally released her toes from the back of the splintered cubicle door, and as she stood and flushed the lavatory just to allay any suspicion, and as she made her way outside to the basins to stare at herself in the scratched bevelled mirror that stretched the length of the far bathroom wall, she said a prayer for the only other two people in the world who understood exactly where Miss Deirdre McCall was coming from.

Maybe the day will come when I can actually help them, she thought, imagining her two young grandchildren folding into her arms. But then the image of her son's face overshadowed her and, hands still wet, she hurried from the bathroom to the comfort of the hall beyond, where the music seemed to soothe her – if only briefly – until the memories returned again.

33

'Hey, DC. Over here,' said Tony Bishop, signalling for David to join him at the far right-hand booth at the back of a crowded Myrtle McGee's. It was almost 9.30am and David only had a half-hour before Barbara Wong-McGregor was meeting them at their offices. He had a million things to do – including catching up with Joe and ME Gus Svenson, but Tony had been insistent that they meet up ASAP. And so here David was, one eye on his old college buddy, and the other set firmly on his watch.

'What's up?' said David as Tony rose to shake his hand.

'This and that,' said Tony, taking his seat again. 'I ordered you the eggs and some coffee.'

'Thanks,' said David. 'I couldn't sleep last night so I got up early to go for a run, which meant I didn't get time for breakfast and . . . in fact . . .' David signalled for Mick who was passing a nearby table.

'Hey, Mick, can you add a fresh OJ to my order?

And some water, one of the big bottles, ice cold if that's okay.'

'Well, as you can see I don't have any other customers to look after this morning so why don't I just hop to the orchard and pick those oranges you requested by hand,' said Mick, his words dripping in sarcasm but his grin betraying his jest.

'That would be great,' smiled David. 'Just make sure they're ripe – you know, and extra sweet with no pips.'

'Don't push your luck, Davey boy,' said Mick as he made his way back to the counter.

'You're busy,' said Tony, stating the obvious.

'I'm flat out,' replied David. 'But you said this was urgent and a man's gotta eat so . . .' And then David sensed, by the furrow in Tony's brow, that this conversation was not going to be easy – and for one horrible moment he suspected that his friend was going to ask him about Amanda Carmichael and what, if anything, she and David meant to each other.

'You're representing Stephanie's son,' said Tony.

Ah, thought David, *so that was what this was about*. 'I know what you're thinking, Tony – that Steph was our friend, that I am defending her killer. But . . . the thing is, there is more to this case than meets the eye. You know there is no way that I would ever do anything that went against what I believe Stephanie would have wanted. I would never spit on her memory, Tony. She meant too much to us – to *you*.'

'That's not it,' said Bishop, instinctively lowering his voice. 'Although, I have heard some rumours.'

'What rumours?' asked David, knowing that this was exactly where it would get sticky. David knew that

Tony's firm represented the Logan/Tyler family interests and, as such, would never divulge any information he had come across as part of his legal responsibilities to his client. But he also knew that Tony had no direct responsibility for either of their accounts, which made him curious as to why he would be . . .

'You know that we represent them,' said Tony, reading David's mind.

'Yeah,' said David. 'But I also know that you are in corporate and Logan and Stephanie's interests were more familial, or media related.'

'Did she do what the rumours are claiming, DC?' Tony asked then, unable to help himself. 'Did she change that much? Did she really abuse her kids to the point where one of them would turn a gun on her and blow her to smithereens?'

'*Jesus*,' said David, completely in shock. '*Where the hell did you hear that?*'

'Let's just say I have a source close to home.'

'Shit,' said David. 'We are trying to keep this quiet until we have a chance to . . .' But he stopped short, knowing exactly where Tony got his information.

'Stephanie was not an abuser, Tony,' he said. 'You knew her. You know she was incapable of such things.'

Tony nodded.

'So what the fuck else has Logan told you?' asked David.

'He's our client, David. And the only reason I told you what he told me about Stephanie was because it won't be privileged for long.'

'He's going to release it?' asked a furious David.

Tony gave the slightest of nods.

'*Shit*.'

'Look, David,' said Tony then, leaning into the table, his voice barely above a whisper. 'I am here because . . .' He took a breath. 'I am here because whatever happens I need you to know that there is more going on than you realise. There is some new information that I obtained via my firm and . . . Amanda is investigating it and . . . it might be a good thing – for your client, I mean, for the kid, Steph's son. It might see him . . .'

'Jesus, Tony, what the hell are you trying to say?'

But Tony was shaking his head, knowing he had probably already overstepped the mark. 'I guess I just needed to know that we were on the same page – about Stephanie, I mean.'

'She was a good person, Tony, which is more than I can say for her husband.'

'He's my client, David.'

'And you rag on me for representing criminals,' said David, rising quickly to his feet. 'It isn't always about you, Bishop. The world doesn't exist so that Tony Bishop can make his millions and ease his conscience all at the very same time.'

'I'm sorry,' was all Tony could think of to say.

'Yeah, well, so am I.'

34

'Well, first up,' said Barbara Wong-McGregor, falling into the seat across from David and Sara, Arthur having taken top spot at the head of their small conference room table, 'one thing is for sure, that when you finally decide on your defence strategy for this kid – and I am convinced, that despite what we all might be *speculating*, that is exactly what you are currently doing . . .' and then she paused, as David stole a glance at Sara, realising that Barbara, like Sara, felt the need to stress that the boy was their priority, and perhaps more to the point, that they had nothing concrete against Jeffrey Logan – at least, not yet, '. . . you will not make the mistake of going with "diminished responsibility".'

Barbara went on. 'I know it seems like the obvious answer, but the boy is very smart, articulate. There was not one suggestion of exaggeration or understatement on his part. He knows exactly what he is saying and does so with confidence and assuredness, and the ADA's experts will find exactly the same thing when they pick him to pieces – which they will, by the way.'

David nodded, not having expected anything less.

'You have to understand,' Barbara continued after both Sara and Arthur had also nodded, indicating for her to go on, 'that these observations are only preliminary, and I'll need more time to listen to the recording and pore over his unusual responses to the great majority of our questions. But, first and foremost, the boy shows classic signs of being the victim of emotional abuse – and if I am right, he has been subject to such abuse since the day he was born.'

'And you know this because . . .' prompted Arthur.

'Because his interview was littered with indicators that show us J.T. was under the abuser's continuous control.' Barbara removed her frameless glasses before moving on.

'First up, there was the thing with the homework times. Not hour blocks or half-hour blocks or even quarter-hour blocks – but shifting allotments scheduled down to the second. This is a classic example of a victim being subject to unusual demands by the abuser purely so that the oppressor might assert their control. The abuser may not gain anything materially from enforcing such demands, but he or she does consolidate their role as the dominant force in the household by dictating the victim's schedule, day in, day out.'

'So it's a power thing,' said Sara.

'Exactly. The specific dinner time was another example and the effectiveness of the controller's dominance is evident in J.T.'s complete disregard of the notion that he and his sister might not adhere to guidelines the abuser has no doubt set for them since birth.'

'They have no concept of rebellion,' suggested Arthur.

'That's right.' Barbara nodded. 'Which makes this whole murder thing kind of hokey, don't you think?'

It was an odd question but David could see where she was going. 'If Stephanie was the abuser as Logan claims, then why would J.T. retaliate now?' he asked. 'Logan claimed it was because he overheard his conversation with Stephanie requesting a divorce, but J.T. was clear that he was studying the mechanics of the rifle on Tuesday so . . .'

'Right again. So if we discount Logan's "divorce" theory, why exactly did J.T. choose last Friday night to rebel . . . or *did* he rebel at all?'

No one said anything. Barbara's question hung like an unattainable 'truth' hidden in a dark and heavy shadow above them, close enough to feel but not clear enough to see.

'Look,' she said then. 'First up, J.T.'s approach to the entire murder is very clinical, right down to the extensive knowledge of the specifics of the rifle and the magazine she was reading when she took a bullet to the chest. He spoke of "intent" rather than desire or need or anger or regret. It was almost like it was a job that needed to be done – another request at his abuser's bidding.'

And still they said nothing, willing the child psychologist to go on.

'Not once did J.T. name his abuser. He said he killed his mother because she was his parent – not because she was in charge of him, but because she *wasn't.* Now at first you good attorneys here might guess that this was the boy's way of expressing his anger at his mother for not intervening to put an end to his father's abuse, but I don't think that is the case. I think he was trying to tell us that he was doing what he had always been forced to do – follow the instructions of the parent who *was* in charge. And this instruction just happened to involve the destruction of the one that wasn't.'

'And now he is too terrified to talk because his sister is still in the care of their abuser,' said Sara.

'His affection and concern for his sister was obvious,' said Barbara. 'I would suggest, with their mother gone, that the two children are holding on to each other for grim death – which is extremely difficult, under the circumstances.'

They paused as Nora entered to pour them another coffee, and Barbara took a sip before going on. 'So, I know what you are all thinking: is this enough to nail Logan? And the answer is an irrefutable . . .'

'No,' said a frustrated David, knowing there was no way this sort of behavioural speculation would be enough to 'outrank' the physical evidence in court.

'That's right,' said Barbara. 'But it does give us something to work on. And there is something else – something a little more concrete that . . .' She hesitated, as if wondering whether she should even voice her next observation, perhaps for fear of giving the three people in front of her any semblance of false hope.

'What is it, Barbara?' asked David. 'Please, we need to know anything, everything that can help us help J.T.'

Barbara nodded. 'Well, I hesitate because in many ways what I am about to suggest screws your client as much as it exonerates him – especially given the nature of what you tell me is confirmed in this morning's forensics report.'

Joe had called early with the details of Martinelli's report – and the three of them had shared the information with Barbara.

'But, I found it extremely interesting,' Barbara went on, 'that he remembers shooting his mother, but has removed himself completely from the much less violent "preparation" stage.'

'You mean getting the key, the rifle, the bullets and so forth,' said Arthur.

'Yes,' she said, pushing her shoulder-length black hair behind her right ear. 'In most cases – in fact, in *every* case I have been involved with that involves memory losses – the child blocks out the most visually distressing element of the crime. In J.T.'s case, the explosion of the weapon and the resultant annihilation of his mother's form before him.

'But he described that stage clearly. His lapses fall before that, during a time where he was not exposed to any visual or auditory chaos.'

'But couldn't the ADA argue that such a lapse was just a case of J.T. feeling guilty for his role in putting it all together?' suggested David. 'Correct me if I am wrong, but couldn't Carmichael get another shrink to argue J.T. blocked out the "before" because in his mind it led him to the "during" and the "after".'

But Barbara was already shaking her head. 'No, it doesn't work that way,' she explained. 'And any psychologist worth his or her salt knows it. If a child wishes to block out an event, an event he or she is not yet ready to deal with, they will normally jump from a time when all was well, to a time when everything was over. But J.T. described the "during" and the "after" in great detail.

'You have to remember that this young boy has been brought up in a household where order, where chronology, where timing meant *everything*. So it is highly unusual that he did not relay the details of the preparation as part of the initial sequence of events.'

'Because if his consciousness allowed him to cope with the high degree of trauma that the murder invoked . . .' began Sara.

'. . . then talking about the preparation stage should have been a walk in the park,' finished Barbara.

'Then why the hell *didn't* he list those movements immediately prior to the shooting?' asked David. 'Or, more to the point, repeat what he had been *told* to say by the person who was ultimately responsible?'

'Because, in my opinion, J.T. never prepared for anything – and as for his failure to regurgitate what he had been coached, well . . .' Barbara took a breath. 'I can't be certain but I think our boy just made his first act of rebellion against his real abuser.'

'He refused to regurgitate his father's version of events,' said Sara.

'He's finally getting up the courage to stand up to him,' said David.

'I hope so, David,' said Barbara. 'More than anything, for J.T.'s sake, I really hope so.'

35

'Katherine, you need to listen to me,' said Logan. They were in her office – a tastefully decorated enclave mere metres from *The Doctor Jeff Show* set. The blinds were up, allowing the midday sun to streak into the room, and Jeffrey was pacing across the coffee-coloured carpet, his brown eyes squinting every time he turned towards the window.

'This is J.T.'s future we are talking about. The papers are already labelling him a psychopath, and unless we do something about it, well . . .'

'But you heard what Cavanaugh said,' replied an uneasy de Castro, her hands lifting to her crisp white shirt collar. She had not worn the necklace, unable to bring herself to actually put it on, and she was wondering if he had noticed that her neck was bare.

'He said we had to sit tight, that we had to plan our approach to the media carefully, thoroughly. There are legal implications here, Jeffrey. You just can't come out and . . .'

'And what?' said Logan then, his arms flying up in frustration. 'Tell the world the truth?'

He shook his head and started pacing again. 'Cavanaugh is a skilled attorney, Katherine, but you have to remember that we inherited him by default when he was called to my home by the *police* – who are set on sending my son to prison.

'Secondly, he was friends with my wife – good friends. And while I would like to think the best of him, you and I both know that he has doubts about Stephanie's true character – or lack thereof.'

'But he seems dedicated to J.T., Jeffrey, and he . . .'

'. . . may not have what it takes to see this through,' interrupted Logan. 'In fact, just last night I sought advice from another extremely qualified attorney who I am sure will be more than able to put his own personal opinions aside to . . .' And then Logan met her eye, and perhaps read the disapproval on her face.

'I'm sorry, Katherine,' he said as he stopped pacing, his shoulders now sagging in defeat. 'It is just that, if only I hadn't asked for the divorce, if only J.T. hadn't overheard me . . . this is all my fault!'

He collapsed in her calf-skinned visitor's chair, and de Castro, despite a nagging instinct to remain behind her desk, rose from her seat to approach him.

'Jeffrey, you have to stop blaming yourself,' she said, perching awkwardly on the edge of her desk so that she might place her hand on his shoulder. To her shock he grabbed it, he took it and squeezed it – *hard* – in an action which she was sure was meant to portray . . . gratitude?

'You did everything you could to protect your

children. But . . . my point is . . . despite your reservations, Cavanaugh has an extremely good reputation and we have to take his advice seriously. We may understand the worlds of psychology and television, Jeffrey, but we are not experienced attorneys skilled in the nuances of the law.'

'But don't you see, Katherine,' Logan said, looking up at her, finally releasing her hand so that she might take the second visitors' seat beside him. 'That is exactly why we *have* to act – and quickly. We know how the psyche of this country works, and we know TV – in fact we know talk TV better than ninety-nine per cent of the country.

'Over the years I have been so lucky, so *privileged* to reach so many people with my show. I have seen them, Katherine, I have seen my guests gaze into my eyes with such awe and adulation that I may just as well have told them how to split the atom, or cure cancer, or reverse the effects of the global warming as work out how to all get on together. I have this power, Katherine, and the ability to reach millions with it – and if I cannot use it to help my son then . . .'

Katherine sensed that despite her concerns, this was not something Jeffrey was going to give up on. 'You want to do a special version of *The Doctor Jeff Show*,' she said then.

'Yes,' he looked at her, his eyes as wide as a doe's.

'But we have been removed from air temporarily, Jeffrey. Allen thinks, and I agree, that until we work out where this thing is going . . .'

'You think Allen Greenburg will hesitate one second when he hears what we are proposing?'

Now it was '*we*'.

'I . . . no,' she said, knowing the network CEO would jump at such a proposal. 'But we have to be careful here, Jeffrey. This cannot look like a one-hour pity party. Your closeness to this issue leaves you open for criticism. Your views will automatically be judged as prejudiced and no matter how understandable that may be, in the end it could negate our cause.'

'So we bring in an independent party,' he said, and Katherine realised he had thought this through.

'We bring in an unbiased interviewer – someone with a solid reputation in news and current affairs. And this person, she acts as our conduit to tell J.T.'s story – she shows the world that video tape and exposes Stephanie for the tyrant that she really was.'

In that moment Katherine felt an uneasiness which came with her suspicion that Jeffrey had planned to involve her all along. 'You want to ask Croft to run the interview.'

'I want her to launch J.T.'s case in self-defence. I want her to present the facts plainly, clearly and without prejudice to an America – a *Massachusetts* – that houses our jury, the ones who will decide my son's fate.'

'And your role will be . . .?'

'To be me – a grieving, caring father placed in the most horrible of circumstances, a learned physician who, despite his best efforts, failed to protect his own. I have done my best, Katherine, but I am only human after all – and my audience will see this and understand, and their hearts will go out to me and my daughter and, most of all, to my son who finally had the courage to act.'

Katherine said nothing, simply lifted her smooth olive-skinned hand and rubbed her forehead before looking at her 'partner' once again. 'You want to try this case on TV before it gets a chance to reach the courtroom,' said Katherine.

'No. I want to *win* this case before it leaves our control.'

'And Cavanaugh?' she asked.

'Don't worry about Cavanaugh, Katherine,' he replied, that famous smile now spreading across his equally as famous face. 'Just leave Cavanaugh to me.'

In 1974, an American psychology student by the name of Scott Fraser undertook an experiment in basic human behaviour to discover if anonymity encouraged aggression. Fraser, who studied under Philip G. Zimbardo from Stanford University's respected Psychology Department, wanted to see if human beings in their purest form would feel more comfortable with behaving aggressively if their identity was concealed – thus giving them the 'freedom' to act without social repercussions.

And so he chose children as his subjects, and Halloween costumes as his props, organising an experimental 'party' where a teacher gave the children a series of games to play – half were non-aggressive and half were confrontational in nature. Initially, while the games were played, the teacher said the costumes were on the way so they would start the fun while waiting. Then the costumes arrived and were worn as the games continued. Finally, the costumes were removed to go to other children in other parties, and the games went on for the third phase, each phase lasting for about an hour.

The data collected was a striking testimony to the power of anonymity. Aggression increased significantly as soon as the costumes were worn, more than doubling from the initial base level average. But when the costumes were removed, aggression dropped back well below the initial level base rate.

Logan knew this was only *one* study on the influence of anonymity on aggression. Other research on the history of war showed that soldiers or 'warriors' who altered their appearance prior to battle – with war paint or masks or the like – were much more likely to torture or mutilate or slay their victims. Psychologists note that it becomes much easier for a human being to injure, to harm, to kill, if they first change their appearance, for anonymity has the ability to alter the usual internal focus of compassion and concern – so that they can act without repercussion, and often without regret.

Now, Logan realised, as he sat at the crowded outdoor café in Boston's famous Quincy Marketplace, that some experts might argue that his 'mask' had been worn for so long that it had relinquished its ability to provide anonymity. That indeed, his façade was so famous, so recognisable, that it had taken on a life of its own – reversing the effect of the previous studies on 'anonymity' and its ability to 'cloister the beast'. But they would be irrefutably wrong. For Logan's cleverly constructed veneer not only provided him with the perfect 'cover' to exercise his insatiable desire to 'control', it also gave him an identity that quite literally deflected any possibility of impropriety. In other words, the public loved him – and any suggestion Jeffrey Logan could be capable of the things that he was, was well . . . beyond ridiculous and outright insulting.

Which is why, after leaving Katherine de Castro's office (his business partner had been quickly and easily cajoled, just as he knew she would be), he had called his son's attorneys and asked for one of them to meet him here, in this frenetic tourist-riddled 'circus'. And he had chosen said attorney so that he might do what he did best: play his learned little game of psychological chess using one seemingly weaker piece to force the demise of its superior.

For despite Cavanaugh's naive assumption that Logan had no idea what he was up to, the good doctor was not only aware of the moralistic attorney's covert attempts to use his children to build a case against him (his efforts to keep him away from his son, his co-counsel's visit to his daughter, had been nothing short of pathetic), but also of his recent efforts to dig for 'evidence' he had no business unearthing. Carleton Blackmore's messages had told him as much and, in all honesty, despite Logan's justifiable level of confidence, the attorney was really starting to piss him off.

But no matter, he comforted himself as he saw the pregnant and somewhat apprehensive-looking Sara Davis weaving her way in and out of the crowd towards his umbrella-shaded table, for this little fishing expedition should prove fruitful on more levels than one. And even if he did not achieve what he expected to today, there were already many other support strategies in place, the first of which would be a national TV extravaganza set to go to air in (he checked his Rolex), fifty-six hours, thirty-two minutes and forty-five . . . no, make that forty-*four* seconds from now.

'Miss Davis,' said Logan, rising from his chair. 'Thanks so much for meeting me here. I know it is short notice, and I certainly didn't want to cause any problems by asking for you personally but I . . . well . . .'

Sara was immediately taken aback. Truth be told she had expected Logan to chastise her from the get-go for visiting Chelsea unannounced. David had urged her not to go solo, but she told him that Logan, who had called her direct line just as Barbara Wong-McGregor was packing up to leave, had requested a private conversation with her and her alone.

'Not that it is any of my business, but I think she should go,' Barbara had said after several minutes of heated discussion between David and Sara.

'*What?*' David had replied.

'Logan sees Sara, a pregnant woman with two male bosses, as an inferior. He wants – he *needs* – to feel in control and if I were you, I would take advantage of his warped sense of ascendancy and send in Sara to see what she can find out.'

'You want me to send my pregnant partner to meet a man who orchestrated the murder of his wife?'

'No,' said Barbara, who had rolled her eyes at the suggestion. 'I want you to allow your fellow, experienced attorney to do her job – to help save your client by finding out as much as she can about his abuser.'

'I didn't mean that . . .' David had begun.

'Yes you did, and I understand why, so that's okay,'

Barbara had said. 'But the meeting is in a public place and there is no way the famous Doctor Logan is going to try anything untoward in such a busy, fan-filled location. Let me put it this way,' she had continued, perhaps reading David's expression and seeing he was still not convinced, 'if he asked to see you or Arthur, would you hesitate?'

'Well . . .'

'Exactly,' she had replied before she had grabbed her briefcase and headed towards the door. 'So I suggest that you shove your chivalry where it belongs, David, and allow your co-counsel to do her job.'

Sara could not help but smile. 'I'll be fine,' she'd said.

'She'll be fine,' Nora had agreed with a nod.

And so, short on time, they had discussed briefly what they hoped Sara might achieve, before she turned to leave.

'Please don't apologise,' said a smiling Sara now, taking out her sunglasses to shade her pale blue eyes from the strong early afternoon sun.

'It's just that,' Logan went on, '. . . Chelsea told me how you came to see her yesterday – and with her mother gone and me so busy, I, well . . . I wanted to say thank you, thank you so much for offering her a shoulder to cry on.'

And Sara was gobsmacked – as Doctor Jeffrey Logan took her first false 'assumption' and batted it way out of the window.

'I fear I have been somewhat short – with both you and David. I was frustrated you see, at not being able to see my son. I am going to see him this afternoon at last, so that has eased my concerns. But I know I have to come to terms with the reality that we are now at the mercy of the system and the delays are not your fault.'

Sara paused, not sure where to begin. 'Honestly, Doctor Logan, talking to Chelsea was my pleasure,' she replied, composing herself. 'Both David and I know how difficult this must be for you. And as for your omitting him from the lunch invitation, I can promise you he won't be offended. He is currently tied up in a meeting with Barbara Wong-McGregor – discussing the validity of our plan to go with self-defence, so I decided not to interrupt him and come meet you here instead.'

A tick in Logan's eye suggested that her comment had surprised him. 'You have decided to go with self-defence?'

'Oh, yes.' She nodded.

'It's just that I thought the more obvious option was . . .'

'Diminished responsibility?' interrupted Sara. 'No, Doctor, you have reared a very bright young man and if we even attempt to claim he has lost control of his faculties, the Commonwealth will shoot us down in flames.

'The law very rarely operates in absolutes, Doctor. True, your son killed his mother, but our strategy is to encourage a jury to look beyond the obvious and remember that there are degrees of innocence and guilt. In J.T.'s case we must convince the twelve that your son was the lesser of two evils. We must make them see that when he killed his mother, he did so to save himself.'

For once the 'King of Talk' was speechless.

'Did I ever tell you why he was born in New Zealand?' he asked after some time, after the waiter had taken their order for salads and coffees and brought long, cold glasses of iced water that came with an array of colourful straws.

'No,' said Sara, feeling a little more confident now that she sensed she was holding her own with the clever psychologist. 'No, I don't think you did.'

'Stephanie was at a corporate development conference. She refused to come home for the birth. She even had him induced a day early – on the Tuesday, so she could give a major talk on corporate finance at the end of the week.'

'I thought she stopped working for Cunningham, Eather and Groves after Chelsea was born.'

'She did, but her old bosses asked her to be a guest speaker at this conference and of course – Stephanie being Stephanie – she could not resist.

'So you see, Sara,' he said, his hand reaching across the table but stopping mere fractions of an inch from her own. 'She was the one responsible for ensuring J.T. was born a full twenty-four hours before he was meant to come into this world – the same twenty-four hours that allowed the ADA to charge him as an adult. So in actual fact, Stephanie started screwing J.T. from the womb – and continued to do so until . . .'

Logan stopped, before tapping his hand briefly on top of Sara's, and retrieving it again to pull his sunglasses from his crisp blue shirt pocket. 'I'm sorry,' he said. 'I seem to be doing a whole lot of crying of late.'

Sara had to stop herself from retching.

Moments later, after their lunch arrived, Sara

decided to approach some of the issues she had really come here to discuss. She was hoping that she might be able to draw Logan into acknowledging his call to Tony Bishop, and ideally get a sense of what they might have discussed. She wanted to feel him out regarding Tony's suggestion that the doctor was about to release information on his wife's abusive nature to the press, and approach the issue of Tony's confusing 'tip-off' to David – his allusion to the fact that Amanda Carmichael was working on something else, something important that might affect the outcome of the case.

'Our next priority, Doctor,' she began.

'Please, Sara,' said Logan. 'You know you can call me Jeffrey.'

'Jeffrey,' Sarah said and smiled. 'Our next priority is sitting down to devise a strategy on how we are going to work with the media.'

'Of course,' said Logan. 'And, forgive me for sounding a little pompous here, Sara, but working as I have in the industry for so long, I would hope you and David would take my counsel on how we might proceed.'

'Do you have any specific ideas?'

'Not really. With everything else going on I haven't had a chance to think on it. But I will.' He smiled. 'If you like.'

And Sara, who was ready for an out-and-out argument about releasing the controversial tape, found herself caught short and thus, stuck for words herself.

'Of course I can understand David's hesitations,' said Logan. 'About releasing the tape, I mean.'

Sara knew he could read the surprise on her face.

'But I can assure you, that despite David's past

friendship with my wife, I know that he is on board one hundred and ten per cent.'

'That's right,' said Sara, now seeing an opportunity to gain back some control. 'It is true Stephanie was part of his social group in college – in fact, I believe your wife once dated his good friend Tony Bishop.'

Logan stopped short, his fork mere inches from his mouth. 'Yes, I knew that,' he said.

'Of course you did,' she said. 'In fact Tony works for Williams, Coolidge and Harrison – the same firm that represents yours and your wife's legal and financial interests.'

'That's right,' Logan replied, putting down his knife and fork as if finally realising her intent. 'You want to know why I called Bishop.'

But Sara was too surprised by his frankness to reply.

'His firm is sorting out the issues surrounding Stephanie's will. I just wanted to see where my children stood – or more to the point where my son stood, given the recent turn of events.'

If he was a liar, he was very good at it, thought Sara, his eyes hidden safely behind his dark Armani glasses.

'I understand,' she said, before taking another risk and adding, 'Did you know that Tony was currently dating the ADA?'

'*What?* Amanda Carmichael?' responded Logan, and Sara sensed she might have finally told Logan something he did not know.

'That's right,' said Sara.

'Wow,' said Logan, his frown now melting into a rather supercilious grin. 'Do you lawyers always date in-house?' he asked, now shoving a large piece of tomato into his mouth. 'I mean Stephanie, Tony, Carmichael – you and David? What's that old adage about not shitting where you sleep? Rather junior high of you all, isn't it? And it most certainly limits the intellectual gene pool from which you draw . . . Oh, I am so sorry,' he said then, as if realising what he had just said. 'I didn't mean . . .' He gestured at Sara's middle.

But Sara knew exactly what Logan had meant, and also guessed he was well aware of the 'seriousness' of Tony and Amanda Carmichael's relationship – maybe even counted on it.

'You know, I must tell you something funny,' he said, his knife now making little circles in the air as if in introduction to the titbit he was about to share. 'When I first set eyes on Amanda Carmichael, I thought she was you.'

'Ah . . . excuse me?' said Sara. 'I mean, the ADA and I, we are . . . well, let's say we look nothing alike.'

'Not true, my dear, for you are both incredibly beautiful women, but that is not where this little story is going. You see, Stephanie and I attended the St Valentine's Day Law Society ball last winter, the same dinner where David caught up with my wife.

'Anyway, I found myself at this table of legal heavies and the discussion got around to David and his growing reputation as one of the best litigators in the city – and to you as his professional and personal partner. So I said something like, "Oh yes, they did a tremendous job at the Matheson trial last year", and asked Gareth Coolidge to point David out. Which he did, of course – at a moment when David and Amanda Carmichael were in the middle of what appeared to be a very private conversation.'

He dug into his salad again.

'They were standing very close, you see,' he resumed in between swallows. 'Close enough for me to assume that this was the Sara Davis that everyone was raving about – the tall, willowy blonde, in the form-fitting sheath now stretching up to whisper something into your fine-looking lover's ear.

'But then, if I recall, they were joined by another attorney. And perhaps, doing what I do, I read too much into David's reaction to the disruption. I felt he was a little annoyed by the interruption, you see, that he was already leaning in to her to respond.

'Of course, in hindsight, they were probably just discussing some extremely delicate legal matter,' he suggested. 'In fact, that is most definitely what it must have been, given the colour in your loyal partner's cheeks.'

Sara sat frozen in her seat, her entire body numb with shock.

'Anyway,' Logan went on, finally taking off his glasses. 'It's funny how these things happen isn't it – the reckless assumptions that we make? Because then I met you and understood of course that David was lucky enough to share his life with this glowing, full-bodied woman beside him. And the fact that you had planned this child together, well, there is a sign of commitment if ever there was one.'

But this baby had not been planned, and Sara guessed that Logan knew it.

'Did I tell you that I met Stephanie at a hotel bar following a work conference? She was so smart and sexy and strong. It's true what they say about those professional dos, Sara – they are the backdrop for many a dangerous dalliance; they throw sexually charged, like-minded people together under the guise of professionalism and the cocktail can be impossible to resist.'

But then Logan was interrupted by a tour group of middle-aged women from Kansas City who approached him, and fawned over him, and sympathised with him, and said they were behind him '*one thousand per cent*'. He smiled and posed for photos, before long triggering a similar reaction from scores of other fans who seemed to flock towards him like moths drawn to the brightness of his now irresistible flame.

And in that moment Sara knew exactly what Logan had been trying to tell her. And his eyes . . . his deep brown eyes, flicked towards her with such penetration, such *power*, that she could swear he was reading her mind. He smiled, and despite herself, Sara felt the contents of her stomach rise swiftly in her throat. She grabbed her bag and ran from the table, determined to find the closest restroom before she vomited in full view of Doctor Jeff and his ever-multiplying following of starry-eyed, faithful devotees.

36

Tony Bishop was sitting two feet away from Amanda Carmichael in the meeting area of his expansive harbour-view office. She was reading, her white-blonde hair tied back in a low bun, her glasses on the end of her long narrow nose, her concentration intense. Tony, Amanda and Harry Harrison had spent the better part of the past hour listening to Stephanie Tyler's controversial phone message – the voice mail being short but to the point. Stephanie had directed Harrison to remove her husband from her will completely, leaving her two children as the sole beneficiaries. She requested that in the event of her death all of her assets and monies, including her stake in the family's Rockwell Wineries fortune which had an estimated worth of $200 million, be held in a trust and managed by her attorneys until the children reached the age of twenty-one. After which they could invest it as they pleased.

Then they had been joined by another visitor, a

man named Shane O'Rourke from a company known as APS Insurance. Tony disliked the man from the get-go, his entire demeanour screaming smarmy insurance salesman – striped suit, garish tie and slick brown hair framing a too-tanned face.

The room was unsettlingly quiet as Amanda sat on one of two burgundy silk upholstered chairs, reading a print-out of an email sent almost two weeks ago. It was accompanied by a copy of another email of confirmation from the receiver of original said email – two pieces of correspondence that would set the whole Logan situation on fire and, as Tony knew, cause a national media frenzy in the process.

From: Stephanie Tyler Logan (Loganhome@webmail.com)
To: Shane O'Rourke (orourkes@APSinsurance.com)
Sent: Fri, 4 May 9.56am
CC:
Subject: Life insurance adjustments

Dear Mr O'Rourke,
Thank you for sending me the recent brochure on your various levels of life insurance cover. The information was incredibly helpful and has assisted me in deciding how best to adjust my current cover to meet my family's on-going needs.

I have read the information in detail and have thus decided to make the following changes to my existing policy effective immediately. From what your documentation advises, there is no waiting period for any increases nor any of the 'riders' I have chosen below and as such would appreciate it if these changes could be made as per the date at the top of this email. The changes are as follows:

1. I would like to increase my existing policy from a basic (lump sum) benefit of $5 million to $20 million.
2. I would like to add the life income option whereby my beneficiary(s) received monthly payments equivalent to my salary (including that pertaining to both my work as an attorney and as a member of the Rockwell Wineries Board of Directors) for a period of my calculated working life (up until I reach 65 years of age).
3. I would like to add the 'supplementary rider' noted as ADB or 'Accidental Death Benefits' to the value of an additional $2 million.
4. I would like to reaffirm my beneficiary as being my husband, Doctor Jeffrey Logan and the contingent beneficiaries (in the event of my husband's death) being my two children, Chelsea Marie Logan and Jeffrey Tyler Logan.

I have, as of this morning, electronically transferred a sum of $10,799.50 to my policy account as a first payment to what will be the adjusted policy effective today. This sum should cover me for the next six months after which additional premiums can be direct debited from my account as was done previously.

Thank you so much for your assistance in this matter. I would appreciate it if a return email to the above email address could confirm your receipt of this request and activation of its recommendations.

Yours sincerely,

Stephanie Tyler

The return email read:

From: Shane O'Rourke (orourkes@APSinsurance.com)
To: Stephanie Tyler Logan (Loganhome@webmail.com)
Sent: Mon, 7 May 10.47am
CC:
Subject: Re: Life insurance adjustments

Dear Ms Tyler,

Thank you for your recent email regarding the requested adjustments to your APS Life Insurance Policy.

We are happy to advise you that your existing policy shall be amended and entered into our system by early next week. The new policy, titled Premium Life Plus (PLP), shall be backdated to be effective as per the date of your original email being Friday 4 May.

As soon as the paperwork is completed our accounts department, which received your initial transfer relating to the increased premium, will send you a follow-up letter to confirm the new premium (direct debit) amount with an accompanying booklet on all policy details.

I would like to thank you for continuing to choose APS as your preferred life insurance provider. Please feel free to contact me if there is anything else you need.

Kindest regards,
Shane O'Rourke
Client Services Manager
APS Security

Amanda's head was down, those petite designer glasses now concealing her expression. She had finished reading, Tony was sure of it, but he sensed she was allowing herself a few seconds of adulation, perhaps even swallowing a smile before she looked up at the other two men sitting on the couch on the other side of the antique walnut coffee table – a still nervous-looking Harry Harrison and a smug-faced Shane O'Rourke who, Tony noticed, had not taken his eyes off Amanda's sheer-stockinged legs since she had entered the room.

'Mr O'Rourke,' said Amanda, breaking the silence. 'Did you have any verbal correspondence with Ms Tyler before or following the sending of these emails?'

'No,' said O'Rourke, now uncrossing his own legs and resetting his expression to read: *'I am a man of great intelligence who will patiently explain to you how I go about my daily business as insurance expert extraordinaire.'*

'Eighty per cent of our correspondence is now done by email – largely at our policyholder's request. The email came from Ms Tyler's home address, the money came from her account. We had done an extensive search on her assets and so forth when Ms Tyler set up her policy a number of years ago and so did not feel it necessary to do so again.'

Amanda nodded. 'And this original brochure she mentioned receiving in her email, how did she request it and how was it sent to her?'

'Both via email. Ms Tyler wrote requesting the information from the same home email address on Monday, the thirtieth of April and I emailed her the brochure forthwith. I have a copy of her original request here also – a simple two-sentence request for the information.'

O'Rourke leaned across the coffee table to hand Amanda the email and Tony noticed his fingers extending slightly so that they might brush against hers. 'The brochure was sent by attachment, which she would have downloaded and read.'

'So no paper trail,' said Amanda.

'None,' said O'Rourke. 'Which, I might add, goes hand in hand with our company's Reduce Waste with Haste program. We are extremely sensitive to the current environmental issues facing our planet, Ms Carmichael. We want our trees – and our policy-holders – to live as long and as healthily as possible.'

Of course you do, you pompous twit, thought Tony. *The longer they live, the more premiums you pocket and the less you have to pay out. Smart-ass son-of-a-bitch.*

'Did you get any further emails from Ms Tyler following the correspondence you have provided here?' Amanda asked, interrupting Tony's thoughts.

'No, that was it,' said O'Rourke. 'But as you can see, we dealt with her request swiftly and efficiently so no further correspondence was necessary.'

'And so tell me, Mr O'Rourke,' said Amanda, her face all stony seriousness, 'why don't the police have this new information? I am sure the homicide detectives on the case would have requested information on Ms Tyler's life insurance status. It is part of procedure in any homicide investigation.'

'Yes,' said O'Rourke, obviously worried he was going to have his knuckles rapped. 'The problem lay in the timing. As I mentioned in my email to Ms Tyler, while the new policy became effective immediately, the paperwork took some time.'

'Paperwork?' interrupted Tony, unable to stop himself. 'I thought you guys didn't use any . . .'

'No . . . I mean, that's right,' said a now flustered O'Rourke. 'No paper, that is just a general term referring to the computer input. That will be completed today.'

'So the police got the original policy details, the ones in place prior to Ms Tyler's recent request for adjustments.'

'Yes.' O'Rourke was shaking his head. 'The policy control officer the detectives spoke to was not yet aware of the changes as they had not been put onto the system. He would have printed out the original information and given it to the police.'

'And you didn't think to holler when you heard of Ms Tyler's death?' asked Amanda, tilting her head to the left in a gesture that said '*please explain*'.

'I . . . ah . . .' And that was when Tony realised exactly what had gone down after Stephanie had died, and he could see the look on Amanda's face, that she had got it too.

'I was not across that transferral of information,' said O'Rourke.

'And there would be no way that you would have deliberately failed to make information of this new policy available, Mr O'Rourke?' asked Amanda, removing her glasses to stare the reclining O'Rourke squarely in the eye. 'I mean, in your email you said the paperwork would be completed in a week, not . . .' Amanda looked at her watch, '. . . twelve days after Ms Tyler's request, which is exactly what today is.

'You seem like a man dedicated to helping your policyholders, Mr O'Rourke, so I am sure you would not bury a new policy so that the company might not have to pay out what would now be an extremely substantial benefit. A benefit worth . . . what?' Amanda lifted her eyes upwards as if calculating the amount. 'Well over fifty million dollars?'

'Of course not,' said O'Rourke, now squirming in his seat and looking suitably offended by the suggestion. 'As soon as Mr Harrison here called and requested the policy information I forwarded it immediately.'

'And the fact that Mr Harrison was an attorney who asked specifically if there had been any recent changes to the policy didn't sway your decision at all?' asked Tony.

'Certainly not,' said O'Rourke. 'I'm here, aren't I?'

'Yes, you are.' Amanda smiled at last, before turning to Harrison. 'It was very astute of you to call Mr O'Rourke and investigate the matter, Mr Harrison,' she said, and Tony could have sworn Harrison blushed.

'My experience tells me that people often change their wills and life insurance policies at the same time,' piped up Harrison. 'It's a matter of "cleaning out the cupboards". Nine times out of ten, people make these decisions and take action across the board – wills, life insurance, health checks and so forth.'

For some reason Tony found himself making a mental note on the health check thing.

'Well, thank you, Mr Harrison,' said Amanda, rising to her feet. 'I will get back to you if there is anything else we need.'

Mr O'Rourke rose to shake her hand.

'Mr O'Rourke,' she said, extending her hand but then withdrawing it as if needing to stifle a cough, leaving an open-palmed O'Rourke with nowhere left to go. 'Thank you for your time,' she said, walking the two men towards the door. 'We'll be in touch.'

And then, she and Tony were alone.

She turned to look at him, and he looked back, neither of them moving as if there was so much to talk about and nothing left to say.

'So what are you going to do?' he said at last.

'What do you think I am going to do?' she said, as if ready for his disapproval. 'I am going to do my job.'

'Your job involves an obligation to provide the defence with all information relevant to the outcome of the impending trial – and includes voice recordings, relevant documentation. You have a responsibility to disclose.'

'Tony, you're jumping the gun. The case against your friend's client may not even go to trial. I have only just received the forensics reports. I am not before the grand jury until later today and . . .'

'Then you have to provide this new information to the grand jury.'

'I have to do no such thing,' she argued. 'This

information remains in this room until I confirm the voice on that message belonged to Stephanie Tyler – until I confirm who sent those insurance emails from the Logans' home email address.'

'Oh, come on,' said Tony. 'The increased insurance request originating from the Logan home computer, the request to have the husband cut from the will? You're taking another shot at the father and you know it.'

'He didn't shoot her.'

'Maybe not physically but . . .' And then he saw it, that familiar look in her eye, that glint that told him she was already focusing on the bigger picture – a rare opportunity she intended to milk for all it was worth.

'You want them both,' he said at last. 'You lost the father and so you went after the son, and now you want them both.' He shook his head. 'Amanda, if what we learned this morning pans out the way I think it will, you can nail the doctor to the wall. The kid could well be another innocent victim in all of this.'

'He shot her.'

'He's thirteen.'

'Fourteen.'

'Jesus, Amanda. You need to talk to David.'

'I need to leave. I have a date with the grand jury at four,' Amanda said, moving swiftly past him towards his desk so that she might retrieve her handbag. But as she turned again to head towards the door, Tony grabbed her by her upper arm, hard, forcing her to turn and meet his eye.

'You cannot hold onto this information,' he said, his voice close and low. 'You cannot fail to report what you know so that you can star in your own media circus extraordinaire.'

'You're not my boss, Tony. I can do whatever I damn well please.'

'But it's unethical.' Tony took a breath. The truth was he liked this woman, hell, he believed he was even falling in love with her. But he couldn't sit back and let her bulldoze his best friend – he couldn't turn a blind eye to her manipulating the system of justice they had all sworn an oath to uphold, just because her ego was greater than her sense of professional responsibility, just because he had feelings for her and did not want whatever they had to end.

'I swear, Amanda,' he went on. 'You do this. You fail to share the information I helped you discover, and you and I are . . .'

'What? *Over?*' she said, shaking her head. 'For God's sake Tony, you were never that Goddamned special to begin with. There is a difference, you know,' she added, moving even closer to him so that they were now standing eye to eye, '. . . between fucking me and fucking me over. You breathe a word of this to your moralistic friend and I'll have you arrested for interfering with an ongoing criminal investigation. I will end your career in a heartbeat, Bishop, and take great pleasure in doing it.'

She shrugged free of his grip, turning her back on him sharply so that she might stride towards the door.

'You're going to regret this, Amanda,' said Tony at last, not knowing if the pain in his chest was a result of the anger or the disappointment. 'You don't know David like I do. He won't stop until he . . .'

'Until he what, Tony?' she interrupted him, turning

one last time as she reached the corner office door. 'Brings me down?'

'No, I was going to say until he sees that justice is done. But if he brings you down in the process, then you have only yourself to blame.'

'Oh *please*,' she said as she reached for the handle and opened the door to leave. 'Cavanaugh doesn't scare me. I eat men like him for breakfast – or in your case, lunch and dinner and dessert.

'So thanks for the tip, Mr Bishop.' She smiled as she moved out of his office and into the reception area, nodding at Tony's assistant as she strode confidently past her desk. 'Your boss is a credit to his profession,' she smiled. 'And the District Attorney's Office shall be forever in his debt.'

37

The Chief Medical Examiner's Office was located in Albany Street, south of Copley, west of Roxbury and across the road from the Boston Medical Center's Harrison Campus. It was a short, squat building with a somewhat sad-looking exterior which, David had always felt, had a fitting relationship with the equally as depressing goings-on inside – matters of grief and loss and tragedy, of injury and illness and death. And today, despite his friendship with Chief ME Gus Svenson, and the fact that he knew he could count on Svenson's unfailing professionalism, he felt an uneasy edge to the air of melancholy that seemed to be flowing through the corridors of the examiner's rooms – perhaps because he had rushed down to meet with Svenson in what the ME had described as his 'only window of opportunity', while he was worried about Sara and her lunch with Jeffrey Logan.

'You look like shit,' said David, as he collapsed into the red-covered visitor's chair across from Svenson's desk. The tall, Swedish-born physician looked even paler than usual, his face dissected by the two dark circles that hung like shadows under his pale blue eyes.

'Should I take your honesty to be a sign of your concern, or a general observation as to my . . .' Gus was obviously looking for the word, '. . . shittiness?'

'Both,' said David, managing a smile.

Svenson shrugged. 'I am tired,' he said. 'Two of my ten medical staff are at home sick, my chief administrative officer has just resigned, my technicians are overworked and underpaid and the governor is calling for my head following our inability to get on top of our backlog.'

David nodded in sympathy. It was no secret that the dedicated bunch who worked at the Boston ME's headquarters were seriously outnumbered by the turnover of cases that came their way – now somewhere north of 30 000 a year.

'That sucks,' said David.

'It is what it is,' returned Svenson.

David nodded again. 'So what can you tell me?' he asked at last.

'Nothing you would not expect,' said Svenson, reaching across his busy desk to find a clear plastic file labelled with the name of Stephanie Tyler. In that moment David felt a deep and hollow sadness at the sight of his old friend's name on the cover of a freshly typed autopsy report.

'Cause of death was a single, high-velocity gunshot wound to the chest. The bullet entered at the sternum and fractured the third, fourth and fifth ribs before tracking through the heart.

'Damage to the heart was extensive and thus difficult to define. But the vascular injuries most likely include damage to structures including right atrium and aorta, main pulmonary artery, aortic arch and right pulmonary vein.

'The bullet also tracked through the right lung, with a linear path of gas containing small metallic and bone fragments from the ribs. The exit wound was large with the directionality and bevelling of bone, along with the gunshot residue on the subject's skin and clothes, telling us she was shot at roughly a thirty-degree downward angle, at point-blank range.'

Gus sat back in his seat and threw up his hands as if to say, '*that's the basis of it – with further detail enclosed to give further macabre descriptions of the harsh finality of death*'.

'What about the rest of your findings, the bloods, toxicology . . .?'

'The basic tests show results all within normal range for a woman her age, but given a number of her organs had been removed I . . .'

'*What?*' said David, unsure he had heard the ME correctly.

'Her organs. Ms Tyler's driver's licence showed she had volunteered herself as an organ donor. And you know the good people from the New England Organ Bank are notoriously quick off the mark.'

'But Stephanie had been dead too long for the NEOB to recover any living organs. Her blood supply was drained, her body deprived of oxygen.' David well knew that in order for an organ to be viable for transplant, either the body must be kept on a ventilator to keep the organs of a brain-dead patient 'alive', or the organs removed and transplanted (often 'on ice') to reduce what doctors referred to the organ's 'anoxic' time – the lapse between the death of the donor and the transplant to the recipient.

'This is true,' said Gus. 'But Ms Tyler was very specific in her request. Tissue – like bone, skin, corneas and so forth – can be used in transplants up to twenty-four hours after death. And in regard to her other major undamaged organs – her liver, kidneys, pancreas, brain . . . they were removed for the purpose of research.

'David,' said Gus, perhaps reading the look of disappointment on his attorney friend's face. 'You know how these things work. The NEOB are zealous in their recovery of usable organs and tissue. If time had been shorter and less damage procured, I am sure they would have taken every viable organ in her body.'

Gus stopped there. Everyone knew the donation recovery people had an important job to do, but David knew that Gus and his fellow workers at the ME's Office were sometimes irked by the bank's workers' efforts to cajole the relatives of recently deceased loved ones into signing away their beloved's body parts mere hours after their death.

'I didn't know,' said David.

'I am sorry,' said Gus. 'But in the end it mattered not.' And David knew that Gus was trying to tell him that despite the organ donations, there was no argument as to what had caused Stephanie Tyler's death.

'Mannix tells me she was your friend, yes?' offered Gus.

'We went to college together,' David replied.

Gus nodded.

'Have you given the report to Carmichael?' asked David after a pause.

'Of course,' replied the ME. 'She called me early this morning, asked me to dispatch a messenger as soon as the report was ready. I believe she . . .' Svenson hesitated.

'It's okay, Gus, we checked with the courthouse. We know that she has an appointment with the grand jury at four.'

Gus lifted up his hands as if to again say: '*It is what it is*'. 'I am sorry you did not know,' he said. 'About the organs I mean.'

'It was the bullet that killed her, Gus,' said David, not wanting to place any heavier burden on the exhausted ME before him. 'You should go home, take a load off,' he added, standing from his lumpy fabric chair.

'Yes, but I have a morgue full of patients to examine. I do believe that I need some rest, however,' he said, standing to see David to the door, '. . . as lately I find myself talking to my horizontal subjects.'

'They ever talk back, Gus?'

'Unfortunately no. For if they did they would tell the world what happened to them,' said a sad-eyed Svenson. 'And we could all go home and get some much needed sleep.'

Five hundred and seventy-five thousand – that's how many people live in Boston, MA. And if you double it, to nearly 1.2 million, that's how many people are estimated to travel to Boston from neighbouring areas to work, shop, eat and play on any given day.

Now work out the odds, David thought to himself as he hit the ground with a thud, *of my running into – literally – the man I currently despise most in the world, a good two blocks from where I was headed.*

'Jesus,' said Logan, steadying himself on a street sign. He had obviously been distracted, walking while reading a sheet of white paper, which he now stowed quickly in his inside jacket pocket.

'David, of all people I . . . I'm sorry. Gosh, are you okay? You *are* in a hurry! Is everything all right?' He offered his hand to help David get to his feet. 'I've just dropped Sara back at your offices and my car is parked in a garage on Tremont so . . . Here,' he took a breath, 'let me help you up.'

'I'm fine,' said David, using the pole to pull himself to standing. 'I'm running late for a meeting. My cab got a flat and . . .' This was half true. There was no meeting but David's taxi had got a flat tyre. He had hailed a checker cab outside the ME's Office and asked the driver to get him back to the city pronto. The cab hit a pothole and blew a tyre on Tremont, forcing David to help the cabbie push the vehicle to the side of the road before running north towards School Street where he had cut east on his way back to his offices on Congress. His cell was out of batteries and for some reason he felt an all-encompassing need to get back to Sara – the anxiety of it all resulting in him failing to look where he was going.

'You look pale,' said Logan.

'I've just come from the ME's Office,' David offered as some form of explanation.

'Ah – the autopsy report,' said Logan, his eyes

now narrowing just a fraction. 'Nothing untoward, I hope . . . I mean, of course what happened to Stephanie was untoward, but nothing *unexpected* . . .?'

'No, Jeffrey,' said David. 'Nothing unexpected – if you are referring to our expectation that the shot from the big game rifle that blew your wife's internal organs to smithereens would be listed as the official cause of death.'

He met Logan's eye, a flicker of understanding between them.

'Well,' said Logan, breaking eye contact, 'I suppose in the very least we know what we are up against.'

'Sure,' said David, unable to stop himself. 'Another kick-ass rifle, but this time in the guise of a system we like to refer to as "justice".'

Logan shook his head. 'If my son had taken a gun to his suppressors some two hundred and thirty years ago, not far from the *very spot* we are standing,' he said, gesturing at his feet for effect, 'during the war that gave us independence – the same war that enabled us to build the very system of justice of which you speak, well . . . he would have been championed as a *hero*. But since his abuser was his mother, his freedom has been snatched by the very . . .'

'How was lunch?' asked David, unable to listen to another word of Logan's bullshit.

'Ah,' said Logan – and David sensed the man was not used to being cut short mid-soliloquy. 'It was fine, lovely. You have quite a lady there, David. A real catch. And now I understand why you hold on to her so desperately.'

'Excuse me?' said David, his blood starting to boil.

'Oh, please. I am sorry. There was no offence intended. It is just that . . . as an expert in relationships, I could not help but notice that . . .' He shook his head. 'Really, it is nothing.'

David did not respond, Logan taking his silence as an indication to continue.

'Well, forgive me for being frank but . . .' Logan took David's elbow, pulling him away from the sidewalk and towards the quieter alcove of an office building entryway. 'Obviously recent events have led to my doing a lot of thinking – about me and my children, about my wife, and where it all went wrong. And I cannot help but think that it is partly my fault.'

'Oh, really?' said David. And if he was making any effort to conceal his distaste, he certainly could not hear it in the tone of sarcasm that accompanied his enquiry.

'Yes,' said Logan, continuing unperturbed. 'You see, I think Stephanie was too young for a relationship as serious as ours became. And in hindsight, I think her decision to give up her career – a decision she made of her own free will, I might add – was the wrong one, at least for a bright young woman like her who thrived on the excitement that a career in the high-powered legal fraternity allowed.

'She was beautiful, David – beautiful, smart, energetic and with enough bright ideas and determination to light up a city. And I think in some way I put an end to all those opportunities by falling in love with her, marrying her and impregnating her before she had a chance to . . .'

'You think Sara regrets having this baby?' said David,

now barely able to control the burning inside. 'Did she say that?'

'Not in so many words, as I believe her devotion to you knows no bounds. But Sara, not unlike Stephanie, is a gorgeous woman, with a brilliant mind and a hell of a lot more to contribute. So I don't think she has had her fill – no,' said Logan, shaking his head as if commiserating over the tragedy placed before them. 'But, as a wise man once said, we all make the most of the situation given us – which, I have no doubt, the pair of you will do with courage.'

David stared at him, the audacity of what he was saying, the daring, the impudence, the pure fucking *cheek* of it sending a new sensation of anger soaring determinably up his spine. And then a memory came rushing back of the last time he had spoken to Stephanie – at the ball, at their table, after he had asked her about her work: '*Oh it was terrific, David, interesting, demanding – a real challenge. But I was only there a year when I met Jeffrey and got married and had kids and . . .*' David remembered the look of regret in her eyes, the look of self-disappointment and remorse and . . .

'Goodness me, look at the time,' said Logan, deflecting his eyes to his Rolex, his slight smile telling David that he had achieved exactly what he wanted and was ready to move on. 'I am finally allowed an audience with my own son this afternoon. Can you believe it? Ridiculous, of course. But David,' he said, taking David's elbow once again, 'if ever you need someone to talk to, if you ever need some professional advice . . .'

'You are offering to counsel me on matters of relationship and family?'

'Why yes – and free of charge.' He smiled before slapping David on the shoulder and pushing past him to head quickly down the road.

David stood there shocked, speechless, literally unable to move, until he finally felt the fire explode inside of him, releasing itself in an almost primitive outburst that drew attention from all within earshot.

'*Fuck you*,' he shouted, realising that if Logan had heard him, he had decided a failure to respond would be more frustrating than any acknowledgement of David's rebuke. '*You're a Goddamned son-of-bitch, Logan, and I will not rest until I bring you down.*'

But Logan had already turned the corner, wearing – David was sure of it – the slightest trace of a smile.

38

Later that night

They were going head to head. The two of them. And Caroline Croft was barely maintaining her cool. Katherine de Castro was trying desperately to flex her 'executive producer' muscles, and Croft was slowly tiring of her tantrum.

'I am sorry, Caroline,' said the olive-skinned de Castro. 'But this is a deal breaker.'

It was 9pm on Wednesday night and the air in de Castro's office was warm despite the cool breeze now forcing its way through the wide eastern windows. Logan was sitting quietly, comfortably, on Katherine's sofa, a vodka tonic in his right hand, Katherine's five-sheet program run-down proposal in his left.

'This is not your standard *Newsline* broadcast,' Katherine went on. 'It must be a variation of the usual *Doctor Jeff Show* format. Where Jeffrey is the key speaker, or at least on par with yourself who is introduced as a respected news journalist "guest".'

'Not going to happen,' said Croft, who was now pacing the office like a caged tiger.

'Then maybe we are wasting our time,' said Katherine. 'Maybe we should just . . .'

'Now, now, ladies,' said Logan, and Caroline could have sworn that his 'partner' stifled a cringe. 'There has to be some way we can reach an agreement. Caroline,' he said, turning to Croft, 'I know we have spent our lives chasing, "owning", that precious currency known as ratings, and that you, like Katherine, have built a career on being forthright, uncompromising and direct. But Katherine is right, people are going to tune in to hear what *I* have to say, and our priorities should be focused on what is best for J.T.'

'But when you called, Jeffrey,' said Caroline, having already formulated her argument, 'you told me in no uncertain terms that this special would be under my control – a *Newsline* presentation on the *Doctor Jeff* set.'

'Except this "*special*",' countered Katherine, her tone suggesting she found the commercialisation of the event distasteful, '. . . would not even *exist* if it weren't for Jeffrey's high profile and regard in the industry, and among the American public. You are being handed the exclusive of the year on a silver platter, Caroline, and therefore I suggest that you . . .'

'I will not be given a list of questions to rattle off like some puppet,' interrupted Croft. 'I am a respected journalist, Katherine, not some two-bit dramatic actress who regurgitates her lines as frequently as she does her breakfast. Further, as I stressed to Jeffrey earlier, the matter we are discussing is sub judice, meaning any preparation of material or pre-setting of questions leaves us open to the charge of contempt.'

Croft was referring to the universal law that forbade counsel or media to speak of information regarding a matter under legal consideration, for fear it might unfairly influence the outcome of the case.

'I mean, what does Cavanaugh have to say about all this?'

'This has nothing to do with Cavanaugh,' snapped Logan, and Caroline could not help but raise her eyebrows in surprise. 'I have consulted with my family attorneys about the matter and proceed with their knowledge.'

This was interesting, thought the savvy Croft, *Cavanaugh was obviously on the outer.* There was a story there somewhere, she knew – but one she would have to put on the backburner, until she nailed down this exclusive on her terms.

'Look,' she said, now turning to de Castro. 'I understand it is difficult for you to let go, Katherine. If I were you, I would be arguing to produce this as a variation of *The Doctor Jeff Show* as well. But don't you see? If Jeffrey is the key speaker, or even on par with myself as the neutral conductor of the interview, the entire program will come off as contrived.

'You're right when you say your guy is famous . . . but he got a whole lot more so when his kid went and blew a . . .' Croft hesitated, '. . . when his son shot his wife less than a week ago. If he does not play humble here, if he appears to be milking his own family's misfortune for a shot at some super huge figures in prime-time sweeps, if he turns this into a "Logan Family Pity

Party" he will not only risk Amanda Carmichael charging the lot of us with sub judice contempt but also risk the public deciding that maybe, *maybe*, this whole thing was not carried out with sincerity after all. And we do not want the American people thinking J.T. Logan was not sincere in his efforts to free himself and his family from the tyranny of his mother. Cute fucking kid or not.'

There was silence.

'She's right,' said Logan at last, turning his attention to de Castro. 'We're looking at this the wrong way, Katherine, this cannot be about me. This special has to be about J.T. and Chelsea and the millions upon millions of other Americans out there – mothers, wives, husbands, kids – who are terrified of defying their emotional abuser and breaking the status quo for fear of the inevitable reprisals. We have to show ourselves as victims here, not leaders. We have to hand Caroline the reins and let her run with it.'

They waited for Katherine to respond.

'All right,' she said at last. 'We go with the interview, but I would also suggest we have a second guest – an emotional abuse expert who will sit next to Jeffrey and speak freely of the true horrors that this domestic maltreatment ensues.'

And Croft, who was quietly revelling in her 'victory', decided that a consolatory 'gesture' was in order. 'That's a good idea,' she said.

Katherine nodded, a 'neutral' Logan now smiling at them both.

'So Friday night it is,' said Caroline after a time, her stilettos making tiny divots in the plush mocha carpet.

'If we find our expert quickly we can tape tomorrow, promote for a full twenty-four hours and run the program as a special two-hour presentation in our regular Friday night slot.'

'No,' said Logan, finally throwing his own 'deal breaker' into the ring.

'*Excuse me?*' said Caroline, all of a sudden feeling like a little girl who had just been given a pony that refused to let her jump on.

'No pre-tape. No promotion. We go on Friday night – but we do it live.'

'You cannot be *serious*,' Caroline said. 'That is unheard of. The network will never go for it.'

'We pre-tape and pre-promote and the ADA will slap us with an injunction which at best delays our telecast or at worst bogs it in legal argument for weeks.'

'*Jesus*,' said Croft. But as she absorbed Logan's words, she could see that what the doctor was suggesting was true. *In fact*, she thought, her knotted brow now relaxing as she considered it, saw it, appreciated it even, *pulling off such an almighty live broadcast could be nothing short of . . .*

'All right,' she said at last. 'Live it is.' She walked across the room to shake Katherine's hand. 'You have a deal, Ms de Castro. I'll talk to Allen Greenburg and make this happen.'

And then she moved beyond Katherine and towards the couch where she extended her hand once again, this time to the man that would be her subject in what no doubt would be the most talked about news event of the year.

'Doctor, you know I was an acquaintance of your

wife's,' she said, as he rose from his chair to take her hand. 'Indeed, I even interviewed her once, years ago, fresh out of college with a hotshot career and a Fortune 500 company in her hands. But I need you to know – that while I knew her, I did not *know* her. I had no idea whatsoever, and I am extremely sorry for what has come to pass.'

'Thank you, Caroline,' said Jeffrey Logan at last. 'And believe me when I tell you that you were not alone. For nobody knew what was going on in our family. And perhaps now, after all these years, it is finally time that they did.'

39

The following morning several phone calls were made simultaneously.

The first was a return call from a Calvin Garretson of Garretson Specialty Rifles in Bangor, Maine, to Joe Mannix at Boston PD Homicide. Calvin, a young man with a very loud voice, reintroduced himself as the company's acting general manager (his father, Gareth Garretson, owned the company but was away at a gun traders' conference in Iowa), before confirming that he had triple-checked the details on the purchase of the 'Tyler' Mark V Deluxe and could assure the lieutenant that the paperwork was 'as straight as a Texas stallion'.

Garretson Jnr also confirmed that 'the tall skinny red head' in the pictures shown to him by local police earlier this week was most definitely the same woman who had contacted him on the internet, paid with her personalised Amex and picked up the rifle in person, before driving it back down to Massachusetts.

Having thanked Mr Garretson for his time and

effort, Joe hung up the call and scratched his head before looking up at his fellow detective Frank McKay to say, 'Shit.'

To which Frank replied, 'Don't worry, Chief. As Thomas Fuller once said: "All things are difficult before they are easy." '

'Yeah, well,' Mannix responded, 'whoever the hell Fuller is, you can tell him to shove his easy up his ass.'

The next call was highly anticipated and came in the form of an apology from a man who had been impossible to find.

'Mr Rigotti?' said the caller when Rigotti picked up his direct line with his usual impatient manner. 'I am so sorry it has taken me so long to return your call. You see, I have been in Africa, and I only just got your message from Carleton Blackmore and . . . my apologies again, Mr Rigotti, I am getting ahead of myself. My name is Jason . . .'

'. . . Nagle,' interrupted Rigotti as he felt his insides give an involuntary leap for joy.

And then, after Rigotti dismissed Nagle's apologies and Nagle explained he had been on a hunting Safari in Kenya and they both spoke of Mr Blackmore's diligence and Nagle expressed his sorrow at the Logan family's loss, the Nevada rifleman finally stuck a sturdy thumbtack into Rigotti's balloon of possibilities and deflated his potential headline within seconds.

'It wasn't my gun, Mr Rigotti, and I know this because *Ben Hur* has been in Kenya with me for the past fortnight. Took out an elephant with one fell swoop, he did, nailed the bastard right between the eyes.

'Anyway,' Nagle went on when Rigotti failed to find

the words to respond, 'Mr Blackmore made a very rare mistake, Mr Rigotti, and I am sorry if his information has caused you any inconvenience.'

'Not at all,' Rigotti replied.

'It was nice talking to you,' Nagle said then.

And Rigotti hung up the phone.

'Shit,' he said to himself, at almost the exact same second Joe Mannix was uttering the identical expletive barely two miles across town. 'Time to ruin Cavanaugh and Mannix's week,' he added as he picked up the receiver, not realising that the week for both of them had sucked big time – and things would only get worse.

'Mannix?' asked the voice, an old familiar grunt.

'Hey, Starkey,' said Joe, recognising the retired cop's mumble. 'How goes it? They still got you guarding the masses at Boston Municipal?'

George Starkey was Joe's captain when he first started on the force, one of the toughest but fairest cops Joe had ever had the pleasure to work with. He was now a part-time security guard at Boston Municipal Court, his retirement fund eaten up by his kids' college fees, his dependency on cigarettes and alcohol, and his weekly sojourn to the track at Suffolk Downs.

'Just like they still got you chasing dead bodies,' replied Starkey with a cough.

The widowed Starkey was lonely, Joe knew as much, which is why, no matter how busy he was, Joe always took the time to shoot the breeze when Starkey called to share or collect a bit of 'gossip from the beat'.

'Nothing much to report today, George, except for the fact that Frank McKay seems to have taken up origami. He's sitting in front of me right now, folding up the paper in my outbox into the shape of a God-damned crane.'

'Frank's a faggot,' said Starkey.

'I'll make sure I pass that piece of information on to his wife.'

And then, after a pause . . .

'You working the Logan thing?' asked Starkey.

Joe's eyes flashed at McKay's. 'Yeah, I always pull the short straws, you know that, George.'

'Then maybe you'd like to know the TV show pony just got spirited in through a side entrance for a private hearing before a judge.'

'What court?' asked Joe.

'Civil,' replied Starkey.

'At whose request?'

'The show pony's.'

'You sure it's him?' Starkey had a tendency to 'speculate' and 'embellish' when it came to 'seeing' or 'hearing' about the goings on of some of the court's more famous visitors, and Joe was concerned this might be one of Starkey's well-meaning exaggerations.

'I'd know that smarmy mug anywhere.'

Joe paused. 'What's he up to, Starkey?'

'Don't know as yet.'

'He got a lawyer with him?'

'One of them fancy rich ones with the perfect faces and the shiny shoes.'

'But not Cavanaugh,' said Joe.

'Since when did Cavanaugh qualify for any of the above?'

Starkey had a point.

'Keep your ear to the ground, Starkey.'

'As far as my fucked up lumbar will allow. Tell Frank to go fuck himself.' It was a term of endearment.

'I am sure he sends the same greeting back.'

And Starkey laughed – a low, gritty grumble, before hanging up the phone.

40

'Did you tell him?' asked Nora, after knocking quietly on Sara's office door. It was Thursday afternoon and David was down at Plymouth with Arthur, the pair of them determined to keep as much contact with J.T. Logan as possible now that his father was making use of his daily visitor's access and maintaining his control.

'No,' said Sara, signalling for Nora to come in.

Yesterday afternoon, after a persistent Logan had pulled himself away from his adoring fans to find Sara just outside a Quincy Marketplace ladies' room, he had insisted on walking the ashen-faced Sara back to her office. And Nora had met them at the door, taking Sara's cold and clammy hand, Sara insisting she was fine, a melodramatic Logan arguing she was anything but . . .

'The girl should not be working so hard,' he had said to Nora as she led Sara to the reception area sofa. 'As much as I admire Cavanaugh's dedication to my son, I do hope he is also finding the time to look after his pregnant partner!'

Nora had pursed her lips in annoyance, assuring Logan that Sara was in good hands and apologising for not showing him out. And then Sara had told her all that Logan had shared – about David and Amanda Carmichael and what he saw at the St Valentine's Day Law Society ball. Nora had listened quietly, caringly, her heart going out to the puffy-faced young woman before her, the 'child' she thought of as her own.

'I couldn't do it, Nora,' said Sara, easing closer to Nora on the small fabric-covered office sofa. 'I went to tell him last night but he was so distracted. I guess he'd had a bad afternoon – the visit to the ME's Office, my pathetic attempt to milk information from Logan setting us ten paces back.

'I trust him, Nora – I do. And I know that Jeffrey Logan was just trying to bait me. But somehow, the way that he said it, the way that he described David and that woman, I . . .' Nora saw the tear start to trail down Sara's smooth left cheek. 'I let him get to me.'

'Oh my dear, that's only natural. You've had so much on your plate of late.'

'No,' interrupted Sara. 'I know what you are going to say, Nora – that I am pregnant and pregnant women have a tendency to be overly emotional.' She took a breath. 'But my pregnancy shouldn't have any bearing on the way that I do my job. I am worried that I've been letting David down. I've been tired and my back has been driving me crazy and . . . maybe I am not at the top of my game right now, just when David needs me to be.'

'Absolute rubbish, lass,' said Nora, taking Sara's hand and cupping it in her own. 'You *are* pregnant, Sara, so the tiredness is to be expected, but your mind is as sharp as ever. You should not be so hard on yourself. David thinks the world of you – personally and professionally.'

'Then why has he been so . . . withdrawn?'

Nora shook her head. She had noticed it too. 'You should have told him what Doctor Logan said, dear – and that you were not feeling well.'

'Nora, I screwed up big time. David already has me wrapped in cotton wool. I need him to know I can pull my weight on this one.'

But Nora was not convinced. This case was having an adverse effect on both Sara and David – and she could not help but think it was only going to get worse. David's behaviour yesterday afternoon was nothing short of extraordinary – storming in, listening to Sara, explaining he had some work to do before rushing to his office and *shutting the door*. David never shut his door, and Nora suspected Doctor Jeffrey Logan was at the source of both her young attorneys' distress that afternoon, neither of them wishing to discuss the matter with the other.

'Listen, lass,' said Nora, turning to face Sara. 'I am the first one to chastise young David when he steps out of line – and his behaviour yesterday afternoon was certainly a little . . . intense.' It was the only word she could think of. 'And as much as we all want to win this for the young boy, in the end, we also have to understand that we have our own lives to lead – and in a manner we see fit, not in the way some two-bit excuse for a psychologist suggests one way or the other.

'The man is a liar, Sara. A criminal. But he is also very cunning, shrewd – a fox. He was playing with you yesterday, Sara, and as much as his words cut to the quick, you have to realise that they are grounded in malice and coated in deceit.'

Sara looked at her, her pale blue eyes glistening as she swallowed back the tears.

'David loves you, dear. That much I know – and while you have made him the happiest man alive, your child is going to bring untold joys to you both.'

Sara nodded. 'I know,' she said, pulling Nora into an embrace. 'I love you, Nora.'

'And I love you too, dear,' said Nora after a pause. 'Everything is going to be fine. Just you wait and see.'

41

Caroline Croft was in her office when the call came – drinking a double shot, half decaf, skinny latte.

It was early, her shoes were off, her stockinged feet stretched out in front of her as she read over her questions – and tweaked them, just a little. Despite Katherine de Castro's concessions, the woman had still managed to voice her concern that the wording of each query had to be just so. She claimed she was worried that any mispronouncement might come back to bite J.T. in court, but Caroline knew it was more a case of de Castro being unable to 'let the fuck go'. Legal schmeagle! There was no way that Caroline Croft, news magazine front woman extraordinaire, was going to forego drama for legalese, sub fucking judice or not.

'Yes,' she said, reaching across her glass-topped desk to punch the speaker button on her private line. Not many people had her direct extension and the few who did knew her well enough to accept that when she was working, she did not appreciate being interrupted.

'Ms Croft,' said the smooth female voice on the other end of the line. 'This is Amanda Carmichael.'

Caroline immediately sat up in her high-back, distressed leather, ergonomic chair.

'Ms Carmichael,' she returned, the honey now dripping from every syllable. 'Thank you for returning my calls.'

Caroline wasn't stupid – while she had spent the past week trying to get the defence on the line, she had also been calling the stunning ADA several times a day. She had a talent for playing one off against the other, and knew that ingratiating yourself with both teams was key to getting at least one, perhaps even both, to agree to using *Newsline* as their preferred conduit to the masses.

'Are you still interested in an exclusive on the J.T. Logan case?' asked Carmichael, getting straight to the point.

'Of course,' said Croft, her heart now leaping in anticipation of the possibility of a double coup.

'You said in your messages that you and Stephanie Tyler were friends,' said Carmichael.

'Why yes, we were very close,' lied Caroline. 'Her death is a tragedy for many. To those in the legal profession, to the family members not involved in her death – and, dare I be selfish enough to say it, to myself personally, for I lost a beloved confidante on the night that she died, Ms Carmichael, and I miss her dearly.' *God, I am good,* she thought.

'Then you will appreciate my determination to get to the bottom of her murder.'

'Certainly,' responded Caroline.

'I must warn you from the outset that the information I have will not be popular,' continued Carmichael. 'And before we speak I need your assurance that you will not be influenced by the concerns of the network which airs your program – the same network that broadcasts *The Doctor Jeff Show*.'

Jesus, thought Croft, *this woman has balls.* She was liking Carmichael more by the minute.

'Ms Carmichael,' she began, '*Newsline* may be broadcast on CBC but I can assure you we are a totally independent news magazine program dedicated to exposing the truth.'

'And benefiting from the ratings that accompany it,' said Carmichael.

'Just as your reputation benefits from the pursuit of justice on behalf of the Commonwealth,' countered Croft, and she could have sworn she heard Carmichael release the slightest of laughs in agreement.

'Tonight then,' said Carmichael. 'My office at seven.'

'I am afraid that is impossible,' said Croft.

'I do not understand,' said Carmichael.

'Tonight will be too late.'

'I am sorry, Ms Croft. But if you are seriously interested in . . .'

'It is almost 8.30am,' said Croft. 'I will be at your office in one hour.'

'I am afraid I have a very busy morning, Ms Croft,' countered Carmichael, perhaps a little miffed at Caroline's desire to assert her authority over the conversation and the instructions Carmichael had delivered.

'I apologise for the rush, Ms Carmichael, but believe

me, if you allow me the opportunity to explain, I think you will understand that speed is of the essence. For calling me this morning was an incredible stroke of luck on your part.'

But Carmichael was not convinced. 'I am not one for playing games, Ms Croft. So unless you are willing to elaborate on any information you possess that would be of use to the District Attorney's Office, I would suggest this can wait until this evening when . . .'

'I have spent much of the past two days with Jeffrey Logan,' said Croft – and there it was, that wonderful pause that signified a shift in control.

'I see,' said Carmichael after a time. 'Then perhaps I can see my way to clearing my schedule – as long as you believe that what you have to share is worth my rearranging my day.'

'Oh, you have no idea, Ms Carmichael,' said Croft. 'You have absolutely no idea.'

When Stephanie Logan was a young mother – running a small private practice from home, catering to the needs of her two children, and playing the discreet, supportive wife to a famous husband who had mastered the art of wearing two faces many years ago, she used to like to play 'what if'.

'*What if*,' she would begin – and her children would follow with a scenario.

'*I was a trapeze artist at the circus*.' Chelsea would giggle.

'*Or an astronaut on the moon*,' a five-year-old J.T. would scream with delight.

'*Or a bird who could fly*,' Stephanie would add until

all three were transported to another world where the days were bright and the nights were peaceful and the burden of time ceased to exist.

And so, as strange as it may have seemed, it felt natural for Chelsea to look up at her little brother – who sat across from her in his too-big maroon jumpsuit – and ask the same question once again.

'What if?' she asked with a smile, the only genuine smile she had offered in almost a week.

'What if,' he said back, meeting her eyes now, the two of them connected by an unbreakable bond that came from years of experiencing the same secret torment.

'I was a bird who could fly,' she said, recalling her mother's favourite response.

'Or a wizard with magical powers,' he added.

'Or smart enough to know what to do,' Chelsea said then, her eyes now pooling with tears.

This was not fair, she told herself. *I am meant to be the strong one. I have learnt enough over the past sixteen years to realise that hiding my true emotions is the only defence I have.*

But this was her little brother she was speaking to – the only one she could have this conversation with without fear of the inevitable reprisals. And so she straightened her back and swallowed her sobs and looked him squarely in the eye.

'I made a mistake,' she said.

'How?'

'I talked to the woman – Sara Davis.'

J.T.'s eyes met hers as his smooth brow knotted. 'I thought we said we wouldn't . . .'

'I know. But I saw the opportunity and took it.'

Then she explained to her pale-faced little brother what had happened three days ago.

'I had to do something,' she said. 'Father is watching my every move. He had a meeting with Katherine this morning so I put a piece of cardboard in the door jamb so that it wouldn't slam shut – I put the timer on pause and I'll punch in the code and reset the clock when I get home so it appears like I only went out to collect the morning paper . . . but still,' she added, glancing at her watch, 'it would be dangerous for me to stay too long.'

J.T. nodded. 'So you told her the *truth*?' Her brother was obviously distressed. She knew he was not angry at her for trying to 'break through', more worried for her welfare given their father was cleverly manipulating their current 'separation' by playing one sibling's safety off against the other.

'I tried to.'

'And do you think she . . .?'

'I think she thought I was on drugs. Seriously, I sounded like I was tripping. But I do think she understood that we were being recorded – so that in itself is something.'

But the flush-faced J.T. was too distressed to see any positive in their predicament.

'I'm sorry, J.T.,' said Chelsea, wishing beyond anything that she could ease his fears. 'I know we were supposed to stick to the strategy, and I know you are worried that he will follow through on his threats.' J.T.'s eye darted upwards to meet hers. 'It's okay, I know he has told you that if you didn't do as he says, that he would take it out on me.'

'He told you?'

'He didn't have to.'

J.T. nodded.

'The thing is,' Chelsea went on, now reaching across the table to take his hand, 'I can't help but think that if Mom were here, maybe she would *want* us to tell them. She trusted them, J.T., and maybe we should too.'

'No, Chels. Even if we did decide to tell, we'd have to tell it the way we all agreed upon. Mom told us never to tell anyone.'

'Mom didn't count on things going the way they have.'

J.T.'s breath was quickening. 'I'm sorry, Chels,' he said, his wide eyes meeting hers. 'It's just that, being in here – so far away – I can't stop thinking about what he might do if you try to help me.'

Chelsea loved her brother more than ever at that moment – her little hero, her valiant little bro.

'I know,' she said, as she squeezed his hand – realising that for J.T.'s sake, she could not take this any further, at least, not now, not yet. 'Maybe you are right. Don't worry, J.T., from here on in I will stick to the story.'

J.T. nodded, relieved that she would not try to save him.

Chelsea looked at her watch once again. 'Something else is going on,' she said after a pause, not wanting to upset him further but desperately needing to get his take on the latest events at the Beacon Hill home.

'What is it?' asked J.T.

'The police were at the house again yesterday – they took all of our home computers.'

'Why?'

'I don't know.'

'Was Father there?'

'Yes.'

'And was he . . .?'

'Cooperative? He practically carried them out to their cars for them.'

J.T.'s forehead furrowed in confusion, that familiar crease now dissecting his brow in two.

'And that's not all. I heard Father on the phone, talking to another lawyer by the name of Bishop. They had an appointment in court yesterday – but I don't think it had anything to do with you.'

'I don't understand,' said J.T.

'Neither do I. But then they started discussing something about sub judice, about what they could and couldn't say on TV.'

'Father is going on TV?'

'I don't know.'

J.T. said nothing.

'I am so sorry, J.T.,' Chelsea said, swallowing back the lump in her throat. 'None of this is working out like we thought it would. And I just feel so . . .'

'You wish it had been you,' he said, reading her mind.

'Yes.'

'Don't. I was where I was and it is what it is, and if anything I am safer in here than you are out there.'

She nodded. 'Is it all right?' she asked – the first time she had asked it. 'In here, I mean.'

He looked at her then and she could see that her brave little brother felt an all-encompassing need to comfort her. Everyone thought he was the mirror image of their father, but in truth, he was just like their mom.

'I've stayed in worse.' He smiled.

And she understood.

'What if?' she asked, as if trying to raise a smile.

'What if?' said J.T., the slightest crack in his otherwise steady voice.

'We were playing "what if?"' she said, placing her other hand on top of his.

'Just you, and me, and Mom.'

42

The *Doctor Jeff* studio set was a mammoth circular construction which sat low and round opposite a wall of plush, violet-coloured audience chairs that hugged the main stage in a semicircle of anticipation. The floor was carpeted in a complementary mauve, with various wooden platforms (used for guests' entrances and exits) leading like the spokes of a wheel from the circle's nucleus where Jeff would sit in his modern but comfortable cream-coloured armchair.

His higher-than-usual perch was angled so that he could be easily seen by the spectators before him and be equally as accessible to his guests *de jour*, who hunkered down on the slightly less comfortable wood-framed chairs beside him. The basic lighting was all subtle pinks and blues – but, as Katherine de Castro had explained, could be altered depending on the subject matter, wavering from the deep purple illumination used for more serious topics, a more upbeat lilac for the lighter episodes which, she went on to elaborate, '*balanced with the heavier topics and gave Jeff a chance to show the down-to-earth cheerfulness that audiences loved*'.

Caroline almost puked. *These talk show divas thought they ruled the airwaves*, she thought. *But throw them into the battlefield that was news and current affairs and they would not last a Goddamned week.*

It was after eight and Caroline Croft was in her element. She had compromised by allowing Doctor Jeff to stay in his usual leading man's chair but asked that another seat – identical to that of her 'subject's' – be provided so that in the very least she and the clinical psychologist star would appear on equal footing.

She was buzzing, her hair and make-up already in place. She was re-checking her questions, talking to the camera operators about angles and demanding that the lighting on her own right profile remain particularly soft. She could not believe she had talked Logan into it – adding the third guest, that is, and was even more surprised when he agreed it was best not to tell de Castro. As tough as Katherine de Castro was purported to be, there was no doubt that Logan wore the pants in that business relationship. Which, if she were honest, surprised Croft somewhat – as she sensed the 'power' had only shifted of late.

Maybe he was fucking her, she thought. *No, de Castro was not his type*. Caroline got the feeling Jeffrey Logan liked his women minus a pair of balls – which was why, after tonight, she suspected she would probably have made herself an enemy for life, given de Castro was not the only one who was in for a surprise this evening.

*

'It's Frank,' said Marie Mannix as she handed Joe their red telephone handset – the one in the kitchen, with the extra long cord.

They had just finished dinner, the four Mannix boys, aged from seven to thirteen, now raiding the freezer of the oversized refrigerator for chocolate-chip ice cream.

'*Boys!*' whispered Marie. 'Keep it down. Your father is on the phone.' But Joe had already pulled the lead around the corner into the living room annexe so that he could hear his partner properly on the other end of the line.

'What's up, McKay?'

'No idea, Chief – but nothing it is not, and something it definitely is.' Frank had a tendency to talk like Yoda when he was agitated, and this didn't sit well with a now curious Joe.

'I just got a call from O'Donnell down at the station,' began Frank, 'who just got a call from Carmichael, asking him to meet her downtown.'

'What?'

'O'Donnell said he just wanted to give us a heads up. Carmichael told him to high-tail it to CBC's studios. He said he knew it had to have something to do with the Logan case – which was originally our collar so . . .'

'It's almost nine o'clock on a Friday night. Why the hell is she going to the studios?' Joe asked himself out loud.

'Like I said, Chief, no idea. But O'Donnell says the ADA asked for at least two units of back-up.'

'It'll be on the police wires,' said Joe, thinking ahead. 'The media will pick this up.'

'Maybe that's the idea,' said McKay.

Joe nodded.

'I wonder if Cavanaugh knows about this?' he asked after a pause.

'Well, given Jeffrey Logan was last seen in the company of some other big shot lawyer, my guess is probably not. You think we should call him?'

'I think that is exactly what we should do.'

'Maybe we should have told him about Starkey's call as well, boss,' said Frank, referring to their decision not to tell David about George Starkey's 'gossip' until they discovered exactly what had gone down.

'Yeah, Frank. I think maybe you are right.'

Joe had rung David late the day before with the disappointing news of his conversations with Calvin Galveston from Maine and they then had discussed Rigotti's news regarding Jason Nagle and his kick-ass rifle. But he had stopped short of telling his disheartened friend about George Starkey's 'intelligence', hoping he could find out (a) if what Starkey claimed was correct and (b) if it was, what the hell Logan had been up to.

But the day had gotten away with him, and thanks to a fatal hold-up in Mattapan, Joe had missed a Friday afternoon call back from his court administrator friend – which meant he still did not know if Jeffrey Logan had indeed been at Boston's Municipal Courthouse yesterday afternoon, and if he was, what his slick visit was all about. Just like he had no idea what he was up to right now.

'I could be wrong, Frank, but I don't think Amanda Carmichael is going to cut us into her loop on this one – given we haven't got the call and the woman hates our guts.'

'I would tend to agree with you there, Chief – but I think if we chew on this one a little, we can probably figure it out for ourselves.'

'What are you thinking, Frank?' Joe asked, guessing Frank had his own take on what was about to go down at CBC's studios tonight.

'Well, it seems to me that Carmichael likes the attention, and her way of getting it is to think out of the box.'

'She likes to screw judicial convention for personal gain,' said Joe.

'Couldn't have put it better myself, Chief. That's why she arrested the big-time TV star, dragged him into court, and then chose that high-profile forum to release the guy and arrest his kid while the cameras were still rolling.'

'A kid she is trying as an adult,' said Joe.

'Two for two. So my guess is, she is on a roll. She thrives on two things: the element of surprise and the opportunity to drop her bombshells in front of the biggest audience possible.'

'She's planning something on TV.'

'Well, considering this is a woman who defines the word "court" as something you do to the media when you want to see your own mug on the box . . .'

'She doesn't want us crashing her party, Frank,' said Joe, continuing McKay's thought process. 'She likes playing everything solo, and given she knows she cannot count on us for applause . . .'

'We can safely assume we didn't drop off her invite list by mistake.'

Joe said nothing.

'You got a problem with writing our own invitations to this studio shindig, Frank?' asked Joe after a time.

'Seems to me it was rude of her not to include us in the first place.'

'And you're free this evening?'

'Well, I was planning to catch that *Columbo* re-run on A&E.'

'I'll pick you up in ten then.'

'And I'll grab my raincoat.'

'It's not raining, McKay.'

'True, but it worked for Columbo.'

'Ladies and gentlemen,' said Caroline Croft after the opening credits had rolled and a voiceover announced this presentation as a special, exclusive, two-hour *Newsline* 'event' live from CBC's studios in Boston.

Katherine de Castro had made a mistake. In her dogged determination to win at least one victory over the dictatorial Caroline Croft, she had demanded that they introduce a studio audience into the mix – *'so that Doctor Jeff's loyal followers would see the broadcast as an open, honest presentation as was every production of his show'*.

But now, as the excited spectators sat on the edge of their seats like a pack of predatory animals – animals who were squashed in edgewise, thanks to CBC running promos throughout the day saying a 'special live broadcast' needed a live studio audience that night – she realised that she had allowed her bruised ego to get the better of her. She had a bad feeling about this – and was praying that, for once, her instincts would be proven wrong.

'We wish to welcome you tonight to a very special television event,' Croft began. 'There is no doubt each and every one of you has seen the recent headlines, read the latest internet blog, heard the TV and radio news and basically been bombarded with a great deal of conjecture and speculation regarding the events surrounding the death of Stephanie Tyler – the local Boston attorney who was killed in her Beacon Hill kitchen exactly one week ago tonight.'

Pause.

'You are also no doubt aware that her husband, Doctor Jeffrey Logan, the respected television clinical psychologist who has dedicated his life to advising others on how to achieve healthy, respectful and loving relationships, originally confessed to accidentally shooting his wife in order to protect his fourteen-year-old son, J.T. Logan, who was eventually charged with his mother's murder.

'What you do not know,' said Croft then, tilting her head just a little to the left, 'what you have not been told, what has not been *revealed* until tonight are the facts behind this killing – the reason young J.T., at only fourteen, is about to face an adult jury in an adult court where, if found guilty, he will face the ultimate sentence of life without parole.'

Small shake of her head.

'The Logans are a private family in the public arena. Both J.T. and his older sister, Chelsea, have been largely protected from the limelight by their father – and their mother who, fiercely private herself, chose never to become involved in her husband's popular television career.

'But while Jeffrey Logan encouraged his children's anonymity in order to assure them a stable upbringing, his wife saw her role as "protector" in a completely different light. A light that we can finally reveal, involved the constant, incessant, daily ritual of unfathomable emotional abuse. An abuse we will explore in full detail as I am joined by Doctor Logan and others involved with the case.'

Others? thought de Castro. *Others involved in the case? Croft must be referring to Professor Georgia Hinds,* she reassured herself, thinking about the emotional abuse expert she had organised for tonight's broadcast. Georgia Hinds was a Harvard-educated behavioural psychologist who had a PhD in emotional abuse and what she called 'relationship extortion' – an attractive and intelligent-looking strawberry blonde with a calm and studious demeanour.

'But before we go on,' said Croft, tossing her shoulder-length blonde hair over her left shoulder so that she might twist slightly in her cream armchair to face the special 'guest' beside her, 'I would like to thank Doctor Jeff for inviting me to his television home this evening – a place where he has welcomed thousands before me in the spirit of consideration and hospitality. I would like to assure him that I understand the difficult circumstances under which he has agreed to speak with me here tonight and thank him for his bravery in coming forward.

'Doctor,' she said.

Logan nodded . . . and the entire audience was unable to hold back. It was the first time their dear Doctor Jeff had faced them since the tragedy, and their sympathy flowed in torrents. The applause was deafening as the spectators rose to their feet, prompting

Katherine to take a breath. *They love him*, she told herself. *Perhaps everything is going to be all right, after all.*

'I would also like to introduce the special guest sitting next to Doctor Jeff, emotional abuse expert Professor Georgia Hinds from Harvard University,' she said, tilting her head back towards camera one to gesture at the conservatively dressed woman sitting adjacent to Logan on one of two 'lesser' chairs.

And then she rattled off Hinds' impressive credentials, spoke a little further about the nature of the interview to follow, and assured her audiences that this event was unrehearsed (a lie, considering Jeffrey had seen most of her questions in advance), unscripted (a half truth, given Jeffrey had discussed some of his prospective responses with Croft so that she might '*bounce off the genuineness of his distress*'), and guaranteed to move and shock the millions of viewers watching this exclusive exposé tonight (and that one, Katherine knew, was right on the money).

Croft threw to the first three-and-a-half minute ad break, giving all a chance to take a breath – and Logan the opportunity to stand and strut around his own familiar set like a Goddamned peacock. And in that moment Katherine felt a distinct wave of nausea rise in her throat – at the sight of her partner's confidence, at his ease with the whole fucking mess. And then, as if Croft had been reading her thoughts, Katherine saw her glance towards the posturing Logan before shifting her eyes to meet Katherine's straight on, and then, of all things, offering her a smile.

*

'Shit,' said Joe as his cell phone rang in his hand – he had just fished it from his left-hand shirt pocket so that he might call David and expand their little gate-crashing party to three.

'This is Mannix,' he said then, manoeuvring the phone to his ear as his foot hit the brake for the umpteenth time – he and Frank were on Huntington, travelling east, the traffic leading up to the popular Copley Square now in a Friday night gridlock.

'Chief,' said the familiar voice of FBI Agent Susan Leigh. Susan was Frank's old partner – an over-enthusiastic workaholic who traded her Boston PD shield for its FBI equivalent a little over a year ago.

'Susan,' he said. 'How's it going?'

'Pretty good. I put in my form for Boston today,' she said, referring to what Joe knew was her application to be transferred to the FBI's Boston Field Office – an office run by their mutual friend, Special Agent in Charge Leo 'Simba' King.

'They getting sick of you down there in Virginia, Leigh?'

Susan laughed. 'Well, my supervising agent says he came down with a bad case of gluteus painous maximus the day that I arrived in Quantico.'

'I'd be disappointed in you if you weren't being a pain in somebody's ass, Leigh . . . but listen, I hate to be rude, but me and Frank got something going on here.'

'Okay sure, so I'll be quick.'

Susan went on to explain that SAIC King had been trying to reach Joe all afternoon, but that Joe had failed to return his calls. And this was true, Joe had got a message that King had called late, but once again Joe had simply run out of time to call him back. The two were friends, so Joe assumed it was more of a social call than anything else, and he figured he would ring him back on Monday and set up a time for them to catch up.

'Anyway,' Susan continued, 'since SAIC King had some bureau dinner to attend, I told him I would keep trying to reach you so that I could confirm the results on the voice mail and email analysis. As far as the voice comparison thing goes, the gang from Forensic Audio, Video and Image got you a one hundred per cent match – and our Computer Analysis and Response Team confirmed the exact laptop the emails came from, along with the username and password used to log in mere moments before the emails were sent. And those two bits of information put together well . . . let's just say, as sad as it is, everything falls into place.'

Joe shifted in his seat. He had just hit another red light on Boylston, he had no idea what the hell Leigh was talking about, and something about this whole night was starting to piss him off.

'Susan,' he began, 'I don't know anything about any voice mail or computer analysis.'

Susan paused on the other end of the line. 'But it came from the DA's Office,' she said after a beat. 'And I assumed, given you and McKay are working the Logan case that . . .'

'Jesus,' said Joe. 'Listen to me Susan, Carmichael's playing "cut the cop out of the picture". If someone gave her a recording of a voice mail, we know nothing about it. She must have got Simba to send an ERT to the house,' he said, referring to the FBI's Evidence Response Teams, '. . . and confiscate the computer so that it would be sent straight through to you guys in Quantico.'

'What a bitch,' said Susan, never one to hold back when it came to sharing her opinion of others. 'What's up her ass then, Chief?'

'We're not sure, but we're on our way to find out if that's any consolation.'

'Well, she already has this info. SAIC King would have called it through to her sometime today. But if it makes any difference I can give you a jump on what she's up to by reading you the conclusions on the two reports.'

Despite his predicament, Joe could not help but smile. 'Fire away, Leigh,' he said. 'And I'll put you on speaker so that Frank can hear you too,' he added, pressing the speaker button on his cell.

'What's up, McKay?' she said. 'You still as crazy as all hell?'

'He's wearing a raincoat so he looks like Columbo,' said Joe.

'And you two might want to can it so you can fill me in,' returned a grinning McKay.

'Okay,' said Susan. 'And you better listen up, because if this stuff means what I think it does, this new evidence is gonna blow this case sky high.'

'Joe,' said David, staring at Sara from across the candle-lit dinner table. As soon as his cell rang he had intended to turn it off, but then he saw Joe's number shining back at him on the miniature blue screen and Sara urged him to pick it up. 'This better be good because I'm at L'Espalier having dinner with Sara.'

He had been feeling like a heel for days for allowing Jeffrey Logan to get under his skin – and worse still, for taking it out on Sara. In the end it was Nora who had set him straight – his serious-faced secretary waiting until Sara had gone out for coffees late that afternoon before bounding into his office and delivering him a good ten minutes of her acerbic Irish disapproval.

And she had been right; he'd been acting like an ass, which is why he'd made a reservation at one of the best restaurants in the city so that he might apologise and explain to Sara exactly why he'd been acting the way he had.

'Well, I hope you've made it past your entrées because I need you at CBC studios in ten.'

'What? Why?' asked David as Sara mouthed '*What's happening?*' from across the table.

Joe filled him in – told him everything he knew about O'Donnell and Carmichael and Susan Leigh's extraordinary analysis report, before backtracking to Starkey's tip-off about Logan and his slickly dressed lawyer friend.

'Jesus, Joe, what is going on here?'

'I have no idea. There is a lot of shit to sift through, David. But as for our immediate priority, Frank thinks Logan and Carmichael are planning something on air – either separately or together.'

'Caroline Croft has been after him,' said David – and he could almost hear Joe ticking this over.

'Which makes me all the more nervous,' said Joe. 'Especially since you're the kid's lawyer and Logan failed to give you a heads up. The guy is playing with us, David.'

'I know,' said David, relieved that Joe had a similar take on the situation. 'That is what I have been trying to tell you, Joe. I don't care what your gun nut from Maine told you, or what the mysterious Jason Nagle told Rigotti. I just know . . . in my *gut* . . . that this whole thing leads back to Jeffrey Logan, and that we just haven't been able to work it out – at least, not yet.'

'Take Sara home and get her to turn on the TV,' Joe said after a few moments. 'If Frank's instincts are right, and if Carmichael is playing true to form, this thing is probably going to go live.'

'And if Croft is involved they could already be on air. It's just gone nine, Joe – which means *Newsline* has already started.'

Joe was silent again.

'We're moving,' said David as he met Sara's eye and she nodded, collecting her handbag and raising her hand at a passing waiter for the check. 'I can be at the studio in fifteen. Just promise me one thing.'

'What's that?'

'That you let me have a go at him.'

'Can't do that, David.'

'And why the hell not?'

'Because I plan to get to him first.'

'Abuse is any behaviour that is designed to control and subjugate another human being through the use of fear, humiliation, intimidation, guilt, coercion, manipulation and so forth,' said Professor Hinds, her expression calm but serious. 'And emotional abuse is any kind of abuse that is emotional rather than physical in nature. It can include anything from verbal abuse and constant criticism to more subtle tactics, such as repeated disapproval or even the refusal to ever be pleased.'

Croft nodded, urging the professor to go on.

'It has often been described as a form of brainwashing in that it systematically wears away at the victim's self-confidence, sense of self-worth, trust in their own perceptions, and self-concept. Whether it is done by constant berating and belittling, by intimidation, or under the guise of "guidance", "teaching", or "advice", the results are similar. Eventually, the recipient of the abuse loses all sense of personal value as the mistreatment cuts to the very core of the person, creating scars that may be far deeper and more lasting than physical ones.'

'And in fact, the research shows exactly that, doesn't it, Professor?' asked Croft, her blue eyes narrowing in curiosity. 'That emotional abuse victims suffer the consequences of such cruelty for years.'

'Yes,' said Hinds with a nod, her pale green eyes glistening under the deep indigo lights. 'With emotional abuse, the insults, insinuations, criticisms and accusations slowly eat away at the victim's self-esteem until he or she is incapable of judging the situation realistically. The victim becomes so beaten down emotionally that they blame themselves for the abuse. In many cases the victim's self-esteem is so low that they cling to the abuser.'

'And while we often associate the dominating figure in a family to be the patriarch,' Croft went on, 'is it not also true that the number of female abusers is on the rise?'

'Yes,' agreed the professor. 'I have seen numerous

cases where the mother is the domineering force in the family. There have been cases where the woman, who may lack the ability to proffer physical domination, uses manipulation, verbal aggression and emotional blackmail to establish her authority.'

'So a mother – or mother figure – might belittle, criticise and demean her fellow family members. She might deny their emotional needs, denigrate their feelings and use blame, sarcasm and humiliation to maintain her control.'

'Exactly,' said Hinds. 'Of course it is all a matter of degrees, but in my professional experience, abuse from the mother figure can be even more damaging to the victim psychologically, given the societal stereotypes whereby children expect their mother to be loving, understanding, kind.'

Croft nodded again before casting a glance at her now mesmerised audience and turning to the man beside her.

'Doctor Logan,' she said, acknowledging the expression on Logan's face – pained, but with just the right amount of concern and sympathy. 'I know this is difficult, but perhaps you could tell us – is what Professor Hinds describes familiar? Does this emotional abuser prototype mirror the personality and behaviour of your late wife?'

Logan hesitated.

'Yes,' he said finally – his head downcast, his shoulders slumping but the determination in his voice suggesting he needed to get this out. 'In fact, the professor's description is spot on. Of course, I was aware of the habits of emotional abusers through my training – but somehow had difficulty, at least initially, recognising such abusive characteristics in a person I loved.

'Stephanie was an incredibly bright woman who appeared outwardly hospitable to those she met but was secretly obsessed with maltreating those closest to her,' he went on. 'And I was remiss in not acting sooner, in not removing our children from her influence. But then,' he paused, shaking his head, 'all of this is easy to say in hindsight, as for a very long time my coping strategy was simply to act as a shield for my children by doing everything I could not to rock the boat. A cowardly approach, I know, and one I will regret passionately, deeply for the rest of my life.'

'Excuse me, Doctor,' said Professor Hinds then. 'But cowardly does not factor here and from my perspective you should be congratulated for offering yourself as a protective barrier between your wife and your children.'

With that they were up again – the entire audience, on their feet, clapping and cheering for the 'heroic' TV Good Samaritan before them. And Katherine felt an unexpected second wave of nausea – unsure as to why the adoration she had counted on for all of these years suddenly reeked with the stench of exploitation.

One ad break later, after Croft had spent a good ten minutes quizzing Logan on examples of his wife's tyranny (during which Logan spoke of the rationing of food and unwavering daily schedules, the unrealistic academic expectations and monitoring of phone calls, the coveting of the children's possessions and control of their limited social activities, and Stephanie's general obsession with regulating every aspect of their lives), Croft finally got to show that all-important video.

Katherine could see the horror of it play across the spectators' faces – the shock, the revulsion and finally the acceptance of it all. And she realised that she, along with Logan and Croft, had taken this case and set it on a course from which there was no return.

'Doctor,' said Croft, just as the video went to black, 'I believe I can say, on behalf of everybody watching, that we had no idea what your family has had to deal with – how every day was a nightmare, every second spent in anticipation of what minefield you would have to negotiate next.

'And I also believe that I speak for all concerned when I congratulate you on your ability to hold it all together, to function, to protect your children in a household run by fanaticism and intolerance and fear.'

Logan shook his head and lifted his hands at his audience – all of them on their feet by now – in a gesture which said: '*I do not deserve your applause*'. 'I appreciate your sentiment – all of you. But in truth, it was I who was at fault, for I left it too long to ask for a divorce. And even when I did, I made matters significantly worse by doing so in an environment where my son was able to overhear.'

'J.T. heard you ask your wife for a divorce?'

'Yes, the night before she died.'

'And you believe that his terror, his absolute panic at the prospect of being left in the sole custody of your wife was the trigger that led him to . . .'

'Yes,' said Logan, as if he did not wish Croft to voice it.

Croft nodded. 'A natural assumption to make, Doctor,' she said. 'But, as I think we will all soon agree, one which is totally unfair to yourself.'

Katherine felt an icy sliver of concern slip quickly down her spine.

Croft then gave another knowing nod and looked towards the camera, as a producer in headphones lifted his hands to count her down into another break. And just as the *Newsline* theme music rose to swallow the audio, she promised viewers another explosive, exclusive surprise guest – immediately after the break.

'O'Donnell,' said Joe as he strode across the studio car park towards the side entrance O'Donnell had directed them to. 'What gives?'

'Hey, Lieutenant,' said the grey-haired cop, moving slightly to the side so as not to be overheard by the four uniforms marking time near a now darkened loading bay filled with lighting equipment, audio wires and props. 'I have no fucking idea to be honest. Carmichael called a minute ago, says she is on her way. She told us to sit tight and not to make a move until she got here and gave us our instructions,' he said, rolling his eyes.

'What's going on in there?' asked McKay, pointing to the far right-hand corner of the room – at the red studio 'on' light, now blinking brightly in the semi-darkness.

'It's the *Doctor Jeff* set – and they're filming,' said O'Donnell. 'According to one guy we saw passing, they let a studio audience in about an hour ago. He said nothing had been scheduled for tonight but that he heard the rumour the show was going live. He also said when the light is on that the door is locked. Which it is – I checked.'

'Shit,' said Joe. 'We need to get to a TV.' It was ironic, he thought, that they had been on the road for close to an hour trying to find out what the hell was going on – but everyone else in this fine fucking country was getting a live-to-air preview into the 'case' that he had been ceremoniously 'bumped' from by a media-obsessed ADA. It was even more ironic that they were in a television studio and could not find a single God-damned television – until Joe forced the door to an office next to the main entrance of the loading bay and found a small-screen Sony sitting on top of the filing cabinet against the far back wall.

'Frank,' he yelled as he tried to get a signal on the fuzzy set. 'I need you to ring Cavanaugh and see how far away he is.'

Just as Frank dialled David's cell once more, a car sped up to the side entrance of the loading bay carrying a tall, slender blonde wearing a pair of designer glasses and an impeccably cut suit.

In that moment the red blinking light above the studio door caught his eye again and Joe could have sworn he heard a loud voice inside say *'three minutes everybody',* just as Carmichael came striding in the door.

'Jesus, Caroline,' said Katherine de Castro. 'What the hell is going on?' Katherine knew she only had a few minutes before they were back on the air, and she was determined to find out what the manipulative interviewer was up to.

'Who is this mystery guest?' she asked. 'And why the hell haven't I been told about it? Jeffrey,' Katherine turned to her partner, 'did you know about this – because if you did you owe me an explanation?'

Katherine met his dark brown eyes, his face wearing

that '*I am doing the best that I can*' expression he had used so effectively of late.

'Look, Katherine,' he said. 'This is difficult for us both – we are not used to having to transfer the control of our show to another, but we all agreed in this instance that the shift was best for J.T.'

'You mean, you know what this is all about and you haven't . . .'

'Caroline had an idea and I supported it,' he said, an edge of intolerance creeping into his voice. 'Trust me,' he said, reading the shock on her face. 'This is not going to be a problem, Katherine. Everything is going to be okay.'

'Shit,' said Carmichael as soon as she saw Joe. 'What in the hell are you doing here, Mannix?'

'This is our case, Carmichael,' he said loudly as he moved towards her. He wanted to humiliate her in front of the uniforms, and everyone else within earshot.

'Wrong, Lieutenant,' she said, pushing past him and heading directly towards O'Donnell. 'Sergeant O'Donnell here is quite capable of handling an arrest and considering you and your Keystone Cop partner here have managed to fuck this case up from the get-go, I suggest you step back and cut your losses.'

'We haven't needed to fuck anything up, Carmichael. You seem to have been doing a pretty fine job of that all on your own. I mean, what the hell are you going to do now – arrest the whole Goddamned family until you can make a murder charge stick?'

Carmichael stopped in her tracks, before swivelling on her toes and striding back towards Mannix with determination, stopping mere inches from his face, her long neck stretched up so that she might meet him eye to eye.

'All right, Lieutenant. Feel free to stick around. For you might even learn something about the art of competent criminal investigation. Have you been calling your friend, Mannix?' she asked.

But there was no need for him to answer, for at that moment Joe saw a familiar Toyota LandCruiser screech into the car park behind them.

'Jesus,' said Carmichael, reading Joe's expression before following his eyes to the loading dock behind her. 'You people are truly pathetic. Not that it matters,' she added. 'Because nothing, not even your glorified hero of a friend, has a chance of successfully defending this one.'

'What the fuck is going on here?' It was the question of the night. David came running around the loading bay doors aiming his query directly at Carmichael, the attractive ADA now placing herself physically in front of him, her hands on her hips, right hand extended as if ordering him to stop.

'None of your business, Cavanaugh,' she said.

'It certainly is my business if it has anything to do with the Logan case,' said David, taking a step forward.

'Wrong again, Cavanaugh. You only represent the kid.'

But David would hear none of it, for he was already moving past her, nodding at Joe before he headed directly towards the studio door.

'You can't go in there,' said a young studio hand with

earphones, pointing a set of keys at the solid red light indicating the broadcast was now live to air.

But David ignored him completely, nudging the kid aside before snatching his keys, unlocking the door and grabbing at the thick stainless steel handle before yanking at the heavy soundproof door and moving into the studio beyond.

'Welcome back,' said Croft, calm, composed but with a new level of intensity in her expression.

'A moment ago I spoke of another guest on our program this evening, a guest who I believe can cast even more light on the goings-on in the Logan family household – and indeed, on the events leading up to Stephanie Tyler's death.

'I would like you all to welcome . . .' she said, as David, Joe and Frank, and behind them a determined Amanda Carmichael and an entourage of police entered the studio and adjusted their eyes to the lighting, '. . . Chelsea Logan.'

'Jesus,' whispered David to Joe, who had immediately followed him into the studio. 'I think he's about to fuck over his other kid, Joe. The bastard is going for broke.'

Chelsea Logan appeared the vision of innocence, wearing a pretty white dress with a perfectly cut jacket over the top. Her hair was pulled back in a ponytail, her face free of make-up as she walked towards the stage and Professor Hinds moved to a fourth chair, allowing Chelsea to sit next to her father. Logan embraced her, a perfunctory, awkward gesture which Chelsea appeared reluctant to return. She took her seat, her blue eyes wide, her body language anxious, her short nervous breaths causing her shoulders to rise and fall in double time.

'Chelsea,' said Croft. 'We want to thank you for being here tonight, for we understand how hard this past week has been for you.'

Chelsea nodded.

'Your father has explained to us the depth of abuse both you and your brother suffered at the hands of your late mother and I think I can say, on behalf of all of us watching tonight, we want to acknowledge your bravery, your stoicism and your determination to go on.'

And then they were up again – the audience members rising to their feet, the applause loud and full and heartfelt.

Croft proceeded to ask the now shell-shocked Chelsea a number of questions, not so much about Stephanie Tyler and her apparent rule of tyranny, but more about Chelsea's role in the family as a whole, and in particular, her desire to break free from a household grounded in condescension, vindictiveness and fear.

'It is awful,' she said, and David *knew* the girl was telling the truth. 'For right is always wrong no matter how hard you try.'

'So you lived in fear?' asked Croft. And David saw Chelsea's shoulders tense.

'I do.'

'Knowing that to defy your abuser would result in further admonishment.'

'Yes.'

'And what was it like for you – being not only a beautiful, intelligent young woman in the prime of her youth, but also the older of two siblings, unable to protect your little brother from . . .'

'J.T. protects me as much as I do him,' she interrupted, as if needing to make the point, and David could see Caroline Croft's brow furrow ever so slightly, no doubt at the girl's determination to speak in the present tense. 'We look out for each other. We always have and we always will.'

'So I suppose what you are saying is that you understand your brother's actions? That you relate to them – applaud them even?'

Chelsea looked at her, before her eyes tracked sideways to her father beside her. And in that moment a horrified David realised he was right about what was happening, and he guessed Chelsea had realised it too.

'I love my brother,' she said, her eyes now darting around the studio as if scanning for a route to escape.

'And you have always survived together as a team?'

'Yes.'

'And isn't it true that J.T. rarely acted without your advice, especially when it came to matters regarding your mother?'

'Not just my mother but . . .'

'Chelsea,' Croft said then, now perched so far on the end of her chair that she was practically obscuring Jeffrey Logan from the audience's view, 'did your brother tell you what he intended to do on the evening of Friday, the eleventh of May?'

The audience gasped, as Jeffrey Logan did a perfect double take – from Croft to his daughter – as if the concept was *way* beyond his comprehension.

'Did you speak of it together? Plan it even?'

But Chelsea said nothing, just scanned the studio

once again, her hands twisting in her lap, the bright lavender lights now causing her eyes to water.

'Do you know how much you and your brother stand to inherit following your mother's death, Chelsea – an inheritance that would have fallen directly to you if your father had been removed from your mother's will, or worse still, found guilty of a serious crime such as homicide?'

Still Chelsea said nothing, her eyes now welling with tears – and David realised that the young girl was not so much looking for something but rather for *someone*. She was trying to find him, he was sure of it.

'And further to that, were you aware,' Croft persisted, 'that someone in your house emailed your mother's life insurance company mere days before her death to ask that they increase her potential benefit to a figure running into the tens of millions – an email, I might add, that has been traced directly back to your own PC?

'And that someone purporting to *be* your mother, left a message for her lawyers to remove your father from her will barely hours before her death – leaving you and your brother as her sole beneficiaries, or rather, considering your brother is now incarcerated, yourself alone as the *sole* recipient of her *massive fortune as the owner of Rockwell Wines?*'

The audience cried out in unison.

'I don't believe this,' said Joe.

'We have to get her out of there,' said David.

'*No!*' yelled Logan, now on his feet, turning to his daughter. '*Chelsea, tell me this isn't true?*' And David realised that one question alone had officially hammered the nail into the doctor's sixteen-year-old daughter's coffin. '*You didn't have to do this – I should have . . . I was going to . . .*'

But it was too late. For in that moment Amanda Carmichael pushed past David, Joe and Frank, before barking 'Follow me' to O'Donnell and his fellow uniforms and striding onto the studio floor.

O'Donnell shook his head in apology at Mannix before following the ADA to the centre of the room, dragging his feet and squinting his eyes and looking for all the world like an embarrassed child as he reluctantly returned Carmichael's nod and opened his mouth to say, 'Chelsea Logan, you are under arrest for the murder of Stephanie Tyler. You have the right to remain silent. Anything you say can and will be used against you in a court of law. You have the right to an attorney. If you cannot afford an attorney, one will be provided for you at the time of interrogation and at court.'

Then the audience took in an almighty gasp of breath, and at least one distressed spectator yelled, '*Oh my God!*', just as David whispered in Joe's ear. Joe passed David's instruction onto Frank, before following David and running towards the stage.

Then . . . everything went black, as Frank McKay pulled every light in the house . . . and David took a slight comfort in knowing that, whatever else, Amanda Carmichael's catastrophic finale was now swallowed in the darkness it deserved.

'*What the hell?*' yelled Croft.

'*Shut it down!*' yelled de Castro, who David spotted demanding a camera go to black before barking at her producer to: '*Throw to a break – now!*'

David jumped over a stack of cables to run onto the

stage before grabbing Jeffrey Logan by the shirt and shoving him out of the way so that he might form a human barrier between Chelsea Logan and a now furious Amanda Carmichael.

'My name is David Cavanaugh and I represent Chelsea Logan,' he yelled through gritted teeth, as if the proclamation needed clarifying, setting down in stone. 'My client will not be answering any questions until she has had an opportunity to speak with counsel.'

'I won't allow it,' said Logan, pushing his way into the huddle. 'I don't want you representing her – or my son, for that matter. My children are minors, and I have legal responsibility for them. And they . . .'

'. . . are about to be tried in a fucking adult court for a crime that they did not commit, you two-faced son-of-a-bitch.'

David could not help himself; it was all welling up inside him. He wanted to grab Logan, punch him, nail him to the ground so that he would never get up. But in the end he decided the only way to catch this maniacal mastermind was to show him that two could play at his game of veiled threats and psychological manipulation – and so he moved within inches of Jeffrey Logan's face, before shifting towards his ear.

'You're a murdering bastard, Logan, a sick and twisted psychopath who uses his own helpless children as bait. You believed you are in control, and I'll grant you, so far you have done a pretty good job of convincing the world of your sainthood. But your luck turned, my friend, the moment I walked into your kitchen and saw what you had done.

'So guess what, Jeffrey?' David said then, grabbing

the man's tie and pulling him that much closer. 'The clock is ticking – tick, tock, tick, tock, second by second – so make sure you are keeping track. For I will work day and night to bring you down, my friend. And I will not rest until you are punished for what you have done. For then, and only then, will Stephanie be at peace, and your children be set free from the true tyrant they have the misfortune to call their father.'

David felt the slightest tap on his shoulder and, thinking it was Joe, shrugged it off before releasing Logan's tie and turning to face his detective friend once again. But in that second David felt like he had been catapulted into some perverse alternative reality, as his other best friend, Tony Bishop, his bloodshot eyes red under dark and heavy lids, handed him a piece of paper before taking a breath to say, 'I'm sorry.'

'What's this?' asked David.

'A 209A,' said Bishop.

'Logan has taken a restraining order out against me?'

'He's taken legal action to prevent you from going near his kids.'

'The order is for the kids?'

Tony nodded.

'So I can't represent them? *I can't fucking stand up for them when they face the trial of their lives?*'

'No,' said Tony, his right eye flinching as he spoke. 'I'm sorry, DC.'

But David did not hear him as the images all came at once – Tony's embarrassment, Chelsea's tears, Carmichael's smirk, Joe's look of outrage, and above all else, the look of pure victory that glowed like a beacon on Jeffrey Logan's face.

PART TWO

43

Ten weeks later

'Oh my God,' said Sara as she grasped David's hand and squeezed. She was lying on her back, her neck craned to the right, the reflection of the monitor's light turning her pale blue eyes green.

'It is so beautiful. David – look,' she said, pointing to the image of their unborn child on the screen before them.

'It's . . . wow. It's unbelievable,' said David, his smile so wide it hurt. 'Is that . . . Doctor?' he said turning to Sara's OB/GYN, a pretty brown-eyed woman by the name of Michelle Taylor. 'Is the baby actually opening and shutting its eyes?'

'Yes,' replied Taylor. 'In fact it's probably been doing so for some time. The baby's eyelids started to separate about a month or so ago and by now it is responding well to light. If you put a torch on Sara's belly it might even move towards it – if it had the space, that is.'

'Wow,' said David again, unable to stop himself. And Taylor smiled.

'Your baby is now about nineteen inches long which is normal for thirty-seven weeks or so. It probably weighs about six pounds and it is more than likely amusing itself by practising breathing movements with its lungs, as it prepares itself for life outside the womb. Oh, and he or she can recognise your voices well by now – sort of like you do when you hear things under water.'

'Amazing,' said Sara.

'It's just incredible,' David confirmed.

'The good news is that he or she looks to be in perfect health. The baby is already making its way into the anterior position which will see it move down with its face towards your spine – and that fares well for a safe, natural delivery somewhere in the next three weeks. But don't worry if you feel some tingles down your lower abdomen or legs in the next couple of weeks. Junior here is running out of space,' she said, as she lifted the ultrasound camera from Sara's stomach. 'And with less room to move, he or she might be pressing on some nerves when it goes to play football in such a confined space.'

She moved to her desk to get a digital camera before taking a picture of Sara and David with the ultrasound image in the background. 'Your first family photo.' She smiled. 'I'll email it to you in the next few days.'

David returned her smile. 'You mentioned football, Doctor Taylor. Can we take that as some sort of hint?'

David and Sara had decided against finding out the sex of their baby, but they knew Doctor Taylor was fully aware of whether the miracle they had just witnessed was actually a boy or a girl.

'I'll have you know my daughter Lulu scored three goals at her soccer match on Saturday.' She smiled, switching off the monitor. 'And back in college,' she added, 'I played a mean game of touch.'

'So it *is* a girl,' said David.

'Or a boy,' teased Taylor. 'In which case I'd sign him up for ballet classes within the week.'

They laughed. This felt good. *So* good. It had been almost two and a half months since that horrible night at CBC's studios, and despite David's continued resentment – his anger at being banned from trying to help the two Logan kids – moments like this, with Sara and his unborn child, gave him a temporary respite from the frustration that still boiled silently inside him. He had tried to let it go, largely for Sara's sake, for they had talked out their concerns and decided that no matter what, having people like Jeffrey Logan in your life was not healthy for any relationship. But the aggravation still raged and there was many a moment when he found himself wondering how the hell he could reverse that ridiculous restraining order and rescue Stephanie's kids for good.

The 209A was a joke. In Massachusetts, restraining orders were called 209As or 'Abuse Prevention Orders', and the fact that Logan was able to secure one – or in effect *two* – against David and Sara, was nothing short of preposterous. Logan had claimed, before a Civil Court judge, that David, motivated by his past friendship with Stephanie, had abused his role as J.T.'s attorney to browbeat the boy by calling him a 'no-good killer' and trying to convince the kid that he would never win in court and so he might as well plead guilty.

Logan further claimed that Sara, at David's request, attended Logan's home without his permission so that she might harass Chelsea Logan and convince her to give evidence against her brother. And the judge, who requested proof of Logan's claims and was subsequently given such evidence in the form of a statement taken from J.T. Logan under his father's guiding eye, found he had no choice but to grant such a request – a request then extended to include Chelsea Logan who, Jeffrey Logan argued, 'was in just as big a threat from David Cavanaugh and his co-counsel's bullying tactics as his fourteen-year-old son'.

And so David had had no choice but to sit back and watch the whole bloody mess play out daily like a soap opera in the tabloids and news shows. Until everything seemed to go quiet – including any news on J.T.'s and Chelsea's defence, and who Logan might have chosen to represent them.

'A penny for . . .' said Sara after they left Doctor Taylor's rooms, the spring in her step almost contagious, the pure happiness in her eyes bright enough to light up a city.

'Sorry,' David said, pulling her close. It was Monday morning and they were on their way back to the office, photographic stills of their baby clasped firmly in Sara's hand. As much as David hated to admit it he was actually glad to be out of the confines of the OB/GYN's offices. That emerald green light coming from the ultrasound machine had unnerved him a little – reminded him of another, less happy jade-hued room, where the occupants were shrouded in despair rather than hope.

'I was just wondering what Nora is going to say

when we show her the photos,' he lied. 'Something like: "Lucky it looks like its mother", or "Little Nora is coming along just fine".'

'You're still convinced it's a boy, aren't you?' Sara smiled.

For some reason David had developed a habit of calling their unborn child Harry – a habit Sara would feign distaste at despite the fact that, David was sure, she found it strangely endearing.

'Does that mean the name Harry is growing on you?' He smiled.

'Absolutely not. Every time I picture a "Harry" I imagine a kid with glasses and a fire bolt engraved on his forehead. Not that the Potter kid isn't cool, but I don't particularly want to rear a wizard hell bent on saving the world. I mean, I already married one of those.'

David smiled, while inside he felt more frustrated than ever.

Fifteen minutes later they were back in the office, Nora immediately commandeering their photos before explaining that any group discussion on the images of 'little Nora' would have to wait – as they had an unexpected visitor who was currently in with Arthur and awaiting their return.

'Hey,' said David, walking across Arthur's office to shake Joe Mannix's hand. 'Since when do we rate a Monday morning visit from the head of BPD Homicide?' he asked, even then, at that early stage, praying it was some positive news on the Logan children's case.

'First things first,' said Joe, lifting his hand in

greeting to Sara. 'Arthur here tells me you have some hot-off-the-press photographs of young Joseph.'

'Oh, for God's sake,' smiled Sara. 'My poor child has more names than an Arabian prince or princess. And I am afraid you have to wait in line for an exclusive look at the shots, Joe. Nora has first dibs so . . .'

'Fair enough,' said Joe, before meeting David's eye. 'We have to talk,' he said, shifting his gaze to Arthur who Joe had obviously already filled in. And Arthur responded by moving around his antique cherrywood desk, to join Sara, David and Joe on the office sofa.

'Joe here has some news on the Logan case,' said Arthur, as David's eyes instinctively flicked to Sara to try to gauge her reaction to such news – news that threatened to jerk them back into the world controlled by Doctor Jeffrey Logan. 'And I think we should hear him out.'

And so, as Nora made some fresh coffees, Joe began at the beginning – or, more to the point, the middle, which is where they had left off.

'Early this morning I got a call from Gerald Garretson from Garretson Specialty Rifles in Bangor, Maine. If you remember, I originally spoke to his son, and it seems that young Calvin was, well . . . not completely honest when it came to the transaction and delivery of the Mark V concerned.'

'*What?*' asked David. 'But the paperwork clearly listed Stephanie as the purchaser, and Calvin Garretson even identified her as the person who picked it up.'

'Stephanie didn't collect the gun in person,' said Joe, rendering all in the room speechless. 'You remember Calvin Garretson claimed there was no video surveillance tape of Stephanie picking up the rifle because their camera was out that day? Well, when Gerald Garretson finally had some technicians take a look at their video system, and when the technicians assured him there was never anything wrong with it to begin with, he took his son to task on the whole issue over this last weekend – which is when the kid finally came clean.'

Joe went on to explain how Calvin Garretson had told his father that Stephanie Tyler had emailed and offered to pay him $5000 cash if Calvin agreed to overlook his professional obligation to do the required paperwork in person – and if he agreed to erase the surveillance tape on the day he would list as the purchase date, and drive the rifle down to Massachusetts personally. And Garretson junior, whose dad pays him little more than pocket money for working in the family business, barely hesitated before agreeing to blank the tape, fudge the paperwork and deliver the gun to Boston, dropping it at a Somerville post office where an envelope containing a key to a private security box which held the cash was waiting for him just as 'Stephanie' had said.

'That's illegal in how many ways,' said Sara.

Joe nodded. 'And if we were in a situation where we could go public with all of this, Garretson would most likely be paying for his mistake with the cancellation of his father's gun trading licence – but the dad is an okay guy and . . . well, first things first . . .'

David sat forward on the edge of his seat, nodding for Joe to go on.

'When Calvin Garretson finally told his father

exactly what he had done, an embarrassed Garretson senior, determined to make amends by finding out exactly what had gone down before placing his call to the police, undertook some further investigation as to the origins of the rifle.

'It turns out that the Garretsons had only had this specific gun, sold to them by a private owner, for a few days when they received Stephanie's email asking for a rifle that fit the particular Mark V's description perfectly – right down to the Claro walnut, raised comb, Monte Carlo stock, the rosewood forend tip and pistol grip cap and so forth.

'And so Garretson thought all his Christmases had come at once – because he had bought the gun for a song one week and sold it at a premium price the next. It was almost as if the original owner and the new one had been thrown together by fate, like the gun was destined to remain in the possession of someone who appreciated it – or, in this case . . .'

'Its previous owner who had no intention of letting it go in the first place,' finished David.

Joe nodded, before taking a breath to go on. 'Anyway, Garretson explained how he went back to check the paperwork on the original seller who had listed his place of residence as a house in Waterbury, Vermont. And in an effort to get as much information as possible, Garretson put in a call to his brother – a cop from Montpelier, who did a check on the seller's address.'

'Let me guess,' said David. 'The address was a fake.'

'Not exactly – it was the location of a Ben and Jerry's ice-cream factory in Waterbury, VT.'

'Jesus,' said David, unable to keep the excitement

out of his voice. 'This gun was protected by a maze of smoke and mirrors. The seller used Garretson to launder it so that any connection to him would be erased.'

'Exactly,' said Mannix. 'And believe it or not, there's more.'

'Garretson also told me the Waterbury seller had given his name as James Golan – a name I immediately ran through the Vermont DMV only to come up blank. I even got Garretson to ask his brother to run the guy's name through the local police wires while I did a nationwide search. But once again we came up with nothing – zero, nada, zip.'

'So you hit a brick wall,' said Sara. 'Which is not surprising given the name Golan is probably as false as his address and . . .'

'Yes to the alias, but no to the brick wall,' said Joe, the slightest of smiles starting to creep across his face. 'In fact, while I was talking to Garretson I was doodling the name Golan on a pad, and it sort of triggered a hunch which prompted me to call Rigotti and get him to ring Blackmore one more time. I wanted him to confirm the spelling of Nagle's name. I knew it was a long shot but . . .'

Joe stopped, before looking at David as if he wanted him to see it before it was actually 'said'. And then David met his eye and . . . it came to him, just like that – the almost invisible thread that finally connected it all.

'Oh my God,' said David.

Joe nodded.

'What?' asked Sara. 'What is it, David – what the hell does the spelling have to do with connecting Logan to any of this?'

'Logan is a master manipulator,' answered a now excited David. 'He plays games with people's minds, their emotions, their perceptions. And the name Golan, the name Nagle, it is almost like he is challenging us, baiting us to catch him out.'

But the look on Sara's face told him she was still confused.

'We got the Nagle wrong,' he said, glancing at Joe before turning in his seat to face her. 'We assumed it was spelt N.A.G.L.E., but it wasn't, was it, Joe?' He swivelled back to Joe. 'It was N.A.G.O.L.

'The Golan is an anagram,' he went on, turning his eyes back to Sara. 'And the Nagol, if you spell it backwards . . .'

'Oh my God,' she said at last.

'David was right,' said Arthur.

Joe nodded. 'The gun belonged to Logan all along.'

44

The first shock was bad enough.

Amanda Carmichael had been waiting for Jeffrey Logan to make the decision on his children's legal representation for almost two months. And while her overactive mind had anticipated some high-powered names such as Gloria Shapiro, a high-profile criminal defence attorney who had at least thirty successful murder trials under her belt, or Baker O'Reilly, an attorney who had a penchant for defending the rich, or Tucker Gates, a beast of a man who practically bullied juries into finding his clients 'not guilty', the fact that she was now presented with the man before her was quite surprise enough.

But the revelation that the elderly Charles Harrison, from Tony Bishop's blue chip firm of Williams, Coolidge and Harrison – a greying corporate attorney who had not dipped his wick in the lower salaried criminal courts for over two decades – was named as the Logan teenagers' counsel was just the first surprise to smack ADA Carmichael square between the eyes this morning. For what the deteriorating Harrison had to say was even more unexpected than the fact he was here in the first place . . .

'The Logan teenagers want to plea,' he had said, mere seconds before.

Amanda was finding it difficult to recover.

Now, on the surface of it, the fact that J.T. and Chelsea Logan (who had been charged as an accessory before the fact – a charge which, given it assigned her equal responsibility for her mother's death, would see her, like her brother, facing an equated charge of murder one), were willing to change their plea from 'not guilty' to 'guilty' might sound like a welcome proposal to the DA's Office, which could negotiate sentences and claim a victory without all the trouble of having to wrestle the case through court. But from a personal perspective this was the *last* thing Amanda Carmichael wanted. For almost two months she had been working towards, building on, *craving* her 'once in a lifetime' opportunity on the centre stage. She wasn't even taking pleasure in the fact that her ex-lover, Bishop, was now standing in the corner of her office looking more dishevelled than ever. And she had *always* taken such pleasure in her exes' demise following her exit. But not today. Not today.

'Well, gentlemen,' said Carmichael at last, addressing Harrison, Bishop and Doctor Jeffrey Logan who sat fresh-faced and confident before her. 'I must say, this is somewhat of a surprise.'

'It shouldn't be,' said Harrison, his voice a grainy croak. 'We are aware the original court date was set for Monday the thirteenth of August and given this deadline is a mere two weeks away, and the unusual . . . ah, defence counsel issues surrounding the case, I would have thought you might have anticipated Doctor Logan's desire to make certain decisions so that he might get his children help as quickly as possible. The children planned and executed the murder of their mother in an act of desperation, and this needs to be considered in view of both the nature of the charges against them and the sentences applicable to such charges.'

'So what are you thinking?' asked Amanda, her eyes darting quickly towards an obviously unhappy Bishop. She had heard around the traps that Logan had 'adopted' Tony Bishop as his personal legal advisor in recent weeks, a role, she had no doubt, Tony abhorred but was professionally obligated to, considering his firm had always made – and continued to make – bucketloads by having the Tyler/Logans as clients.

'A reduction of the charge against J.T. Logan from murder one to murder two and a similar reduction for Chelsea Logan on the charge of accessory before the fact.'

Jesus, thought Amanda Carmichael, *what kind of defence attorney was this idiot?* It was true that Chelsea Logan faced the same charge and potential penalty as her brother (that being life without parole), but considering she was not the one who physically 'pulled off the job', Amanda figured that in the very least Harrison might be asking for the lesser charge of voluntary manslaughter in the case of the sister. But no, Harrison here was handing Carmichael her victory on a silver platter – which made the ADA even angrier given said 'victory' would not be played out in court.

'I see,' said a straight-faced Amanda, sure that she had not allowed her thoughts to betray her. 'And how do your children feel about this, Doctor Logan? I would have thought this discussion would have best been had in their presence.'

While Amanda was certainly not one disposed to unnecessary consideration for the defendants in the cases that she prosecuted, there was something about Harrison's offer, and Logan's approval of it, that did not sit easily with the learned ADA. Amanda was all for winning, but she was still her father's daughter and this one was . . . well . . . she found it quite a stretch that the two young people in question would have agreed to the proposal that their lawyer and only remaining parent were proposing on their behalf.

'They understand their situation,' said Logan. 'And to be honest with you, Ms Carmichael, they are both extremely distraught. I am trying to shelter them as much as possible from the incredibly stressful nature of these legal proceedings. They know what they have done, Ms Carmichael – and first and foremost we need to get them some help.'

Amanda nodded, not missing the colour now rising in Bishop's cheeks. 'Let me think about it,' she said. And if she was expecting an argument from Harrison she didn't get one – for the lawyer simply nodded at Logan, who subsequently flicked his finger at Tony to follow as they all rose to leave.

'Thank you, Ms Carmichael,' said Logan, offering his hand. 'I am so sorry about . . . well, you know, all of it.'

'Ah,' said Carmichael, who in that second found

herself highly tempted to say, '*not as fucking sorry as your wife*'. 'I understand, Doctor Logan, and I can assure you I shall give Mr Harrison's offer my every consideration.'

Five minutes later, her secretary at lunch, her door closed and her phone diverted to voice mail, Amanda Carmichael was up and pacing.

How dare they, she thought. *How dare they waltz in here and surrender like a trio of dickless halfwits. How dare they throw in the towel, a mere two weeks before trial, with such gutless inanity and leave me with the ultimate of career anti-climaxes. This isn't a win, it's a forfeit. What kind of victory is it when the opposing team is too spineless to even show the hell up and fight?*

Worse still, she knew there was no solution. Even if she rejected their offer – an offer she would never have been stupid enough to put on the table if the shoe were on the other foot – Harrison could still advise his clients to plead guilty and pray for the leniency of the court. On the other hand, if the rejection of their offer saw them do another about face and stick with their original plea of not guilty . . . sure she would get her day in court, but beating Harrison would be like taking candy from a baby, like kicking the walking stick out from under a man who already had one foot in the grave and was too damned past it to know which way in the hell was up.

No, she thought. *This is not good*. In fact, it was worse than not good, it was a massive opportunity missed, a once-in-a-lifetime chance squandered – a bona fide professional disaster. Truth be told, she knew why she was so pissed. (And it was *not*, she told herself, because of her earlier suspicion that the Logan children were being 'swayed'.) It was not just the exposure of this high-profile trial that she craved, but a chance to face off against David Cavanaugh – the only man to have refused her, the only one insolent enough to turn her down! The very thought of it made her blood boil, made her want to strike out and slap him *straight across the face*.

But given the impossibility of that no doubt satisfying retaliation at present, she compensated by kicking off one high-heeled shoe and bent to take off the other so that she might throw it – hard – against the far office wall. And that was when she saw her office door open quickly and the most unexpected of visitors stride determinedly into the room.

'Jesus, Tony,' she said with a start. 'What in the hell . . .?'

'I forgot my briefcase,' he said, his face flushed. And in that moment she sensed that Bishop, whose brown leather case was indeed sitting by the visitors' chair leg, had left it there on purpose – that he had come back for more than just a piece of luggage, that he had come back to . . .

'My God,' she said. 'You left it here deliberately so that you had an excuse to come back.' She shook her head. 'For God's sake Tony, grow some balls. It's over between us, has been for months, and I have no intention of . . .'

'Jesus Christ, Amanda, for once in your life stop assuming that everything in this Goddamned universe revolves solely around you. Logan and Harrison are downstairs waiting for me, which means I don't have much time, so I need you to shut the fuck up and listen.'

And with that she caught her breath and nodded. She was dumbstruck – for the second time in less than an hour – but this time something told her it was in her best interests to do exactly as Tony had asked.

'Harrison is an idiot,' he started. 'He is tossing this case away and you know it. The man is a senile fool who thinks he can score some points with the media by settling this case for the big TV star and his mentally disturbed kids, but that is a load of crap and I am pretty sure you agree.'

Amanda said nothing, so Tony went on.

'The kids deserve decent representation, Amanda – for no matter what the hell went down in that Logan "House of Horrors" over two months ago, those two young people have the right to their day in court. Their father is steamrolling them. I can feel it. And no matter *which* side of the legal fence you sit on, that is not how our system of justice is meant to work.'

Amanda hated him then, for making her pull at her conscience once again.

'So here's the thing. I know you are pissed – seriously pissed – at not getting the opportunity to strut your stuff in front of a national, hell, an *international*, audience. You are good, Amanda – brilliant, in fact. And the fact that this rare opportunity is being snatched from you by a savvy psychologist and his fool of a lawyer is eating you up inside. And don't try to deny it because I can see it in your eyes.'

Amanda blinked, but did not protest.

'So what if I told you I have a way for you to take it

back – for you to get your day in court and play your best shot at prosecuting one of the most groundbreaking, high-profile cases this Commonwealth has seen in decades? What if I told you I could give you a way out – or "in" for that matter – which, as you and I both know, is exactly what you want.'

'For God's sake, Tony,' she said at last. 'I am not stupid – and I know what you are going to say. You are about to tell me that you can convince Harrison to bail on the plea and take this case to court. But in all honesty, I have no desire to face off against a man who is probably wearing diapers under his $3000 suit. It doesn't interest me, Tony – and you *know,* when something fails to interest me I . . .'

But then he was in front of her, and lifting his hand to her mouth so that she could not say another word.

'Shut up,' he said, before finally lowering his hand. 'There is another way.'

She met his eye and slowly but surely got a sense for what her clever ex-lover was proposing. And in that moment she knew, without question, that Tony Bishop could well be her lucky charm, after all.

45

It had not taken long for their high to crash and burn. Logan may be Golan and Nagol and myriad other characters for all they knew, but in the end, they had no concrete proof of the connection and, even more importantly, no solid evidence that he was behind his wife's death.

Worse still, while Garretson's admission that Stephanie did not pick up the rifle in person certainly helped validate their suspicions, it did not provide any direct link to Logan as the buyer. If anything, they realised the ADA could argue that Stephanie, given her devious and abusive nature, was indeed the one who offered Garretson junior the $5000 to deliver the weapon personally – a tactic Carmichael would say she adopted to keep her 'birthday purchase' secret. It was Stephanie's email address (albeit a new one she had supposedly created on Webmail – explaining why the email would not have been found on Stephanie's home computer's Outlook), credit card and FIC linked to the purchase, after all – which meant that in reality Logan's 'fingerprints' were nowhere near the gun purchase, whether they liked it or not.

'There has to be a way we can tie Logan to these other characters – Golan or Nagol,' said David.

'But how?' asked a tired-looking Sara who had moved to a straight-backed chair in an effort to relieve the ache in her shoulders. She was over eight months pregnant and, David knew, feeling more uncomfortable by the day. In fact, while he was selfishly excited at these new revelations, he had noted the immediate disquiet on her face the moment the name 'Logan' had been uttered.

'Even if we do find a link,' Sara went on, 'what can we do about it besides going to the ADA. And who is to say she would even *believe* what we were claiming, given she is the last person wanting to cut us a break. Don't forget, there is still the matter of those dual restraining orders against us, which means we can't take this to the children – which means we have no hope of . . .'

'Sara's right,' said Arthur, taking an icy cold water from Nora before she rushed from the room to monitor their calls. 'The 209A is a problem. And besides all that, our evidence is sketchy at best.'

'So we have to find the link,' said Joe. 'Golan is a long shot, but in the very least we know someone who knows Nagol – and if at some stage Nagol came in to buy his guns from Blackmore's outfit personally, then we might be able to get an ID and match it with the smarmy Doc Hollywood himself.'

'But you said it yourself, Joe,' said Sara. 'The gun laws in Nevada don't require you to front up in person, and if anything we can assume Logan has been super careful when it comes to hiding his multiple identities.'

'Sure,' said David, picking up on Joe's tack. 'He's careful now, but what about years ago before he became so famous. Blackmore told Rigotti that Nagol had been a customer from way back. Maybe he wasn't always as cautious as he is now.'

Before he had a chance to change his mind, David rose from the sofa and moved towards Arthur's desk, picking up the phone before pressing four digits and waiting for the operator to pick up.

'Nevada, please,' he said, when the operator asked him for the state before enquiring if the number he wanted was residential or commercial. 'It's a business. Hunting Rifles Inc in Las Vegas.'

'Jesus,' said Joe, rising from his seat. 'What in the hell are you doing, David? I thought we all agreed we can't alert Blackmore to . . .'

But it was too late.

'Mr Blackmore?' asked David, and the others in the room immediately picked up on his accent. Marc Rigotti was a born and bred New Yorker and thus had the tendency to speak in that edgy, punctuated dialect that those from the Big Apple favoured.

'This is Marc Rigotti. I am sorry to bother you again.' And in that moment David switched the phone to speaker, hoping beyond all hope that Blackmore would not notice – or, even worse, protest.

'Honestly, Mr Rigotti,' said an obviously exasperated Blackmore. 'Your calls are now verging on harassment. I have spoken to Mr Nagol and he has assured me he has spoken to you. I have a business to run, sir, and I . . .'

'I am sorry, Mr Blackmore,' said David. 'There is just one more thing – and I am happy to say it has nothing to do with the Logan case. It's just that after all of our conversations another idea came to me. Mr Nagol seemed like a very nice man and I was kind of in awe of his shooting accomplishments. And I thought that maybe he might make a good subject for a character piece – you know, man against elephant – that sort of thing.'

Silence . . . as Blackmore took a breath and all in the room waited anxiously for his response.

'Well, that sounds more like it,' said Blackmore. 'We have been supplying him with rifles for years, you know. He must have a tremendous collection by now. I would be happy to talk about our business and how we go out of our way to supply our loyal customers and – as in Mr Nagol's case – lifelong gun enthusiasts with the pieces they desire.'

'So you've obviously known Mr Nagol for some time then? It's funny, I have been sitting here trying to imagine what kind of man takes on the most powerful animals on the planet – I mean, the guy must be pretty big to have the guts to . . .'

'Oh no, sir,' said Blackmore.

'He's of average size then,' said David, barely able to hide his excitement. 'Is he tall or slim or . . .?'

'My "no" didn't refer to Mr Nagol's stature, Mr Rigotti.' And David felt his heart begin to sink. 'But to the fact that I have never seen him. He orders most of his guns by email or telephone and we send them to various places around the country, depending on where he is at the time.'

It wasn't much better.

'But Little Willie has seen him,' added Blackmore.

'Excuse me, Mr Blackmore?' asked David, lifting his head to meet his colleagues' eyes.

'Little Willie – or more specifically William Dukes, my second-in-charge. Willie used to compete against Jason Nagol when they were teenagers – you know, at local shooting competitions, target rallies and the like.'

'And is Mr Dukes available to . . .'

'Well sure,' said Blackmore. 'In fact, if you hold on a moment Willie is just finishing up with a customer. He could call you back if you like. I have your number at the *Tribune*.'

'No!' protested David, almost a little too enthusiastically. 'I mean, I can hold if that is okay.'

'Well, all right then.'

Moments later, Dukes was on the line.

'Jason Nagol was the best damn shot I ever come across,' said Dukes after their introductions. 'I'm a darn fine shooter, Mr Rigotti, but my talent comes from hours and hours of practice. Jason, on the other hand, could well have been born with a gun in his hand. With Jason, the ability to shoot come natural, the gun was like an extension of his arm.'

'So you are saying that the fair-haired Jason had always been big,' David was fishing. 'Strong enough to control his weapons even at a young age when . . .'

'No, sir, you get me completely wrong. First up, Jason was dark – long brown hair that always covered his face, tanned skin and, if I recall correctly, dark brown eyes. And he was never a physical kid, if anything he was average in build – maybe even what you would call scrawny. But my point was, Mr Rigotti, that Jason knew how to control a weapon with his *mind*.'

David said nothing, hoping that Dukes would go on.

'I remember him arriving at various pistol shoots in the back of his mom's '82 Buick. He'd jump from that car like a boy obsessed, already summoning the calm it would take to kick our asses to hell and back.'

'His mom used to drive him to the contests?'

'As far as we could tell she had no choice. Jason said he used to force his mom to take him – even joked about holding a gun to her head so that she would get into the car.' And Little Willie laughed, a strange high-pitched giggle. 'That Nagol was some controlling son-of-a-bitch, all brooding and tormented and smug.'

David nodded, knowing the 'controlling' comment was probably the understatement of the year.

'And his mother,' said David. 'Do you remember her too?'

'Well, sure,' said Dukes. 'In fact, she was particularly hard to forget because she was such a looker. If I recall correctly, Jason's mom was a sort of celebrity in her own right – she used to headline at the Bellagio or the Sands or . . . anyway, I believe her moniker was Lovely Legs McCall.'

'His mother was a Vegas showgirl?' asked David.

'That's what I heard. But that was years ago and from what I recall there was some story about her passing early, in some car accident I think – something about her and Jason's dad being taken out by a semitrailer heading west on the Interstate 15.'

David shot a glance at Joe. 'So they are both deceased,' he said.

'Like I said, that's what I heard.'

'And Lovely Legs McCall was the show name she used when she danced in the Vegas clubs?'

'I think so, and judging by those pins, Mr Rigotti, I am guessing she certainly did not disappoint.'

Just then, a loud noise rung out across the office and David looked up to see Nora in the doorway, the pitcher of cold water now in pieces around her feet. And in that same moment, Dukes said he was being called away to help another customer. Sara rushed to mop up the debris and David took Dukes' home number before thanking him for his help and hanging up the phone. Then he met Nora's eye, knowing – just *knowing* – that his beloved secretary had something important to share.

'God save us,' said Nora, before turning to hurry from the office, the others standing to follow as she went to her desk and emptied her in-tray by tipping it upside down in total disregard of her usual sense of order.

David moved around her desk and, taking her by her shoulders, forced Nora to look at him. 'What is it, Nora, what's wrong?'

But Nora only shook her head in frustration, before turning to face the confused group beside her, then once again meeting David's eye. 'The article on Ms McCall – it's missing, lad. Your only link to Jeffrey Logan – it is gone.'

46

The *Vanity Fair* arrived at 3.45pm. She was at home, which was not unusual considering Jeffrey seemed to be requiring her less and less at the studio these days. It came via messenger, 'hot off the presses', as the saying goes – one of the first copies of the soon-to-be-released August issue, with a strikingly handsome Jeffrey Logan on the cover. The shot, taken by world-renowned *Vanity Fair* photographer Annie Leibovitz, showed Logan at the wheel of a large white cruiser, the wind lashing across his olive-skinned face, the grey clouds massing overhead, the hint of sea spray glistening on his left cheek, and his knuckles tensed, white, as he steered the massive powerboat through the rough seas.

The image, Katherine noted, while meant to portray a sense of loss and loneliness also spoke of determination and resolution. It was, she thought, incredibly powerful, the expression on Jeffrey's face saying: '*I will not be beaten no matter what life throws at me – and I dare anyone, **anyone**, to divert me from my course*.'

There was a truth to this, she knew – just as she also knew that the tide was turning. That Jeffrey was cutting her out of the loop. That she was no longer captain of their ship. The evidence was in the small things – his asking her to execute menial tasks, making decisions without consultation and, most unnervingly, treating her *differently* around their staff. She had seen the looks on their faces – the flashing glance here, the raised eyebrow there when Jeffrey complimented her on her appearance, put a subtle hand on her shoulder, or stood that fraction closer to her than he did to anyone else.

And how must that look? How must that *look*? She asked herself the unnerving question over and over again as she took a long slow swallow of the deep-red claret before her. Did they . . . *could* they be thinking that she was somehow involved in all that had come to pass – that Jeffrey . . . that she . . . that the children . . .? It was far too dreadful to contemplate – and way too distressing to address.

So much had changed of late. For starters, Jeffrey had done a complete turnaround when it came to the handling of his children's cases. His defence strategy was suddenly that there *was* no defence strategy – that his two teenagers were guilty and would plead accordingly.

Then there was his new demeanour – that fresh spring in his step as if things had been dealt with and the fact that his family had been whittled from four down to one in less than three months was, if anything, a pleasant change in the mix – which made Katherine wonder if Jeffrey had not been captain of his ship from the outset.

She grabbed for her wine. She looked at the magazine again, and this time noticed the two yellow post-it notes protruding from separate pages; one at the front of the issue, and the other closer to the back. Her finger flipped to the second post-it first, and she realised that this page had been highlighted, with a note from Jeffrey which read, '*What Do You Think?*', because it marked the beginning of the feature article, a 'painstakingly honest exclusive' written by a journalist by the name of Hamilton Trent.

The next post-it, the one at the front, was stuck on one of the many pre-feature advertising pages that *Vanity Fair* seemed to specialise in – this one from Cartier, of some incredibly gorgeous woman wearing little but an expensive diamond bracelet around her flawlessly skinned, slender right wrist.

Just as Katherine took another sip of her wine, just as she dismissed this post-it as an anomaly and was about to flip back to the feature to read what she knew would be one of the best public relations exercises in decades, the doorbell rang again, this time determinedly, prompting her to rise from her sofa and make her way down her long, plush, carpeted hall.

'Package for Ms de Castro,' said the UPS man, already holding out one of those electronic receiver gadgets for her to sign – which she did, quickly, before walking back to her living room, collecting the magazine and wine, and moving to the kitchen annexe where she retrieved a pair of scissors. Sitting down at the table, she unwrapped the small cardboard box.

The flash of scarlet caught her eye immediately, and as she removed the tissue and picked up the small, leather bound box beneath it, her fingers began to shake.

'No,' she said to herself as she prised open the clasp on the bright red container.

'*No!*' she repeated, but this time aloud.

Sure enough, it was exactly as she had anticipated – the Cartier bracelet from the magazine, with the briefest of notes – '*To K with love*' – attached. And as she sat there, at the end of her kitchen table, a wine and a *Vanity Fair* placed just within her reach, she looked up towards the kitchen door and realised just what role she had been cast to play.

47

'Hello,' said Nora Kelly, after the young female voice on the other end of the line answered the phone with: '*Miss McCall's Dance Studio. This is Tracey speaking, how can I help you?*'

'I . . .' Nora cleared her throat. 'Tracey, I was wondering if I could speak to Miss Deirdre McCall. This is a friend of hers calling, and I won't take but a moment of her time.'

After they had found the number of Deirdre McCall's dance studio through Las Vegas directories, their decision had been unanimous. Given Nora's description of Deirdre McCall's extreme nervousness during their last conversation, they concluded that, while not ideal, it was best if Nora be the one to approach her again. They knew McCall would be apprehensive, but still believed that Nora's gentle Irish manner was the better alternative to that of the three lawyers, or one homicide cop, currently occupying the room.

'Oh,' said the girl after a pause. 'I . . . ah, I'm sorry. Did you say you were a friend?'

'Yes,' said Nora. The phone was once again on speaker and Nora's eyes were set firmly on the plastic handset before her. 'We last spoke a couple of months ago, about a friend of mine who wanted to join her "Follies".'

'Well, I am afraid your friend . . . What I mean to say is . . .' They all noted the shakiness in the receptionist's voice. 'Ms McCall has been the victim of a terrible incident. The police say it was a case of mistaken identity – or a random act of violence.'

At that point, with his heart racing, David could not bear to sit back a moment longer. 'Tracey,' he said into the speaker, not wanting to scare the girl but determined to get to the truth. 'My name is David Cavanaugh and I am a lawyer from Boston. I am standing here with a lieutenant from the Boston Police, a man named Joe Mannix – and if you want to take his name down you can call BPD and check.'

'Ah . . .' began the girl. 'Okay, but I . . .?'

'The thing is, Tracey, we believe Ms McCall may have unwittingly become involved in a case we are defending. She has done nothing wrong, but she may be linked to an individual who does not have her best interests at heart.' It was a slight stretch of the truth, but even as he said it, he prayed that the girl would neither run a mile, nor worse, contradict his use of the present tense when it came to his references to McCall.

'Ms McCall is in a coma,' said Tracey, and David knew that she was crying. 'She was shot a few Fridays ago – she was walking home from class and was almost at her apartment when a car full of Asian guys pulled up alongside her and shot her in the head.'

David's breath caught in his throat.

'The police say it was a gang-style shooting,' the girl went on. 'The detectives came in here and questioned us and asked all sorts of things that we did not understand.'

'What kind of questions?' asked David. 'And what didn't you understand?'

'They asked if any of us knew that her real name wasn't Deirdre McCall. That McCall was a name she used to use on stage. That her real name was Diane Nagol and that she had been hurt once before.' The girl took a breath. 'The thing is, Mr Cavanaugh, I have known Ms McCall for over ten years – first as a student and then as a teacher here at the studio, and she never once told me her name wasn't her own. She said she never married, had no kids – that her students were her life.

'I always believed I was the closest thing she had to family. But when I went to the hospital, after the shooting, the doctors asked me all these questions about her medical history, about why a CAT scan showed she was missing a small section of her brain, about the previous traumas she had experienced, about any possible next of kin.

'They thought she would die, you see, but in the end they could not find anyone else to call – and I was so glad that I could be there for her. She has been holding on for almost three weeks now, defying those know-it-all doctors at University Medical who told me she would probably not last the week. But Ms McCall is a fighter, and she simply refuses to give in.'

'Tracey,' said Joe, before stealing a glance at David. 'This is Lieutenant Joe Mannix. Do you remember the name of the Las Vegas detectives handling Ms McCall's case?'

'Yes,' she replied. 'The main guy on the case is a detective named Michael Lopez. He gave me his card.'

And as Tracey went to retrieve Lopez's card from her purse, David whispered something into Joe's ear. Joe was still shaking his head fervently in the negative when Tracey returned to the phone.

'Tracey,' said David, after the girl had read out the number. 'Just one last thing. I don't suppose Ms McCall ever mentioned someone by the name of James Golan or Jason Nagol or Jeffrey Logan?'

'No, Mr Cavanaugh,' she replied. 'She never mentioned any of those names – although Jeffrey Logan is the same name as that poor guy on TV. But Ms McCall didn't know anyone famous. At least if she did, she never mentioned it. She lived a very quiet life, Mr Cavanaugh – a good, decent, very quiet life.'

By 10pm that night, after Joe's lengthy conversation with Michael Lopez of the LVPD, they had concluded several things.

Jeffrey Logan had stolen the photocopied newspaper article about Deirdre McCall and her dance studio accomplishments from Nora Kelly's desk. He had most likely done this the day he brought Sara back to the office after their lunch, after Nora told him to 'show himself out', after which he most likely spotted the article sitting face-up in her in-tray. The article told him his mother was alive and based in Las Vegas – or, in other words, they had unwittingly paved the way for her attempted murder.

Deirdre McCall had died before. Detective Michael Lopez confirmed it. She and her husband suffered a fatal car accident in late 1983, when a transport truck hit their sedan on Highway 15 near Barstow, California. McCall – or Diane Nagol as her fingerprints confirmed her to be (a savvy Lopez took her prints when the name Deirdre McCall failed to appear on the social security register and then matched them to a set collected some forty-five years ago from a Diane Nagol who had been arrested for shoplifting from a supermarket), had actually passed away beside her husband before being revived in the ER of Barstow Community Hospital. There were records of the couple having a son named Jason, but police attempts to contact him proved unsuccessful.

Diane Nagol's California-based rehabilitation took close to ten years, during which she learnt to 'function' with what remained of her brain. After that, as Lopez put it, she had basically 'fallen off the map' – and David and his friends surmised that this was when Diane Nagol had decided to adopt her stage name and make the gutsy move back to Las Vegas. She was a dancer by trade, after all – and in the very least, her rediscovered talent could earn her a decent living.

Judging by McCall's reaction to Nora's initial call and Lopez's findings, they believed the woman had lived incognito in the hope her son would never locate her again. What he had done to terrify her to such an extent was still an unknown, but in his heart David guessed that Logan was somehow behind that car accident – and perhaps other atrocities as well.

Of course, there were also many unknowns – the first one being how the Asian gang members came to be involved in Deirdre McCall's shooting. David and Joe had no idea how someone like Jeffrey Logan would know a group of notorious criminals who Lopez described as 'members of the influential Chinese street gang known as the Asian Boyz'. And while Joe knew the gang also had a presence in Massachusetts, he could not see a link between these gangsters and the wealthy, Beacon Hill-based Dr Jeff.

Worse still, any identification of Logan as the young Jason Nagol seemed close to impossible. While William Dukes gave a vague description of the dark, long-haired boy he used to shoot against as a teenager, a return call to Dukes confirmed he did not remember the boy well enough to identify him as an adult. In fact, the closest comparison Dukes could give, when asked if the young Nagol resembled anyone famous, was that he 'looked a little like a young version of that long-haired guy who played Aragorn in *Lord of the Rings*, except a little taller, a little darker and with longer hair and dark brown eyes'.

A bona fide dead end if ever there was one.

David came up with the idea of talking to Katherine de Castro who, in the very least, first knew Logan almost twenty years ago. But they guessed that by that stage Logan had already 'reinvented himself' to be the man he was now. They also feared that, despite de Castro's assistance in cutting the cameras on the night of the TV exposé, that she remained loyal to her business partner – and any move to unsettle their career objectives might result in her expressing her concerns to Logan. And no matter how much faith they had in what they had discovered, as Joe had put it, 'tipping off that asshole could seriously fuck things up'.

Finally, Nora's second piece of mail – the other anonymous piece of information that had come from the unidentified correspondent in the same envelope as the article on Deirdre McCall – made no sense to them whatsoever. The piece was simply a brochure on a famous upmarket resort in Cape Cod called the Chatham Bars Inn. And while it meant nothing to them at the moment, it was a priority for David to try to work it out.

In the meantime, considering the envelope had been discarded (despite David's protests, Nora felt dreadful about this, as she did about her failure to make the link to the Las Vegas-based McCall earlier), Joe said he wanted to check the brochure for prints. And David felt sure he knew whose long slender prints he would find on it – that of his old friend Stephanie Tyler.

Finally – and most importantly – despite the unanswered questions and, even more frustratingly, the lack of stand-up-in-court proof, David desperately *needed back in*! He not only needed it, he *wanted* it – perhaps more than he had ever wanted anything in his whole entire career. It was a selfish yearning, the timing of which could not have been worse. But in the end he knew that finding a way to defend the Logan children and expose their father for the monster that he was would be his first testimonial as a parent – for mothers like Deirdre McCall and Stephanie Tyler deserved justice, and children like J.T. and Chelsea deserved freedom from the man who was destroying their lives.

48

The following morning

'What is good?' Jeffrey Logan asked himself, quoting Nietzsche as he sucked the cool morning air into his lungs. 'Everything that heightens the feeling of power in man, the will to power, power itself!' he replied.

And Nietzsche was right.

Logan, who had been running for a good forty minutes along the now silver-surfaced Charles River, stopped to catch his breath. He closed his eyes, placed his hands on his hips, extended his chest and saw himself – literally *saw* himself – as that incredibly good-looking cruiser captain defying those riotous seas. Here, on his own, the cool easterly breeze cutting into his sweat, his legs pumped with blood, his breaths warm and powerful, he felt stronger than he had in his entire life – and he wasn't even carrying a gun!

Oh, he missed them – the guns, that is. But he had controlled his need to carry one of his thousands of rifles and handguns that rested safely in a storage facility, and realised, in the process, that he was now beyond need of a physical weapon, given the highly tuned efficiency of his brain.

He had sensed it since childhood – the 'gift' he had been given to influence, to dominate, to command. True, when he was younger he needed a gun in his hand to do it, but he had learned that people respond just as quickly, perhaps even more so, to the subtle workings of manipulation.

Take Stephanie, for example – he had completely possessed that woman, taken her seemingly inextinguishable spirit and doused it repetitively, constantly, until she belonged 100 per cent to him. Of course, 'therein lies the rub', he admitted to himself as he began a series of difficult stretches, balancing his long tanned leg on a rusty balustrade before him. Once they reach a certain level of submission their subservience tended to repulse.

But thanks to his children, both of whom, unfortunately, had turned out to be miniature clones of their mother, that problem had been solved. Their pathetic little game had backfired and now they were paying the price. Carmichael would eventually accept their plea. He was sure of it. She was a whore – a smart whore, but a whore nonetheless – who would always sell her wares to the man who would 'advance' her the most. If circumstances were different, the thought came to him, he would like to have a go at her. Perhaps at another time, if his next 'subject' failed to submit.

His mother had been disposed of. *Ah, see – now that is where luck enters the equation.* Who would have thought that his brief encounter with local Asian Boyz leader Damien Chi would have reaped such significant rewards? The police would never make the connection, and with that pesky Cavanaugh well and truly out of the picture everything was, well, as close to perfect as it possibly could be.

He would have his hands on Stephanie's more than substantial fortune within weeks (the prospect of buying himself one of those multi-million dollar cruisers had been in his mind constantly since the *Vanity Fair* shoot), his lawyers had told him as much – and then, with his children incarcerated for God knows how long, his life would be close to perfect.

And all this from a boy born to a strip club dancer and a number-crunching halfwit. Quite brilliant really. Really quite brilliant indeed.

Sara was sick. She had a migraine and had been throwing up since 4am.

He felt awful leaving her, but she assured him she would be okay and would call Doctor Taylor as soon as it was 9am. In the meantime, he had called his sister Lisa – a nurse in Massachusetts General's busy ER department – and asked her to stop by on her way to work. Lisa was a five-foot-three firefly – her windswept dark hair and bright green eyes providing the typical Irish aesthetics to her 'think before you speak' enthusiasm. The minute he had called her, at little after seven, she abused him for neglecting her again, before launching into a diatribe about some loser intern she was dating and finally shutting up long enough for David to get a word in.

'You know I don't mind coming over, DC, but why

aren't *you* staying home to look after Sara?' asked Lisa, straight to the point as usual. 'Are you due in court?'

'No, I, ah . . . I got something going on, Lis,' he had answered, feeling guiltier by the minute.

'Something big enough to leave your pregnant partner barfing on your bathroom floor?'

'Well, I wouldn't be leaving her if it wasn't,' he barked then – but part of him knew she was right.

Truth be told, he really didn't have anywhere to go and no one specific to talk to. He was legally forbidden to approach the two people he needed to access the most, and his only other link to Logan's true nature was now lying in a coma halfway across the country, trying to survive without a decent chunk of her brain.

Logan had done that. David was sure of it. He had killed his father and twice tried to do the same to his mother. He had annihilated his wife and framed his children and manipulated Sara and condescended to David and caused a massive rift in David's friendship with Tony Bishop and, to top it all off, reduced his beloved secretary Nora to a state where she believed her lack of action had resulted in Deirdre McCall's shooting.

Logan did not play fair. He broke all the rules and covered his tracks like a professional.

Well, perhaps it is time, David thought to himself as he left his building, *that I play him at his own game – legally or not.*

Ten seconds later, the opportunity presented itself.

'Mr Cavanaugh,' said the voice. At first David dismissed it, as he could not see where it was coming from.

'*Mr Cavanaugh.*' This time louder, and David turned to his right to see a man in a nondescript black SUV poking his head out of the passenger-side window.

'Do I know you?' asked David, his heart skipping a beat. He wondered if you ever lost that slight tingle of fear when a stranger pulled up beside you. Mothers were very good at planting that seed early, and it never left you, no matter what.

'Ah, no,' said the man. David took him in quickly – pale skin, balding head, expensive suit, conservative tie. 'My name is Harry Harrison, and I am an attorney at Williams, Coolidge and Harrison. Specifically, I have a request from . . .'

But David's blood was boiling.

'Mr Harrison,' he began, advancing towards the window to stick his head squarely in Harry Harrison's face. 'If this is Tony Bishop's spineless way of trying to make amends you can tell him to go fuck himself.'

'No. No, sir,' said Harrison.

'I'm not interested, Mr Harrison,' said David, banging the roof of the car before turning his back on the sickly faced lawyer behind him.

'*Please*, Mr Cavanaugh.' Harrison was out of the car now, and pulling David by his arm.

'Jesus,' said David, shrugging himself free. 'Believe it or not, Mr Harrison, I am really kind of busy right now and not in the mood for this communication by proxy bullshit. If Tony doesn't have the balls to come talk to me in person, then . . .'

'Look,' said the slightly built lawyer, his hand back on David's bicep and squeezing surprisingly hard. 'Truth be told, Mr Cavanaugh, this is not how I usually spend my Tuesday mornings either. In fact, if my uncle found out that I was involved he would . . .'

The flushed-faced Harrison had David's attention now, enough for him to turn to meet Harrison eye to eye. 'What are you talking about?' he asked.

'You need to come with me,' said Harrison, gesturing towards his car.

'What? Why?'

'Mr Bishop needs to see you, and you need to come with me now,' he said, looking at his watch. 'The timing is everything and we are already running behind schedule.'

'Now hold on a minute,' said David. 'I am not going anywhere until I understand what is going on.'

'Tony said you would argue,' said Harrison. 'And so he told me that when you did, I should tell you: "*amicus primoris*".'

Amicus primoris – the memories came rushing back. It was Latin – something Stephanie used to say back in college every Friday night before exams. Her argument was that a good night out would release the anxiety before a long weekend of cramming. And more often than not she was right.

Amicus primoris – 'friends first'.

'All right,' said David, as he moved towards the car. 'Just tell me where in the hell we are going.'

'Mannix,' said Joe, as he picked up his direct line. He had only been at work twenty minutes and already he was flat out – the report of a murder/suicide in Dorchester had thrown the entire department into action. And so when the caller did not respond, it was no surprise that Joe did not have the time or patience to humour them.

'Jesus,' he said, before removing the receiver from his ear only to hear a distinctly female voice finally emanating from the other end of the line.

'Lieutenant Mannix,' said the woman, a tone of nervousness in her voice. 'I am sorry. I . . .'

'Who is this?' asked Joe.

'It's Katherine de Castro. I am friends with, I mean, I work for – *with*,' she corrected herself. 'I work *with* Jeffrey Logan.'

Joe lifted his hand at Frank McKay, who was just outside his door and using his thumb to indicate he was also about to hit the road with a fellow homicide detective named Rico.

'Ms de Castro,' said Joe, gesturing for Frank to come in. 'What can I do for you?'

'I just . . .' she began. 'I just had a question for you, Lieutenant, and it is going to sound very silly. I mean, something came to me last night. It is ridiculous really.'

The woman was on 'the tightrope'. Joe could feel it. He had heard that tone before – the one where a family member or friend hadn't quite made the decision to come clean on something they knew about a loved one. It was the tone people adopted when they were overcome by guilt or shame or fear – when they were 100 feet above the ground, knowing a fall was inevitable, but still not sure which way was the right way to jump.

'I wanted to know what issue of *Vanity Fair* Stephanie Tyler was reading before she died?'

And jumped she had, Joe sensed. The question

meant nothing to him now, but his gut told him that it would – eventually.

'To be honest, Ms de Castro, I am not sure,' answered Joe, careful not to make light of her query. 'Is there a problem – with the issue, I mean?'

'No!' she said, almost too quickly. 'Oh God, it really doesn't matter, I'm sorry to have bothered you.'

'It's no bother,' said Joe, trying to keep her on the line, grabbing a pad and pencil and writing a quick note for Frank that said: '*Tyler,* Vanity Fair. *What issue?*' 'I can find out. It is really no trouble. I have it here somewhere.' He was fudging while Frank bounded from the room to call the guys in evidence. 'Did the issue belong to you?'

'No. I mean, it might have, *yes*. You see I collect *Vanity Fair* and I was missing a few issues.'

Now she was lying – Joe knew it. 'You want it back?'

'God, no. I am so sorry, Lieutenant. I must sound so petty. It was a random thought . . . I . . .'

She was on the verge of jumping the wrong way, Joe sensed, his heart now beating in double time. She went all the way out onto that cliff and now she was jumping the Goddamned wrong fucking way.

'Hold on,' he said, frantically waving his arms for Frank to hurry up. And then Frank hung up the phone and bounded into his office, before shoving the hastily scribbled note under his boss' nose.

'It was the October '93 edition,' said Joe at last. 'A tenth anniversary issue, with Julia Roberts on the cover.'

And then there was silence.

'Funny, that is what I thought it was,' de Castro said, a tone of dull realisation in her voice. 'Thank you,

Lieutenant, and I promise I won't be bothering you again.'

Plymouth, Massachusetts, is about forty miles south of Boston on what is known as the state's South Shore. It is most famous for being the landing site of the *Mayflower* – and, David recalled, for the somewhat less than spectacular rock which was said to be the first piece of American ground William Bradford and his fellow Pilgrims stepped onto in 1620. The rock was an anti-climax – and David prayed that his unexpected 'abduction' south would not prove similarly disappointing.

The weather had turned. After weeks of sun the city had been swallowed by a mass of clouds and accompanying sea fog. It was cool but humid, the air thick with a damp that hung heavily on David's skin, a red-faced Harrison sweating copiously beside him – his left leg shaking nervously, his grey eyes shot with tiny flecks of red.

'Almost there,' said Harrison, the first words he had spoken in over half an hour. All that Harrison would tell David was that they were meeting Tony in Plymouth. And David, knowing that was where J.T. Logan's detention unit was located, decided not to push any further, hoping Tony had actually gone out on a limb and got him some sort of quasi-communication with the young boy he wanted so desperately to represent.

But his hopes were dashed as Harrison turned off just before the large block structure that was the DYS Plymouth Juvenile Detention Unit. David immediately asked where the hell they were going, and Harrison, who had obviously had enough as he pulled into a roadside diner parking lot, looked David squarely in the face.

'I have never broken the law before,' he said. 'I come from four generations of attorneys and I could lose my licence over *you*.'

Despite Harrison's misery, David felt his heart rise again and he nodded. 'Thanks.'

Moments later they were inside, David looking desperately around the sparsely populated diner for the man whose friendship he was now feeling incredibly guilty for doubting. Then Tony Bishop, sitting in a far corner booth, lifted his head with a nod, before leaning across the table to tell his companion that the person they were waiting for was here.

And in that moment, as an incredibly thin, pale-skinned J.T. Logan turned and rose up on his knees so that he could see David approaching from over the top of the high-backed booth, the young man's eyes met his, and for the first time since David had known him, J.T. Logan smiled.

Moments later, Harrison having chosen a separate table at the other end of the room, David was in a huddle with his friend and the young teen who looked more like a child than ever. And after several questions regarding J.T.'s welfare, David finally got to the point.

'How many ways are we breaking the law here?'

'I lost count when I hauled J.T. from the detention unit next door. Told them I was his attorney, said I was transporting him to a private conference with the ADA.'

David nodded. 'I hate to state the obvious, but I am in breach of the APO,' he said, referring to the abuse prevention order still in place against him.

'Yeah well, that's our first order of business – reversing the 209A.'

'I appreciate the sentiment, Tony, but in case you haven't noticed, neither of us is a judge and . . .'

'No, but I was lying when I said I was lying before – when I told you about pulling J.T. here from Plymouth, about meeting the ADA.'

'He *does* have a meeting with the ADA?' said David, just as it hit him. 'Jesus, Tony, has Logan convinced the kids to plea?' David knew that although J.T. was sitting right next to him, this was no time for platitudes and he figured J.T. was smart enough to know that too.

'Yes,' said Tony, immediately dashing David's hopes. 'And no,' he finished before looking quickly at his watch.

'Tony,' said David. 'I still don't . . .'

But Tony was already on his feet, lifting his right hand in greeting to two other visitors who had just entered the front door of the diner.

David swivelled in his chair so that he might see them, and blinked twice just to make sure they were real – ADA Amanda Carmichael and behind her the prettiest red-haired teenager David had seen since he first met her mother all those years ago, Chelsea Logan.

49

'Doctor Taylor was adamant,' said a breathless Lisa Cavanaugh, putting away the sugar before walking around the kitchen annexe and handing Nora Kelly a cup of English Breakfast tea. After Sara had called the office to explain she was off to the doctor, with Lisa Cavanaugh (who had swapped shifts with the afternoon nurse) as her companion, Nora had promised she would pop by at lunch – which, of course, she did.

'Sara has to take it easy,' Lisa continued. 'So I am telling you, and my workaholic brother when I can get him on the phone, so that this one here . . .' she said, gesturing at Sara, who was now sitting rather awkwardly on her sofa, '. . . does not do too much!'

'She's right, dear,' said Nora, looking at Sara.

Lisa nodded, before grabbing her bag, flipping her long black hair over her shoulder and heading for the door.

'Keep at her, Nora,' she said, winking. 'And you call

me if you need anything,' she pointed to Sara. 'And tell my brother he is an inconsiderate ass.'

And with that she was gone.

The truth was, Sara was worried – about the baby, about herself, about David and his obsession with this case, about her lack of contribution at work, about what the manipulative Jeffrey Logan might be up to next, and about Nora who, despite her attempts at bravado, was obviously still wracked with the misplaced guilt of 'being responsible' for the McCall woman's fate.

This was not going the way it was supposed to. She was pregnant – a mere three weeks away from giving birth – and she and David were meant to be happy, excited, ecstatic, fulfilled! But ever since Stephanie Tyler's death, David had been different. It was as if a dark cloud had descended upon him, growing thicker and heavier each day. His feeling of responsibility to save those kids, to avenge his friend's death, was now at the point of fixation, despite the danger it might be putting him in, and, by association, her and their unborn baby as well.

David had been away for most of the day and had not yet bothered to call. Lisa had tried his cell three times but got his voice mail at every attempt. And Nora, despite her efforts to make light of it, did not know where he was – which meant he could be anywhere with anyone and, despite herself, Sara saw a quick flash of the beautiful Amanda Carmichael streaking swiftly through her mind.

She re-focused. 'I'm okay, Nora, really.'

Nora smiled. 'No, dear,' she replied. 'No, you are not.'

'The doctor said I would be fine. Just that I have to

rest a little more. The baby is almost to term but Doctor Taylor said she would prefer it if he or she had that extra couple of weeks . . .'

'It's not the baby I am worried about. This is not good for you, Sara. This case, this pressure, young David's determination to . . .' But Nora stopped there, obviously not wanting to state what they both knew to be true.

'What is it about this one?' Sara asked. 'I mean, he has always been determined but even on his toughest of cases, he still manages to see past it – to see *me*.'

'And he still sees you, Sara. It is just that this one – well, there are children involved and he is about to become a father and, sometimes, men like David, they want to make a better world for the child that they have created and that results in their priorities going a little askew. He is afraid, Sara, of not doing enough.'

'I know,' said Sara. 'So afraid that he is not doing enough.'

Nora nodded, before taking Sara's hand and pulling her into a hug.

'I have a bad feeling about this, Nora,' said Sara after a time.

And the normally comforting Nora did not reply – her silence telling Sara she was thinking: *Me too, dear, me too*.

50

'For Christ's sake,' said Amanda Carmichael, staring at the two hugging teenagers before her. The minute Chelsea Logan had walked into the room, J.T. had turned in his seat, climbed over David and run directly towards his sister. And now the pair stood right in the middle of the diner, their heads buried in each other's shoulders, the slight vibrations in their bodies telling David that both were now sobbing.

'Jesus, Tony, everyone is watching. Someone needs to pull those two apart,' Amanda continued. And while her tone was cool, David saw in her eyes the slightest tinge of discomfort – perhaps at being witness to such a raw outpouring of emotion. Or maybe it was embarrassment, considering her job was to see these two kids were separated for the rest of their lives.

'Amanda,' said David, now rising from his bench. 'I am not too sure how or why you swung this but, honestly, I am so grateful.'

'Shut the hell up, Cavanaugh,' she barked, swivelling

on her high heels to address him face to face. Then she swallowed, and David knew that this woman – this incredibly beautiful, highly manipulative, extremely ambitious woman – was trying desperately to 'recover'. And David guessed that as much as she would never admit it, putting these two kids together had got to her.

'Don't for one second think my arranging this little get-together has anything to do with my concern for you or for the Logan children's futures. In case you have forgotten, I am the lead prosecutor in this case and I will do everything in my power to make sure these two murderers are sent away for life.' Another swallow.

'My interest here, Cavanaugh, is not with *if*, but *how* I get this done. Bishop might have told you I had the chance to take a plea, or square off against a man who should have done the world a favour by turning off his pacemaker years ago. But this case is my ticket to the big league, and that ticket is worth all the more if I whip your ass.' She took a step forward then, her body mere inches from his.

'So you can have your five minutes with these matricidal maniacs, and if they consent to withdrawing their statements against you, I will talk to the district judge and get that APO reversed. Then you can defend Dick and Jane here with all the determination you can muster, and then I will bring you down – all three of you – and you will wish that you had made certain decisions differently, and regret your mistakes for the rest of your Goddamned life.'

Every now and again, when the extremeness of a situation calls for it, when the pressure is so tight, the risks so high, the human body has the ability to rise above its current circumstances and transcend to a completely different universe where reality ceases to exist.

As Amanda and Tony turned to join Harrison, and as J.T. and Chelsea took their seat in the bench across from him and instinctively drew themselves into his huddle, David felt it – felt the three of them *remove* themselves from the environment around them so that they might finally say what needed to be said.

While David was terrified that the sheer force of Jeffrey Logan's power might still be enough to paralyse his children into submission, he hoped that this reunion – the combined force of J.T. and Chelsea's dedication to each other and perhaps, ironically, the sense of freedom they felt to be out of their father's house – would finally give them the courage to tell it as it was.

'Okay,' he began, leaning an inch further into their private little group. 'We don't have much time so I am going to cut to the chase and say some things that I believe to be true. These are my opinions, and while I must warn you that I don't have any real evidence substantiating these views, I can promise you, with all my heart, that if you tell me I am right and if you want me to represent you, I will do anything, *everything* in my power to prove these allegations and set you two kids free.'

He was talking like a lawyer and he knew it, but somehow he sensed that was exactly what these kids needed – a grown-up they could lean on, perhaps the only adult they had been able to put their trust in since the death of their mom. And when Chelsea's eyes met her brother's and J.T. gave her a nod, David took this as a cue to continue – which he did, starting at the beginning.

'Your father had been planning it for weeks, months, perhaps even years,' he said. 'His strategy was long and complicated. He knew that beyond all else he had to supply you with a motive for your mother's death,' he said, looking at J.T. 'And so he set about creating the myth that Stephanie was an emotional tyrant – the one who had been abusing you both since birth.'

The kids did nothing bar squeeze each other's hands, which David took as an indication that they were ready for him to continue.

'He compiled his evidence. He started telling Katherine de Castro about Stephanie's relentless need to control. He preyed on Katherine's loyalties knowing she would repeat the stories when asked, taking comfort in the knowledge that she would want to help *him* – and in the process think that she was helping you too.

'And so the next step was getting the evidence – in the form of that hellish home video where he directed your mother to hold a gun to your head.' David saw J.T. flinch. 'And he wrote the script and made you learn your lines and he forced you to play along by . . . by . . .'

'Placing a gun on the table,' finished Chelsea. And in that moment David felt a distinct wave of relief flow through his entire body, for Chelsea had opened the gate and finally let him in.

'He said it was a Smith and Wesson .38 special. He said it was made out of titanium and alloy. He said it weighed less than a pound. He put it in the . . .'

'Gravy boat,' finished David.

'How did you know?' asked a wide-eyed Chelsea.

'I sensed he was controlling you with something, and I knew your mom,' he said. And this explanation was enough.

'We didn't have to learn our lines though,' Chelsea went on, 'because Father had set up one of those machines from work – an electronic autocue which scrolls at a preset pace.'

An autocue, of course! Logan would have had access to one at his studio. He had seen one of these machines before; they emanated a distinct computerised glow which in this case must have been green – not unlike the ultrasound in Doctor Taylor's office.

'Your father held the tape until it was needed,' said David. 'His final preparations for your mother's death being the increases to her life insurance – which he did from your computer, Chelsea, using your username and password so that any investigation would lead straight back to you.'

'Yes, but I didn't know about the life insurance until the night I was arrested. He must have done that while I was at school.'

David nodded. 'And then he set about teaching J.T. how to use the gun – the same high-powered rifle that had always belonged to him. And he did this like he did everything else when it came to your education,' he met J.T.'s eye. 'By forcing you to study the weapon inside and out, by learning its mechanics, so that nothing would be left to chance.'

'Yes,' said J.T., the tears now falling freely down his cheeks, just as David was jolted back into reality by a forceful jab on his shoulder.

'This is taking too long,' said Carmichael, standing over him.

'Five more minutes,' said David.

'No,' said Amanda. 'This love fest has to end now. I need to get Chelsea back to Brockton,' she added, referring to the female juvenile detention unit where Chelsea was being held.

'Come on, Amanda,' said David. 'You want me back in, and in order to do so I need the briefest of consultations with my clients. All I need is five more minutes. Six or seven tops.' He knew he was stretching it.

She looked towards the children. 'You have three,' she said, before walking determinedly away.

'He tested me,' said J.T. 'He made me memorise every component of that gun. He instructed me on how to fire it. He said if I didn't go through with it that he would simply pick up a rifle and kill us all – me, Chelsea and Mom.'

David nodded once again as the boy took a breath, hoping that if there was ever a time that J.T. was going to trust him, that this was going to be it.

'He planned it down to the second,' continued J.T., his boyish voice raising just a notch. 'He made us synchronise our watches every morning before we went to school because he said he did not want us to know exactly which night he planned to do it. He said it could happen today, or tomorrow, or next week, but we had to be always on the ready. He said if we warned our mom he would kill us all,' he repeated. 'He had already loaded the gun. He had locked it in a drawer in the garage so that on the night he was ready, when he came in from work, he could move quickly, out of the car, and take out the gun before meeting me at the bottom of the stairs.

'And on that night we were upstairs, and like every night in recent weeks we were dreading the sound of his car pulling into the drive. But then we heard it, and I went down, *like he told me too*. And then he walked down the hall holding the gun and Chelsea was looking down at me from the landing and we knew what was going to happen. Chelsea started to cry and he grabbed my arm as I tried to run to Mom, who was in the kitchen, exactly where he knew she would be.'

'How did he know that, J.T.?' asked David, his heart pounding hard in his chest. 'How did he know your mom would be sitting where she was, doing what she did?'

'Because that is what she always did before dinner. It was her routine. If she did not do it, he would take it out on us. He made her drink the wine. He said it made her submissive. She had to read the same magazines over and over. They were very old.'

David nodded for J.T. to go on.

'And in the end,' J.T. continued, his voice now a high croaky sob, 'no matter how many threats he made, I could not do it. I knew I had to, but I couldn't. I didn't care if I died. I looked up at Chelsea and she was shaking her head. He told us to shut the hell up and I tried to scream '*No*'. But he placed his hand on my throat and I was scared. Chelsea was crying. And then he turned the gun on her and he whispered that he would shoot her if I did not obey.

'And I *still* could not do it. I hated myself, and was proud of myself all at the very same time. Then he held the gun on Chelsea and released my neck and pulled out the handkerchief from his pocket and told me to rip it in three. He screwed up two small pieces and shoved them in his ears before putting the rest back into his pocket. Then he grabbed me around the neck again and he pushed me HARD,' J.T. caught his breath, '. . . fast, towards the kitchen door. And then he wrapped one arm under my T-shirt around my waist and held the rifle high in the other and then he forced us both through the door with a BANG! And I saw her, I SAW HER. I shouted. And I screamed for Mom to run. I tried to break free, but he slipped his hand under my T-shirt and through the sleeve and forced my right arm up so my finger was locked against the trigger. And then my mom looked at me and she said that everything would be okay. She looked at my father and she begged him please to STOP. And then, I felt the force of his finger against mine. I closed my eyes, TIGHT. And then I heard the loudest noise I had ever heard in my life. And my ears burned like they were on fire. And then I felt the warmth of her blood upon me – and then I felt sick, and then I felt dead.'

Chelsea held him, as David placed his own forehead against J.T.'s. And then J.T., perhaps sensing that time was running out, swallowed hard before taking a breath and finishing his story.

'My father took the handkerchief pieces from his ears and pulled me from the room and then he dragged me to the toilet and flushed them. Chelsea could not stop screaming and my father told her to shut up. Then he grabbed the rest of the handkerchief from his pocket and wiped down the gun and his hands, which were clean from being under my T-shirt in any case, before moving back into the hall and calling 911. And then he called Katherine, and made us go back . . . INTO THE KITCHEN.' He shook his head. 'And then we saw her, and I shut my eyes again and Chelsea was crying and my father said if we did not follow his lead he would kill us too, and if one talked he would kill the other. And then the police arrived and he CONFESSED and we knew, both of us, that this was part of his plan, and that if we did anything that he would kill the other, and that our mom was gone and that she was the only person who could save us and . . .' The boy's head bent down as he fell exhausted against the diner table, and David knew he had finally said his piece.

'You're wrong,' said David. 'Stephanie was not the only one. Your mom . . .' He took a breath. 'She knew, in choosing me, that I would help you. She knew that this was going to happen, which is why she changed her will.'

Chelsea nodded. 'We were scared of Father – that he might kill us all. And I think somehow we thought if we kept quiet about it like he told us to, that he might change his mind. Mom did not say anything, but I think she must have known about the changes he made to her insurance. I also think she found that receipt, the one for Katherine's necklace. And that told her that Father was getting ready – to move on.

'The morning of the day that she died, she asked me if I could borrow a friend's cell phone at school. Father monitored the home telephone, and Mom knew this call would have to go undetected so . . . She told me to find somewhere quiet at lunchtime and call her lawyer, a man named Harrison. And she told me to pretend I was her and to give him specific instructions about how she wanted to change her will.'

David held tight to Chelsea's hand.

'She never thought about herself,' Chelsea went on. 'She only thought about us – and how she could protect us from . . . this.' She lifted her free hand at her surroundings. 'But Father was too smart. He had an answer for everything. And now that Mom is gone, we are . . . we can't . . .'

'No,' said David, taking the girl's hand and squeezing it. 'Your father is a clever man – granted. But in the end, I believe your mother was smarter. She had her own ideas about how to stop him, and I promise you I will see them through.'

Chelsea looked up at him. 'She liked you,' she said after a pause. 'When you won that case last year she told us she was your friend, and that you were the lawyer she would have liked to have been.'

David looked into Chelsea's eyes and saw her there, his old college friend, with the open heart and the big ideals.

'You mom wasn't just a brilliant lawyer, Chelsea,' he said to her, his own eyes now filling with tears. 'She was one of the best people I have ever known, and if the situation had been reversed, if you had been my children, I know she would be sitting here, doing the same for me.'

Ten seconds later Amanda Carmichael, an anxious-looking Tony Bishop behind her, was upon them once again – pulling Chelsea and J.T. from the booth and dragging them to their feet.

'You have two weeks,' she said, causing David's mouth to drop open in shock.

'Two weeks?' he said, not believing what he was hearing. 'That's impossible, Amanda. I have only been back on this case for what . . . fifteen minutes. There is no way I can prepare for trial in a fortnight.'

'The trial was originally scheduled for mid-August, Cavanaugh, and if you hadn't fucked up with the kids' father you would be ready for the showdown now. So if you want me to follow through with helping you reverse that pesky 209A, I suggest you save your arguments for court.'

'Amanda,' David hated to beg, but under the circumstances . . . 'I can't guarantee these kids fair representation if I don't have the time to . . .'

'Time?' she interrupted as she turned to face him before advancing towards him as he rose from the booth. 'Is your schedule full, Cavanaugh?' she asked then. 'You got somewhere else to be from mid-to-late August?'

The thought raced through his head – *of course* he had somewhere else to be. He would be with Sara, for the delivery of their baby, and more likely than not, Amanda Carmichael knew it too.

'No,' he said, the word alien even to him as Tony Bishop's eyes met with his from behind the ADA.

'Two weeks it is then, or considering it is already Tuesday afternoon, thirteen days to be exact,' she said, the slightest of smiles on her porcelain-skinned face.

And despite himself, David nodded. 'I'll be there, Amanda. You have a date.'

51

It was Sinatra. He was singing 'Come Fly With Me'. Deirdre McCall could hear it but she could not see it – or rather, him. She must be back at one of his shows. She loved Frank's shows. She remembered one night at The Sands, she had just got her first gig in the chorus line and Frank was performing in front of a wall-to-wall sell-out crowd. He was wearing a fedora, holding a cigarette, his blue eyes bright under the mellow stage lights. He was singing 'Embraceable You', he was smiling, at *her,* at every starry-eyed woman in the room.

But wait – *no* – that was too long ago. It was back then, before . . . she wasn't sure? Maybe if she could just open her eyes she might be able to . . .

Deirdre McCall concentrated – a task that seemed even harder than usual. Sinatra's voice was still there, but now she heard other noises too – the beep of a machine, the distant sounds of footsteps, more voices somewhere beyond. Slowly she prised her eyelids apart, the first slit of light shocking her pupils into contraction. She shut her eyes again and then tried once more, this time preparing herself for the force of the overhead fluorescents.

She was in a hospital – that much she knew. But not like before, when they had her whole body in traction. She lifted her hand to her forehead, dragging the drip with it. She felt the wad of bandages – thick, tight. Something had happened, something new, with her head or whatever was left of it.

And then an image shot across her consciousness, a blinding, powerful vision that wrenched her cruelly from the past. She could see the setting sun, the dust-covered street, Mrs Abercrombie watering her lawn just across the way. She was walking, slowly, wanting the journey home to last those extra few minutes. She lifted her arm to Mrs Abercrombie who smiled and yelled something about the heat and then she saw them – *no,* she *heard* them first. Not them. Their car. The screech. And her nose contracted at the smell of burning rubber. A now frowning Mrs Abercrombie moved across her lawn to get a better look. Deirdre turned, and squinted, and lifted her left hand to act as a visor against the sun. And then the car – the big, long, red sedan carrying four, maybe more, dark-haired young men – swerved right, straight towards her and she jumped back, off the pavement and onto a patch of grass. But then the young man in the back seat had his arm out the window – a long, slender arm with a thick silver hand. But it wasn't his hand. It was a gun. She knew this because she had seen many of them before. And even though it wasn't him it *was.* It was Jason. Jason was going to shoot her and follow through on his threats after all these years. She saw the spark. And she smelt the burning. She lowered her hand and saw that it was covered in blood. And then . . . then she heard Sinatra.

Run.

Run. The thought raced through her head like a tornado. It was ridiculous of course; she could barely focus, let alone run.

But, run she had to. This much she knew. She had survived her son's attempts to kill her twice, but something told her the third time she would not be so lucky.

She yanked the cannula from her hand, ignoring the blood that followed, and removed the sticky pads from her chest. She kicked the blanket from her legs and forced herself to a sitting position before waiting for the dizziness to subside. She registered the small cupboard in the corner which held a soft cotton dress she had owned for as long as she could remember.

Tracey has been here, she thought, and smiled. *She must have left the Sinatra tape playing in the cassette player by my bed. She brought the dress, just in case I . . .*

But the very same thought now made her panic. If her young friend returned, she would surely prevent her from *running*.

In that moment, just as Ol' Blue Eyes took a breather before slipping into a smooth and easy version of 'I've Got You Under My Skin', she knew that running was only *part* of the solution. If she was going to survive, she had to work out a way to stop her son for good. She would have to do what she *should* have done all those years ago, when she could have gone to the authorities and had him committed – perhaps even treated – for whatever made him like he was.

And so, as she unwrapped the still bloodied bandages from her now pounding brow, and assessed the damage in the scratched cupboard door mirror before her, she decided, then and there, that she would finally fulfil her maternal obligations, as unspeakable as they may be. It may be too late for 'treatment', but it was not too late, she decided, to put an end to her son's path of carnage, once and for all.

52

'Sara,' said David, clasping his cell phone hard against his ear. He was on his way back from Plymouth, a sour-faced Harrison doing ten over the speed limit beside him – obviously determined to get back to Boston and 'wash' himself of this whole bloody mess as quickly as was humanly possible.

'David,' she said.

He felt comfort in the sound of her voice, and a dire need to tell her what he had learned. 'I called the office and Nora said you were still at home. Are you okay? What did Doctor Taylor say?'

'I'm fine,' she replied, but her voice was flat – and David felt incredibly guilty for not calling earlier. 'It is just a stomach virus. Doctor Taylor said I am overdoing it – that I need to rest if the baby is to go to term.'

'Oh God, Sara, I am so sorry. This is my fault. I should have insisted you stop work earlier.'

'No,' she said, now with a trace of irritation. 'I have actually felt really calm the last few months. Work hasn't been too bad – since we stopped working on the . . .'

She was about to say 'Logan case' and David knew it. And now he had thrown them back in. *But these were exceptional circumstances*, he argued with himself. *This was not a case but a responsibility – a life or death commitment to a brave old friend.*

'Where have you been?' she asked, interrupting his thoughts.

'In Plymouth,' he answered.

'*What?*'

'Sara,' he began, now unable to hold back. He loved her so much and knew that she would be the one person who understood just what an opportunity this was to save these kids, *to bring Logan down*. 'You won't believe what happened. I was picked up – or more to the point abducted – by a guy from Tony's office.' He glanced sideways at Harrison, not giving a damn if the pole-up-his-ass lawyer could hear. 'He took me to Plymouth – to see Tony and J.T. and . . . then Amanda Carmichael turned up.'

'You spent the day with the ADA?' bit Sara.

'Yes . . . I mean, no. She had Chelsea with her. The kids are going to withdraw their statements against us. And Carmichael is going to get the judge to withdraw the APO.'

'And why the hell would she do that?'

'Because she wants us back in.'

'Us?' asked Sara.

'Yes. She wants to come up against me.'

'She wants to come up against you,' repeated Sara.

'Yes. In court. It's what she has wanted from the very

beginning, and lucky for us that woman never lets go of what she wants.'

There was silence.

'Sara?'

'I'm here,' she said.

'The kids told me the truth, Sara – everything from beginning to end. They implicated their father. They told me how it went down. And I know we are short on time, and I know we still don't have any concrete proof,' he took a breath, 'but I also know we can find it. If we look hard enough, if we follow Stephanie's leads and . . .'

'How short?' she asked then.

'Sorry?'

'On time – how short are we?'

He hesitated, knowing there was no easy way to tell her. 'Two weeks,' he said.

'*The trial starts in two weeks?*' she said.

'It was Amanda's condition – on helping us lift the APO.'

Silence.

'Sara?'

More silence.

'Sara?'

But Sara said nothing – before hanging up the phone.

53

The following day

Whirrr . . . whirrr . . . whirr . . .

It was the only sound in the room – the Mannix family dishwasher playing its own rhythmic, hypnotic tune.

Marie and the four Mannix boys had just left – Joe's wife running against the clock to get them to their respective summer camps on time. The breakfast table was now spotlessly clean despite having, just moments ago, been covered by myriad breakfast cereals and beverages. And the room still smelt of traces of coffee and toast and honey, as David sat anxiously waiting for Mannix to read the two children's statements which had been faxed to David by Tony Bishop late last night.

'Jesus,' said Joe, as he finished Chelsea's statement and placed it on the scratched red formica table before him.

'I know,' said David. 'They have taken it all back, Joe – they have let me in.'

David told Joe everything – from Logan using

Chelsea's computer to change his wife's life insurance to his use of the autocue in that telling home video. From his schooling the kids on how the murder would go down, to his constant threats to kill them all if they refused to play by his rules. David relayed J.T.'s version of the events of that night in detail – telling Joe about J.T.'s protests, Logan's use of the handkerchief and his eventual storming into the kitchen so that he might use his son as a 'shield' while he forced his finger onto the trigger. He spoke of the aftermath – of the disposal of the handkerchief, the further threats and the calls to 911 and Katherine de Castro, before telling Joe how he 'safeguarded' his own plan by offering the police a confession.

Joe sat silent, taking it all in, not once interrupting until David had finally finished – until he told him of Stephanie's instructions to her daughter that she borrow a classmate's cell phone to call her mother's lawyers and change her will, and how this and other clues suggested that Stephanie had been awaiting her own murder for months.

'Unbelievable,' said Joe.

'I know.'

'It explains it all – including J.T.'s ear problems but the lack of shoulder pain or bruising.'

David nodded. 'Logan got himself in and under J.T.'s oversized T-shirt. He bent down and rested the rifle on his own shoulder while he forced his son to be the one to fire.'

'We should have checked Logan's shoulder on the night,' said Joe, blaming himself.

'He had a quick physical at Suffolk County, Joe,'

countered David. 'The rifle didn't burn his shirt because it was under J.T.'s clothing. Logan may have been in pain, but there was no way he was going to rat himself out.'

Joe nodded. 'So in a way,' he went on, 'Logan's biggest mistake to date was to have both children arrested – because as soon as Chelsea was "safe" behind bars at Brockton, J.T. was no longer afraid to speak.'

'And vice versa,' agreed David. 'But Logan is going for broke, Joe. He wants both of his children sent away for good. And as for the kids, well, despite their new places of residence they are still terrified, Joe. They have lived their entire lives watching him manipulate their futures. The man never loses, and even now I can tell they still think he will find a way to destroy them.'

'Which is understandable, considering he has done a pretty good job to date,' said Joe.

David nodded.

'The one thing I can't get,' said Joe after a pause, 'is why the hell Stephanie didn't run. I mean, if she knew this was going to happen, why didn't she get those kids out of there. Why didn't she . . .?'

'I don't know, Joe,' said David. 'I guess maybe she was terrified – scared to the bone – of the repercussions of defying him, of him taking her two children's lives.'

'So she just sits there, waiting to die?'

Truth be told, David found this one thing difficult to swallow too. The Stephanie he knew was a fighter. But then again, as it had been stressed so often of late, that was the Stephanie he *knew* – not the one she had been forced to become.

'She gave her life for her kids, Joe.'

'And in doing so she left them with that maniac.'

'What choice did she have?'

'She should have gone to the police.'

'And risk her husband shooting her kids?'

'There had to be another way, David.'

'Yeah, well maybe under the circumstances we can forgive her for not being able to find it.'

Joe nodded once again, before lifting his eyes from the table. 'You have a problem,' he said.

'You think?'

'No – what I mean to say is, you have a shitload of problems but one huge one which at least at this point appears kind of insurmountable.'

'We don't have any proof that what the kids tell me is true,' said David, reading his mind.

'Exactly,' said Joe. 'There is no way Carmichael would have put you lot together if she thought there was any chance of you actually being able to win this thing. The forensics still point singularly at the boy. The kids go implicating their father and she will paint them as maniacal little psychopaths – two greedy Machiavellian geniuses who murdered their mother and then pointed their finger at their famous do-gooder dad so that they might get their hands on that seriously substantial inheritance.'

'You think Carmichael will use greed as a motive?'

'I think she can take her pick – greed, rebellion, anger at their mother's abusiveness, anger at their dad's failure to get them out.'

'But the video . . .' David began.

'. . . is a gift for the prosecution and you know it,' finished Joe. 'That green light/gun in the gravy boat bullshit will get you nowhere. It's the kids' word against their father's and if I was an average Joe, forgive the pun, I'd be backing America's most loved TV hero every time.'

Joe punctuated this point by reaching behind him to grab two copies of *Vanity Fair* magazine off the kitchen counter, before taking the one on top, and sliding it across the table to his friend.

'Jesus,' said David, glancing at the cover for the very first time – his eyes taking in that powerful shot of the seafaring Jeffrey Logan before glancing down towards the accompanying cover line which read '*Jeffrey Logan – a father's fight for justice*'.

He shook his head. 'There has to be something I can do, Joe. I am running out of time.' David realised then that he had forgotten to tell Joe about his two-week deadline – Amanda Carmichael's parting 'condition' in return for her help in reversing that APO.

'Shit,' said Joe. 'Monday the thirteenth is twelve days away.' And then David saw Joe's eyes light up with a new sense of realisation. 'That means right in the middle of the trial you will be . . . How does Sara feel about all this?'

'We argued,' said David. 'Yesterday, after I told her. But she came around last night, said she would do everything she could to help, from home – until the baby comes. It's just that Logan gets under her skin and . . .'

'She has every right to be scared of him, David – and maybe you should take a leaf out of her book. You don't have to do this, you know. There are other lawyers, who will have more than enough grounds to have the case postponed.'

'No, Joe. Stephanie asked for me. She cried out for help in that video, she sent that newspaper clipping and brochure to tip us off.' Joe had called Arthur while David was AWOL yesterday – confirming the fingerprints on the Chatham brochure belonged to Stephanie.

'And maybe there was more. Maybe there were other clues that I still haven't picked up on, messages she left that I'm not smart enough to see.'

Then Joe did something David did not expect. He picked up the second magazine, the one with what looked to be a picture of a young Julia Roberts on the cover, before sliding that towards him as well.

'*Vanity Fair*, October 1993 – Stephanie was reading it when she died. Not this copy, of course. That blood-covered piece of evidence is under lock and key at headquarters. I had this one couriered from Conde-Nast late yesterday after Katherine de Castro made her call.'

'De Castro?' said David. 'I don't understand.'

'De Castro is showing some signs of coming around,' said Joe, '. . . which could play to your advantage. But before I get to that, flip to the middle – the page where I bent back the corner.'

David did as his detective friend asked, landing on an article by the renowned celebrity columnist Dominick Dunne. It was a story on Sunny von Bülow – the mega-wealthy socialite who fell into a mysterious coma back in 1980.

'The magazine was open at that page when Stephanie was shot,' said Joe, and immediately David knew that Stephanie had been calling for his help once again.

'Sunny von Bülow's husband Claus was accused of

attempting to murder her,' said David, the pieces falling into place. 'They arrested him for allegedly poisoning her with insulin. But he got off on appeal and inherited her millions and he . . .'

'Still roams free today,' said Joe.

David said nothing, until: 'She was telling me her husband was her killer, Joe. I have to find a way to do this.'

'I know. But if you go down this road, David, you have to remember something else that Stephanie has taught you – about what happens when you take on the enemy, when you climb way out on that limb.'

'And what is that?' asked David, not sure he really wanted to know.

'That everything comes at a price, my friend. Everything.'

54

'I'm sorry I'm late,' said Katherine de Castro as she took a seat across from Jeffrey Logan. Jeffrey had called late the night before and left a message on her home voice mail saying that he wanted to meet her for breakfast at the upmarket Fairmont Copley Plaza Hotel at eight to discuss their lucrative new network deal and the equally as substantial syndication deals that would follow. And despite her reservations – hell, her downright anxiety – at accepting such an invitation, Katherine knew there was no way she could not, for she was still Jeffrey's business partner and these new deals, negotiated under such highly unusual circumstances, were nothing short of miraculous.

'Don't apologise,' said Jeffrey. 'Although, I have to admit, given we missed each other at the studio yesterday, I feared you were, you know, a little embarrassed by my recent gift and as such perhaps a trace uncomfortable about meeting me here this morning.' He smiled.

'Uncomfortable?' she said, wiggling in her seat. 'Of

course not, Jeffrey. We have known each other for close to half of our lives. But I must say, in regards to the gift, I don't think I can . . .'

'Nonsense,' he said, waving his hand in protest. 'You deserve it, Katherine.'

And Katherine found herself wondering if a Cartier diamond bracelet was what most executives gave their business partners as thank you gifts.

'Jeffrey,' she said, 'honestly, it is too much. Your money – it should be going towards your children's defence.'

'I told you, Katherine,' he lowered his voice a little. 'We have decided to plea.'.

'For their ongoing care then.'

'Sadly or not, Katherine, the good US taxpayers are up for that hefty bill.'

Katherine sat back in her seat, unsure as to how to take this last comment.

'Look,' said Jeffrey, perhaps reading her confusion, 'you know how much I love my kids, but truth be told, they did plan and carry out the murder of my wife. They are sick, Katherine – terribly, terribly sick. And I fear that unless they are incarcerated they might try something like this again.'

'You think your kids would turn on you?' she asked in shock.

'No, no, of course not. But those years of abuse, they had to take their toll in some fashion. They are disturbed, Katherine – deeply, deeply disturbed, and until they learn to deal with their feelings I would suggest it is better for all concerned that they are securely removed from the general public – for their own sakes.'

And for yours. The thought stole into Katherine's brain.

'Besides.' He smiled, before leaning across the table. 'Money is not an object. Stephanie's share in Rockwell Wineries has finally been transferred to me. So I have more than enough – to help my children, and show my gratitude and . . . devotion to you.'

'Jeffrey, I . . .' she began, the bile now rising in her throat.

'No,' he interrupted, taking her hand and squeezing it. 'I am embarrassed to say, Katherine, that this is more than just a little hard for me. *Me*,' he lifted his other arm to his chest in a dramatic gesture of irony, '. . . Doctor Jeff, relationships expert extraordinaire.' He smiled again.

'But if you will indulge me, if you will deign to hear me out, I think I can finally voice what I desperately need to say.'

Jeffrey met her eye, and Katherine felt herself shudder, and then Jeffrey smiled – either in delight at her physical reaction, or perhaps, at the power he had to unsettle her.

'For many years, Katherine, I lived in a house filled with fear and trepidation. My entire existence was devoted to protecting my children, my every thought was of how I might negotiate the minefield that was life with a woman filled with anger and frustration and rage. And, rightly or wrongly, I forgot what it was like to feel the simple comforts that come from an affinity with someone with a good and generous heart.

'It has been so long,' he said, waving away an approaching waiter so that he might finish what he had started, 'that I have allowed myself to relax.'

Katherine wondered how in the hell that was possible given his two teenage children were currently facing life sentences for murder.

'But, now that Stephanie is gone, I realise that I feel – perhaps *have* felt for a very long time – an attraction to you, Katherine – to your kindness, your intelligence, and, in all truthfulness, your beauty as a strong and vibrant woman.'

Katherine felt her stomach turn.

'I want our relationship to change, Katherine,' he said, caressing her fingers then. 'I want it to grow. I want you to know that now that I have secured the inheritance, now that *I* have consolidated these deals . . .' and sadly, that part was true, Jeffrey had negotiated the latest broadcast contracts with little assistance from her – largely because he had not made her aware of the meetings or telephone conversations that had been conducted in the course of such negotiations, '. . . that you never have to worry about financial security for the rest of your life. I can look after you, Katherine. I *want* to look after you.'

'Jeffrey,' she said, pulling her hand away. She was starting to panic – half of her wanting to run, the other half terrified of what such a reaction would trigger. 'This is so very . . . unexpected. We have a working relationship, a good one, and I am not sure if you are perhaps confusing my recent support – of you, of your children – for something else.' It was the best she could manage.

'Nonsense,' said Logan. 'Of course I have appreciated your support but this is not about Chelsea or J.T. We have an opportunity here, Katherine, to start a new and wonderful life alone.'

Alone.

'And, call me old-fashioned, but I want the woman in my life to be able to relax, to fulfil the passions she has not had the time to explore because of the rigorous nature of her work. Which is all my fault, by the way – the hours you have been working. You have built me up to become an all-American phenomenon, Katherine, and supporting you – giving you some freedom – is the very least I can do in return.'

And then, just as Katherine felt her head begin to spin, just as the waiter approached again, this time with à la carte menus and a pitcher of iced water, Jeffrey's cell phone rang – the unmistakable jingle of *The Doctor Jeff Show* theme, amusing nearby patrons who had recognised the famous celebrity in their midst, but had the 'I take breakfast in one of Boston's finest hotels' upper-class decorum not to approach him.

'Logan,' he said, lifting his right pointer finger to Katherine as if to say '*this is just a pause in our negotiations*'.

'Yes, what is it, Charles?' he asked.

And then there was silence, as the voice on the other end of the line delivered what appeared to be some very disturbing news.

'I don't believe this,' he said, his face now filling with colour. 'You are my attorney and I hired you to handle this, Charles. How is this possible? Did the man breach his restraining order?

'*What do you mean it was reversed?*

'The children? But I am their parent. They do not think for themselves, for God's sake.'

Katherine recoiled from the table.

'For fuck's sake, Charles.' Jeffrey lowered his voice. 'Don't tell me there is nothing you can do. This is completely unacceptable.'

Another pause, as Jeffrey ran his white-knuckled hand through his smooth, dark hair.

'All right, I've heard enough. You go and find out where I stand legally as the man who is supposed to fit the bill for this cockamamie defence and see where my children stand when they are left without a penny.

'And as for Cavanaugh,' he added, as Katherine saw his hand bunch tightly into a fist. 'You can leave that asshole to me.'

Other men would have reacted differently – other, lesser men driven by the neanderthal impulses of rage. *But not Jeffrey Logan, no, sir*, he thought to himself as the valet brought his car around to the front of the hotel, for despite his *considerable* displeasure it had only taken seconds for Logan to contain his anger and formulate a plan of attack.

That being said, his train of thought continued as he tipped the valet a tenner and climbed into his new Mercedes CLK class cabriolet, this latest piece of news had unnerved him. If he was truly honest with himself, which he had always had the wisdom to be, he would acknowledge the fact that the old (and pleasant) low-lying urge, the one that he had forced into dormancy so long ago, had reared its head – just a little.

It came in the form of the guns – visually, sensually – the way they felt when he caressed them, ran his fingers down their barrels, enjoyed the weight of them in his hands. And then there was the psychological cross-referencing – the source of the irritation with the means to eradicate it. Cavanaugh, guns, guns, Cavanaugh – and so on.

All right, he told himself as he headed towards his intended destination, *you have had your fun for the day*. And he gave himself another mental pat on the back for being able to turn this 'negative' into a pleasant mini fantasy.

Not that it would be a negative for long, he reminded himself, *for I know how to flip, slide and turn with the best of them, and the guns would not be needed – at least, not yet.*

'Okay,' said David, removing his jacket to pace around Arthur's office. 'So what do we know?'

After leaving Joe's, David had headed directly for the office. Sara was going to work from home until the baby came, which meant she was on conference while David, Arthur and intermittently Nora were formulating the 'game' plan from Arthur's now sun-filled office.

'We know that Jeffrey Logan was born Jason Nagol,' Arthur began. 'And grew up to be an obsessive young gun enthusiast with a dire need to control those around him – namely his mother and father, both of whom he has attempted to kill – his father, so far, successfully.'

They all took a breath, instinctively knowing that poor Nora still felt responsible for her role in the events that led up to Deirdre McCall's shooting.

'I called Ms McCall's friend Tracey late yesterday and she said her condition was still unchanged,' said Nora, the slightest trace of distress in her voice.

David nodded for Arthur to go on.

'We also know that Nagol must have what appears to be an extremely impressive collection of weapons – judging by the number Mr Blackmore suggests he has sold him, and the other guns we can assume he has purchased from additional sellers around the country. We know that he is fond of using aliases that are an anagram of his last name – with a penchant for choosing the letter 'J' as the first letter in his Christian name. And we also know that he laundered his own rifle – the personalised Mark V Deluxe – so that he might use it to murder his wife.'

'Correct,' said David, picking up his pace as the adrenalin started to flow.

'Psychologically,' Sara piped in on speaker, 'we know he is the ultimate control freak. According to Barbara Wong-McGregor, he sees himself as the definitive alpha male.'

Early this morning, after a night of soul searching and numerous apologies to Sara for failing to check on her earlier, David had not had the heart to argue when his incredibly understanding and 'desperate to help' partner said she could still have a role in the lead-up to trial. Having promised she would stay at home and keep her working hours to a minimum, Sara had then come up with the idea of asking Barbara to compile a comprehensive psychological profile of a sociopath such as Logan, which the dedicated expert said she was more than happy to do – starting by giving Sara some immediate insights before promising to compose a more detailed report as quickly as she could manage it.

'Barbara suggests Logan's IQ is extremely high. He has the innate ability to read people – which he uses, some might say for 'good' on his television show, but for much more sinister purposes when it comes to manipulating his family and any who intend to cross him.

'He knows how to get under people's skin,' she added, and David knew she was talking from experience. 'He finds people's weaknesses and he uses them to his advantage. He thinks one step ahead at all times, hopscotching to the position which will give him the greatest advantage.'

'Which makes you wonder what he is up to now, lad,' said Nora to David, given they all knew Logan's lawyer, the elderly Charles Harrison, would have had word of the Logan children's latest decision on who would represent them in court. 'There is no way he could force them to . . .?'

'No, Nora,' said David. 'The children are set. They will refuse to see him, which is their prerogative. I have offered to represent them for free so money is not an issue. The law states that in the end it is the defendant's call who stands up for them at trial, especially in a case where juveniles are facing serious charges in an adult court.'

Nora nodded.

'What else?' asked Arthur, getting them back on track.

'We believe he is making advances towards Katherine de Castro,' said Sara.

'Yes,' said David. 'And given her call to Joe yesterday we can take a guess that she is feeling a little less than comfortable with how this whole thing is going down.'

'Do you think it is safe to approach her?' asked Sara.

'I think we have no choice. Unfortunately, the time to approach anyone subtly has passed.'

'Then let me be the one to do it,' suggested Sara.

David saw Nora shoot him a look. 'No, Sara. I can handle it,' he said.

'I am sure you can, but no matter how hard you try, you are not going to come across as a woman who is sensitive to her fears. We got on well that afternoon at her house, David, we had a natural rapport. I can do it all from here,' she insisted. 'I can call her, feel her out, see if she wants to meet for a coffee.'

Nora was still giving him the eye.

'Okay,' he consented, his eyes falling away from his obviously displeased PA. 'But let's start with a phone call – nothing more – and we'll discuss how it should play out from there.'

'Okay,' said Sara. 'Done.' And in that moment David loved her more than ever.

'So what *don't* we know?' Arthur asked, once again keeping them focused.

'Well, there is the unexplainable link to the Asian Boyz – but Joe and Frank are working on that.' David took a breath. 'And we still don't know what that brochure means – the one Stephanie sent me for the Chatham Bars Inn.'

'Maybe one of us should head down there,' suggested Sara.

'Maybe,' agreed Arthur. 'But it would be best if we had an idea of what we are looking for before we did. We don't have the time to go running around blind.'

'Then I shall call the Chatham Bars Inn,' suggested Nora. 'I shall ask if a Logan or Nagol or Golan is known to them. And if there is a link . . . well, I would be happy to make the trip south to investigate.'

'Nora . . .' began Sara through the speaker.

'I know what you are thinking, dear, but I would really like the opportunity to make amends.'

'There are no "amends" to make,' David insisted, moving towards his trusted secretary and taking her hand. 'You are half the reason we have made such headway in this case.'

'I am not sure Ms McCall would agree,' Nora said, her green eyes once again filled with regret.

'David's right,' said Arthur. 'You've been a terrific help as always, Nora. And we need you here, holding the fort while we all prepare for trial. No matter how much we think we know, this isn't going to be easy.' His eyes shot across to David.

'I know,' David agreed. 'But even the smartest of criminals have their weak point, Arthur – including sociopathic geniuses like Jeffrey Logan. And besides,' he said, turning to meet his mentor's eye, 'something tells me there is one thing that gives me a distinct advantage.'

'And what is that, son?' asked Arthur.

'Logan is the typical bully. He has the habit of carefully picking his victims – preying on women and children and those without the resources to fight the bastard back. But I am not afraid of him, Arthur. In fact, the prospect of facing off against him, the idea of finally nailing the monster who forced his son to kill his own mother with a rifle powerful enough to split her in two is . . . well,' he paused, '. . . in all honesty, he can bring it on.'

55

He did not flinch when he said it. He did not hesitate or pause or suggest by the tone of his voice that what he was proposing was anything out of the ordinary. And Amanda Carmichael knew she should be celebrating; she understood that what Jeffrey Logan was offering would consolidate her victory. But she had to admit that, despite the considerable benefits, Logan's suggestion had made her skin crawl, and if she wasn't the career driven prosecutor that she was, she might have even described his offer as repulsive.

'Forgive me for being surprised, Doctor,' she said. 'I am appreciative, of course, and I understand your motives are in the best interests of your children.'

'Of course.'

'But – and I have to ask this – I do not want to go down this path if your offer is, how shall I put it . . . a knee-jerk reaction to your children's decision to seek independent counsel?'

'Knee jerk?' he said with amusement. 'If there is one

thing I am not, Miss Carmichael, it is a person prone to acting on impulse.' Amanda did not doubt it; she had the feeling every move this man made was calculated right down to the tiniest detail, his latest proposal included.

'You understand that your children's attorneys will need to be informed of your decision. I have a legal obligation to provide them with a list of . . .'

'Of course,' said Logan again, with the same casual assurance.

'And we will need some time to prepare.'

'I'll look forward to it,' he said.

A pause.

'Well,' she said, in an attempt to stem the awkwardness, 'I'll be in touch,' she added, starting to rise from her desk, 'over the next few days, to set up some appointments.'

Jeffrey Logan smiled. 'It's been a pleasure,' he said, as he extended his hand to shake hers.

She extended hers in return, and as Jeffrey Logan held on to her palm for that touch too long, she had to admit that just for the briefest of seconds, she sensed that she was dealing with the devil.

Deirdre McCall was missing. Joe got the call just after lunch. After apologising for not calling earlier, Detective Michael Lopez from the LVPD explained that the patient was last seen in her hospital room at about 6pm yesterday evening but that he was only informed of her MIA status after the hospital's security staff had failed to find the woman on the premises and had confirmed with a Miss Tracey Scabo that she had not returned to her apartment.

'We went to her place a couple of hours ago,' he told Joe. 'It was tidy but empty. The bed hadn't been slept in, there was no coffee in the pot. My guess is the woman has bailed – probably scared those Asian Boyz who popped her a few weeks ago might come back to finish the job.'

And Joe sensed that was exactly what Deirdre McCall was fearing.

'You got anything else you wanna tell me that might help with my investigations, Lieutenant?' asked Lopez, obviously curious as to why Joe had been less than forthcoming in regards to his interest in a sixty-something dancing teacher who lived on the other side of the country.

'We believe we know someone who might have a bone to pick with her.'

'Anyone I know?' asked Lopez.

Joe almost laughed at the irony. 'Let's just say the person in question is a man of many talents.'

Lopez said nothing, obviously sensing that Joe would tell him more if he could. 'I don't mean to push, Lieutenant, but this woman was shot on my watch.'

'I know, Lopez, and I apologise for the cloak-and-dagger stuff, but if you could keep me posted on your efforts to find her, I promise I will fill you in as soon as I am able.'

Lopez read between the lines. 'You got a live one?'

'You could say that.'

'Would it help if I pulled some of the Asian Boyz in for questioning? I don't have anything concrete on them but I am sure our guys from narcotics could find something to hold them, at least for a day or two.'

'That would be a huge help,' said a grateful Joe.

'All right then,' said Lopez.

'Thanks, Detective,' replied Joe.

'Don't mention it. You know what they say, one less asshole on the street is . . .'

'. . . one less asshole on the street,' finished Joe. 'Keep in touch, Lopez.'

'Will do.'

'I'm sorry, David,' said Sara, resting her head against his shoulder. It was late and the air in the room was stagnant, despite the fact that David had opened every window in their apartment to try to give Sara a little relief from the heat.

'First McCall's disappearance,' she said, referring to Joe's call to inform them of Lopez's communication late this afternoon, 'and now Katherine. She just didn't want to talk to me. It was so awkward. When we first met I felt like we made some sort of connection, but this afternoon it was like she could not hang up the phone fast enough.'

David understood how Sara was feeling. For days now he had been hoping Deirdre McCall would wake up so that she might provide that desperately needed link between her son Jason and his new identity as Jeffrey Logan – but he never guessed his wish would be granted and then stolen away from him almost immediately, when the obviously terrified woman came out of her coma and literally ran for her life.

Katherine de Castro's dismissal of Sara was a second blow. Joe had been right. While de Castro had made moves to come forward with whatever she knew, or at the very least suspected, her fear had got the better of her also. She had become yet another victim of Jeffrey Logan's despotism – and another potential 'life line' who had fallen through the cracks.

'It's not your fault that de Castro dismissed you, Sara,' said David, pulling her a little closer. 'I think part of her wants to reach out, but she is just too scared.'

'She's petrified,' returned Sara.

He felt her nuzzle in to him just that little bit more.

'I'm sorry, Sara,' he said, '. . . about putting you in this situation, only weeks before the baby is due.'

'And I am sorry for overreacting,' she said, referring to her hanging up on him and their subsequent argument last night. 'It is just that Logan has a way of getting to me – with what he said about Carmichael and my pregnancy and . . .'

Last night Sara had come clean to David about her discussion with Logan at Quincy Marketplace all those weeks ago. And David had finally told her about Logan's 'counter-attack' on his own sensibilities – his claiming David had impregnated Sara long before she was ready to put her career on the backburner.

'And you were being so distant,' Sara went on. 'I was worried you thought I was not strong enough to cope.'

'You are strong enough for both of us,' he said.

'Well, I wouldn't go that far.' She smiled as she held his hand on her stomach. 'But we have definitely got your back.'

They sat in silence for a while, taking comfort in one another's embrace.

'We are going to run out of time,' David said after a while, knowing that jury selection would begin next week and his priority at that stage would be making sure they secured the best panel of twelve possible.

'I know,' she said.

But he did not reply.

'I want to stand up for Chelsea,' she said then.

David turned towards her. 'No, Sara. No way.'

'No, listen to me, David. It makes sense that the children have some sort of independent counsel. I went to see Doctor Taylor this afternoon and she said my blood pressure was back to normal and that all was looking fine. She now thinks the wait could be longer than we first expected, and that three weeks could well run into four.'

But David was still shaking his head.

'You know what I'm like, David,' she went on. 'Sitting at home during the trial will be way more stressful for me than being involved in it. If Doctor Taylor is right, I could be there for all of the prosecution's case, and some of ours as well. You *know* I can be of help. Just my presence in the courtroom – a pregnant woman holding Chelsea's hand – will show the jury that we truly believe these kids can be trusted.'

He looked at her.

'Besides,' she said, perhaps sensing that in the very least she had his ear. 'I irritate her.'

'You irritate who?'

'Amanda Carmichael. I unnerve her simply because I have what she does not.'

'I think falling pregnant is the last thing on that ambitious woman's mind, Sara.'

'I am not talking about the baby, silly,' she said. 'I am talking about you.'

David was already shaking his head. 'The only thing that woman wants to do is kick my ass.'

'And the only thing I want to do is kick hers back.'

They could not help but smile at each other.

'I'm not saying yes,' David said then, wrapping his arms around her.

'But you *are* saying maybe,' Sara replied, before lifting her chin to kiss him. 'And that is good enough for now, Mr Cavanaugh – that is good enough for now.'

56

In the Commonwealth of Massachusetts, jurors are empanelled according to a process known as the One Day/One Trial system. First trialled in Middlesex County in 1980, the system expanded the number of those eligible to sit for jury duty by eliminating many of the usual exemptions. It was also designed to make jury service less cumbersome by promising those selected that they would either serve one day or, if the proceedings were likely to run over that one day – one trial only. Prospective jurors are selected at random from the lists of residents supplied annually to the Office of Jury Commissioner by each of the 351 cities and towns within Massachusetts. In the case of the Logan trial, an unusually high 400 summonses were sent out before a final list of 150 were requested to attend the Suffolk County Superior Court for the meticulous selection process. That process, which began in the massive, high-ceilinged jury pool room before moving to a specified courtroom, would eventually see the large group reduced to sixteen, twelve of whom (the other four would eventually be named as alternates) would go on to decide the fate of the two defendants.

It was a long, generally exhausting process, during which both the Commonwealth and the defence would call on specialists to help them use their sixteen peremptory strikes (one for each potential juror) to maximum effect. And in David's case that expert came in the form of the brightly dressed Phyllis Vecchio, a large, garrulous woman with a mouth like a sewer and a mind as sharp as a tack.

'You're fucked,' said Phyllis, just as the judge called for the luncheon adjournment and she and David followed the group of sixty remaining potential jurors now moving excitedly from the courtroom. Arthur had gone back to the office to return some calls while David and Phyll planned to do some more brainstorming over lunch.

'Jesus, Phyll,' said David, whispering in the woman's ear. 'Selection has barely started. How can we be fucked already?'

'For Christ's sake,' said Phyll with a roll of her eyes. 'Have you learned nothing from my years of unparalleled advice?' And despite her undeniable self-confidence, David knew Phyll's tongue was firmly in her cheek.

'Look at the . . .' she began, but then held that thought as they reached the elevators and, taking note of the small placard near the now opening doors which reminded all that cases should not be discussed inside the confined space of an elevator, remained silent until they reached the ground floor.

'Look at the high ratio of women to men,' Phyll went on, her fuchsia stilletos clicking on the tiled lobby floor. 'Look at their ages, their dress code, the huge fucking stars in their bright fucking eyes. That's the Doctor Jeff fan club right there, David,' she said, as they hit the front doors and moved outside into the sunshine. 'You saw the looks on their faces this morning. These woman are greasing their pants to get on this jury for one reason and one reason only – they want to get close to their favourite shrink, the same George Clooney lookalike they dream about fucking every night after they put their children into bed and their slob of a husband lies snoring like a hippo beside them.'

And, at least on this point, David knew she was right.

'The thing is, David,' Phyll continued, directing him towards a café at the bottom of the steps that led up to Pemberton Square, 'these women are going to believe everything the TV star tells them. If he says his wife was the devil incarnate then they are going to swallow it whole.'

'But we've already discussed this, Phyll. I have no intention of calling Logan and there is no way he will ruin his reputation as the concerned father by appearing as a witness for the prosecution. So Logan doesn't get a voice in this trial – at least not until I am ready to destroy him.'

Late last week David and Arthur had brought Phyll into their confidence – a necessity considering her role in the jury selection process. And given they trusted her 100 per cent, and given her mind worked as well as that of any lawyer David had ever come across, they knew she could also be an asset in their plans for the days that followed.

'Bullshit Logan has no voice in this trial,' said Phyll. 'He doesn't need a courtroom to express his views, David. He is a national hero, for fuck's sake. He can open his trap any time he likes and the masses will walk into it willingly with sweet smiles of surrender on their perfectly made-up lips.'

'He will be sitting on our side of the room, behind his children,' countered David.

'And you think that will be enough for the jury to want to acquit them?' Phyll was shaking her head as they took a seat in a sunny corner of the busy café.

'Look at me, David, and read my lips: *You are going to go after him* – maybe not at first but when you get your chance you are going straight for the charismatic counsellor's jugular. Those women are going to hate you – they are going to think you are launching an attack on Saint Jeff simply because you have no other way of defending your clients.'

Phyll signalled for the waitress who took David's order of a club sandwich and Phyll's request for a mega burger with the lot, before taking a breath and moving on.

'From what you tell me, that bastard is one smart fucker and as soon as you go on the attack, he will play the poor, distressed father who is caught between a rock and a hard place. Don't forget he *confessed* to the murder in the first place, so the entire nation believes he will do everything to help his kids.'

'He wants them incarcerated,' said David.

'Sure, so all he has to do is insinuate to his friends

in the media that he believes his kids need help – lots and lots of long-term help in the appropriate psychiatric institution. No,' she said then as she tapped her long pink acrylic nails on the red formica table, '. . . we need *men*, David, young men who have never watched *The Doctor Jeff Show* in their lives and so couldn't give a flying fuck what the hallowed psychonut says.'

'But the women will have more sympathy for the children.' It was David's turn to shake his head. 'By nature they tend towards leniency.'

'True,' said Phyll. 'But if the ADA manages to convince them that the kids' motive for murder was not just one of self-preservation but of greed, then those big-hearted moms won't blink an eye before committing your junior jackals to a life behind bars. And even if they *do* feel sorry for them, that doesn't mean they won't vote to have them committed to a mental facility for long-term treatment. And is that what you want for your clients? A life in a loony bin filled with psychos who kill for fun?'

David let out a sigh, pausing to collect his thoughts as the waiter placed their meals in front of them. The past few days had been exasperating. While he was confident the children were now stronger, united, as prepared as they could be for the tough weeks that followed, they still had no concrete evidence against Jeffrey Logan, nor any word on the whereabouts of the missing Deirdre McCall. Nora's enquires at the Chatham Bars Inn had come up blank, and Sara had had no luck with reaching the increasingly evasive Katherine de Castro.

'I see what you are saying, Phyll,' said David after a

time. 'But aiming for a jury of close to all male jurors . . . isn't that a little extreme?'

'Let me help you out here,' she said, leaning into the table, the strength of her perfume now filling the space between them. 'You think any woman with half a heart is gonna wanna see those kids walk after Miss Barbie Doll ADA holds up pictures of the crime scene? You think any woman is gonna look at J.T., no matter how cute the kid happens to be, and let him skip happily into the sunset after she sees how he turned his mom into a bona fide carcass?' Phyll took a breath. 'No, David, it will be the violence that disturbs them, and given you will *not* be arguing that they acted in self-defence then . . .'

And there they were, Phyll's true feelings on the matter. The woman was a realist and made it very clear that she thought they were mad for not going with self-defence. She understood that Jeffrey Logan might be the abuser from hell but she did not think they had a chance of proving it.

'Bottom line, kiddo,' she said, perhaps reading the despondency on David's face, 'you've made your bed on this one – and don't get me wrong, I certainly admire your chutzpah. But not everything they teach you in law school is correct, my friend.' She took his hand and patted it. 'And Clarence Darrow was lying when he said the truth will set you free.'

57

Deirdre McCall popped another two super-strength Advil into her cracked, parched mouth and swallowed. She had run out of water hours ago, being careful to ration her money considering all she had was the $287 that she had luckily left in her faux leather purse.

She was on a Greyhound, travelling east. The bus had just passed Denver, which meant there were still two days to go on this close to three-day trip. The idea had come to her a few days ago, when she was staying at a filthy roadside inn just outside of Boulder City. And once she thought about it – once she felt, in her gut, that what she was guessing was correct – she used her ATM card to purchase the $204 ticket and worked out a $15 a day budget to tide her over. Even if the police or whoever else might be looking for her traced the transaction, she would be a long way from Nevada when they finally 'came to collect'.

When she hit Boston she would immediately jump

a ferry to take her within shouting distance of her final destination and then . . . well then, she would sit down and wait.

He would come, she thought to herself, as the pain in her head throbbed to the beat of some dull, persistent drum. It had been a long time since she had seen him, but something told her, something way down deep inside, that if he ever found himself in trouble that he would not be able to stop himself from seeking out the one thing that he had always loved the most.

He would go for the guns. He would take leave from his new identity – if just for a little while – so that he might go to them, feel them, and make a decision as to which weapon would suit his purpose best. And considering she guessed she was the only living person who knew where they were stored, she would seek them out also, so that she might do what she should have done all those years ago, and finally put an end to the bloodshed.

58

Prospective juror number fifty-one was a forty-one-year-old from Brookline. Her name was Betty Baker and she looked like something directly out of an episode of *Desperate Housewives*. She had listed her employment as 'home-maker' and her interests as baking and charity work, and she was president of the local elementary school PTA.

'So you have two children, Mrs Baker?' asked Amanda Carmichael, as she read from the woman's questionnaire and moved towards her with the prettiest of smiles on her face.

'Yes,' smiled Baker. 'Sheldon and Kiara – Sheldon is eleven and Kiara is eight – and they are both absolute delights.'

'And your husband?'

'Bob is managing director of an office works company called The Golden Staple. They sell everything from rubber bands to computer ink.' Another smile.

'And do you watch a lot of TV, Mrs Baker?'

'Well,' said Baker with a guilty little smile. 'I must admit I do like that *Dancing with the Stars* and I supervise the children's viewing, of course.'

Carmichael smiled. 'And what about daytime TV, Mrs Baker. Have you seen *The Doctor Jeff Show*?'

'Well, of course I have *seen* it.' Baker smiled again. 'And I do like *Oprah*. But my time during the day is limited, Ms Carmichael, especially on Thursdays when the housekeeper has a day off.'

At this last comment David bent to whisper in Phyll's ear. 'You want me to strike her?'

'Does a bear shit in the woods?' returned Phyll. But then Phyll shook her head. 'Try to get rid of her without using one of our challenges,' she whispered. 'There are several June Cleavers left in the pool,' she said, gesturing at the remaining, mainly female group behind them, '. . . and we only have one challenge to play with.'

David nodded.

'Finally, Mrs Baker,' Carmichael went on, 'do you think that, despite your knowledge of Doctor Logan's program, you could make unbiased decisions when it came to assessing the facts presented to you in proceedings involving the activities of his two children?'

'Well, of course,' said Baker. 'That would be my moral obligation, Ms Carmichael.'

Carmichael smiled again. 'I have no objection to this juror, Your Honour,' she said, before moving to resume her seat.

'Mr Cavanaugh,' called Kessler then, and David noted the judge had attempted some 'self-renovation' for her debut in the Suffolk County Superior Court – her usual brown 'nest' of hair having been coiffed into a bowl-like helmet which sat awkwardly on top of her head.

'Thank you, Your Honour,' said David, getting to his feet. 'While we do not wish to use one of our challenges, we feel that Mrs Baker may have some sort of affinity with the victim given Stephanie Tyler was also a PTA representative when her children were younger.'

'You want to strike Mrs Baker because she is a mom?'

'No, Your Honour,' said David, knowing very well that his argument was weak.

'Because if that is the case we will have to strike half the female population of Massachusetts.'

Kessler was right – but David was desperate to find a way around it. 'But Your Honour, Mrs Baker, like the victim, has a son and a daughter and . . .'

'Rubbish,' said Kessler, shaking her head before turning to Mrs Baker. 'Mrs Baker, I am pleased to inform you, you shall be joining us as juror number thirteen in the total group of sixteen. Please be aware that you will not know whether you will be named as one of the four alternates until the end of the trial.'

Kessler was referring to the 'lottery' system employed when whittling down a jury to the final dozen. It was believed that if the alternates were named in advance of the proceedings then they would not listen as intently as the original 'chosen twelve'. But if each of the sixteen did not know whether or not they would be literally pulled out of the barrel as an alternate, they would all concentrate on the evidence equally.

'Well, you made a dog's breakfast out of that one,' said Phyll, as David returned to his seat.

'Thanks for the encouragement, Phyll,' said David.

'I'm not here to stroke your ego, pretty boy,' she returned as Kessler called their next prospective juror – another of the group Phyll had nicknamed the 'Macy's Sale Parade'.

Two hours later, as the clock struck five, the sixteenth and final juror – a single father by the name of Nick Mandel – joined the mostly female group now sitting in the jury box at the far right-hand side of the room. And as Judge Kessler proceeded to swear them in – briefing them on what to expect during the course of a trial, reviewing their responsibilities and thanking them in advance for the role they were about to play – David looked at Phyll who met his eye to say: 'You're fucked.'

'Well at least you're consistent, Phyll,' said a now exhausted David.

'No, that's not what I meant,' said Phyll, collecting her things as the judge began to rise. 'Yesterday you were fucked but today you got screwed over big time.'

'Jesus, Phyll,' he said, collecting his briefcase at his feet before glancing across at Amanda Carmichael who could barely contain a smile.

Then he saw it – what Phyll was referring to. And he realised just exactly how 'fucked' he was.

'She chose our jurors,' said David as he stormed into Arthur's office, an equally as fired-up Phyll behind him.

'What?' asked an obviously confused Arthur, rising from his desk.

'Carmichael – she gave preference to the type of juror we would have been favouring if we didn't know what we did.'

'Slow down, son,' said Arthur, gesturing for them both to join him on the sofa and accompanying armchairs as Nora entered the room. But David was set on pacing.

'We know what Logan is up to,' he said. 'But if we didn't, if we thought he had his children's best interests at heart, we would have done everything we could have to make sure that jury was filled with women sympathetic to the Logans' cause. We would have *wanted* Logan fans – women who watch his show every day and, as Phyll rightly pointed out, live and die by his advice. Because that way they would have voted for *his* camp – or *our* camp – the one that was determined to set those children free.

'But we *do* know what he is up to. We know he wants his kids incarcerated and we also know that eventually we are going to go after him. So we can't favour Doctor Jeff fans because they are the ones who are going to hate us for turning the tables and gunning for him.'

'Okay,' said Arthur. 'I follow you so far.'

David nodded. 'Then why is Carmichael favouring the jurors who can only hinder her case? She should be choosing the ones who don't give a crap about the famous psychotherapist, because they are less likely to be swayed by sympathy to Jeffrey Logan, and as a flow-on, to his two kids.'

'Carmichael has spent the entire day favouring stay-at-home moms?' asked Arthur, now truly confused.

'Think Carol Brady times sixteen,' said Phyll, before pointing towards Arthur's corner fridge. She had worked with Arthur and David long enough to know the fridge was always stocked with cold Australian beers. Arthur nodded.

'The ADA was sucking up to those housewives like there was no tomorrow,' Phyll went on. 'And sadly she got what she obviously wanted – sixteen jurors of which ten are women and seven of those with kids. It was like a Tupperware party in there today, Arthur, except the only thing they were selling was their devotion to your favourite celebrity shrink.'

'But why?' asked Arthur. 'Why the hell would a savvy young prosecutor like Carmichael be filling the jury box with Logan sympathisers?'

'Because he is going to sell out those poor children in public.' It was Nora, from just inside the door.

David nodded as Arthur met his eye.

'You think Logan has offered to be a witness for the prosecution?' asked Arthur, not believing what he was hearing.

'It certainly explains Carmichael's strategy,' said David.

'But why would he? Surely any desertion of his children will be professional suicide on his part.'

'Not if he paints his actions as a hard decision for their benefit,' said David, '. . . if he says they need to be incarcerated, so they can be treated and kept safely away from the public while their lengthy psychiatric treatment is carried out.'

'You really think this guy is brave enough to go public with a flip like that?'

'I think this guy believes he is invincible – that his masses are so loyal that they will swallow whatever crap he chooses to dish out. And worse, Arthur, I think he might be right.'

There was silence.

'But how can you be sure, lad?' asked Nora. 'Doctor Logan is not on the original witness list Ms Carmichael faxed to us earlier this week.'

'She's delaying the addition,' said David. 'My guess is she'll want him to come last – play him as the powerful sympathetic back-up to her iron-clad evidentiary case. She will start by submitting the irrefutable facts as presented by the police, the ME, the forensics experts and the FBI and then, just when she has all those loyal Doctor Jeff devotees torn between voting with their sense or their sensibilities, she will clinch their guilty votes by getting the children's father to tell them it is *okay* to put his kids away.'

Arthur shook his head, in part realisation, part disgust. 'What do you think, Phyll?' he asked, turning to their savvy jury expert.

'I think your boy is spot on, but you'd be in a much better position if you knew what Doctor Asshole was planning for sure.'

'Well,' said Arthur, taking a beer from Phyll before moving to the corner cabinet to pour Nora a sherry. 'I am afraid that is impossible, Phyll. You see, there is no way in hell Logan is going to let us in on his strategy.'

David stopped pacing, before moving towards Phyll, taking a cold green bottle from her hand and unscrewing the lid so that he might down the bottle's contents in one almighty swallow.

'We don't need Logan to confirm it,' he said, taking a breath before placing the empty bottle on Arthur's desk.

'Then . . . how . . . who . . .?' began Nora.

'Amanda Carmichael,' he said, before grabbing his

jacket and heading for the door. 'It's her legal obligation to disclose all witnesses on her list – and if she thinks she can avoid that responsibility . . . well, I think it's about time I set the woman straight.'

It was raining when he left the office – a heavy, hot summer downpour that made the air thick with humidity. He decided to walk, knowing that at this hour on a Friday night he would be faster on foot than in his LandCruiser. He had tried Sara at home, but the line was engaged, so he'd left a message saying he was held up (he found himself stopping short before telling her he was on his way to Amanda Carmichael's apartment), and would be home within the hour.

He thought the walk might calm him, but if anything it was revving him up – his wet shirt now sticking to his skin as he made his way in and out of the umbrella-toting Friday night crowd. It was as if he existed in his own private cocoon, like a leading character in some high tension movie, locked in a world where the people around him were moving in slow motion, their voices muffled, their footsteps soundless, their smiles blurs as he focused on nothing but the inevitable task ahead.

He reached the waterfront and saw Amanda's building soaring like a glass palace before him. Tony had told him months ago that Amanda had bought a condo in the impressive new Residences at the Intercontinental, and as he entered the prestigious Atlantic Avenue address, he immediately tried to find someone who could direct him to her apartment somewhere up above.

'My name is David Cavanaugh and I am here to see

Amanda Carmichael,' he said when he reached the front desk. 'She owns one of the condos here.'

Within minutes the helpful staff were escorting him to a private elevator – the doorman having made a whispering phone call to Carmichael who, David guessed, was wondering why in the hell her number one opponent was paying her a house call late on a Friday night.

'Well, this is a pleasant surprise,' she said, standing in the doorway of her tenth floor apartment with a glass of white wine in her hand. She was wearing a pair of faded blue jeans with a ribbed white cotton singlet. Her hair was down and fell in thick blonde layers around her make-up-free face, her feet were bare and David was sure she was braless.

'We need to talk,' he said, meeting her at the door. The carpet was thick beneath his feet, that new hotel smell lingering fresh and sweet in the air.

'Come in,' she said, flattening her back against the door so that he could enter the dimly lit apartment. She followed him into the living room, allowing the door to squeeze silently shut behind her until the barely audible click of the lock acted as a trigger for David to finally say his piece.

'What the hell are you up to?' he said, turning from the breathtaking harbour view to face her.

'Excuse me?'

'The past two days – in jury selection – why were you choosing jurors perfect for the defence?'

'That's a good question, Counsellor,' she said, taking a step towards him, '. . . almost as good as the one I could ask you regarding your decision to challenge those very same jurors – the ones any half-assed jury expert would have been advising *you* to favour. Don't forget that I know Phyllis Vecchio, David, and there is nothing half-assed about that woman whatsoever.'

'Stop avoiding the question, Amanda,' David said, taking a step forward himself. 'I know what the hell you are up to, but I just want to hear it from . . .'

'How dare you,' she interrupted him then, placing her wine on a side table as she made the final steps to reach him. 'How dare you come into my home and tell me how I can or cannot run my case. Do you think I am completely stupid, David? Do you think you could come over here and strut your stuff and convince me to give away my entire game plan just because I used to be attracted to you? You may be a good-looking man, David, but . . .'

'Don't be ridiculous,' he said, cutting her off before pacing determinedly back towards the window.

'You think *I'm* being ridiculous?' She shook her head, the gesture making her long blonde locks sway behind her shoulders. 'I am not the one who walked halfway across town in the dark and the rain to knock on my opponent's Goddamned door. Does your girlfriend know you are here, David? Does she know you are standing dripping wet in my apartment begging me to tell you what I know?'

There was silence as David turned to meet her eye once again, the illumination from the city now bouncing off the harbour and filling the apartment with light.

'You're playing with fire, Amanda,' he said. She went to open her mouth to argue, but he held up a hand in protest. 'Let me finish,' he said. 'Jeffrey Logan is a sociopath. He is a manipulative megalomaniac who is – whether you want to believe it or not – trying to control your case.' And then he saw it, the slightest twitch in her left eye.

'He wants to see his children incarcerated – in fact, that has been his plan all along – and he will do anything, including using you as his conduit, to get his way.'

'The boy shot his mother, David,' she replied with exasperation, but David knew at least some of the fight had gone out of her.

'Did he?' asked David, moving back towards her. 'Then why doesn't he have a dislocated shoulder where that cannon of a rifle would have rested when he blew his mother in two?' He was saying too much, but something told him he could reach her, if only he could . . .

'No.' She began taking a step backwards.

'J.T. may have had his finger against that trigger, Amanda, but someone else was pushing him – someone older, stronger.'

'But the forensic evidence . . .' she began.

'. . . is covering up the truth,' he finished. 'Someone else was behind him, using him as a shield. The man is a psychopath, Amanda. He has a desperate need to control people, to take them, consume them, suck them dry and spit them out.'

'Stop it,' she said, retreating once again. 'You shouldn't be telling me this, David.'

But David was determined. 'He controls people, Amanda – he slinks in with his fancy credentials and movie star looks and before you know it you are doing exactly what he wants you to do. But you are smarter than that, Amanda. Your father – he was a working-class Joe who fought his way through the system to become one of the most respected legal minds in this country – what do you think he would say about you bending to some celebrity asshole simply because he swears he can hand you your guilty verdict on a silver platter?'

'You're right, my father is a great man but he would expect me to do everything I can to win this case,' she said. But David knew he had hit a nerve. 'And more to the point, I don't need Logan to do it,' she bit.

'Then why are you allowing him to dictate how you play it? Would you have been choosing housewives over childless men on that Goddamned jury if Logan *hadn't* offered to bat for your team?'

Her lips parted and her eyes blinked as she took a breath and met his eye once again. 'This isn't fair,' she said. 'What in the hell do you expect me to do? The man has a right to give testimony. Do you honestly think I should be gagging the children's father when . . .'

'If his motive is to pervert the course of justice then that is exactly what you should be doing.'

But she was shaking her head. 'Maybe he *does* want to do what is best for his kids. To get them long-term help for . . .'

'Oh for Christ's sake, Amanda, the man is a multi-millionaire psychotherapist. If he wanted to help them he would do everything to ensure their release so that he could admit them to one of the best private clinics in the country. If those kids get sent away, they will be locked into the system – sent to second-rate psych hospitals where the therapists are juggling a hundred and fifty patients a day.'

'Yeah, well maybe they should have thought of that before they plotted the murder of their mother.'

'There were two people holding the gun that night, Amanda – and all the younger of the two was trying to do was work out a way to save his mother.'

They stood there, mere feet from each other, the silence deafening as David took the final steps towards her.

'You know this is wrong,' he said, lowering his voice. 'It is not worth it, Amanda – the exposure, the kudos, the promotion to Roger Katz's job. You are bigger than this,' he said as he instinctively placed his hand on her chin and lifted it so that she might meet his eye. 'If you are going to win this, then win it on your own terms – and not with that bastard as back-up.'

And then, just as a beam of pale green light shifted across her face turning her blue eyes turquoise, she did the last thing David expected – she stretched her neck and rose onto the balls of her feet and reached up to kiss him softly upon the lips.

And in that moment, his entire body filled with a confusing mixture of fear and anger and frustration and regret, he found himself lingering that second too long, before taking a step backwards and heading towards the door.

59

Jeffrey Logan, aka Jason Nagol, aka James Golan took a long slow breath, allowing the refreshing Sunday morning salt air to fill his lungs as he opened the living room doors and stepped onto his ocean front deck to look out towards the ice blue North Atlantic beyond.

He was home.

Of course, many would argue that Vegas was his home, but he had never thought of that filthy desert pit as anything close to being home – more like the prison he was forced to grow up in, until he took destiny into his own hands and cut the ties that bound him.

He felt a need to see it then – the one that had provided the key to his freedom. And so he moved back inside and closed the doors before walking to the far corner of the open plan living area. Lifting the plush, cream thick-pile rug from the floor, he found the groove in the Baltic pine floorboard and used his car key to get under it. He lifted it the necessary six inches and reached inside to grab the rope that would hoist up the trapdoor and allow him to access the basement.

Seconds later, the cool dank air cosseted him in a welcome wave of familiarity. He was there, alone, in his blessed concrete haven, standing in front of his 'children', his *family* – his collection of over a thousand firearms, handguns, long arms and explosive weapons that he had begun 'adopting' at the age of twelve. And he sought 'her' out, the original XM21 – the real Yankee Doodle, 'Born in the USA' sniper rifle he had called upon all those years ago. The one that he had used to put a bullet in the tyre of the '82 family Buick from a good 200 yards away, the one that hit the front driver's side tyre just as the semitrailer was approaching from the other direction, the one that had saved his life! He found it, took it from the wall and caressed its 559 mm barrel and the original M14 wooden stock briefly before making sure that he shared his time evenly with the others, old and new, heavy and light.

Of course, his wasn't your typical gun enthusiast's collection. Many of the world's most celebrated collectors spent decades and millions amassing historically significant weapons that included everything from the first blunderbusses and muskets to the original muzzle-loading hand-cannons and Tommy guns. But the difference between Logan and those sorts of lily-livered wannabes was that Logan had actually used, or *intended* to use, every single piece in his collection for the purpose for which they had been made.

Not that all of his pieces were modern – indeed, he had an original Luger, a Colt .45 and a .38 super automatic aka Bonnie and Clyde. But most of his 'children' were of the high-tech variety – hunting and military weapons including pistols, shotguns, semi-automatics, assault rifles, machine guns, sniper weapons and a much-loved Mark V Deluxe which (sadly) had had to take leave from the rest of his family – at least for a while.

Jeffrey Logan moved towards the far wall so that he could assess his beloved clan as a whole, the nostalgia washing over him as his mind drifted to memories of each and every piece in his precious arsenal – from the early handguns that had whet his appetite by killing the cats and flattening the dogs and, once, even putting a poor homeless man or two out of his misery, to the German-made Heckler & Koch PSG-1 sniper rifle, which had ultimately secured his inheritance.

And when he eventually allowed their beauty to overcome him, when he *finally* gave into his urges and allowed himself to 'let go', he felt an overwhelming rush – of exhilaration, of excitement, of pure and utter bliss. It was a raw sexual uprising that began in his thighs and exploded in his groin and overtook his entire body, climaxing in the fantasy that he might soon be able to call on one of his 'children' again.

While logic told him all was very much on track, and commonsense argued it would be much safer if he did *not* require the services of his much beloved arsenal, part of him wished that he could have his cake by beating Cavanaugh in the courtroom, and then call on his 'children' so that he could ultimately eat it too.

60

Monday 13 August
The first day of trial

'I have a confession to make,' said Amanda Carmichael. Immediately David felt the sting of irony in her words. The weekend had flown by – David having told Sara everything about his altercation with the standing ADA except for that unexpected kiss. He knew he had to tell her – he knew he eventually would – but not now as they faced the imminent birth of their child, and the task of defending a case that would, in many ways, affect both of their lives forever.

The courtroom was packed – the natural light from the high eastern windows casting alternate shadows across the silent masses below. Jeffrey Logan had decided to make his loyalties known from the get-go, taking a seat behind the prosecution's table. And while the jury had not yet registered the significance of his choice of position, the media certainly had – with most of them, including Marc Rigotti and a half-smiling Caroline Croft, unable to take their eyes off him – setting up camp across the aisle from his kids.

A fresh-faced Judge Kessler had spent the first twenty minutes welcoming the jury, admonishing the gallery (who once again, she warned, would be banned from her courtroom for just the slightest hint of impropriety), and reminding the press, who sat shoulder to shoulder in the cramped media benches to David's left, of their obligation to report these proceedings fairly.

J.T. sat by David's side, next to him was Arthur and then Sara, who was holding Chelsea Logan's hand tightly behind the modesty curtain, erected around the defence table so that the shackled defendants' hands would not be visible, and thus act as a trigger for bias to the jury. David had argued repeatedly to Judge Kessler prior to this morning's proceedings that their two defendants be uncuffed for the duration of the trial, but Kessler, perhaps keen to establish her authority early, had denied his request saying that she may reconsider if the children proved they could behave appropriately in court.

'They're being treated like two-year-olds while being tried as adults,' a frustrated Sara had said to David as they left Kessler's chambers in defeat.

'So much for our supposed impartial system of justice,' he had replied.

Now, as Amanda Carmichael made her way towards the jury, her perfectly fitting dark grey suit shining slightly as she moved across the sunlit room, David wondered what in the hell Amanda Carmichael was planning to divulge as part of her much anticipated opening statement. The guilt of his actions – or rather *inaction* – was cutting freshly into his consciousness, the magnitude of the weeks ahead sending a shiver of nervousness running slickly down his spine.

'Now, I know what you are thinking,' Carmichael said, moving slowly towards the sixteen. 'A confession may seem like an odd way for the leader of the prosecution to begin her case, but I truly believe that my job here is to behave with the utmost of integrity, that my duty is to expose the truth and so, in order that you trust me, I need to – if you like – come clean.'

Slight smile, short pause.

'Sometimes I feel for the defendant.'

Another pause as Amanda nodded at her own admission.

'It's true. Sometimes,' she started pacing again, 'I am not *unhappy* when I lose.'

David glanced at Sara, both of them knowing that at the very least this was a lie.

'Sometimes I can even understand why someone takes the course of action that they do. And while I do my job to the utmost of my ability, while I prosecute cases with the full understanding that I represent the victim who cannot speak for themselves, sometimes I have to admit that the world is a better place without the murderers and rapists and abusers who are removed from those they have mistreated for so long.' She nodded as she advanced on the sixteen once again.

'When I first met J.T. and Chelsea Logan,' she said, gesturing at the defence table behind her, the eyes of the jury members glancing towards the two wide-eyed children before returning, mesmerised, to the beautiful ADA before them, '. . . when I became more familiar with their case, I have to admit, I felt that something was amiss. I asked myself, why would two intelligent, good-looking, privileged, outwardly sensible, well-mannered young people plot and execute the murder of their mother?

'I could not see it – and almost *wanted* to find a reason that would explain their heinous actions and, I guess, restore my faith in the virtue of our young.

'The revelation that their mother, Stephanie Tyler, was an incessant emotional abuser – a woman who made these children's life a living hell day in and day out – somehow eased my concerns by answering my question about motive. And while I certainly did not condone their actions, the facts, at least to some degree, assisted me in *understanding* them.'

'She's good,' said Arthur, leaning across J.T. to whisper privately in David's ear. 'The woman is taking away the foundation for any argument we make in regards to self-defence.'

'I'm pretty sure she knows that I don't want to go with self-defence, Arthur.'

'True, but maybe she thinks you may have realised that in the end we won't have any choice.'

David knew this was Arthur's way of telling him that they had run out of time – that they still had no concrete evidence against Jeffrey Logan and, whether they liked it or not, their main priority was arguing a case which would result in the lowest possible sentences for their two young defendants. But this would mean David standing up in court and describing his old friend Stephanie as the dictator mother from hell – a strategy that he and his two clients would never agree to, no matter how dire the circumstances.

'You see,' Amanda continued, 'just as I allowed myself to see things from the defendants' perspective, just as I accepted that perhaps these two young people saw their mother's murder as the only way out, new evidence shattered my attempt to comprehend their actions by revealing the multiple motives behind Stephanie Tyler's death.' Amanda shook her head, before advancing on the jury two steps further to stand directly in front of their dock.

'Fact,' she said, lifting up her pointer finger in accentuation. 'Chelsea Logan used her own computer to increase her mother's life insurance by a sum of millions mere weeks before her shooting.

'Fact,' now her middle finger was up. 'J.T. Logan was studying how to operate the murder weapon – a dangerous game rifle powerful enough to kill an elephant – at least four days prior to her death.

'Fact,' she went on, lengthening her third finger. 'On the morning of Stephanie Tyler's murder, Chelsea Logan impersonated her mother in a phone call to her mother's lawyers, instructing them to cut her father, Doctor Jeffrey Logan, from Stephanie Tyler's will.

'And fact,' she said raising her smallest finger. 'When Doctor Logan, in a desperate attempt to protect his children, confessed to killing his wife, neither J.T. nor Chelsea offered up a single word in protest.'

Amanda Carmichael placed her two hands lightly on the railing before her, looking sincerely at each and every one of her captivated audience of sixteen.

'The thing is, ladies and gentleman, there is no way these children didn't kill their mother. The forensic evidence is irrefutable, the medical examiner's report watertight. So you see, in many ways my job here is easy, for I have the facts to back me up.' She took a breath.

'But you,' Amanda continued, lifting her hands from the railing before bringing them back down as if in punctuation, 'you have the tough call of doing what is necessary. You have the difficult job of facing the two defendants – two young people who, admittedly, appear more like children than the adults their crime states them to be – and doing what is *right*.

'For you see, ladies and gentleman, sadly the great seventeenth-century philosopher, Baltasar Gracian, was right when he said things do not pass for what they are, but for what they seem. Sadly, some hide behind the appearance of innocence and take advantage of those of us who would love to absolve them of their guilt.

'But each and every time you look into J.T. Logan's eyes, each and every time you glance upon Chelsea Logan's face, I want you to see not just Stephanie Tyler who was almost disintegrated by a bullet that propelled her body halfway across a room, but also the defendants' father, Doctor Jeffrey Logan, who, despite his tireless efforts to protect his children, has been betrayed by the two people who he loves most.'

In that moment David knew that despite his desperate pleas, there was no way the ambitious Amanda Carmichael was going to let an opportunity such as this pass her by. For as she pivoted to return to her seat, the entire jury turned towards their beloved Doctor Jeff, and their devotion, their loyalty, their unbridled *commitment* to this man they so obviously adored was unmistakable.

*

After the ADA's flawless opening soliloquy, David had told the court that he had decided to delay his own statement until the prosecution had presented their evidence. This was his prerogative (in fact the defence were not obliged to give an opening statement at all), but he knew it had made them look undecided, disorganised, weak.

'I should have known there was no point in approaching her,' said David, as Sara and Arthur and the newly arrived Barbara Wong-McGregor joined him in a small courtside conference room for the morning recess. David had come to trust Barbara wholeheartedly, and, even if he had not, was not sure if he would have been able to restrain his frustration in any case.

'She's going for it, Arthur,' he said, turning to face his boss. 'And that two-faced homicidal maniac has got her back.'

'You're right,' said Arthur. 'Which is why, as much as you abhor it, you have to consider . . .'

'No,' David snapped. 'There is no way I am going to paint Stephanie as the abuser.'

'But the woman is *dead*, David,' argued Arthur. 'And maybe, if she *could* communicate with you, she would be begging you to sell her reputation up the river for the benefit of her kids.'

David looked at Sara who, after hesitating ever so slightly, looked back towards Arthur. 'David was the one who knew Stephanie, Arthur. The children trust him. This has to be his call.'

David was more grateful than ever.

'I'm sorry, Arthur,' he said. 'But I won't walk into that courtroom and lie.'

Despite himself, Arthur nodded.

'Well,' said Barbara, perhaps sensing it was time she weighed in, 'I wish I had something positive to lift your spirits. But what I have come up with . . . let's just say I am not even sure if it is an option.'

Barbara had compiled a comprehensive report on Jeffrey Logan which she had delivered to them late last week. It basically outlined the psychosis of an identity such as Logan – a man she had diagnosed as a 'charismatic psychopath' – or as her report had put it, *a morally depraved individual whose mental state could not be explained in terms of antisocial rearing or development*.

'As Sara noted when she read my analysis, people like Logan are "born bad",' began Barbara, '. . . meaning they represent the "monsters" in our society, people whose actions cannot be explained by the influence of normal human emotions.'

'Which makes them almost impossible to catch – or even treat,' Sara offered.

'Right, and that's part of the problem. Their lack of emotion reflects a detached, fearless, dissociated state. It's even difficult to pinpoint what motivates them – control and dominance, possibly. But their grandiose demeanour and attitude of superiority, well, don't forget they are called *charismatic* psychopaths for a reason – they are often charming and attractive, fast-talking persuaders who use their talents to bait.'

David nodded, anxious for Barbara to go on.

'One of the greatest challenges you face in coming up against a man like Logan is his fearlessness. Such boldness in the face of danger is a core characteristic of personalities such as his – in fact some psychiatrists describe them as high-speed vehicles with ineffective brakes.

'But,' Barbara hesitated as if trying to express herself carefully, 'this very same fearlessness that gives him an advantage could . . . *maybe*, also give you an edge. Men like Logan,' she continued, turning to David now, 'have an excessive need for stimulation – a constant craving for rousing, thrilling, ego-fulfilling highs. And these sorts of individuals tend to take risks – risks that see them walking the line between going unnoticed and getting caught, between escaping and getting snagged in the trap.'

'You think we can catch Logan while he is in the middle of taking one of these risks?' asked David, starting to see a lifeline but finding it very difficult to hold on to. 'But time is so short, Barbara, how in the hell do we create a situation where he wants to roll the dice?'

'Well, that's where it gets a little tricky,' she said, 'because in order to do so, you have to take some pretty serious risks yourselves.'

Without even meeting her eye, David could practically feel Sara bristle. 'How so?' he asked.

'Well, when it comes to charismatic psychopaths, I suppose if you went looking for a single flaw it would come in their inability to suppress urges – and their frustration at anyone who restricts them from fulfilling such urges, by standing in their way. These personalities often feel a need to be close to something that has never failed them, an object or set of objects that they have collected and trusted for much of their lives.

'What I mean to say is,' Barbara hesitated, and David

got the feeling that she was almost too scared to voice what she was proposing, 'if someone identified this something, and prevented him from accessing it, from feeding his urge . . . then . . .'

Sara shot a look at David, and in her eyes he saw an unspoken plea that he stop this now, that he turn back *immediately* before it was too late.

'Chelsea and J.T.,' said David, who despite his need to do otherwise maintained Sara's gaze with an expression that told her he needed to see this through, 'they told me that on occasion their father would disappear for a weekend, leaving Stephanie strict instructions as to her routine but giving no details of where he was going. He must have been . . . I mean, what if he was going to check on his guns? Logan has sought comfort in shooting since childhood. From what Blackmore told us, he has been purchasing guns for decades – and if that is the case, they must be stored somewhere . . .'

'And you think if we find these guns,' said Sara, her blue eyes now falling resignedly away from David's, to face Barbara front on, 'and we get *between* him and them, that he will . . .?'

'That he will be so angry that he has no choice but to reveal himself,' nodded a serious-faced Barbara, '. . . as the murderer he actually is.'

61

'The Commonwealth calls Lieutenant Joseph Mannix,' said Amanda Carmichael, as she rose from her seat to officially begin the presentation of the prosecution's evidence.

She was shaking, not outwardly but internally. It was a new sensation, and one that scared her – just a little. She knew she should be celebrating, for her opening statement was nothing short of spectacular, but the truth was, what David Cavanaugh had told her last Friday night had unsettled her; his warnings about Logan, the man she could almost *feel* breathing down her neck as she sat at the prosecution's table, had rung bells of clarity and panic, all at the very same time.

But as she rose to her feet, and as she felt every eye in the room watch her approach Joe Mannix, who was now seated in the witness stand, she realised that she had to bury these feelings of uncertainty if she was to reach her ultimate goal. If anything, Cavanaugh had given her a free ticket to victory when in a moment of weakness (or perhaps sincerity) he carelessly confided in her his own theory of the Stephanie Tyler shooting. Despite the overwhelming affinity she had felt with him in that one raw moment of truth, she knew that tossing away such opportunities would be stupid. And Amanda Carmichael had never acted out of emotionally motivated stupidity – never had, and never would.

'Lieutenant Mannix,' she said, after asking Joe to state his name, position and give a basic summary of his duties as head of Boston PD Homicide for the benefit of the now focused jury. 'You and your fellow homicide investigator Detective Frank McKay were the first detectives on the scene of Ms Tyler's murder on the night of Friday eleventh May, were you not?'

'That's right,' Mannix responded.

'And you attended the scene after responding to a communication from your police officers who had reacted to a 911 call made by Doctor Jeffrey Logan at 8.20pm – a mere four minutes after he arrived home.'

'That's correct,' said Mannix, and Carmichael sensed that he knew she was trying to rule out any notion that Jeffrey Logan could have been involved in his wife's murder from the get-go.

'And as such the case became yours – and by that, I mean you and Detective McKay continued to be the lead investigators on the case.'

Joe answered in the affirmative again.

'And as the lead investigator on the case, and as an officer with decades of experience in attending homicide scenes, could you tell us what you saw when you entered the family kitchen? And while I appreciate the scene was particularly gruesome in nature, I would ask you, for the jury's benefit, Lieutenant, to be as detailed as possible.'

David listened in horror as his friend described the scene that was the Logan's Beacon Hill kitchen – and despite Joe's obvious attempts to keep his account as clinical as possible, it came across as a scene from a gory Halloween movie.

He knew what Carmichael was doing; research showed that jurors presented with gruesome evidence – including detailed descriptions and photographs of murder scenes that showed the most horrific of human mutilation – were five times more likely to convict than those who were not. An Australian study carried out by the respected University of New South Wales even found that undue emphasis on such evidence was linked directly to prejudicing the jury against the defendant – resulting in the twelve making biased decisions influenced by an overpowering need to punish.

He also knew that Carmichael's referral to Logan's arriving home only four minutes before the shooting (and even David had to admit that four minutes sounded tight – but he also knew a lot could happen in 240 seconds, when lives were on the line), meant that she had no intention of even considering the possibility that she should, as a representative of the people, explore the possibility of Jeffrey Logan's involvement. For while David had sensed that Amanda Carmichael the woman had opened her mind – her *fears* – at least briefly, to such a possibility, Amanda Carmichael the prosecutor would never let her admit it.

Ten minutes later, after several long-winded questions regarding the physical appearance of the victim, the jurors' faces were as white as sheets. Carmichael then went on to question Joe about J.T. Logan's appearance – about the blood spatter that had covered his clothes, his hair, his eyes.

'So would it be fair to say, Lieutenant, that despite the fact that Doctor Jeffrey Logan actually confessed to his wife's shooting – an incident he described as an accident involving the cleaning of the rifle given to him by his wife – there was no doubt in yours or Detective McKay's minds that J.T. Logan was the shooter.'

Joe took a breath. 'The Logan boy appeared to be the most likely suspect on the night,' said Joe.

'Appeared to be?' questioned Carmichael, with a slight shake of her head. 'Come on, Lieutenant, the boy was the only one in the room covered in blood spatter. In fact, isn't it true that on the following morning you and Detective McKay came to visit me at the DA's office and told me, in no uncertain terms, that you believed the father was covering for the son? That . . .' Carmichael held up a finger indicating that she needed to clarify something further before Joe gave his response, 'and I quote,' she said, as she moved back to her desk to retrieve a yellow piece of paper, '"the blood spatter pattern alone points singularly at the boy". After which Detective McKay confirmed that under normal circumstances you would have arrested the boy at the scene, but when his father confessed, when he offered himself up *selflessly* in his child's stead, you had no choice but to . . .'

'Objection.' David had had enough. 'With all due

respect, this is not an episode of some B-grade daytime soap opera. Miss Carmichael's opinions as to the motives of the children's father are irrelevant and . . .'

'He's right, Miss Carmichael,' interrupted Kessler. 'Objection sustained.'

Carmichael nodded in apology, David noticing that despite his mini-victory the jury were now looking even more admiringly at their Good Samaritan Doctor Jeff.

Fifteen minutes later, Carmichael was winding up, her examination of Joe having gone exactly as David had expected – the later part of her questioning hammering home the fact that the forensic evidence alone was enough for her to secure a grand jury indictment. She stopped short of questioning Joe about the insurance or 'change of will' matters, simply because by the time these pieces of evidence had come to light, she had basically cut Joe from the case. But David knew these elements would be examined in detail tomorrow, when she called her FBI expert to the stand.

'Your witness, Mr Cavanaugh,' said Kessler at last. And David could almost read the relief on his detective friend's face. It was time to turn this court upside down and give them another theory to play. And so it began.

'Lieutenant,' said David, advancing on his witness quickly and getting straight to the point. 'Miss Carmichael asked you to describe J.T. Logan's physical presentation on the night of his mother's death, but was there any other physical evidence, besides the blood spatter and so forth, that may have altered your initial opinion that J.T. Logan was the only person involved in this shooting.'

This opening question alone was enough to cause an intake of breath around the room. David's line of enquiry was obviously not what they had expected. The press had been practically guaranteeing that he and his team would be going with self-defence – and so the sorts of queries he was now making were enough to stun the entire gallery into silence.

'Yes,' said Joe, his simple answer triggering a second round of gasps, this time loud enough for Kessler to lift her gavel in warning. 'But it wasn't an existing piece of evidence that worried me – more a detail that was missing.'

'Tell us what you mean, Lieutenant?' asked David, sure the tiny screech he heard behind him was Amanda Carmichael pushing her seat back ever so slightly so that she was on the ready to object.

'The Weatherby .460 Magnum used to kill the victim is one of the most powerful calibres in the world and as such, when fired, delivers an almighty recoil – enough to dislocate shoulders, to burn through material and into the skin.'

'But you said J.T.'s T-shirt *was* burned.'

'Yes. But his shoulder was fine – no burning, no bruising. The doctor at Plymouth Juvenile Detention Unit confirmed as much.'

'Objection,' said Carmichael. 'Once again, Your Honour . . .?'

'Yes, I know, Miss Carmichael,' returned Kessler. 'Hearsay.' And the judge shifted in her seat so that she might look directly at Joe.

'Lieutenant, it is not your role to report on the findings of the medical profession, and I would ask you to restrict your evidence to investigations made by the police and . . .'

But David was already upon her, a white bound report held high in his now sweating right hand. 'Your Honour, this is an examination report on J.T. Logan made by Doctor Mitchell McManus at Plymouth Juvenile Detention Unit just two days after Stephanie Tyler's death. It confirms the lieutenant's testimony that there was indeed no sign of trauma of any type to J.T. Logan's shoulder.'

Kessler furrowed her brow as she took the report from her clerk. 'All right,' she said, after a pause. 'You may table this report, Mr Cavanaugh, and I'll allow the question. You may continue, Lieutenant.'

Joe took a breath as Carmichael re-took her seat. 'Well, like I said,' he continued. 'The lack of shoulder injury was an inconsistency, and in my profession inconsistencies don't sit easy. It led me to suspect that the rifle was not fired while sitting on J.T. Logan's shoulder – and that perhaps . . .'

'*Objection!*'

'No, I want to hear what the lieutenant has to say, Miss Carmichael,' said Kessler, her arms now perching over her partition in an effort to lean that much closer to the witness. 'You may continue, Lieutenant.'

'The thing is,' Joe continued, obviously knowing that his choice of words was now crucial to David's setting up his unpredictable defence, 'I began to believe that the execution of the crime was not as straightforward as we first might have thought. We knew it was highly unlikely that a boy of J.T.'s small stature could have avoided being wounded in some way by the recoil – unless, perhaps, someone stronger had helped him negotiate the weapon.'

And that had done it. The entire courtroom shrieked, at least two members of the jury began shaking their heads in disbelief, and the press began scribbling urgently in their notebooks as Arthur grabbed J.T. Logan's hand under the modesty panel while Sara did the same with Chelsea. In fact, the only person who did not react was a stony-faced Jeffrey Logan.

'Order!' yelled Kessler, her entire body now bunched up in a force that brought her gavel down with determination.

David's next reaction was to turn to Amanda Carmichael, who was half standing, as if ready to protest, until Logan leant forward to whisper something in her ear. Her brow tightened, before she nodded, and resumed her seat.

'Please clarify, Lieutenant,' said Kessler then. 'Are you saying that it is your opinion that someone assisted J.T. Logan in the murder of his mother?'

'I am saying that every piece of literature and information on that particular calibre suggests the recoil is a bastard,' said Joe, perhaps knowing there was no better way to express it. 'These Big Berthas are like cannons, Judge. Even the most experienced of shooters wear padding to combat the power of their hundred-plus foot-pounds of force.'

Kessler nodded, before turning to David and gesturing for him to continue.

'So just to clarify,' said David. 'In your opinion, J.T. Logan had "help" when it came to the shooting of his mother?'

'Help or instruction,' Joe replied, and in that moment David could have hugged his loyal detective friend. 'It was either one or the other.'

It was late. He was rubbing her back, slowly, gently – the only light coming from the moon which slipped like a ghost through their open bedroom window, the only sound coming from the wind which licked at their curtains like a choreographer guiding them into a dance.

'You can stop massaging if you want,' she said, turning to face him, their arms around each other with their unborn child cradled between them. 'It's late and I know you are tired.'

It was true, the day had been long, and while Joe's powerful testimony had certainly laid the foundations for them to take the route they intended, David knew that the afternoon session had been nothing short of catastrophic.

Amanda Carmichael had called Boston PD's Crime Lab Unit chief, Dan Martinelli, who spent the entire second half of the day explaining how the forensic evidence pointed solely and irrefutably towards J.T. Logan as the killer.

'We knew Martinelli's testimony would be tough,' said Sara, lifting her hand to move a stray sandy-coloured hair from his brow. 'And you made a bit of ground when you questioned him about the lack of fingerprints on the rifle.'

This was also true, David had thoroughly questioned Martinelli about the absence of any prints on the Mark V's stock or barrel – and Martinelli confirmed that the only print he lifted was the one left by J.T. on the trigger.

Martinelli went on to speculate that the boy could have wiped the gun clean following the shooting, but upon further probing David got him to agree that this was unlikely given the blood on the barrel was not significantly smudged and, that if the boy had the presence of mind to wipe the gun clean, then it would also be unlikely that he would have forgotten to wipe the trigger as well. (David also got Martinelli to concede that no cloth or towel, which might have been used to wipe the weapon clean, had been found at the crime scene.)

Finally, David had proceeded to 'grow' on the theory launched by Joe Mannix in his testimony earlier that morning, eventually getting Martinelli to admit that – at least from a forensics point of view – another person could have assisted J.T. in the handling of the rifle.

They were tiny, baby steps, which paled in comparison with Amanda Carmichael's solid, show-stopping first day of evidence. But it was a start – at the very least, it was a start.

'What do you think he said to her?' asked Sara, her pale eyes meeting his. David knew she was referring to Logan – and his subtle instruction to Carmichael amidst the commotion in the court. 'I mean, by the looks of things he told her not to object to Joe's "two people in the room" theory, but what specifically do you think he . . .?'

But David suspected Sara had guessed exactly what Logan had proposed to Carmichael – for he had guessed it too.

'He was telling her to let it go,' he said. 'Mostly likely he reasoned that if it comes down to it – if we manage to prove that J.T. had help with the shooting of his mother – that Carmichael could agree with us and say that it was . . .'

'. . . Chelsea,' she finished.

He nodded.

'So you think that if we fail to prove it was Logan, Carmichael will use our theory to bury Chelsea Logan by proxy.'

'Yes.'

'And Logan knows it too.'

'Yes.'

'In fact, he could well continue to foster it.'

'Yes.'

'And secretly he is probably celebrating the fact that we are doing his work for him – assuring his daughter's guilt which, in theory, is far more difficult to prove than his son's.'

'Yes,' he said again, and Sara pulled him closer as they lay in silence for a while.

'You are going to go looking for them, aren't you?' she said after a time. 'The guns, I mean.'

David said nothing for a long time. Finally, he responded. 'Yes.'

62

The following morning Sara lied. She told David she was feeling unwell, tired – and thought it best she not attend the second day of trial.

'You'll do great with the FBI guy,' she had said, referring to Carmichael's next witness – the FBI analyst who would take the court through his findings regarding Chelsea Logan's home computer and the change of will message left on Harry Harrison's machine.

'If I do, it will be thanks to you,' he had answered.

Sara hoped he was right. Yesterday she had come up with a rather 'left of centre' and somewhat legally risky idea as to how they might counter what they knew would be the analyst's damning evidence regarding the upgrade of life insurance emails sourced to Chelsea's computer. It was a long shot, based largely on what their friend, FBI Agent Susan Leigh, had alluded to regarding the personality of her laboratory colleague. While Susan would never speak badly of one of her fellow agents, she had said enough for them to garner that the analyst in question, a technician who had never seen any action in his twenty-year career, never missed an opportunity to play himself up as a 'super sleuth crime fighter'.

'Put it this way,' Susan had explained, 'the guy is not unhappy that his last name happens to be Bond. He even has a private email address where he uses the numbers 007.'

And Sara had got the idea from there. Even so, she felt as guilty as hell as David hugged her at their door and told her that she should rest. But she also knew that she had no choice, for she did not know what else to do, and enough was finally enough.

The thought of David trying to track down Jeffrey Logan's store of what they estimated could be hundreds of deadly weapons scared the hell out of her. And she knew, deep down inside, that unless she did something to turn this case around, the man she loved – the father of her unborn child – could end up facing off against an expert marksman and psychopathic monster, and there would be nothing she could do to stop him.

And so, as she stood on Katherine de Castro's front stoop, the wind now blowing a gale and sending her long brown hair thrashing about her face, she said a silent prayer that she would be able to talk the woman inside into risking her safety to save their case – and perhaps even their lives, in one way or another.

'Ms de Castro,' she said, sensing movement on the other side of the red door. 'It's Sara Davis – the Logan children's counsellor,' she added, knowing that, given there was a peephole in the thick wooden door, de Castro knew exactly who it was. 'I am sorry to call so early, but I wanted to catch you before you went to work and . . .'

'I'm not going to work,' said de Castro, and Sara noted the hesitancy in her voice, the edge of anxiety, the trace of fear. 'I am not well, Miss Davis. I have a stomach virus, and I would hate for you to catch anything, especially at this time when you are about to . . .'

'You know you can call me Sara, Katherine,' interrupted Sara. 'And you need to let me in.'

After seconds of holding her breath, Sara finally exhaled as she heard Katherine de Castro release the lock from the other side of the door. Katherine pulled on the door carefully, slowly, as if fearful the powers that be would rush into her Back Bay 'safe house' and steal her away from the world. And when she finally revealed herself, her face thin, her hair unstyled, Sara realised that Logan had already started his 'campaign' of possession. This once powerful, independent woman – who just months ago Sara would have described as vibrant, sharp, fearless – had begun to slip into the shadow of the beast.

Just like Stephanie Tyler, thought Sara, before extending her hand towards the obviously anxious woman. 'It's all right, Katherine. You and me – we are going to put an end to all of this – once and for all.'

63

Special Agent Curtis Bond was a trim forty-something with short black hair and piercing blue eyes; his charcoal suit, shiny black shoes and dark sunglasses – now perched in his top right-hand jacket pocket – screamed FBI. Bond stated his job as Special Agent in Charge of several of the Quantico-based FBI laboratory's examination units, including the elite Computer Analysis and Response Unit and the unit responsible for Forensic Audio, Video and Image Analysis.

But it wasn't so much Bond's experience that concerned David this morning, as his smug self-assuredness – an arrogance that told David this computer geek with a badge was more than just a little happy to be the centre of attention at this morning's standing room only proceedings – that and the fact that every time Bond opened his mouth he dissected each word syllable by syllable, as if determined to stretch his 'fifteen minutes of fame' to a good two hours or more.

Amanda Carmichael began by asking Bond to

outline the details of his impressive career – including his extensive experience in the high-tech FBI laboratory. And Bond paced himself as he took the hushed gallery through his myriad accomplishments until Carmichael, obviously sensing it was time to speed things up a little, eventually cut to the chase.

'Special Agent Bond,' she said, 'could you tell the court how you came to be assigned to the analysis of the audio message left on the voice mail of attorney Harry Harrison on the morning of Friday the eleventh of May?'

David stole a glance at Arthur – Carmichael was starting back to front. David had expected her to work in chronological order, starting with the life insurance emails before moving on to the 'change of will' voice mail left the morning of Stephanie's death – and the anomaly unnerved him.

'Yes, I am the laboratory's most experienced examiner in the areas of audio evidence – including authenticity, enhancement and voice comparison, and as such, when the evidence came in marked as a priority, I immediately assigned myself to the job.'

'More like he saw an opportunity to increase his super agent profile by giving evidence in the highest profile case of the year,' whispered David in Arthur's ear.

Arthur nodded.

'And could you explain to the court the nature of the voice mail you examined?' Carmichael continued.

'Yes. It was a one-minute-twelve-second recording from a person purporting to be Stephanie Logan, requesting certain changes to her will.'

'Right, well, before we continue, Special Agent Bond, I might request the court listen to said recording, tabled as item number three.' Carmichael looked towards Kessler for her approval.

'Go ahead,' said Kessler, her left hand gesturing that Carmichael had her permission to continue.

The next minute or so played out like an eternity – the entire courtroom staring directly at Chelsea as the somewhat apprehensive female voice, identifying itself as Stephanie Tyler, requested the lawyer, one Harry Harrison, remove her major beneficiary – her husband, Doctor Jeffrey Logan – from her will. The message was smooth in a scripted sort of way, almost as if the caller had written notes before attempting the call. And while at first hearing the speaker could well have been identified as the voice of an older woman, the slight lifts in intonation at the end of each sentence seemed to suggest the caller was somewhat younger – which indeed she was.

'Special Agent Bond,' said Carmichael then, positioning herself so that she was equidistant from the jury, her witness and the defence table to her left, 'did you and your fellow technicians go on to confirm the identity of the speaker in this case?'

'Yes. The caller was identified as Miss Chelsea Logan.'

Carmichael swivelled slightly to meet the eyes of the transfixed jury. 'And could you explain how you came to this conclusion, Special Agent?'

'Yes. The laboratory was also given a second recording – of Chelsea Logan reciting a speech at a school assembly. The assembly was recorded by a staff member on a hand-held video camera and the FBI issued a warrant to gain possession of said recording. In short, we were able to use this second piece of audio to get a 100 per cent match in voice identification.'

'And this is done by . . .?' Carmichael led her witness.

'Identifying similar and dissimilar exemplars in voice characteristics,' finished Bond. 'Basically, specialised software that produces digitally calculated spectrograms is used to compare frequency characteristics of the graphic representation. We also used specialised forensic voice identification algorithms to identify automated voice comparisons between different voice samples.'

'And all of these investigations led you to the conclusion that it was indeed Chelsea Logan who left that message on Mr Harrison's voice mail?' reiterated Carmichael, her eyes flicking towards David as if in anticipation of his objection.

'Yes,' said a satisfied Bond. 'It was Miss Logan, and I have no hesitation in stating that I believe my investigations to be unequivocally correct.'

Moments later Carmichael moved on to Chelsea Logan's computer and the highly controversial life insurance emails, beginning by asking Bond how his laboratory came to receive the laptop in question.

He explained that the computer was recovered by the FBI Boston Field Office's emergency response team or ERT, and transported to Quantico for further testing. 'As head of the computer analysis unit, the laptop was given to me as a priority and along with two fellow technicians we spent a good twenty-four hours pulling the hard drive apart – searching for the emails in question and the login and password origins. We also studied other emails sent by the defendant to friends and associates in an effort to find similar word patterns and grammatical habits.'

Carmichael then proceeded to ask Bond to outline the nature of the four emails in question – two from 'a person purporting to be Stephanie Tyler' to Mr Shane O'Rourke from APS Insurance, and two return emails from Mr O'Rourke in response.

'The first email, sent on the thirtieth of April from the Logan family's home email account, was written by a person identifying themselves as Stephanie Tyler and requested further information on how Ms Tyler might increase her life insurance cover. The first return email, sent by Mr O'Rourke on the first of May, consisted of an attached brochure describing the upgrade alternatives available.'

'So Mr O'Rourke responded quickly, giving Ms Tyler all the information necessary to upgrade her portfolio.' Carmichael was obviously determined to make this as easy for the jury as possible.

'That is correct,' nodded the ever-efficient Bond.

'All right, Special Agent – please continue.'

Bond went on to give details of the next two emails – the one sent by the person once again identifying themselves as Stephanie Tyler outlining the substantial changes she wanted to make to her already large insurance policy; and the fourth, a return email from O'Rourke saying the changes would be made as soon as possible but effective from the return email date. He explained these two emails were sent on Friday fourth May and Monday seventh May respectively, a mere seven and five days before Tyler's murder on Friday eleventh May.

At that point, Carmichael moved back to her desk to retrieve copies of all four emails, after which she requested Bond read some highlighted paragraphs from the third email – the one where 'Stephanie Tyler' listed her specific upgrade requests. Bond pulled his square-framed glasses from his pocket – the lenses tinted just enough to make them look like sunglasses – before explaining he was far-sighted and placing them on his nose and proceeding to read.

'Jesus,' said David, leaning in to Arthur. 'Can the guy look any more Clint Eastwood?'

Arthur nodded. 'Let's hope we can help Dirty Harry here shoot himself in the foot.'

Despite the fact David had read and re-read the emails scores of times since they had been provided by the prosecution as part of initial discovery, the words were difficult to hear – as Carmichael had chosen the two sections which outlined 'Stephanie's' request for her lump sum payout upon death to be increased from five to a massive twenty million dollars, and the paragraph requesting the addition of the 'supplementary rider' which would effectively give Stephanie's beneficiaries an extra two million dollars if her life ended as the result of unforeseen misfortune.

She also told Bond to read a further section where 'Stephanie' identified her beneficiary as her husband, Jeffrey Logan – and David finally realised why Carmichael had gone with the audio line of questioning first. The ADA needed the jury to see just how clever Chelsea Logan was – how she set up the insurance details *before* cutting her father out of the picture by removing him from her mother's will. She was painting David's client as a teenage murdering mastermind, and there was nothing he could do about it – at least not yet.

'Special Agent Bond,' Carmichael continued, now pacing towards the jury, 'could you please tell us what your analysis showed? Could your investigations identify the sender of the two emails – and in turn, the identity of the person purporting to be Stephanie Tyler?'

She flashed a look at David, once again expecting him to object – but David knew if he contested Carmichael's theory of an imposter emailer by claiming Stephanie had indeed sent the requests herself, he would screw himself later, when he felt the time was right to offer another possibility – that it was Jeffrey Logan who sent the insurance alteration requests.

So he sat mute – in a now familiar sedentary position which had also obviously piqued Judge Kessler's curiosity, given her face was now contorted in a frown of unmistakable bewilderment.

'Yes,' Bond responded. 'The login and password investigations showed the emails were sent by Miss Chelsea Logan,' he said, plain and clear. 'And once again, there is no doubt in my mind, that my findings are unequivocally correct.'

'Pepsi,' said David, jumping from his seat to approach the witness, his bizarre cross-examination opener now having all in attendance on the edge of their seats.

'Excuse me?' said the obviously confused Bond.

'Pepsi,' David repeated. 'You asked me if I liked Coke or Pepsi and I am telling you that I am a Pepsi man. It has a little extra bite or something, a slightly more bitter edge.'

Bond immediately looked to Carmichael who responded by rising from her chair.

'Objection. Your Honour, I have no idea what Mr Cavanaugh is referring to, but I wonder if all that sitting down this morning, teamed with his lack of Pepsi might have . . .'

The entire room laughed – and David knew Carmichael had won them over. Now if only Sara's idea could win them back.

'I am sorry, Your Honour,' said David, with a smile. 'I know my statement is a little left of centre, but I promise my point will soon become clear if you just allow me a little latitude.'

'All right, Mr Cavanaugh,' said Kessler, the only one in the room not smiling. 'But make it quick.'

'Special Agent Bond,' said David, lowering his voice slightly to approach the witness. 'Forgive me for confusing you. I was trying to make a point, see – about email origins and so forth.'

But it was obvious the wide-eyed Bond still did not understand, and so David moved back to his desk to 'assist' him.

'Here,' he said, moving once again towards the witness to hand him a piece of paper. 'It's an email I received from you late last night – and it asks the question, you know . . . the one about the Pepsi and the Coke.'

'I didn't send you an email late last night. I was out, at the theatre with my wife and . . .' Bond grabbed the piece of paper from David, now putting on those trusty tinted glasses once again.

'But the note came from your personal email account,' said David, scratching his head in feigned confusion. 'That is your home email address isn't it, Special Agent Bond – ltk007@hotmail.com? And I am gathering the "ltk" stands for licence to kill – your last name being Bond and all.'

'*Objection*,' yelled Carmichael once again, this time her face contorting in a knot of anxiety as she saw where this was headed. 'Your Honour, this line of questioning is intolerable in a million different ways. Defence counsel is badgering the witness. He . . .'

David guessed Amanda was probably dying to accuse him of hacking into Bond's personal email account, but she was too smart for that – for to make such an accusation and have it *denied* would simply consolidate the point that David was trying to make.

'You're right, Miss Carmichael,' said Kessler, now turning towards David. 'But I want to see where this is going. You can continue, Mr Cavanaugh, but the line you walk is a fine one.'

But David did not get a chance to . . .

'*I didn't send him an email*,' snapped Bond, not waiting for another question, simply turning away from David to look directly up at the judge. 'I mean, why in the hell would I . . .?'

'I agree,' interrupted David. 'Why on earth would you care which kind of soda I prefer? Which leads me to believe that someone *else* sent this email, Special Agent Bond – someone who has access to your username and password and . . .'

'Objection.' Carmichael was up again.

'*He can't do that!*' yelled a now horrified Bond.

'By "can't" do you mean that I shouldn't have invaded your privacy, or that getting access to your personal email information was impossible?' asked David.

'*Mr Cavanaugh*,' said Kessler then, believing she knew what David had done, 'if we find evidence you have manipulated this man's personal emails then . . .'

'On the contrary,' said David. 'I simply rang Special Agent Bond's home last night and identified myself as the defence attorney in the Logan case. The special agent's oldest son, a lovely kid named James . . . which I guess actually *does* make his name James Bond –' and now the jury were smiling again, but this time with David '– Well, James answered the phone and I asked him to send me an email from his dad's home computer. I said he could ask me any question he liked.'

'And he asked you about the Pepsi?' said an incredulous Kessler.

'The Pepsi, and the Coke,' finished David, and for the first time since this trial began the entire jury was now laughing and smiling warmly at a representative from the defence, while a red-faced Carmichael tapped her pen anxiously on the yellow legal pad before her, a straight-faced Logan remaining expressionless, apart from the slight tensing of the muscles at the base of his lower jaw.

'So you see, Special Agent, I guess my point is that anyone with access to Chelsea Logan's computer could have sent those insurance request emails. Wouldn't you agree, Special Agent?' asked David, as the room fell silent, awaiting Bond's response.

'Special Agent?' repeated David, the humour now gone from his voice.

'I . . . yes,' Bond whispered.

'Excuse me, Special Agent?' said David, now lifting his right hand to his ear.

'I said, *yes*,' repeated Bond, the anger in his tone unmistakable. '*But there is no question who left that voice mail*,' he continued in frustration. '*Our tests were unequivocally correct. It was Chelsea Logan, she rang to change her mother's will. It was her voice. She did it, she . . .*'

'Well, of course she did,' replied David to the now shocked courtroom, Jeffrey Logan finally turning his head in disbelief.

'Chelsea Logan left that message, Special Agent,' said David, his eyes never leaving Logan as he addressed the witness. 'And for once, I agree, that in this matter alone, you are unequivocally correct.'

64

Sara could not believe her eyes. Katherine de Castro's living room table was like a Rodeo Drive jewellery store display. There must have been at least twenty boxes on the table – some unwrapped, some not, the packaging heralding gifts from the likes of Tiffany, Cartier, Bulgari and more.

'Oh my God,' she said, picking up the long narrow Tiffany box closest to her to see a ruby-studded bracelet with matching earrings inside. 'Katherine, this is . . .'

'I know,' responded de Castro, her dark eyes resting resolutely on the table before her. 'He started with the necklace – the noughts and crosses. And then came the Cartier bracelet and the Bulgari necklace and the gold ladies' Rolex and . . .'

'He sent all of these by messenger?'

'Most of them. Although we had breakfast at the Fairmont a few weeks ago but . . . he had to leave unexpectedly, when he got the bad news from his attorney that his children had opted for alternative representation. And after he left, after I sat drinking coffee after coffee, the waiter sent me a breakfast soufflé with a fresh white rose as embellishment. And there was a ring – a five carat sapphire – placed along its long thorny stem.'

'Katherine,' said Sara, leading her to the sofa so that they both might take a seat. 'Has Logan actually asked you to marry him?'

'No.' She shivered. 'But I believe he intends to – that he expects it to happen, that it is definitely part of his plan.'

'And his advances – they make you feel . . .?'

'Uncomfortable, helpless, scared,' Katherine responded. 'It is like the man I have known all these years – the savvy business partner whose career I have fostered for almost two decades – has suddenly become someone else.'

'Or maybe he was the someone else before,' suggested Sara. 'And what you are seeing now is the real Jeffrey Logan.'

'You think Jeffrey has always been the type of man who would fight to have his kids incarcerated?' asked Katherine, incredulous.

'I think Logan is the type of man who manipulates everyone who crosses his chosen path – tactically removing those who become a hindrance while subtly seizing control of those he desperately wants to possess.'

Katherine lifted her chin to meet Sara's eye. 'There's more, isn't there?'

'I am afraid so.'

And Katherine took a breath before nodding for Sara to go on.

Sara began at the beginning – starting with their information about the sharpshooter Logan as a child up to his more recent psychopathic activities – including the laundering of the gun, the staging of the video, the manipulation of his wife's life insurance and the reign of terror he had managed to hold over his children until they were both incarcerated and safely behind bars.

Katherine did not flinch; she simply listened, calmly, carefully – a reaction that might have seemed strange had Sara not sensed that Katherine de Castro had come to her own conclusions regarding the agendas of her trusted Doctor Jeff, conclusions that no doubt prompted her to ring Joe Mannix two weeks ago and feed him the information regarding Stephanie Tyler's telltale *Vanity Fair*.

'The thing is,' said de Castro after a time, 'I never suspected anything – for so long. He was always so charming, so clever, so determined to succeed.'

'We have done some psychological investigations on Logan, Katherine, and his intelligence and charm fit the profile of a charismatic psychopath to a T. The man works meticulously, methodically to set his plans in motion and does not waver.'

Katherine nodded. 'Years ago, when we first met, he was a nobody. He was a two-bit psychologist running his own hokey practice out of some down and out duplex in Vegas. But I saw something in him, a determination, a passion, a drive. He wanted it, Sara, and he knew I could give it to him so . . .' Katherine hesitated, a new look of horror now falling across her gaunt olive-skinned face.

'What if this is my fault? What if I contributed to all that has happened by giving him the power to control the views of the public? I was the one who built his career, after all. I have been by his side every step of the way. I even helped set up that TV special where Caroline Croft and Chelsea . . .'

'No,' said Sara, twisting in her seat to face the teary-eyed Katherine. 'Logan – he was born the way he is, Katherine. True, he might have used you to further his agenda but I am sure – no matter what – that he was destined to become the monster that he is.'

Sara took a breath, hoping beyond all else that what she had to say next would not ruin her chances of getting de Castro on board.

'I know how you feel, Katherine, I know how frightened you must be, and while I do not want to make this any worse for you, I do know that you are in a unique position to help.

'Logan murdered his wife, Katherine, as sure as he is now sitting behind the prosecution determined to send his kids away. And those teenagers are helpless victims – kids who face a lifetime in prison just because their father happens to be who he is.'

'I can't help you,' said a distressed Katherine, her eyes closed tightly as if willing Sara away.

'Yes, Katherine, yes you can,' Sara pushed on. 'Whether you like it or not, Logan has set his sights firmly and determinedly on *you*. And I truly believe that the only way you can save yourself is by making sure that the man pays for everything he has done.

There is no way out, Katherine, pretending this isn't happening will not make it go away. Logan wants you, and what Logan wants, Logan . . .'

'The last time he wanted a woman he blew her to pieces.'

'The last time he wanted a woman she took too long to fight back. Logan feels the need to win you over, and if there is some way you can get him to believe that you are on his side, if there is some way you can convince him that you agree with his actions – that you are loyal and devoted and willing to share his secrets and dreams, then . . .'

'Dear God,' said Katherine, clutching at her stomach as Sara took her hand.

'We need you to wear a wire, Katherine. We need you to go to Logan and show him just how loyal a partner you plan to be. We need you to stroke his ego and tell him how free you will both be once the children are incarcerated but explain that in order for you to surrender to his desires, you need to know the truth.'

'I can't,' she said.

'Yes, Katherine. *Yes, you can.*'

There was silence as Sara, teetering on the edge between what could and would not be, prayed beyond anything that Katherine would agree to help. And while she hated the idea of placing this poor woman in danger, while she knew she had not yet spoken to David or Joe about her idea, she also sensed that bringing Katherine on board in a controlled environment might be the only way she could prevent David from going after those guns – and selfishly, just days from the birth of her child, that was the one and only thing she needed desperately to do.

Her thoughts were cut short by the buzzing of Katherine's doorbell – a short, sharp shrill that made both of them jump.

'Do you want me to . . .?' asked Sara.

'No,' gasped Katherine, her breath catching in her throat. 'What if it is Jeffrey – if he sees you here he will . . .?'

'Logan is in court,' said Sara.

'But just in case,' returned Katherine.

And so the terrified Katherine de Castro got to her feet and began down the hallway, her head cocked slightly to the left as if she might have the ability to see through the solid wooden door, her eye poised upwards to that she might line it up with the peephole that would reveal the visitor beyond.

'It's a UPS delivery man,' she said.

'Let him in,' said Sara, which Katherine proceeded to do.

Minutes later, the parcel signed for, the two women returned to the living room, Katherine asking Sara to unwrap the package, explaining she did not believe she was capable of receiving one more gift.

Sara tore the UPS envelope to reveal a medium-sized silver box inside, the label indicating the contents were from some exclusive jewellery store in London. 'More jewels,' she said. 'From the UK.'

And then, as she prised open the lid, what she saw inside was enough to make Sara physically sick to her stomach. It was a clutch purse, embedded with what were no doubt real diamonds and emeralds interwoven with an outline of delicate strands of gold.

'Oh my God,' she said, holding up the purse.

Katherine's hand reached for her throat. 'It's in the shape of a . . .'

'. . . Gun,' finished Sara, unable to take her eyes off the intricately crafted piece, the purse itself no bigger than a modern palm-sized pistol, its clasp wrapping neatly over the barrel, its 'stock' patterned with rubies spelling out the two letters J and K.

And then, as Katherine met Sara's eye, the tears now tracking down her smooth ashen face, she said the three words that Sara, despite herself, hoped beyond all else to hear.

'I'll do it,' said Katherine at last. 'I'll do it.'

65

'Quick, Frank, turn it up,' said Joe Mannix, pointing at the TV on top of his corner filing cabinet. And Frank, tuna sandwich in hand, moved to the corner of his boss' office and hiked up the volume on the twenty-four inch TV.

It was a midday bulletin, and a serious-looking journalist with freckled skin and orange hair was reporting live from Suffolk County Superior Court – saying something about the bizarre events that had just taken place in the overcrowded courtroom 908, where defence counsel for J.T. and Chelsea Logan had admitted one of his clients had impersonated her mother.

'Nobody knows what David Cavanaugh is up to,' said the journalist whose name, according to the graphic beneath him, was Dillon O'Brien. 'One minute he is claiming J.T. Logan was not alone when he fired the bullet that killed his mother, and the next he is admitting his sister was the one to change her mother's will.

'His unusual actions this morning have sparked

speculation that Cavanaugh has decided to lay all the blame on the older of his two clients, so that the younger one gets a better shot at a lighter sentence.'

O'Brien paused there as the screen cut away to his anchor in the studio.

'And the prosecution?' asked the anchor, an attractive middle-aged woman with Peter Pan hair and large green eyes. 'What do they make of Cavanaugh's bizarre approach to the defence?'

'Well, Olivia,' said O'Brien, 'I was able to catch up with ADA Amanda Carmichael just moments ago as she left the courtroom for the lunchtime recess and she told me, and I quote: "*If Mr Cavanaugh ever wants a job in the DA's office I would be happy to accommodate*", obviously meaning that she too is shocked that Cavanaugh and his normally competent team did not go with the more obvious strategy of self-defence.'

'But as you say, Dillon,' said the serious-faced Olivia, 'Cavanaugh is a solid criminal defence attorney and has a reputation for being able to pull a rabbit out of a hat.'

'True, but in all honesty, Olivia, the general feeling here is that Cavanaugh is swimming in circles on this one, and it does not help that the children's father, Doctor Jeffrey Logan, has become a steadfast supporter of the prosecution. We spoke briefly to Doctor Jeff as he entered the courthouse this morning and he reiterated that, as difficult as it was to admit to himself that his children had conspired to murder their mother, he would do whatever he could to make sure his children get the best psychiatric care available.'

An interested Olivia nodded as the screen split to show both presenters.

'There was also a theory that Cavanaugh's performance this morning may have been compromised by the fact that his heavily pregnant partner and co-counsel Sara Davis was absent from the courtroom – which led some to speculate that perhaps Ms Davis had gone into labour, leaving Cavanaugh in two minds as to where he was needed most.'

And that was when Joe noticed her, standing stock-still in his doorway. He could see the anger in Sara's eyes as he muted the TV and moved around his desk to lead her into his office, as Frank's feet shuffled nervously on the carpet and Sara grabbed Joe's hand and said: 'They can shove their theories up their ass, Joe. I've found a way out of this thing but it will only work if you agree to help me.'

'What is it, Sara?' asked Joe as he directed Sara to his small office sofa. And when he held her elbow, he felt it shaking and Joe knew that despite her bravado, this case had finally got the better of her, and that she was barely holding on.

'We have to stop him, Joe. We have to use Katherine de Castro to end this thing. Because if we don't, David will go after the guns and Logan will kill him. Of that much, at least, I am sure.'

Half an hour later, Sara's cell phone calls from David ignored, Joe Mannix finally took a seat in the visitor's chair across from Sara. He had been pacing his office while he listened, perching himself on the edge of his desk every so often in between wearing tracks in the grey government-issue carpet. Frank McKay had remained silent, his untouched home-made tapioca pudding now sitting flat and dry in a scratched pink Tupperware container on the small coffee table before him.

'David didn't tell me,' said Joe, 'about Barbara's conclusions about the guns.'

'Of course he didn't,' said Sara. 'Because there was no way he was going to risk you trying to stop him. What Barbara says makes sense – that if we seek out Logan's obsession, if we get between him and his urge to be near them, then we will draw him out. But the cost is high, Joe, and David being David, he wouldn't want to put you or anyone else in the firing line.'

Joe knew she was right.

'The thing is, Joe, that reporter was spot-on,' she went on, pointing at the muted TV in the corner. 'Our defence is scrappy and disorganised, and without any proof of Logan's true agenda it is only going to get worse. And as much as I don't want to put Katherine in danger, she may be our only option. We need her, Joe – and I need you and Frank to help her help us to get to the truth.'

Joe said nothing, the magnitude of it all sitting heavily in the air between them.

'Does Cavanaugh know where the guns are?' he asked after a time.

'No, but . . .'

And then it came to him. 'You think he thinks they are at Chatham. You think that David believes Stephanie's brochure was a roadmap to Logan's lethal stash.'

Sara nodded. 'He hasn't told me as much because he doesn't want to scare me. But it fits, Joe. Chatham is close, accessible, quiet.'

Joe paused once again.

'And de Castro is on board?' he asked after a time.

'Yes.'

'And she understands the depth of this man's depravity?'

'Well, I told her most of it – editing some of the scarier details such as the fact he just attempted to kill his mother.'

'And you think de Castro is cool enough to be able to pull this off?'

Sara hesitated.

'Sara?'

'No,' she said, realising it was better to tell the truth.

Joe nodded, before rising from his seat once again.

'Frank,' he said turning to his fellow detective friend, 'go see Ms de Castro and see if you can't teach her a thing or two about effective audio surveillance. But take it easy on her; keep her calm until we all have the chance to get together on this thing later tonight.'

Frank nodded, before patting Sara on the shoulder and rising to leave the room.

'Sara,' Joe went on, 'call that pig-headed partner of yours and give him a briefing of your meeting with de Castro. Tell him you've spoken to me and I've suggested we all meet at nine tonight at Myrtle McGee's – Frank will bring de Castro and Mick can supply the beers.' It was the only thing Joe could think of to say to take the edge off the situation.

'David's gonna kill me for leaving the house, Joe.'

'And I'm gonna kill him for thinking he could go this one alone.'

'I love him so much I hate him, Joe.'

'Yeah, I know. David tends to have that effect on people.'

66

'David Cavanaugh's office, this is Nora Kelly speaking. How may I help you?'

Nora's voice echoed around the empty offices. With David and Arthur in court and Sara resting at home, she felt the dual sensation of anxiousness and responsibility – anxious to find out exactly how her co-workers were progressing during the second day at trial, anxious about the fact that Sara was due to give birth in a matter of days, but pleased she could be here holding the fort, while her colleagues did their best to set those poor children free.

'Mrs Kelly,' said the girl. 'My name is Tracey Scabo, we spoke some weeks ago when my friend, Ms McCall . . .'

'Of course, Miss Scabo,' said Nora, sitting up in her seat. 'How can I help you? Has there been some news of Ms McCall's whereabouts?'

'Call me Tracey and . . . the answer to your question is no, but . . .'

'What is it, Tracey?' asked Nora, her heart beating double time.

'She rang me.'

Nora could not believe what she was hearing. *McCall had made contact* – which meant she must be well enough to move about, which meant she had not collapsed after fleeing the hospital moments after waking from a coma.

'Thank God,' said Nora, a wave of relief washing over her. 'What did she say, Tracey? Where is she?'

'She said she was okay – I mean, that is why she rang, to tell me she was all right. She was worried I would be worried – which I have been, of course.'

'And her whereabouts?' asked Nora again, her pencil at the ready.

'That's the thing, Mrs Kelly, she refused to tell me where she was. She said she was calling from a payphone, but that she didn't want to involve me – that it was too dangerous!'

A disheartened Nora hesitated before going on. 'She obviously cares for you very much, Tracey. But listen, dear, did she say anything that might give you an inkling as to where she might be. Did you hear any noise in the background or . . .?'

'No,' said Tracey, and Nora exhaled in disappointment. 'But she called my cell, which meant the number came up on my screen.'

'You have the number she called from?'

'Yes, it was a 508 number.'

'508,' said Nora, turning her computer screen around quickly so that she might Google the area code.

'I looked it up,' said Tracey. '508 is one of the area codes for Cape Cod.'

'*Cape Cod*,' repeated Nora, when finally it came to her. 'Tracey, what parts of Cape Cod does that exchange cover, dear?' she asked as she continued to Google the area herself. 'Does 508 include the area of . . .?'

But she did not need the girl to answer. Nora had Googled the Chatham Bars Inn and, sure enough, its number was listed with a prefix of 508.

'Tracey, I need you to give me the full number, dear, so that we might talk to the police and try to find out exactly where Miss McCall might be.'

'But she told me not to look for her.'

'Which is exactly why we must, dear. Miss McCall may be in danger,' she said, before realising she was probably scaring the girl half to death. 'What I mean to say is, she should be examined by a doctor to make sure she is all right.'

Tracey agreed, giving the number to Nora before asking her to please keep in touch.

As Nora hung up the phone, her heart now pounding with a mixture of nervousness, excitement and fear, she knew there was only one way she could truly help her loved ones to win this seemingly unwinnable case. She would call Joe Mannix and provide him with the information Tracey had shared, and then, when the time was right, she would drive to Chatham and find Miss McCall herself.

67

Chelsea Logan's skin was pale. She had just been taken to the bathroom by a female security attendant who waited outside while Chelsea barfed into the toilet. The afternoon session had been nothing short of catastrophic, Medical Examiner Gus Svenson having spent a good three hours detailing Stephanie Logan's extensive internal injuries, Amanda Carmichael making the most of a series of photographic 'blow-ups', until juror number three, a middle-aged home-maker by the name of Cassandra Clements, requested a much needed recess so that the jury might hold on to their lunch.

David's head was spinning. Half of him was furious at Sara for not staying at home to rest and the other half wanted to kiss her for finally convincing Katherine de Castro to come on board. Not that he was sure what her efforts would accomplish, given Jeffrey Logan's superior intelligence and his innate ability to read a set-up a mile and a half away.

He had not had a chance to tell the children about de Castro – and in all honesty he was not sure he should. For giving them false hope at this stage seemed beyond cruel, especially given what the pair had just had to sit through, seeing their murdered mother, in poster-sized, digitally enhanced colour, mutilated by a bullet powerful enough to create a bloody crater in her back.

'They don't believe us,' said Chelsea. 'They think we killed her for her money. They think we masterminded the entire scheme so that we could cut our father out of her will and live like royalty for the rest of our lives.'

David glanced at Arthur, knowing that what their distressed client was saying was true.

'It is early days, Chelsea,' said Arthur, moving across the small courtside interview room to sit beside the trembling teenager. 'Unfortunately, there was no way we could refute the ME's testimony as it was a basic statement of fact. But we can refute who is responsible for leaving your mother in such a condition. And we will.'

'But nobody is going to believe us,' argued Chelsea, rising from her seat to pace the room. Her brother was sitting in the opposite corner, his head down, his right foot tapping nervously on the floor. 'My father is invincible. The people love him – and now they hate us even more for conspiring to cut him out of that will.

'Don't you see,' she said, and in that moment David wished Sara were here to comfort her, 'those people, on the jury, they just spent the entire afternoon looking at pictures that will haunt them for the rest of their lives – and then they looked across at us, and the hatred in their eyes was unmistakable.

'They don't just *want* to put us away, David, they *need* to,' she said, meeting his eye. 'Like we are some evil blot on their perfect utopian landscape – two deranged malformations with blood on our hands and greed in our hearts who blew our mother to bits in cold blood just so we could get our hands on her estate.

'No,' she went on, stopping in front of her brother. 'Our father had three victims in his sights when he plotted to get Mom's inheritance – it's just that me and J.T., well, we're taking longer to die.'

There was silence as David felt an all-encompassing realisation spread through his consciousness. It started as a chill in the base of his back before moving up his spine and consuming his entire body in a wave of horror and clarity. Chelsea was right, this wasn't just about the power, it was also about the money. Jeffrey Logan had recently inherited hundreds of millions of dollars thanks to the demise of his wife, and while he may have been a wealthy man in his own right, to a psychopath like Logan, enough was never enough, until he had bled all those around him dry.

'Chelsea,' he said, moving towards her, 'your mother was the sole owner of Rockwell Wineries, am I right?'

Chelsea's brow furrowed, obviously having no idea why David was asking the obvious.

'Yes,' she said.

'But a year ago this wasn't the case. A year ago she was the major beneficiary, a director and salary earner of your grandfather's company – a company he built from scratch.'

'Yes,' said J.T., the first word he had spoken all afternoon.

'But your grandfather, Stephanie's dad,' said David as he crouched down to take both J.T.'s and Chelsea's hands, 'he died in a boating accident – what, sometime late last . . .'

'It was just after last Christmas, he was sailing off the Cape,' said Chelsea.

'Where abouts off the Cape, Chelsea?' asked David.

'Ummm, I am pretty sure it was as east as the Cape takes you – on the elbow, just off the town of . . .'

'Chatham,' said David.

And Chelsea nodded.

David shot a look at Arthur before moving on. 'And do you guys remember if there was ever any investigation into his death? Did the local police make any queries, was an autopsy ever arranged?'

'No,' said J.T., his right leg now stopping mid-shake. 'They told us Grandfather was sailing in stormy weather when the boom most likely swung around to hit him – and that the force of the impact sent him overboard where the water was cold and rough and . . .'

'Oh my God,' said Chelsea. 'Do you think . . .?'

But David was already on his feet. 'Arthur, we need to talk to Joe – and then we have to get hold of a judge who is crazy enough to grant us a court order.'

'I don't understand,' said a wide-eyed J.T. 'A court order for what?'

'To exhume your grandfather's body, J.T., and find the hole that marks the track of the bullet that killed him.'

68

Later that night

When David finally entered the front door of the harbourside café known as Myrtle McGee's, he was overwhelmed by the sight before him. Looking up at him were nine people, his team of dedicated friends and supporters, people who were willing to put their lives on the line in order to fight for his cause – to save the Logan children and bring their father to justice.

He was late. After leaving the Logan kids he had gone back to the office to research the precedent of exhumation of the deceased – particularly those close to twelve months after death with no concrete evidence that the cause of death was anything except accidental. He was even trying to see a pattern – if one judge may have been more conducive to granting such a request compared to others – but in the end he had come up blank. There just weren't that many cases that required such a petition, which was obviously a good thing, except in this case, where finding a link to Logan's culpability seemed close to impossible.

Joe was there, with a dedicated Frank McKay by his side. And then there was Arthur, and Nora, psychologist and friend Barbara Wong-McGregor, the brave Katherine de Castro, and his beloved partner Sara. The eighth person in the room was perhaps unexpected – his old college friend and Logan's lawyer Tony Bishop who, after taking a swig of his beer, walked across the room to shake David's hand.

'Stephanie was my friend, DC,' he said. 'Tomorrow morning I am going to go straight to my boss and officially remove myself from Logan's payroll so that I can help you squash the bastard.'

David smiled. 'That must have hurt,' he said. 'I believe Logan has a buck or two to spend.'

'He can shove his money up his ass,' said Tony.

'Hear, hear to that,' said the café's proprietor, and team member number nine, Mick McGee who, David knew, knew little of their cause but shared such a strong friendship with most of the people in the room that he would support them regardless. 'This TV pansy sounds like a right asshole,' Mick said with a grin as he handed David a beer. 'And you can rely on me to supply all the refreshments necessary for the rest of the evening.'

'This ginger beer is great, Mick,' said Joe then, lifting his full-strength Bud into the air. Mick's breakfast and lunchtime café had no liquor licence, a small technicality Joe and Frank had turned a blind eye to more than once.

'Then I'll keep it coming,' said Mick, as he moved back into the kitchen. 'And I have a bottle of cranberry juice that tastes mysteriously like sherry out the back, Mrs Kelly.'

'Then I shan't say no,' said Nora with a smile.

And David felt more grateful than ever, as he moved to Sara and took her in his arms. 'You lied to me,' he said quietly into her ear.

'So what are you going to do?' She smiled. 'Ground me?'

'That doesn't seem to work.'

'Funny that,' she said.

And then they got down to it, pooling all their information so that they might decide upon a plan to finally put an end to this nightmare. In the end it was Barbara who came up with it – her idea being inspired and terrifying all at the very same time.

'No,' said Barbara, now rising from her corner booth to arch her back and stretch her legs.

They had been going at it for hours, spending most of their time establishing what they had and deciding upon which angle to work given time was short and Carmichael was blitzing them at trial. It had not taken long for them to realise that, despite what they believed they 'knew' about Logan, they had *nothing* concrete, *no one* at their fingertips to put on the stand and prove it. And that was why Katherine de Castro's role in this whole mess had become so important – as when she did meet Logan wearing a wire, her approach could be nothing short of foolproof.

'It's not going to work,' said Barbara, continuing her train of thought.

'Why not?' asked Sara, now joining Barbara on her feet. 'Katherine is the only one who can reach him. He is enamoured by her. You said it yourself – Logan will see winning her affections as a victory, so why not let him think he has won this battle, so that we can win the war?'

Sara had spent the past twenty minutes posing her idea as to how de Castro should approach her conversation with Logan. David could tell she had been thinking of nothing else all afternoon – and he had to admit, her proposal sounded impressive. Basically, Sara had proposed that Katherine apologise to Logan for not being more conducive to his advances, that she tell him she had been concerned he was too emotionally distressed by recent events to make clear decisions, to know his heart, to know his mind. But now she could deny her true feelings no longer – she was in fact falling for Logan too – and if she was completely honest with herself she would have to admit that she had probably had feelings for him for some time, feelings she had never acknowledged, out of respect to Logan, to his children and his wife.

Sara's plan had Katherine expressing her devotion to Logan, voicing her belief that their long-term business partnership was proof of their ability to work together as a team. And now she wanted something more, to be his confidante not just in matters of business but also in matters of the heart. She needed him to open his soul to her, to express his most secret desires and feelings, to tell her about the *real* Jeffrey Logan – and how he came to be the man he was.

'I thought we agreed that Katherine had to appeal to Logan's vanity,' Sara continued after a breath, the slightest tinge of frustration in her voice. 'That she had to lead him carefully into a position where he wanted to share his diabolical plans, *brag* about them even, and show her exactly how clever he is.'

But Barbara was already shaking her head. 'No, Sara. Katherine shouldn't be appealing to his vanity but *challenging* it. Your plan makes absolute sense,' she said, now confusing all in the room, 'if we are talking about your average egotistical asshole. But you have to remember Logan is way up there on the scale of psychopathological intellect. He may be vain, but his superior intelligence will always act as a monitor to his emotions. In other words, as much as he *wants* to "secure" Katherine here as his own,' Barbara gestured at a now ashen-faced de Castro, 'he will see her little act for exactly what it is – a feigned attempt to get him to show his cards. And the consequences of this could be disastrous – as it would place Katherine in . . .' But Barbara stopped there, her eyes darting to Katherine, before making their way over to David. She was telling them that in her opinion Sara's plan would put Katherine's life in serious danger – and they could not afford to risk it.

'So what approach *does* Katherine take?' asked Joe, perhaps feeling the need to cut the silence short.

'She tells him the truth,' said Barbara.

'She *what*?' asked an incredulous Sara.

But Barbara hesitated before answering, her eyes once again meeting David's, as if sensing that he knew exactly what Katherine de Castro had to do, and should be the one to voice it.

'Katherine has to tell him what we are up to,' he said. 'She must go to him and tell him that you came to see her.' David looked over at Sara. 'She must repeat a version of your conversation – tell him what you claimed, tell him we think he is a diabolical monster and that we want her help to bring him down.'

'No,' said Sara. 'David this is . . .'

But then David saw the realisation in her eyes – that it was the only thing Logan *would* believe. That it was the only approach that would keep Katherine de Castro safe – and force Jeffrey Logan into a position where he would do exactly what they wanted.

'I'm sorry, Sara, but David's right,' said Barbara. 'We have to flush him out. We have to convince him that we are closing in – and that he has no choice but to act. Don't forget the man has an inherent need to feed whatever his particular urge might be, and if his urge is a need to be near his weapons, then we need to give him a reason to seek them out.'

'You want to use Katherine to feed Logan's desire to go after his massive collection of weaponry somewhere in Chatham so that he can return to Boston and hunt David down?' said Sara, her cheeks now flushed with anger. '*This was not how this was supposed to go*,' she continued, her eyes pooling with tears.

'Sara,' said Joe, feeling the need to reassure her, 'I don't like this any more than you do.' He looked across at David. 'But this may be our only way out. If Logan goes for his guns we will be on his tail within minutes and sticking to him like glue. And the minute we find his arsenal we can trace each and every one of his guns back to their original purchaser – Jason Nagol. And if David is right about Stephanie's father, if we get that exhumation order and find a bullet in his head, we may even be able to match the bullet to the weapon and nail this bastard for good.'

'And what about his mother, Joe?' asked Sara. 'What if that poor woman finds the guns first? We all know she must be aware of Logan's arsenal – I mean, why else would she have dragged herself from her hospital bed to trek from one side of the country to the other?'

'We traced her call to a payphone in Chatham, Sara,' said Joe. 'There are only so many places she could be staying. We'll find her before she puts herself or anyone else in danger, and then me and Frank will be free to . . .'

'To *what*, Joe? Paint a target on David's back?'

There was silence as Sara met David's eye, her chest heaving in a series of short, sharp breaths. She looked to those around her, perhaps sensing that there was no way she was going to convince them. And in that moment David wished beyond anything that things were different – but they weren't, and they wouldn't be, until Jeffrey Logan was brought to justice.

'I can help,' said Tony Bishop, a new voice in the mix, his eyes following a now defeated Sara as she slowly re-took her seat.

'Help how?' asked David, reaching under the table to take Sara's hand.

'You want to make him angry enough to go for the guns? I think I know exactly how that can be achieved.' Tony took a breath before going on. 'Maybe all that evidence you *don't* have could be used to your advantage – I mean, you may not have a list of witnesses to rat this lowlife out, but Logan doesn't need to know that, does he?'

'I don't understand, Tony,' said David. 'What the hell are you saying?'

'I am saying that maybe it is about time Logan's ghosts came back to haunt him – and I know exactly the person to open their cage and let them loose.'

69

The banging was loud enough to wake her – the banging and intermittent buzzing and now thumping on her high-rise apartment door.

'*Jesus*,' said Amanda Carmichael, as she prised open her pale blue eyes, the brightness of the moonlight now squeezing her pupils into pinpricks. '*Who in the hell?*'

She rose from her bed, grabbing her pink silk gown from the nightstand before making her way across the apartment. Her heart was racing, partly because she had been pulled from a deep and much sought after sleep (it had been midnight before she had managed to drift off), and partly because she was instinctively suspecting (hoping) the person on the other side of the door might be the same one she had kissed, unexpectedly, mere nights before. But a glance through the peephole showed it to be none other than Tony Bishop, the expression on his face pure panic.

'Jesus, Tony,' she said, as she pulled the door open.

'It's nearly 1am for Christ's sake. What the hell is your problem?'

'I'm not the one with the problem, Amanda,' he said, moving past her to pace her expansive living room. 'I did not know what else to do . . . I mean, I have a moral obligation, to my client.'

Amanda studied her ex-lover before her; Tony was genuinely flummoxed. She had never seen him so agitated before.

'What is it, Tony?' she asked, shutting the door behind him.

'It's David – I mean . . . shit, Amanda, you have no idea how hard this is for me. DC is one of my oldest friends, but Logan is a long-term client and you are prosecutor in his children's case and . . .'

'You know something . . . about Cavanaugh?' she asked, her curiosity well and truly piqued. 'You have some information about his defence which you have a moral obligation to disclose.' She knew she was leading him, but she did not give a damn.

'Yes,' said Tony, now moving quickly towards her. 'He . . . he has a new list . . . an extended one, which he obviously does not intend to disclose until he begins his presentation of evidence and . . .'

'Slow down, Tony,' she said, taking his arm. 'What list? What is Cavanaugh hiding?'

'His witness list. I saw it . . . I mean, it was by accident, of course. I met him for a drink after work. We've been friends for years and I was worried this case had come between us . . . which it hasn't, at least not *yet*, but . . . then he went to the men's room and this drunk guy, he walked past our bar stools and knocked over

DC's briefcase and this folder fell out and . . .'

'You saw his witness list?' she asked, her eyes now wide with excitement. 'But the list he provided for the court contained only a handful of names – character witnesses for the children, the kids' psychologist, the kids themselves.'

'This one is different,' said Tony.

'Different how?'

'There are at least five new names – and their addresses are from all over the country, from Nevada and Maine to . . .'

'Jesus, Tony, who are these people? Did you memorise them? Jeffrey Logan is your client after all and . . .'

'I wrote them down,' he said, pulling a small piece of notepaper from his crumpled shirt pocket, his face a mixture of resolution and self-disgust.

'Tony, I . . .' She could barely contain herself. She would have even embraced the sweaty, panicking man before her if she had not been in such a hurry to study the names on the list. But then her brow furrowed.

'I don't understand,' she said. 'Who the hell are these people? Carleton Blackmore, William 'Little Willie' Dukes, Gerald and Calvin Garretson – well, they are the gun traders but . . . a Mrs Deirdre McCall, a Detective Michael Lopez of the Las Vegas Police . . . who . . . why in God's name would he be . . .?'

'I have no idea, Amanda, but these names have to mean something to somebody.'

The cogs in Amanda's brain turned in double-time, as she tried to put it all together. 'Cavanaugh has a bee in his bonnet about Logan, Logan was born in Vegas, this has to have something to do with him.'

'Then maybe he will know who these people are?' said Tony.

Amanda nodded, before looking at her watch. 'It's the middle of the night.'

'It's the middle of the trial,' countered Tony.

And Amanda sensed that Tony was right – there was no way she was waiting another six hours to find out what the hell Cavanaugh was up to.

'Grab that telephone behind you,' she said, pointing to the hands-free on the coffee table. 'And get Logan on the line – now!'

Moments later, just as Tony Bishop was listening to the ring of Jeffrey Logan's telephone, Sara Davis was lying two miles east, praying for an end to this madness and wishing, beyond all else, that her unborn child would not be brought up without a father.

'I'm so sorry, Sara,' said David, knowing she was not asleep. They had spent the previous hour arguing, their heated to-ing and fro-ing getting them nowhere, before Sara had finally caved in to exhaustion and made her way to bed.

'I wish things were different. I wish I knew how to let things go, to turn my back and move on.' He took a breath. 'But you knew who I was when you . . .'

And Sara knew he was about to say '*married me*' – but he stopped when he remembered they had never actually got around to the marriage thing – something they knew would come eventually, but had been delayed by their work, by her pregnancy, by . . .

'I don't know what else I can promise you,' David went on, 'aside from my assurance that I won't take any unnecessary risks. I mean, if all goes to plan, Joe and Frank will have Logan in custody before he gets anywhere near me.'

'No,' she said after a time. 'He's too smart, David, and you are all too busy playing caped crusader to see it. Logan will go after those guns with a clear and singular purpose – to rid him of the one person who has the power to bring him down. He'll be going after you, David, and there is nothing you can do to stop him.'

David said nothing for a long, long time.

'Sara?' he whispered at last.

'Yes.'

'Will you marry me?'

Then more silence until: 'Yes.'

And they lay there, quietly, gently, the two of them – or, more to the point, three – until finally they fell asleep, the images of what was meant to be playing hopefully in their dreams.

70

On, off. On, off.

It was early, barely past seven, and the lights in the almost empty courtroom 908 were flickering, creating a strobe-like effect on the one inhabitant who, at first glance, appeared to be dancing around the high-ceilinged expanse with a long white stick.

'Judge,' said David, obviously scaring the dogged-faced Kessler who was now jumping up and down with her head craned towards the ceiling above her.

'*For goodness' sake, Counsellor*,' she said, the lights finally returning to show the aforementioned stick now stuck in the soft wood ceiling above her. 'Now look what you've done,' she said, pointing to the circular light fitting above.

And finally David realised what she was doing. Years ago many of the courtrooms in the Superior Court building had been fitted with sensor lights – designed to come on and go off when people entered and left the room. They were installed in an attempt to conserve energy – which now seemed somewhat ironic considering the red-faced judge before him.

'The ceilings are too bloody high! These lights are made for your average-sized room – not one with eighteen-foot ceilings. So I thought if I got that pole,' she said, pointing to the long stick suspended above her, '. . . the one the clerks used to open the high eastern windows, that I could wave it around underneath the lights and force them to . . .'

'Come on,' said David, who smiled, despite himself.

'Exactly,' said Kessler, smiling in return, a rare expression which, David had to admit, made the normally hard-faced woman look surprisingly genuine, sincere, approachable.

'Couldn't sleep?' she asked, making a final gesture at both David and the stick as if suggesting he move into the room and help her dislodge the long white pole.

'Something like that,' he said, tugging hard on the pole to release it.

'And why doesn't that surprise me?' she said, taking the stick with a nod before returning it to its usual place by the window. 'This may be my first murder trial, Mr Cavanaugh, but something tells me most of them don't go quite like this. I can't say I am a fan of the one-horse race, Counsellor, which, in all honesty, I did not expect this to be.'

'I suppose I should take that as a compliment,' said David.

'Or an insult,' she countered.

And David knew she was right.

'I need a favour, Judge.'

'I would suggest you need more than a favour, Mr

Cavanaugh,' she said, leading him to a bench so that they might take a seat.

'I know,' he admitted. 'But for now, this one favour – well, I am hoping it might snowball onto something else.'

'Sort of like one small step for man, one giant leap for the Logan children's defence?'

And David had to admit there was something quite admirable about this woman's refusal to beat around the bush.

'Something like that.'

Kessler nodded. 'Well, what is it, Counsellor? To what do I owe the unexpected delights of this early morning visit?'

'I need a court order to exhume a body.'

Kessler jumped. 'You *what*? Is this some sort of joke? I mean, unless I am mistaken, Counsellor, the cause of death in relation to the victim in this case is irrefutable.'

'Not the victim,' he interrupted. 'The victim's father.'

'Malcolm Tyler.'

David was impressed, Kessler had obviously done her homework on the Tyler/Logan clan as a whole.

'Didn't he die in some boating accident . . .?'

'He was sailing, off the Cape, about a year ago.'

'And you want to exhume his body because . . .?'

'I think he was shot.'

Kessler gave that little jump once again. 'And you suspect this hypothetical killer is the same person who . . .?'

'. . . shot Stephanie Tyler.'

Kessler nodded – a nod that soon transformed into a shake. 'Do the police know about this?'

'Lieutenant Joe Mannix is waiting outside, Judge. He is on board with this – but we need to do it quickly and quietly so that . . . well, timing and discretion are everything.'

'I gather Miss Carmichael has not been informed about your desire to undertake this merry excavation?'

'Ah – not yet,' said David. 'But I promise she will be if anything relevant to the case turns up.'

'Hmmm,' considered Kessler. 'Well I do respect Mannix.'

'He's the best,' said a hopeful David.

'But such an order would be highly controversial. What about permission from the man's next of kin?'

'J.T. and Chelsea Logan are giving "permission to exhume" statements to my co-counsel Sara Davis and another attorney by the name of Tony Bishop as we speak, and as the man's grandchildren . . .'

'Children is correct, Mr Cavanaugh. Normally these things require the permission of an adult relative.'

'If they are old enough to be tried as adults in an adult court, Judge, I would suggest they have earned the right to speak in the best interests of their grandfather's remains.'

Kessler nodded. 'Touché, Mr Cavanaugh,' she said, before meeting David's eye once again. 'Is this going to come back to bite me, Counsellor?' she asked, and David knew she was asking if the media would be involved. There had been cases in the past where desperate defence attorneys had used stunts such as an exhumation to divert attention from their lack of evidence – but David suspected Kessler knew him better than this and was praying he was right.

'No,' he answered.

Kessler took a breath. 'Then I need some comprehensive documentation explaining your grounds for this highly unusual request – and you have to get me those children's statements before I commit to anything solid.'

David let out a sigh of relief. He sensed that, given her level of interest, and her obvious desire to be as thorough as possible on her first murder trial, it was unlikely she would deny any request that could come back to bite her at appeal.

'Thanks, Judge,' he said.

Kessler nodded before rising from her seat. 'Just promise me, if anyone asks about that hole in the ceiling,' she pointed skyward, 'that you will deny any knowledge as to how it got there.'

'What hole?' said David.

'Exactly,' said Kessler. 'What damned hole indeed.'

71

'*Make the lie big, make it simple, keep saying it, and eventually they will believe it.*' And here was another one – '*Great liars are also great magicians*.' And another – '*The victor will never be asked if he told the truth*.'

These were all spoken by history's greatest manipulator, a man Logan admired beyond all others, the Führer with great foresight and power who understood that '*The broad masses of a population are more amenable to the appeal of rhetoric than to any other force*'. In other words, as long as you told people what they wanted to hear, then they were more than happy to believe it. And what better way to do so than as a man who *talks* as a profession. It really was quite beautiful – the profoundness of it all.

Jeffrey Logan looked at himself in the mirror as he adjusted his Ralph Lauren tie and ran his hands over his freshly shaven cheeks. He was a good-looking man – and that had certainly helped, but his charisma went beyond the aesthetic. He had a way with people, an inbuilt ability to charm and beguile and sway. And while he would like to think that much of his 'talent' was due to his insatiable appetite for self-advancement, he knew that much of his skill had come down to luck – at being born the person he was, devoid of morality and that pesky emotional anchor known as a conscience.

Logan lied with ease – and people believed him. And the chosen few who had seen his true self were either too terrified or too dead to retaliate. His whole life was a lie – a brilliant, cleverly constructed work of propaganda which had made him incredibly popular and exceedingly rich. Even better was his ability not to feel fear. Some people were born blind and never knew what it was like to see, but Logan had been born valiant and never knew what it was like to fear.

He had not panicked at Tony Bishop's late night call. While it had not been expected – and, truth be told, it had made his heart race just a little – he had almost immediately turned this unanticipated development into a source of invigoration. David Cavanaugh had balls. He was in fact (and this was the ultimate compliment), probably the greatest adversary he had ever encountered. But it was about time Logan found himself someone worthy of his talents – someone whose destruction he suspected would bring unknown levels of pleasure.

He took a moment to ponder once more on the list. Carleton Blackmore, Willie Dukes – well, of course they could provide Cavanaugh with information on Jason Nagol, but Logan knew they were fishing in that empty pond weeks ago when Carleton first called him (as Nagol) and told him they were asking about his treasured 'Ben Hur'. Logan had spent his entire life covering his tracks and there was no way Cavanaugh had any proof that Logan and Nagol were one and the same. Of this, beyond anything, he was sure.

As for the Garretsons – that pair of half-witted gun traders did not worry him an ounce. The son may have come clean about his lies regarding the gun's delivery but there was no way Cavanaugh could trace the Mark V's purchase to Logan.

And when it came to the last two people on Cavanaugh's list – well, once again, if Logan was completely honest with himself (which he was, given his lies had always been limited to everyone else in the universe apart from himself), he would have to admit that they *did* concern him just a little.

His mother was a dead woman walking, of this he was sure. But she might be stupid enough to be persuaded to tell her story in a pathetic moment of gallantry, given she had already defied death twice and may (rightly) assume that she had nothing to lose as the third and final effort would inevitably do the trick. He had been holding a gun to his mother's head since the very moment he had been born – and while, at this time, he may not be physically forcing the barrel against her brow like he had done so many times in his youth, he knew she could still feel it there, cold and hard – and she might see 'talking' as her last valiant act before execution.

As for the Las Vegas detective, his Asian friends had assured him that the Nevada dick had nothing. And considering his good 'friend' and former prison mate Damien Chi had control of his Boyz, and Logan in turn had complete control of the sexually deficient Chi, he felt reasonably confident this last name on Cavanaugh's list would lead to nothing.

And so, he resolved to himself as he reached for his Armani jacket and checked his watch making sure he would be well and truly on time for his third day in court, he would make some discreet enquiries as to the whereabouts of his mother. And if by a long shot recent events were not enough to keep her quiet, if she was not content to stay holed up in whatever Nevada back-water she had buried herself in, he would simply wait until she raised as much as an eyebrow before blowing her fucking head off.

As for Cavanaugh, he smiled to himself, *when the time is right I shall not rule out the possibility of rewarding myself with a face-off. For as my beloved Aldolf Hitler also said: 'Strength lies not in defence but in attack and the very first essential for success, is a perpetually constant, and regular employment of violence.'*

72

'Well?' asked Joe Mannix, when he saw David round the corridor of the Superior Court's buzzing level nine.

'Walk with me,' said David, as they entered the lift and headed back down to the ground floor.

'Kessler's in,' he said, as soon as they hit the lobby and he was sure they would not be overheard.

Joe smiled. 'That's great. To be honest, I didn't think she would go for it – thought she might want to play it conservatively, this being her first murder trial and all.'

'She surprised me too – I think there's more to Kessler than meets the eye.'

Joe nodded. 'So what do we have to do?'

'Get the kids' letters of authority and file a motion to exhume. I'll be in court all day so I'll ask Sara to do it.'

Joe grabbed David's elbow as soon as they moved outside into the sunshine. 'How is that going by the way? With you and Sara, I mean.'

Joe was never one to pry but David knew that after

last night's heated discussions, his good friend would have been concerned about how this case was affecting him and Sara. Just the fact that he was asking told David that Joe could see just how deep this one was dragging them.

'I asked her to marry me,' said David, immediately seeing the surprise in Joe's eyes.

'Was that your idea of perfect timing?'

'I've never been the violin-and-roses type of guy, Joe.'

'No, you're more of the "*I am going to ask you to marry me before I go and get myself killed*" kind of operator.'

David smiled, despite himself. 'Well, whatever I did, it worked.'

'She said yes?'

'I guess she's a glutton for punishment.'

An obviously delighted Joe took David's hand and shook it with gusto. 'Sara is an idiot and you are the luckiest man on earth,' he said, slapping his friend on the back.

'I know, Joe. I know.'

Moments later they were ordering coffees at a nearby café in the semi-circular Centre Plaza Building, running quickly over their immediate plans before David had to leave for court.

'Frank, Barbara and I will be working with Katherine de Castro for most of the day – helping her with her approach to Logan, giving her some tools to maintain her calm.'

'We need this to happen soon, Joe.'

'I know. Today is Wednesday so we're looking at the end of the week at the latest, we want to give Logan a stretch of time to head to the Cape and those precious guns of his. A Friday evening rendezvous would be perfect – gives him the weekend to start heading south.'

David nodded. 'I haven't heard from Tony.'

'Give him time, it's only early. The witness list thing was a good idea.'

'It was, but something tells me it will take more than that to rattle Logan. This guy is cool, Joe – he knows he has covered his tracks.'

'I agree – but his mother is a wild card, David. Her name alone will give him cause to wonder.'

And then, as if on cue, Joe's cell rang – Joe immediately retrieving his worse-for-wear Nokia before putting it to his ear. 'Mannix,' he answered.

'Lopez, how goes it?' he said after a pause, his eyes lifting to meet David's across the table.

A few more moments passed with Joe saying close to nothing, merely breaking up the almost one-way conversation with 'yeahs', 'okays' and 'I see what you means'.

'You think this kid will fold?' he asked, before giving the slightest of nods in acknowledgement to Lopez's response. 'Okay then – and thanks, Lopez. Just let me know the moment you want me to shake things down this end.'

And Joe hung up just as David opened his mouth to say, 'That was Lopez from Vegas?'

'Yeah. I rang him yesterday to tell him about McCall's telephone call from the Cape. He offered to contact the cops in Chatham so that they could start door-to-dooring some local hotels and B&Bs. This Lopez is switched on, and it was his case from the get-go, so I saw no harm in keeping him in the loop – in fact, the guy may have just handed us a breakthrough, depending on how this plays out.'

'How so?' asked David, moving his coffee aside so that he might lean that bit further onto the table.

'Well, Lopez has been trying to work the Asian Boyz angle for weeks, but up until late yesterday he was having no luck. These Chinese kids are tight, David. They have a "no tolerance" policy when it comes to informing based on the premise that anyone who snitches gets his tongue cut out and is left locked up somewhere until he bleeds to death.'

'Sounds like a deterrent, all right,' said David. 'So what happened last night?'

'There's this young kid – seventeen, name is Mickey Tsi. Last night Lopez arrested Tsi after he was apprehended in an alley where he'd nabbed a pedestrian, taken his wallet at gunpoint and proceeded to pistol whip the guy for good measure. That's robbery and assault with a deadly weapon – or in other words, a serious felony. And considering young Mr Tsi already has three felonies to his name . . .'

'He is classified as a habitual offender,' finished David, Lopez's breakthrough now starting to make sense.

David knew that Nevada had their own version of California's famous 'Three Strike Rule' in the form of the Habitual Offender Stature or the NRS 207.010. Basically, the statute stated that any person charged with a felony and who had been convicted previously for three felonies can be classified as a 'habitual criminal' and face severe penalties such as life imprisonment.

'The kid's going away for life,' said David. 'Unless he gets a sympathetic prosecutor willing to cut him a break and not file for habitual criminality when he goes for an indictment.'

'Exactly,' said Joe. 'Which means our man Lopez has a bit of rope to play with. The local ADA is a friend and Lopez has already spoken to him about playing a little tit for tat.'

'So they are going to ask this Tsi to give up who gave the order on McCall in return for Tsi getting a break with the ADA.'

'That's the idea.'

'And when will they . . .?'

'Today. Lopez wanted the kid to sweat overnight.'

David nodded. 'If we can link Logan to those Asian Boyz we have him, Joe.'

'I know,' said Joe. 'But let's take this one step at a time . . . speaking of which . . .'

'I have to go,' said David, draining his lukewarm coffee before rising to his feet.

'Who's up today?' asked Joe, referring to Carmichael's witness list.

'Carmichael's calling that psychologist from the TV show – Professor Hinds from Harvard. The ADA's going to spend most of the day painting my old friend as the abusive bitch from hell – by getting Hinds to run commentary as she runs that video on a loop.'

Joe shook his head before looking up at David once again. 'We're making progress,' he said. It was his attempt at comfort.

'I know, but we're still flying blind, Joe, and in the end I can't help but think this whole thing will come down to luck.'

'Then maybe today will be your lucky day?'

'Maybe, Joe. Maybe.'

73

It had started when that excuse for a lawyer Charles Harrison had offered his plea, and reappeared last week when Cavanaugh had come to her door – that tiny little niggle. But Tony's unexpected arrival in the early hours of this morning had now made it stronger than ever – that feeling that not all was right with the world, that she was missing something or rather, that something was missing *her*.

Logan's reaction had surprised her. She had spoken to him at length last night and his calm nonchalance was nothing short of unsettling. He said he knew no one on Cavanaugh's supposed list besides the Garretsons – and that was only because he had heard their names mentioned in the process of pre-trial investigations.

'I don't see the problem, Miss Carmichael,' he had said. 'Cavanaugh is obviously bluffing. He and Bishop are old friends, you know – in fact I believe they both may have slept with my late wife at one time or another, which is rather troubling in its own way, don't you think?'

And that had pretty much been it – Logan had basically disregarded Carmichael's concerns outright which should, at least in theory, reassure her that there was nothing to worry about. Except for the fact that she knew Cavanaugh was above dirty tricks like bluffing – which meant those names had to mean something . . .

'*Miss Carmichael*,' boomed a rosy-cheeked Kessler over the hubbub. And Carmichael noted a slight lift in the judge's normally gruff tone this morning. 'Are you ready to call your next witness?'

'Yes, Your Honour,' said Carmichael, now shelving her private concerns so that she might rise to her feet and approach this day as she did any other – with confidence. 'The Commonwealth calls Professor Georgia Hinds.'

Amanda watched as the members of the press sat up at the ready, and the gallery fidgeted in hope, and she knew everyone in this packed courtroom was praying she would be rolling out that now infamous birthday video which had been screened only once on the Doctor Jeff *Newsline* special before being banned from any further viewings for fear of its potential to influence the trial.

And despite her recent misgivings, she would not disappoint them. In fact she would be using that incriminating masterpiece to tilt her approach to the case as a whole. For she could see only one problem in the way her prosecution was progressing to date – the fact that the general public, the media, and the all-important sixteen seated and wide-eyed to her right, were lacking one key ingredient that would guarantee their decision to convict . . .

'Professor Hinds,' said Carmichael, after allowing the much celebrated physician to spend a good ten minutes outlining her academic record. 'I believe your area of specialty is emotional abuse.'

'That's right,' said Hinds, her emerald blouse complementing her bright green eyes.

'Could you explain to us what led you to become interested in this specific field of behavioural psychology?'

'Certainly. I suppose I have always had a fascination with extremities in human behaviour, particularly in those in positions of power. More specifically, I was interested in the role of parents in children's development and what might cause a mother or a father – someone who should have an inherent instinct to nurture – to in fact do the opposite and parent by violence, cruelty and threats.'

'So you're interested in the area of physical violence?'

David knew Carmichael was asking only so she could be corrected.

'No, in fact to the contrary. The violence I refer to is of the emotional variety – the one that leaves deep, lasting scars which, if left untreated, can alter the course of a young person's life. Some might even end up mimicking their abuser's aggressive tendencies – with their violence in retaliation taking alternative forms.'

'So emotional violence from a parent can result in the victims – in this case the abuser's children – to lash out physically, viciously, in an attempt to counteract . . .'

'*Objection*.' David was up before an open-mouthed Hinds could respond. 'Your Honour, the prosecution is leading the witness.'

'He's right, Miss Carmichael. Objection sustained.'

But Carmichael did not falter, merely nodded her head before moving on. She spent the next half-hour asking Hinds question after question about the different types of emotional abuse and their consequences, and Hinds – with her flawless skin, shiny auburn hair and intelligent green eyes – had the jury mesmerised. The professor was not only an expert in her field, but a brilliant communicator as well, so much so that David noted a number of the sixteen were now perched on the edge of their seats, nodding in agreement with her every word.

'And, Professor, I know you have seen the video tabled in this case as exhibit twelve – the home recording taken on the night of Doctor Jeffrey Logan's birthday. Would you say Stephanie Tyler's behaviour in this video was typical of the types of abusers you have studied in your research?'

'Most definitely,' agreed Hinds. 'In the video in question, Stephanie Tyler displays many characteristics of the psychological bully – even the physicality of her presence, the only one standing in a room of three seated people – tells us reams about her self-allocated role in the family dynamic.'

'Only because Logan directed her that way,' whispered a frustrated David to Arthur.

'Patience, David,' returned Arthur. 'Our time will come.'

'The video also shows us many things about the

psychology of the three subordinate family members,' Hinds went on, 'the father figure trying to placate in order to prevent further agitation, the children subservient – but not out of respect, out of fear.'

'And what on earth would make a mother turn on her children like that, Professor?' asked a seemingly perplexed Carmichael. 'For as you mentioned earlier, such behaviour is not the norm.'

'There are many reasons and I am afraid, given Ms Tyler's demise, we may never know the true cause of her psychological condition. Some people are born with such inbuilt tendencies, others abused as children grow to mimic the environment in which they were raised. And still others are sadly influenced by neurological factors – factors over which, without the right treatment, they simply have no control.'

And in that second Carmichael turned, ever so slightly, to meet David's eye. It was a look that said 'hold on to your hat' – a glance that told him she was about to pick up the jury and run with them so that they were well and truly beyond David's reach.

'And given your extensive experience, Professor,' Carmichael turned back to the witness, 'your personal assessment of Stephanie Tyler would be . . .?'

'Well, by all reports she was reared in a loving environment, and those who knew her in her youth say they saw no evidence of aggression or a dogged need to dominate. So my guess is that Ms Tyler was most likely suffering from some form of neurological disorder – something that resulted in her . . .'

'*Objection!*' Finally David could see it. Carmichael was even cleverer than he thought. The ADA was trying to convince the jury that the 'abusive' Stephanie was not to blame for her sadistic behaviour – that she was *sick,* that she went *untreated,* that *none of this was her fault*!

Carmichael had found the only missing piece of her puzzle, the one that would give the jury a conscience-free reason to convict – she was giving the sixteen a reason to feel *sympathy* for the victim, for the poor mentally-ill woman who was unceremoniously blown to bits.

'Your Honour,' David began. 'Stephanie Tyler's autopsy gave no evidence of any neurological disease or malfunction.' But David knew he was cornered – especially since he never intended to argue Stephanie was the abuser in the first place. Worse still, Carmichael had obviously anticipated this argument as well, and was already at her desk retrieving some sort of document to counter David's attack.

'Your Honour,' she began. 'Ms Tyler's driver's licence indicated she wished to be an organ donor after her death, and as such, her brain, as well as some of her other major organs and body tissue were harvested only hours after she was killed – for transplant and research purposes.'

David knew this, of course, but had never considered it relevant given the cause of death had been irrefutable.

'Regardless of her donor status, Your Honour,' David continued, 'Professor Hinds' comments are based on pure speculation. The professor herself pointed out that she never had the opportunity to examine the victim.'

'That's true, Mr Cavanaugh, but the witness has

every right to make speculations based on her expert opinion.'

David could see nowhere to go.

'Forgive me, Your Honour,' offered Carmichael then. 'But Mr Cavanaugh has every right to explore further reasons for Ms Tyler's abusive nature in his cross-examination. But until that time . . .'

And she had him again. Carmichael knew very well that David had no intention of portraying Stephanie as a tyrant – but she was forcing him into a corner, telling the jury that the defence knew very well that Stephanie Tyler was the mother from hell and that the only reason they weren't pushing it was because it gave the kids a motive.

'True, Miss Carmichael,' said Kessler. 'You'll get your turn on cross, Mr Cavanaugh, but for now you can retake your seat. In fact, I might suggest that before we go any further we watch this video known as exhibit twelve. I for one would like to consider Professor Hinds' comments in light of the aforementioned recorded material and I am sure seeing the material would help the jury in their understanding of the witness' testimony.'

And David, his eyes flicking over his two terrified clients before swivelling past those of the press and towards the hallowed sixteen on the other side of the room, knew that every person present, bar the two children sitting beside him, were on the verge of applauding the serious-faced Judge Kessler before them – for her suggestion meant that at long last, the oh-so-patient spectators were about to be shown the much anticipated 'main feature' – the show that everyone had come to see.

And just as Carmichael asked the court clerk to lower the lights, and as the television was wheeled in and set up front and centre, another pair of eyes found David's – a dark, glistening pair alight with satisfaction. And even after they were long swallowed by the shadows David could still feel Logan's gaze upon him – and it spoke of jubilance, of triumph, of victory.

74

The air was thick with salt, the sun high, the clouds thin, and her fine grey hair whipping in the cool summer breeze around her. She was on the beach – the white sandy expanse that stretched in front of the historic five-star resort known as the Chatham Bars Inn – and her dress was loose and her feet were bare and in that moment she felt free.

Her head had finally stopped pounding and, despite her dire predicament, Deirdre McCall felt an unexpected surge of optimism, as she filled her lungs with the brackish sea air and allowed the view before her to swallow her whole. She loved the ocean – felt at peace in its presence, which was ironic really, considering she was a desert girl born and bred. But there was something about its endlessness, about the power and beauty of the eternal expanse of blue which soothed her fears and made her feel – well, *capable* – a sensation she had not felt since the day that her son had been born.

Jason had stolen it all – her confidence, her contentment, her self-esteem. And from what she could tell, she and her beloved husband were mere understudies for those who would follow. Those dear children, his poor departed wife, who had been worn away, slowly, carefully, filed down to bits of nothingness until he was satisfied with their debility and ready to move on. And move on he would, she was sure of it, unless she could end things now.

I have one advantage, she reasoned to herself, *the element of surprise.* Jason had no idea that she knew the exact location of his 'store', and was certain as to what it contained.

Years ago, while she was still in rehabilitation after the first attempt on her life, someone had sent a letter to Jason at their old home address. That letter, among others addressed to herself and her husband, had been collected by a loyal and devoted neighbour who, not knowing where to redirect their mail (she had been told both parents had been killed in a dreadful highway accident), nor the whereabouts of the young man who had never returned, decided to forward said correspondence to Deirdre's old place of employment, hoping her 'show business' colleagues might know of a suitable next of kin to forward them to.

This mail then ended up in the possession of a lovely man named Jackie 'Tingles' L'hoy, Deirdre's former stage manager who, out of pure respect to 'Lovely Legs McCall', had kept said letters for many years until one day when a certain article in the *Las Vegas Weekly* had widened his eyes and sent his seventy-five-year-old heart aflutter.

Just days later, and much to Deirdre's surprise, dear Tingles had visited her at her dance school and, after a teary reunion, delivered Deirdre's mail – some twenty years after it had been posted. And that had been when she had opened the letter addressed to her son. The one sent by Chatham Reality as a notification of purchase. And that had been how she had discovered her son had bought a beach house just across the way from the Chatham Bars Inn. And that had been when she realised Jason was operating under at least two separate aliases – that of the famous Doctor Jeffrey Logan – and Chatham real estate owner, Mr Jeremy O'Glan.

75

'J.T.,' said a voice out of frame.

'Yes, Mother,' replied J.T.

'Did you finish your biology project?'

'Yes, Mother.'

'And the DNA bases – are you sure they were in the right order?'

'Yes,' replied the boy, his eyes flicking towards the front of the room.

David was holding J.T. Logan's hand while breathing slowly, deliberately, trying to remain calm and transfer such strength in composure to the poor shattered young boy beside him. But he did not need to look at J.T.'s shaking hand to realise the hairs on its back were rising, a cool sweat breaking in his palm, as the video progressed in all its ugly finality.

'*Are you trying to lecture me?*' asked the ghost that was Stephanie – the extra large LCD screen Carmichael had organised blowing the whole horrific image up into cinematic proportions. '*I was dux of my high school, you know, and could have just as easily chosen medicine over law – if I had so desired.*'

David heard the short, sharp breaths of Chelsea Logan crying at the other end of the defence table, her own fingers now clutched in Arthur's large, weather-beaten hand. The tears in her blue eyes reflected the sickly green light from the recorded image before them, as the next voice to speak sent a visible shiver through her entire body.

'*Stephanie, really,*' said the flat screen Logan – the 'director' having placed himself in the starring position of centre stage. '*Is this really necessary? It is my birthday, for Christ's sake. I have no doubt J.T. has done a stellar job as always. Just for once do you think you could sit down and behave civilly? Just tonight could you try to . . .?*'

As the on-screen argument progressed, and despite David's knowing it was his duty to pay attention, he felt an overwhelming urge to block out the sickly drama before him and think of nothing but Sara and their unborn child.

And in that moment, as the muted colours of the murderous Jeffrey Logan production danced like devils across the faces of the now captivated audience around him, David's mind floated to another memory – to the morning just weeks ago when he and Sara had watched in wonder at the ultrasound pictures of their thirty-seven-week-old child. And he recalled the pure happiness they had felt as the reflection of those images had played out across their own awestruck faces – their little one's movements casting intermittent light and shadow over its two besotted parents who . . .

And then he saw it. It was almost as if his own child had directed his eyes to the detail.

The gravy boat.

The shiny silver gravy boat glistening with intermittent sparkles of green.

Logan had placed it in the centre of the table so that it might act as an innocent hiding place for his pistol. But in doing so it had also captured the full intensity of the autocue's light. And now that it was on the big screen David realised its significance.

And despite the fact the video now showed Stephanie Logan pointing that kick-ass rifle at her son, David was overcome with an overwhelming sensation of hope. For the gravy boat was performing a dual function – neither of which was originally intended.

It was hiding a weapon and it was reflecting the truth.

And David knew – right then and there – that Jeffrey Logan, in his sadistic determination to place one of his beloved weapons right in the middle of the action, had unwittingly yet undeniably shot himself in the foot.

76

The tape, the tape, the tape. It was all Carmichael could talk about. She was having a field day with it, following Professor Hinds' testimony with that of not one but two audio/video experts – one from the FBI (but not Special Agent Bond, who, despite running the unit concerned, had been unceremoniously dumped from the ADA's list of credible witnesses after yesterday's debacle), and one from an independent forensics laboratory in Philadelphia who spent a good hour explaining how she had enhanced the video for playback in court.

The technician, a small, mousy-looking woman by the name of Lindsay Farris, explained that she agreed with the FBI expert that the video was indeed 'authentic' and she had not altered or compromised its content – merely improved its viewing quality by using a software program which 'applied appropriate algorithms to sharpen, enlarge, enhance, edit and correct visual details'.

Secretly, David could have kissed her.

Carmichael also got the judge's permission to re-run sections of the video – specifically, the more aggressive sections at the end of the 'show', making sure that every single juror would be dreaming about it tonight. *Hell*, thought David, *they would probably be able to recite the damned thing for years to come.* Which, despite how it may appear to the rest of the universe, including Arthur who was obviously more than just a little confused as to his co-counsel's lack of 'objections', did not worry David one bit.

David had not yet had a chance to tell anyone about what he had seen in that all-revealing gravy boat given he spent the entire lunchtime recess in conference with his two clients who were obviously terribly distressed at the courtroom screening of the video. Arthur had gone back to the office to check on Sara's motion to exhume Malcolm Tyler's body and David had made the decision that there was no point in giving his two teenage clients any sense of false hope until he was certain he could read the words on the autocue from their reflection.

And so, as the third day of testimony in the Commonwealth Vs Logan and Logan came to a close, the entire room was abuzz with the amazing progress of the prosecution – and more to the point, the lack of intervention from the increasingly lacklustre defence.

As the crowd fell out into the corridors, the elevators, the lobby and Pemberton Square beyond, David felt an all-encompassing need to shout to the hills that nothing was as it seemed – and that finally he had a way to prove it.

*

'Mr Cavanaugh, Mr Cavanaugh,' called a reporter at the front entrance of the building, one of many who had obviously been waiting for the main players to emerge. 'Do you have any comments on the significance of that video? Is there a reason why you did not . . .?'

But David, with Arthur's assistance, was waving them away. He had asked the security personnel to hold his clients in the DYS transferral vans so that he might have one last word to them before they headed off to their separate detention units for the night, and he needed to hurry if he was going to make it before their 5pm departure.

'But, Mr Cavanaugh.' One particularly determined hack persisted. 'The general consensus is that you are dying in there.' This one didn't beat around the bush. 'Some are even speculating that you have no choice but to negotiate a plea bargain.'

'There will be no plea,' said David, whose upbeat mood was taking a rapid dive as he and Arthur tried to push through the throng.

'But how on earth do you expect to come back from . . .?' But then the reporter turned his head, perhaps sensing the movement of the masses around him. And David realised he was about to be upstaged by a more media-friendly Jeffrey Logan, who had just emerged from the court's front doors, a look of pure satisfaction on his smarmy, famous face.

'Jesus, Arthur, they're like moths to the flame,' said David, turning to watch the action.

'He had a good day,' said a still confused Arthur, perhaps needing to make the point.

'Not as good as you think,' said David, lifting a hand

towards Logan in a gesture which told Arthur that an explanation of this last comment would have to wait.

'Doctor Jeff, Doctor Jeff,' they screamed. 'Can you comment on the day's events? How did it feel to see that video once again? Do you feel like your children betrayed you by taking the road of violence instead of . . .?'

But the ever diplomatic Logan was already shaking his head, as an equally satisfied ADA Carmichael finally emerged behind him.

'I want to get one thing straight,' Logan said, lifting his arms so that the entire mob would fall obediently into silence, the reporters' long arms now finding every available gap to shove their microphones towards Jeffrey Logan's perfect face, their notebooks at the ready, their cameras fixed on record.

'I love my children,' he said, his expression one of earnestness. 'They have made mistakes, and many of them are a result of the unfortunate circumstances life has dealt them. I feel responsible, for not rescuing them sooner, and I wish I could take that back.

'But above and beyond all else, I know that my children need help. Whether their motives be that of defence or revenge or greed. And I agree with ADA Carmichael that they should not be released into the general community until such time that they have been treated, rehabilitated, saved by the system of justice which we all hold dear.'

David felt the blood boil inside him.

'That video was an atrocity,' Logan went on, the masses now hanging on his every word. 'But it was just a small snapshot of what my children and I had to endure. So if you ask me what I think about today's events, if you want to know how I felt as I watched that disturbing drama unfold, I say this and only this . . .

'I now understand that my wife was ill, very ill and if any good is to come of this terrible tragedy I ask that everyone trapped in the cycle that is emotional abuse seek help – be you the victim or the perpetrator. And if my comments help one child, one parent, to salvage a life from the remnants of the catastrophe that is domestic maltreatment, then all is not lost after all.'

And then, after turning to shake Amanda Carmichael's hand, Logan nodded to a tall dark-suited bodyguard beside him – the guard assisting Logan through the crowd until they reached the kerbside where he opened the back door of a tinted-windowed black Mercedes sedan.

Just as Logan bent to enter the car, his head turned ever so slightly so that he might make eye contact with David who was now standing with Arthur across the other side of the square. And then he lifted his right hand so that it rested close against his chest, formed a fist, extended his pointer finger, and lifted his thumb. And then, with his hand now forming the shape of a gun, he jerked his thumb ever so slightly as if he had just pulled the trigger.

'Bang!' he mouthed, making no mistake of his communication.

'Bang!' he mouthed again, as if for good measure.

And then he disappeared into his $200 000 ride, and within seconds, he was gone.

77

'*No, no, no*,' said a distressed J.T. Logan to his sister. They were in the back of the DYS security van. They were whispering. It was dark.

It was the first moment they had had a chance to be alone together since Chelsea had been arrested – the van to Brockton was running late, so the DYS security guards had placed Chelsea in the Plymouth van until the second transport arrived – and they both knew they had to make the most of it . . . to talk, and fast!

'This isn't working. It is falling apart. Did you hear what that professor said – about Mom and her being a donor?'

'They were talking about her brain,' argued Chelsea, sitting as close to her brother as possible. 'And there was nothing wrong with her brain.'

'I know. But, but . . .' J.T. was deteriorating and Chelsea knew it. He was losing weight, his eyes were heavily shadowed, his hands were shaking. He needed her to look after him and she could not properly do it. Within minutes they would be yanked apart once again, and she failed to see any hope of change in their predicament.

'Why do you think Mom signed that donor card in the first place, J.T.?' asked Chelsea, trying to lift her brother's spirits.

'Because she thought it would protect us.'

'And she was right.'

'No, none of this is right. None of this has been right from the very beginning.'

Chelsea let out a sigh. 'Listen to me, J.T.,' she said, negotiating her handcuffs so that she might take his hand. 'We have gone as far as we can; to say any more could make things worse.'

'We are about to be separated for life, Chels,' said J.T. 'How could things get any worse?'

Chelsea stopped herself from nodding. 'Explaining it won't help – not now.'

'But maybe I don't care,' he said, the tears falling freely down his smooth, sunken cheeks. 'Maybe I just want to tell him everything, so that someone besides *us* will finally understand.'

'You don't need to tell David everything for him to understand,' she said, placing her forehead against his, her breath slow and warm, her skin hot against the coolness.

'But I want him to *know* – about how good she was, about what she was willing to do.'

'He knew her, J.T., and even though he did not see her after Father took hold, he has not forgotten – I can see it in his eyes.'

J.T. exhaled, before giving his sister the slightest of

nods, their tears now merging as they fell in droplets upon their shackles.

'Then we say nothing,' he said.

'Nothing.'

'And if David finds out?'

'Then we pray he knew her well enough for him to forgive us.'

78

'The order came from a Damien Chi,' said Joe Mannix as he took a seat on the worn velvet stool across from David.

They were at the Idle Hour, a smoky pub in South Boston that smelt eternally of malt and cigarettes and that musky odour that came from old men wearing even older clothes and Brylcreem in their hair.

The Idle was one of Joe's favourite haunts, and every time he suggested it as a meeting place, David protested with vigour. But not tonight. Tonight David was more than happy to be hiding in the corner of the cosy wood-panelled pub, making the most of the fact that happy hour at the Idle ran around the clock, and there was no way they would be interrupted or overheard here – in a room full of men content to drown in their sorrows while Roy Orbison sang about 'Crying' on the 1960s jukebox.

'Chi is captain of the Asian Boyz New England outfit. In other words, he holds a hell of a lot of clout in our corner of the Asian underworld.'

'Can we link him to Logan?' asked David, noticing that Joe could not help but smile.

'Chi just got out of Suffolk Country Jail, where he was being held awaiting trial for several counts of drug distribution. But our guys from narcotics hit a snag when their major witness went AWOL – which I can tell you is a recurring problem when it comes to prosecuting people like Chi.'

'So this Chi walked.'

'And kept walking. Chi knows our guys are still trying to run down this witness, so he's left the state for a while, the latest intel having him somewhere in Florida. The guy is escaping the heat by getting some sun, if that makes sense.'

David nodded. 'Isn't that a problem?' he asked, knowing that beyond all else they needed to link Logan to Chi's outfit in order to tie him to McCall's shooting.

'Yes, in that we don't have access to Chi, which means we can't ask him if what Lopez's snitch Tsi said about the connection is true. But no, in that Chi would never give it up anyway.'

'So in the very least, we have Logan and Chi in the same jail together for at least a space of two days.'

'Same jail, same floor. We even have the guards saying they shared a conversation or two together – apparently Logan reached out to Chi and had the guy in tears.'

'Logan had a gang lord in tears?' asked David, incredulous. 'He must have manipulated him somehow.'

'That's the way it looks – a theory that holds up given Lopez's snitch claims the McCall shooting was carried out gratis.'

'No money was exchanged?'

'Not a cent. In fact, this Tsi told Lopez he got the impression Chi was returning some sort of favour by popping the old lady. As crazy as it sounds, Logan must have something on Damien Chi – but I have no idea what it could be.'

'You got someone looking into it?' asked David.

'McKay is shaking it down,' replied Joe.

David nodded in gratitude. 'So now we have Malcolm Tyler's exhumation in the works, a viable link to the Asian Boyz, and that autocue reflection,' said David, taking a sip of his thick, sour Guinness before looking up at Joe once again. He had told Joe what he had seen in that gravy boat the moment he had walked into the dimly lit pub – unable to hold it in any longer.

'That's right. Susan will give us a heads up on the gravy boat thing tomorrow or Friday at the latest,' he said, referring to their FBI agent friend and the fact that he had already called her to arrange the isolation and enlargement of the images in question. 'She has a mate in Special Agent Bond's unit who promises to do it after hours, away from 007's prying eyes. She says she's pretty sure they can blow up the gravy boat and enhance the reflection so whatever words might be on it are readable, and if those words match the audio then . . .'

'Bang!' said David, who had told Joe about Logan's 'friendly' gesture of late that afternoon.

'Bang!' said Joe, pointing his own finger as he lifted his Guinness in cheers.

'We're getting there, Joe,' said David at last. 'Which is good, considering my clients are at cracking point.'

'They're strong kids, David.'

'They've had to be. But I . . .' David hesitated as if not sure he should go on.

'What is it?' asked Joe.

'Well, I don't mean to sound greedy, I mean, at this stage Chelsea and J.T. are looking as guilty as all hell. But if we do manage to pull this off, Joe, in the unlikely chance that we beat Logan at his own game, what will become of those kids – with no mother, no father.'

'They have each other, David.'

'That's not enough.'

'Then maybe there is someone else out there – someone who the kids have come to trust and respect, who might open her heart to . . .'

But Joe was interrupted by the ringing of his cell – and, as if by fate, the very subject of their conversation was now on the other end of the line.

'Katherine,' said Joe. 'What's up?'

'Lieutenant,' she said, David now hearing de Castro's voice as Joe flipped his cell onto speaker. 'I . . . we have a problem. I don't know what to do. This isn't going to plan. It is too soon, I am not ready.'

'Whoa,' said Joe, his eyes set on David. 'Slow down, Katherine. What is it? What's happened?'

'It's Jeffrey, he called me five minutes ago and said he wanted to see me. He said that he needed some fresh air, so he was going to shower and then walk across the Common, which means he could be here in less than an hour. And I . . . I am not ready.'

'Can you fob him off so we can go with the Friday night rendezvous as planned?' asked Joe.

'*No!* I mean, I can't do this twice, Lieutenant. I am not sure I can even do it at all.'

'Katherine,' said David. 'This is David Cavanaugh. Did he tell you what he wanted to see you about?'

'No. But he said he had a great day in court. That the tide was turning and luck was coming our way and all of this would soon be over. Oh God, David, I can't do this, I can't.'

Joe put his hand over the phone. 'She's losing it. If this is going to happen it has to happen tonight.'

'But she isn't wearing the wire.'

'We can get Frank to grab George from audio and be at her place in fifteen, wire her up before Logan gets there.'

David nodded, pulling out his cell to call McKay while Joe was still talking.

'Katherine,' said Joe into the speaker. 'Listen to me. Detective McKay and a police audio technician will be at your place in fifteen minutes. The tech will wire you up while Frank goes through what we've practised step by step. You're a smart woman, Katherine, smart and strong and more up to this than you think. And if Logan tries anything we will be right outside your house in an unmarked audio van, and in your front door in seconds.'

'I don't think he is ready to hurt me yet,' she said after a pause. 'He needs to own me first.'

'That's right,' encouraged Joe. 'So as long as you stress you are on his side . . .'

'Yes. I will tell him that Sara came to see me today, and that she tried to turn me against him, and that I was glad he called so that I could warn him, that Sara and David claim to have evidence that he organised Stephanie's murder, and you want me to mention his mother and . . .'

'That's it, Katherine. You got this nailed.'

Then Joe offered some last words of encouragement, promising Katherine that all would be okay before hanging up his cell and looking to David once again.

'It's too early,' said Joe.

'It is what it is.'

'She's not ready.'

'She has to be – in fact . . .' David's brain was in overdrive. 'Listen, Joe, this may not be such a bad thing after all. I mean, there is no way Logan is going to miss tomorrow – his much-anticipated day in the sun.' Carmichael was due to call Logan as her star witness tomorrow afternoon.

'You think that even if Katherine's baiting pops this psycho's cork, he will hold on and delay going for the guns until after he gives his testimony.'

'He has no choice.'

'On the contrary, David, this fucker has the habit of doing whatever he damn well pleases.'

But David was shaking his head. 'No. I know this guy, Joe. He won't miss his opportunity to put the final nails in his children's coffins, which means you can use tomorrow to set up the surveillance as planned. We can track his car, Joe, follow him all the way to Chatham.'

But Joe was already on his feet, pointing at his watch and throwing a twenty on the table as David grabbed his jacket from the stool behind him.

'You better be right about this, Cavanaugh,' he said.

'I know him, Joe.'

'No, you don't, David. Nobody knows this guy, and that's been his advantage all along.'

79

Jeffrey Logan was in exceptionally good spirits. In fact, he could not remember the last time he felt so fine. It had been a great day, topped off by that somewhat self-indulgent gesture he had granted himself, and now this – the appearance of the woman before him, *his* Katherine, wearing both the Bulgari necklace and the Rolex he had sent her weeks before. She was coming around. She was succumbing. He could imagine himself swallowing her – and she tasted good.

'Katherine,' he said, not hesitating before moving into her hallway and drawing her into an embrace. 'You look beautiful.'

'Thank you, Jeffrey,' she said, her arms resting lightly across his shoulders.

'Did you get my other gifts?'

'Yes,' she said, stepping back with a smile. 'Jeffrey, it is all way too much. I should have called to thank you, but it was all so overwhelming. I . . . I don't know what to say.'

'You could say yes.'

'To what?' she asked evenly.

'To the question I am building up to.' He smiled, before shaking his head and leading her down her own corridor. 'But I am getting ahead of myself. I have had a very productive day and I would like nothing better than to share it with you.'

'And I with you,' she said, as they entered the living area, Katherine making a detour towards the kitchen to pour them both a glass of wine. And then she hesitated, her attractive face breaking into a frown.

'What is it, Katherine?' he asked, taking the chilled sauvignon blanc and leading her towards the sofa.

'Well, I don't know how to tell you this. It really is quite distressing.'

'You can tell me anything, Katherine.' He ran his hand down the back of her right arm.

'But – you have been so busy, trying to do what is best for your children and . . . well, it is nothing short of criminal.'

Despite his recent elation, Logan found his own brow starting to furrow. Something was going on, and he had no doubt that David Cavanaugh was behind it.

She began at the beginning – or at least where Detective McKay had instructed her to start – with her general concerns that the children's defence attorneys had an unhealthy view of this case from the outset, that David Cavanaugh's past relationship with Stephanie had robbed him of his ability to be objective. And then she explained how she had always felt quite intimidated in David and Sara's company – she sensed they had a desperate need to ignore the truth that Stephanie was a hardened emotional abuser, which meant they were determined to find somebody else to blame.

'There is something not right about them, Jeffrey. I know David Cavanaugh has a stellar reputation, but now I think I understand why you were wary of his involvement in the first place.'

'I agree,' said Jeffrey wholeheartedly. 'Which is why I applied for that APO.'

'Yes,' she said, allowing him to take her hand. 'I know they are losing in court, Jeffrey – and this will all be over soon.'

'Over in one sense, Katherine.' He gave her a smile. 'But it will be just the beginning for us.'

'Yes,' she said, forcing her own mouth to widen. 'But, the thing is, after today, I . . .'

Katherine diverted her eyes, hoping beyond anything that she was doing what Frank McKay had suggested – drawing Logan out, slowly, carefully, pulling him along with the finest of invisible strings.

'What is it, my dear?' he asked. 'What happened today to upset you so?'

'I . . . I wasn't going to tell you. I mean, you already have so much on your plate but . . . It's Sara Davis, she came to see me – here, at home, while you and her co-counsel were in court.'

Logan shifted in his seat. 'What did she want?'

'She wanted to blind me with her lies.' The line was a little over-dramatic but Katherine met Logan's eye and was reassured when he did not flinch. 'She told me things, Jeffrey, horrible things about you and what you are supposed to have done.'

Logan's eyes narrowed, his dark orbs boring into her own pale brown ones. He was looking into her soul, she knew, but she did not falter, she did not blink.

'It was awful, Jeffrey,' Katherine went on. 'She told me they were getting proof that you forced J.T. to murder his mother, that you were the one who altered Stephanie's life insurance policy, and that you framed your own daughter as a co-conspirator and . . . and . . .'

'What else?' asked Logan, his voice now rising just a little.

'She said they knew about other things – things you had done in your past, something about your father dying in a car accident – and your mother . . . Jeffrey, they told me she was alive but that someone had recently tried to kill her and . . .'

'Both my parents died in a car accident a long time ago, Katherine,' said Jeffrey. 'I told you that when we first met.'

'I know,' she said, reaching for her wine with her free hand and taking a long, slow drink. 'So how can they make this stuff up, Jeffrey? I mean, Stephanie, your parents – and then there were their claims about the gun.'

'What gun?'

'The one that killed Stephanie, of course – that big-game rifle. She said it was *your* gun, Jeffrey. That you had bought it years ago, under another name, and sold it and bought it back and . . .'

She paused then, trying desperately to read his reaction without giving the game away. But Logan said nothing, merely reached for his own glass of wine and sipped it, slowly, as if rationing every drop.

'Is that all she said?' he asked.

'Yes, but she said there was more and they would find proof. I am afraid, Jeffrey. These people are very determined. What if they start making these accusations in public? I mean, we both know they are ridiculous, but if the press gets hold of such claims . . .' And Katherine let that one hang.

'You have worked too hard, Jeffrey, we both have, to build a career where trust and believability are paramount. But their lies – their dirty filthy fabrications – could do some serious damage if they were to get out. And I would not put it past them to leak this. They are dying in court, Jeffrey, and desperate times call for desperate measures.'

And then she paused again, hoping for some indication of how Logan's complicated mind was reading the information she had shared. But he gave her nothing – a good thirty seconds of pure stoicism, until his features broke suddenly, disconcertingly, into a wide and reassuring smile.

'Dearest Katherine,' he said. 'I do not want you to worry. These people are maniacs – slanderous criminals who are committing career suicide by taking the route that they have. You and I both know that the phenomenon of celebrity is both a blessing and a curse – and we have ridden a wave of positivity for a very long time. But everyone faces a storm at least once in their career, my dear, and I am afraid ours is more tumultuous than most.'

Katherine nodded, forcing herself to squeeze Logan's now cool and clammy palm.

'Sara Davis asked me if I had any other evidence

against you, Jeffrey – anything else that would help their cause. But of course there is . . .'

'Nothing,' finished Logan, his voice resolute.

'Of course not.' She smiled. 'Don't worry, Jeffrey, if she calls again I shall not answer the phone, if she knocks I won't be in.'

'That's a good idea, Katherine,' he said, inching that little bit closer. 'In fact, I would not open the door to anyone but me until this trial is over. For as Shakespeare once said: "*Love me, trust few.*" '

'I believe that was "*Love all, trust few*", Jeffrey,' she found herself correcting him, as he moved towards her.

'Then consider me your new Shakespeare, Katherine,' he said, his lips now mere inches from her own. 'And from here on in, you can stick to my script, the one I am writing especially for you.'

'Jesus,' said David, pulling one of the headphones from his ears. 'That Katherine is something.'

'She is one tough cookie,' agreed Joe as they listened to the disconcerting sounds of Logan and Katherine kissing. 'And we owe her big time,' he added.

David nodded, his stomach turning with a mixture of revulsion and guilt for forcing Katherine into this corner in the first place. 'Do you think it was enough?'

'If it wasn't, this psycho is more in control than we figured. If Barbara is right, the guy should be fighting some very powerful urges right now.'

'He'll hold on to them until after tomorrow. Considering what Katherine just told him, he'll be bursting to have his say in court.'

'And then . . .?' asked Joe, perhaps needing to hear it one more time.

'Then he'll go for his guns, and we'll be playing shadow every step of the way.'

'Unless that unknown factor rears its ugly head.'

'What unknown factor?' asked David.

'Human nature,' said Joe. 'The abandonment of logic, the need to hunt, the need to protect, the need to win.'

In that moment, just two miles across the Charles, the 'unknown factor' was packing herself a bag. Nora Kelly, had just received another call from Tracey Scabo, who had told her that Miss McCall had telephoned once again to assure her she was fine, but also once again refused to divulge her whereabouts. But the savvy Ms Scabo had then 'Star 69-ed' the last call received, and come up with another 508 number, also based in Chatham.

'The number belonged to a restaurant known as the Captain's Table,' Scabo had told Nora. 'They confirmed an elderly woman of Deirdre's description had made a call after a light dinner – before taking off on foot.'

'Chatham is a small community, dear, she has to be staying nearby.'

'Yes,' agreed Scabo. 'I think so too, because the person at the restaurant said that this was her third meal there, which means she could well . . .'

'Head for the same restaurant again,' Nora had finished.

And so, knowing there was little she could do in the office, given Arthur and Sara had completed their motion requesting the exhumation of Malcolm Tyler's remains, and David was busy in court, Nora decided to head for Chatham first thing in the morning – in the hope of tracking down Deirdre McCall by nightfall. If she could just talk with the woman she was sure she could convince her that they had the situation in hand. With a little luck she figured she could have McCall safely back here in Boston by this time tomorrow. And she was Irish – and they were always in luck.

80

'The Commonwealth calls Doctor Victor Siebel,' said Amanda Carmichael, calling her first witness of the day. Siebel was the child psychologist she had hired to examine J.T. and Chelsea Logan, and David knew they were in for a beating.

Carmichael looked particularly fresh and confident this morning – in a pale pink suit and flat ballerina shoes. Her hair was down for the first time all week, and this softer look told David the woman was trying to humanise herself for today's 'emotional' examination of Doctor Jeffrey Logan. He knew the ADA would want to be seen as a sympathetic bystander when it came to Logan's testimony, simply guiding the skilled orator through the events of the night of eleventh May, allowing his words to wash over the jury who, there was no doubt, were already true believers – devoted Doctor Jeff sympathisers who wanted nothing more than to help this helper of others to finally regain his life.

'Where is he?' asked Arthur, bending across J.T. to whisper in David's ear.

'Don't worry, he'll be here,' said David, who had woken his boss early to bring him up to speed on the events of the past night. Jeffrey Logan was yet to make an appearance at court this morning, but David was not concerned. Joe already had two uniforms tailing the famous TV doctor and as of five minutes ago, his car, along with the driver he had hired to chauffeur him around all week, was still sitting safely just inside the back garage of his Beacon Hill home.

'Joe's got him covered,' whispered David. 'Logan's probably going over his lies for this afternoon's one man show.'

Arthur nodded as they both refocused on the events at hand.

Child psychologist Victor Siebel was a cold and opinionated man who seemed to have an answer for everything. Unlike many in his chosen profession he did not appear conducive to the nuances of variation in human behaviour. Rather, Doctor Siebel was one of those annoying individuals who viewed every diagnosis in black and white – and had no problem with labelling David's two clients as amoral assassins from the outset.

'They are sociopaths,' he said, plain and simple. 'And no, it is not uncommon for one family to produce two such psychological misfits. Psychiatrists have long believed there is a gene for sociopathy so it only makes sense that every now and again, one family spawns two or more offspring of similar . . .'

'Objection,' said David. 'Your Honour, I understand

the witness, at the prosecution's request, is giving his own clinical analysis of my clients' psychology.' David wanted to make the point that this man had been hired specifically by the ADA. 'But I would ask he refrains from talking about the two teenagers next to me as misfits, or spawn, or . . .'

'He's right, Doctor Siebel,' said Kessler. 'Perhaps you would like to rephrase without the dehumanising vernacular.'

'Your Honour.' It was Carmichael's turn. 'Doctor Siebel is highly experienced in his field of child psychoanalysis, and as such his terminology . . .'

'Must be such that it is accessible for the jury and does not unduly prejudice their view of the defendants,' finished an obviously frustrated Kessler. For some reason David got the sense Miss Pretty-In-Pink was pissing the judge off this morning. 'The objection is sustained. Move on, Miss Carmichael.' Which the ADA did.

Moments later Siebel was giving his extremely harsh analysis of both Logan children – two kids he had visited for barely an hour apiece in the past two months. And while David continued to object as much as was reasonably possible, he knew the jury were absorbing every word of Siebel's testimony – their eyes flicking from Siebel, to J.T., to Chelsea, their brows folding into knots as Siebel's disturbing diagnosis unfolded.

'Sociopaths such as the Logan children do not possess the normal characteristic of basic humanness known as empathy. Without empathy an individual cannot possibly interpret or process the feelings of another. And without the instinctive internal barrier which signals when a moral line is crossed, there is nothing preventing them from carrying out wanton desires on innocents.'

'*Jesus*,' said David under his breath.

'And as for the issue of rehabilitation?' asked Carmichael.

'As much as we as a society would like to believe that criminals can and should be rehabilitated, Miss Carmichael, especially criminals as young as this, the point is moot when it comes to certain individuals, those who show a pattern of sadistic impulses and who clearly lack compassion for anyone but themselves. A sociopath does not commit a one-time impulse of crime to never return to their perverse behaviour; they live a pattern of crimes. And while some sociopaths can be deterred, none can be rehabilitated.'

'Objection, Your Honour.' David could take it no longer.

'I understand your frustration, Mr Cavanaugh, but you will have your opportunity to examine this witness on cross.'

But David was interrupted by a tap on his shoulder, as a court clerk handed him a message written on white Superior Court notepaper.

'*We have a problem*,' it said – and David knew it was from Joe.

'What's up?' asked David as soon as Joe answered his cell. He was striding down the deserted corridors of the Superior Court's level nine. Most of the other courts were still in session, but Kessler had granted his request for an early lunchtime adjournment.

'It's Logan. He's gone.'

'*What?*' And David felt the chill rush up inside him. 'How? When?'

'We don't know. His driver was sitting in the garage in Logan's car but it was too far up the drive for us to see. When he finally pulled out, my uniforms followed him, assuming he was taking Logan to court. But he headed south-west, took the car to a Mercedes service centre in Westwood. Our guys tracked him all the way before realising that he was travelling solo.'

'And did they ask him . . .?'

'They radioed in and I told them to approach the driver. And the driver told them Logan called him late last night and asked him to come by early and take the Merc in for a service.'

'But then why was he waiting in the garage?'

'Logan told him to turn the engine over a few times to warm it up – said he had to run it for a good half-hour so the battery wouldn't go flat.'

'Shit,' said David.

'I know,' said Joe, who hesitated before going on. 'And David . . .?'

'What is it?' he asked, hearing the apprehension in Joe's voice.

'Frank and I,' Joe began, 'we've been calling Katherine de Castro all morning – you know, to check on how she is doing.'

David and Joe had not entered Katherine's house after Logan had left the night before. They wanted to keep their distance in case he returned, but they did call and thank her profusely for her amazing 'performance', telling her she could well be the key to their finally bringing Logan down.

'But she's not picking up,' Joe went on. 'It's now after midday and she still isn't picking up.'

'Maybe she's gone out?' David suggested in desperation, instinctively moving towards the elevators.

'Maybe. But just in case, we're heading over there,' said Joe, just as David entered the elevator. He used his pointer finger to pound the 'G' button with determination.

'How far away are you?'

'Ten minutes or so,' he replied.

'I'll see you there.'

Eleven minutes and thirty-two seconds later, just as Sara was arriving at Suffolk County Superior Court to file their motion to exhume to Judge Kessler personally, and Arthur was receiving a text from his AWOL co-counsel that read '*something's come up – no time to elaborate, need you to X Siebel*', and Nora Kelly was travelling south on Route 3 to Cape Cod, and Joe Mannix and Frank McKay were rounding the corner of Katherine de Castro's Back Bay street, David was slamming the door of a Checker cab in front of Katherine's brownstone and running towards her milky sandstone steps.

'Katherine,' he called. 'Katherine, it's David, are you there?'

'Her car's gone,' said Joe, catching his breath as he ran up the steps with Frank close behind him. 'We did a circle around the back; her garage door is open but her SUV is nowhere in sight.'

'How do you know she drives an SUV?' asked David, in the very least reassured that de Castro could simply be running an errand.

'It's a Lexus. I checked with the DMV.'

David nodded, his eyes meeting Joe's and then Frank's.

'*Katherine.*' He banged again.

'Katherine,' joined in Joe.

And David knew that, despite the absence of de Castro's car, the two men beside him were also fearing the worst.

Frank asked them both to move back, and neither of them gave him an argument. And then a surprisingly strong McKay ran at Katherine's bright red door with his right shoulder, breaking the lock on his very first try. Within seconds they were inside, Joe and Frank drawing their guns, David leading the way as he broke into a sprint down the corridor. His legs were heavy and his heart was fast and his lungs held tight to the balloon of air now trapped like a prisoner inside of him. And then he lost his footing, his right leg beginning to slide as the carpeted hallway gave way to the expensive limestone tiles. He caught himself on the living room doorframe, his eyes tracking down to the dark red slick beneath him, before lifting up, in horror, at the vision of carnage beyond.

Katherine de Castro was sitting upright on her bright white designer sofa, her perfect posture frozen with rigor mortis. Her eyes were open. The single bullet hole centred between her perfectly manicured brows. The blood tracked down her face in two separate tributaries which made it appear as if she was crying, before spilling over the sofa, onto the crisp white rug and finally into the pool that David had slipped on the moment he came through the door. And on her lap she held what appeared to be a ball of sequins, or some other colourful ornament that caught the light from the far window and sent miniature bursts of rainbows dancing across the room. And David saw that it was the gun purse that Sara had told him about, and realised that Logan had personalised his kill.

'This is my fault,' he gasped as Joe Mannix moved around him, Joe's own lungs letting out an audible sigh as his brown eyes fixed on the corpse of the brave, selfless 'heroine' before them.

'I'm the one that set up the meet and greet,' said Joe.

'And I'm the one who helped wire her up,' said Frank.

There was silence then, the only sound coming from the single fly that had made its way through the window to settle on Katherine's right cheek.

'Logan is a dead man,' said David after a time.

And for once, Joe Mannix could not bring himself to disagree.

81

David jumped, his cell phone exploding in a series of vibrations in his top shirt pocket. He had turned off the sound in preparation for his day in court and now its tremors were jolting him back to reality, reminding him that it was time for action – that he needed to MOVE!

'Sara,' he said, her name coming up on the front of his blue-screened cell. David felt his heart sink – how could he tell her? She was the one who convinced de Castro to wire up in the first place. It was her *idea*, for Christ's sake – her brilliant, disastrous idea.

'David, where are you?'

'Ah . . . I'm not far . . . I'm with Joe and Frank and . . .' he could not bring himself to say it. 'You're ringing about the exhumation motion.'

'No, I mean, yes, Kessler granted our motion but . . . that's not why . . . I'm . . . David, I'm worried, I got a message on my phone and . . .'

'What is it?' he asked, waiting for the next bomb to drop.

'It's Nora, she's gone to Chatham. She said she knew we were all busy this morning so she went into the office and put our phones on voice mail and left messages on our cells . . . She got a call from that Tracey Scabo, something about a restaurant that McCall is frequenting in Chatham – and she's going there, David, to try to pull her in.'

David had to steady himself on the doorjamb once again, as the fear rose in his belly.

'David,' she said, after he did not respond, 'I know she feels responsible for everything that has happened to McCall, and I know it isn't her fault but . . .'

David swallowed hard, knowing that on top of everything else, Sara was also about to fall headfirst into that soul-wrenching quagmire known as guilt.

'She is desperate to make things right, David,' Sara continued. 'To rescue McCall before she puts herself in any further danger. But if Logan is going to head up there after his testimony, we don't have much time to find her, and bring her back and . . .'

'Logan's already left,' he said then, knowing there was no way to avoid it.

'*What?*'

'We think he left late last night and most likely took Katherine de Castro's car.'

'*What?*' she repeated, and he could hear her brain ticking over in panic. 'But why would Katherine let him take her car? She didn't call us to tell us. She would have . . .'

And then David closed his eyes, knowing full well that his clever fiancée had worked it out.

'David, where are you?' she asked for a second time, her voice now dropping into a low, hesitant croak.

'We're at Katherine's.'

'Oh God,' she said.

'I am so sorry, Sara.'

And then it was as if he could see her – clutching her swollen middle as she collapsed against a wall, or a chair, or . . .

'This wasn't your fault.'

But all she could manage was, 'Oh God . . . Nora.'

'Don't worry,' he said. 'I am on my way.'

Tick, tock, tick, tock. It was almost as if David could see it – one of those red digital clocks from those cliff-hanger TV shows counting down to when the bomb would inevitably go off, unless he could cut the right wire, unless he could intervene with fate.

'I need your car,' he said to Joe.

'No,' said Joe, anticipating his question. 'At least not yet. I'm coming with you.'

'No,' argued David as the three of them moved further into the kitchen, away from the sight that was a lifeless Katherine de Castro – sensing that the regrets would have to come later, and that this was a time to MOVE! 'You need to secure the crime scene. You need to trace this one back to Logan.'

'Martinelli and his CSR team are on their way. As soon as they get here I can brief them.'

'You are head of homicide, Joe.'

'You're right!' Joe was yelling now, placing his handgun onto the kitchen counter before he took a step towards David. 'And given I have just played a part in the perpetration of a crime I have dedicated my entire fucking career towards preventing, my priority is stopping this carnage now.' Joe took a breath. 'Logan is out in the open now, David. Our little plan worked. He gave the fuck in to his urges and you might as well be wandering around with a huge fucking X on your forehead.'

'Nora's gone to Chatham.'

'*What?*'

'She got a new lead on McCall, she's going to try to bring her back in.'

'*Fuck!*' Joe shook his head and ran his white knuckled hand over his thick black hair. '*Jesus.*'

'You need to call the Chatham locals, Joe.' David was playing the voice of reason. 'Put out an APB.'

Frank piped in: 'I'll handle that.' He pulled out his radio. 'And I'll put out an all-alerts on Katherine's Lexus as well.'

'Sara got Kessler to grant the exhumation order,' said David, knowing exactly what he was doing. 'You have to get that grave excavated ASAP. You need to check on how Susan is going with the gravy boat and how Lopez is doing with locating Damien Chi. We need as much information as possible, so that we can . . .'

'Bullshit, you're trying to bog me down in details so that you can make the trip to Chatham solo.'

'I am trying to get this done, Joe.'

But then they could hear the sirens out the front, as Joe and Frank's radios buzzed in unison, and at least three units of uniforms and Martinelli and his CSR team were pushing through the front door. And then Frank was directing them to the living room, as David's cell rang. And then he moved around the kitchen counter and into the corridor as if wanting to be able to take it away from the hubbub.

Seeing it was Arthur, he pressed the disconnect button knowing that, at least for the time being, his boss would have to wait. He feigned a conversation as he moved out into the street, and then he opened Joe's unmarked car door, and thanked God that the keys were still in the ignition. He felt a rush of adrenaline as he reached under his jacket and pulled out Joe's gun – the same one he had just lifted from the kitchen counter – and placed it on the seat beside him as he turned the key and started the engine and knew that, after all this time, he was finally *on his way*.

82

'What the hell is this?' asked Amanda Carmichael, her pink jacket now discarded. Sara Davis had just stormed into the small Superior Court conference room Amanda had been using as a preparation area during the trial, and she had not bothered to knock.

'I need you to be quiet and listen to me,' said the very pregnant woman before her.

'You need to get the hell out of this conference room,' returned Amanda, moving from behind her desk.

'This trial ends now.'

'Excuse me?' Amanda could not believe what she was hearing. 'Are you completely delusional?'

'Your star witness isn't coming.'

A disbelieving Amanda took a breath. 'If you are referring to Doctor Logan I can assure you he will be here for the afternoon session. What the hell is your problem, Miss Davis?' The woman was really starting to piss Amanda off. 'Has your boyfriend done a runner? I know you have been absent for most of the week,

Miss Davis, but in case he hasn't told you, he is losing this one big time – the jury know it, the press know it, and judging by Cavanaugh's mysterious disappearance this morning, he knows it too.'

'Katherine de Castro is dead,' said Sara.

'What? *Who?*' None of this was making sense.

'Logan's business partner. The good doctor found out she knew what he was up to, so he shot her.'

'I don't understand,' said Amanda, trying to take it all in. 'When? Where?'

'Late last night or early this morning at her Back Bay home. The police are at the scene now.'

'I don't believe this.' And in that moment it was like a million butterflies were released inside Amanda's head, thousands upon thousands of illusive little details – and she knew that once they came to rest, the one thing she had been missing (or perhaps ignoring), would finally become clear.

'And that is why David was . . .?' She called him David, and she saw Sara flinch.

'He found her – along with Joe Mannix and Frank McKay.'

Amanda shook her head, as if assisting the butterflies in their mission to find a place to rest.

'How can I be sure what you are telling me is true? I mean, Logan has a stellar record, he is America's sweetheart, his son shot his wife. He . . .'

'Carleton Blackmore and William Dukes run and work at a gun shop in Las Vegas called Hunting Rifles Inc., and Jeffrey Logan, whose real name is Jason Nagol, has been buying weapons from them for decades. He owned the rifle that killed his wife – but laundered it through the Garretsons so as to erase any link to his culpability. Deirdre McCall is Logan's mother; Logan killed his father years ago and so far has made two attempts on his mother's life. Michael Lopez is the Las Vegas detective investigating McCall's recent shooting which Logan arranged via his links to organised crime.'

Amanda realised what Sara was doing – she was rattling off the people on that mystery witness list, the one Logan claimed to know nothing about. 'Where is Logan now?' she asked, the fluttering finally starting to abate.

'We believe he is either on his way to, or already in, Chatham, Cape Cod.'

'Does he have a weekender there?'

Davis hesitated. 'We believe so – or one of sorts.'

Amanda nodded. 'What is it you want from me?' she asked after a pause.

'I . . . we, my boss Arthur Wright and I, we want you to call the State Police and arrange for us to fly to Chatham by helicopter.'

Sara was referring to the State Police's Airwing Section. The Massachusetts State Police had the largest and most comprehensive full-time public safety aviation unit in New England, and considering Amanda Carmichael was a high-ranking ADA, she had the power to call one of their three bases and organise a transport ASAP.

'Where is your partner?' she asked.

'I am not exactly sure,' answered Sara, and Amanda noticed her shudder. 'But if I know David, he is already on his way to Chatham.'

Amanda met her eye, and in it she saw the controlled

panic, which was when the buttlerflies finally settled and she moved back behind her desk.

'I'll need to confirm all of this with Mannix,' she said.

'All right,' said Sara.

'But first I'll call the MSP's base in Plymouth,' she said. 'And see if they have a chopper that can pick us up at Logan Airfield. I am coming with you, Miss Davis. It is my duty as the prosecutor on this case.'

Sara did not argue, simply let out a sigh of relief.

'Thank you,' she said, as Amanda picked up the phone.

And then, as Amanda got on to MSP headquarters and waited to be put through to the Airwing Service in Plymouth, her eyes lifted to meet Sara's once again.

'I suppose I should say I am sorry,' she said.

'What for?'

And Amanda knew her apology had nothing to do with the Logan case – and the look in Sara's pale aqua eyes told her that she knew it too.

'For persisting.'

'It's okay,' said Sara. 'To me, it doesn't count if your persistence was never returned.' A question rolled up in a statement.

'Never,' said Amanda, a half lie.

And Sara nodded with the slightest of smiles, just as the Airwing Commander came on the line.

Jeffrey Logan could smell it. It was a subtle aroma, the salty, organic scent of the ocean and the plant and marine life that resided beneath it.

He had heard the early forecast and spent the better

part of the morning waiting for the fog to come. He had sat out on the deck, watching the fishermen leave the dock and marvelling at the powerful harbour seals that had followed them out in hope of snaffling the rejects of their catch. And now, as he walked along the scenic Shore Road into the tiny township of Chatham, he could not only smell it but *feel* it, the periphery of its ghostly mass licking across the water – the living, breathing, incoming fog that within the hour would swallow the little seaside town in a dense and impenetrable mist and give Logan (who was wearing dark glasses and a low-riding Red Sox cap), a natural cover of anonymity.

They would be looking for him. They would know he had taken her car. Of course it was garaged now, hidden at the back of his whitewashed timber-shingled cottage, but they would find him, David Cavanaugh would find him, and the thought of it was *bliss*.

Killing Katherine was sublime. Witnessing Stephanie's ultimate demise was satisfying but given the nature of the situation – the fact that his children had *intervened* – meant that it was nowhere near as enjoyable as it should have been. In effect they had robbed him of the experience – but at the very least, they were paying for it now.

But killing Katherine was sublime. He had known what she was up to the moment she brought up the Davis woman. *I mean, seriously, how Goddamned stupid did she think I was*? He had been wrong about her, he knew that now. The bitch would never have gotten off her high fucking horse no matter how much he worked on her. She did not deserve him. She'd had the audacity to think she was *better* than him – and deep down he knew that she had always believed that he should be the one bowing and scraping to *her*. She thought she had discovered him, but in reality it was he who discovered *her*. He would have become the identity that he was with or without her fucking assistance, and the fact that she had been more than happy to spend close to the last twenty years riding his coat-tails just proved what a fucking sponge she was.

That is why killing her had brought him such pleasure, seeing the shock on her face as he casually walked into the living room a good two hours after he had left. Watching her eyes widen and her skin sit up in a million miniature bumps of horror as he pointed the trusty little Smith and Wesson .38 at her head and pulled the trigger.

The weapon was so light and reliable, like a diffident little friend. Not that there was anything modest about the hole it left in Katherine's forehead; he gave her a third eye so that she could stop using the other two to spy on him – fucking Goddamned whore.

Taking her keys had been easy – she left them on the hallway dresser as she always did, and she was in too much of a flap to notice him slide his hand over them and scoop them into his pocket as she showed him out the door.

He knew they were listening – he had felt the rise of wire under her bra. He even saw the van out the front, and it took all of his restraint not to wander on over to the tinted windows and offer Cavanaugh and his useless detective pal a friendly how-de-do!

So now they knew, and Logan was glad of it. Hell, the

thought of Cavanaugh seeking him out was enough to make him . . . well, let's just say, for fear of drawing attention to himself, he had to send the thought away as he neared the strip of colourful shops and cafés that sat like decorations along the scenic Main Street.

He would create another identity as he had done so many times before. He might even travel abroad, start somewhere fresh, find himself a woman and . . .

And then he felt it, that delectable tingle of anticipation that rose like a tide inside him. He had not expected it to come so quickly, but there it was nevertheless, prompted by the sight of the elderly ginger-haired woman now walking quickly up the other side of the street. It was Cavanaugh's secretary – the self-important one who paraded around Cavanaugh's place of business like a fucking mother hen. She was here. They knew!

And so Logan could not help but smile as he crossed the street and settled into a rhythm behind her, the mist now swelling around him, as he took a long slow breath of it and revelled in the ecstasy of what was to come.

It was like someone turned off the lights. From the moment David crossed the Segamore Bridge onto the Cape, the fog swallowed him whole. For much of the trip he had used Joe's portable siren light. But it would be of no use to him now as he made his way through the soup that covered Route 6, and thickened by the minute as he tracked east towards Chatham.

His cell phone had been ringing incessantly, but he hadn't bothered to pick it up. Logan had made this personal the moment he slaughtered Stephanie and proceeded to drag David's loved ones into his sick little game of cat and mouse. Now Nora was down here – alone – thanks largely to David's determination to beat his murderous nemesis. He would find her, and make her safe, before hunting Logan down and ending this thing for good.

'This is Mannix,' said Joe, raising his voice over the siren. He and Frank had taken one of the Boston Police Department's blue and whites the minute they realised their unmarked sedan was missing, and they had been flying down the freeway ever since.

'Chief,' said FBI Agent Susan Leigh, 'Martinelli just gave me the heads up.'

Joe had asked his CSU commander Dan Martinelli to take control of the forensics end of this investigation while he and Frank high-tailed it to the Cape.

'I'm sorry, about the business partner and all,' she said, and Joe knew that she meant it.

'Me too. You got news on the gravy boat?' he asked, knowing there was no time for chitchat, and Susan would not expect it.

'Yeah. Cavanaugh was right. We enlarged the gravy boat and enhanced the reflections using video imaging capability software, then we used a colour video printer with the most superior resolution on the planet to capture the images frame by frame and effectively freeze the reflections. The script is word for word, Chief. You have the fucker.'

But Susan had no idea how wrong she was.

*

Deirdre McCall was starving but she daren't leave her room, at least not yet. She was staying at the Chatham Bars Inn – one of the most expensive places on the Cape – with no means of paying the bill whatsoever. She had given the desk reception manager her credit card (knowing that even if they traced it, it would soon be over one way or the other), before calling upon her skills as a performer to spin a story about her retired corporate executive husband who would be joining her in a day or two.

She'd had no choice. The resort was the only place in the township with a view of his cottage – the inn's main building sitting like a historical bastion of yesteryear, its semicircular form capturing sweeping views of the waterfront cottages and the silver ocean beyond.

And early this morning her patience had finally paid off. She had seen him, she had *seen him* after all these years, and sadly and yet not unexpectedly, she felt no sadness or maternal nostalgia at all, only anger and determination and resolve.

And so, she would wait, her empty stomach rumbling as the sea mist engulfed the quaint east-facing balcony and shrunk her visibility to zero. She would wait at least an hour until the fog was at its thickest before making her way down towards his bunker. And then she would confront her son and do what she should have done all those years ago – put an end to this thing, once and for all.

Nora Kelly had been at the Captain's Table for over an hour, eating her chowder slowly, hoping beyond all hope that Deirdre McCall might walk in the café's front door at any moment, and order a late seafood lunch. But the likelihood of that happening was diminishing by the minute, given it was now half-past two. So Nora took a calculated risk and approached the waitress at the cash register, knowing that she needed to locate McCall by nightfall, and that she was running out of time.

'Excuse me,' she said. 'But I was wondering if I might ask for your help?'

'Your chowder okay, ma'am?'

'Oh, yes,' said Nora, with a smile. 'It was delicious but . . . the thing is, I have come to the Cape to look for my sister.' It was a reasonable lie, given she and Deirdre did look somewhat alike. 'She is in Chatham on a brief vacation and she told me on the phone last night that she had enjoyed a number of meals here, and given today is her birthday, I drove down from Boston in the hope of surprising her and . . .'

'I am sorry,' said the woman. 'I haven't been working here for most of the week and . . .'

'Is this the woman that other girl was ringing about?' asked a voice from behind, a young man, who had obviously overheard their conversation from just inside the kitchen.

'Ah . . . yes, that would have been her niece, Tracey. I guess she wanted to wish her happy birthday too.'

'Well, she hasn't been in today,' said the young man.

Nora's hopes depleted.

'But she's staying at the Chatham Bars Inn, if that helps. I saw the big gold key in her purse. The inn is one of the few five-star outfits that use an old-fashioned key instead of those plastic key cards. Kinda cool considering their heritage – you know, the grand historical seaside resort thing and all.'

Nora could not help but smile. 'Well thank you, young man. That is a great help.' She fished into her handbag before pulling out a fifty. 'And the chowder was wonderful.'

Nora could not believe her luck. She had found her – or at least had their first reliable lead. And then the thought struck her – the fact that this was indeed a team effort. She had left so abruptly and she knew that her colleagues would be worried.

So an energised Nora, given she did not possess – and had never possessed – a cell phone of her own, walked towards the closest convenience store with a 'Payphone Inside' sign on the window. And then she went to the phone which was located way down the back and dropped two quarters in the shiny aluminum slot to call David's cell.

'*Nora?*' David picked up, he could see the 508 number on his cell's screen and was praying that it would be her.

'I . . . yes. David, dear boy, I did not expect you to answer. I thought you would still be in court and I was going to leave a message but . . . well, you must be on a recess so I'll be brief. I am sorry I have not called earlier but I have news – good news. I think I have found Deirdre McCall and . . .'

'*Jesus, Nora*,' he interrupted. Nora was obviously on a high and while he did not want to come down on her, he was unable to stop himself. 'We have been so worried about you. You shouldn't have gone off on your own like that – not with Logan and . . .'

'I'm sorry, lad. I know what you are saying, but you are all so busy in Boston, whereas I had the time to . . .'

'Logan is in Chatham,' he said, not wanting to scare her but needing her to understand.

And then there was a pause.

'Dear Lord,' she said. 'His mother, she will be in danger. She is here, staying at the Chatham Bars Inn.'

'Where are you?'

'At a convenience store on Main Street, just down from the ice creamery and the candy store.'

'I'm almost there. I'll pick you up in five. And Nora, you don't think anybody . . .?'

'The fog is so thick, David, and getting thicker. No one has seen me. I am sure of it.'

David's next call was to Joe, whose first utterance went something like: 'You fucking idiot. Where the fuck are you?'

'I'm in Chatham. I found Nora. I am about to pick her up.' David assumed Joe would know about Nora by now, and he was right.

'Thank Christ. Sara is beside herself.'

Sara, thought David, the guilt now rushing through him. But Joe was not going to let him go so easily.

'You took my fucking gun.'

'I didn't take it, Joe. I borrowed it.'

'Jesus Christ, David, you need to listen to me. You have to grab Nora and go hide somewhere safe.'

'Nora found McCall.'

'*What?*' said Joe.

'McCall is staying at the Chatham Bars Inn. I'm

going to pick up Nora and head over there now. You can meet us in the lobby.'

He could almost hear Joe sigh with relief.

'Okay. Just stay put until we get there. And whatever you do, don't touch that freaking gun. We're only fifteen minutes away.'

'I'll be waiting,' lied David, before hanging up the phone.

'Get in,' he said, pushing the passenger side door open without coming to a stop. He had almost forgotten that Joe's gun was still on the seat, but had managed to put it into the glove box just as he pulled up in front of the convenience store.

Nora moved quickly. 'I'm sorry, lad,' she said. 'I should never have left without discussing it with you first.'

David took a breath. 'It's okay. None of us knew this would happen so fast.'

Nora nodded. 'I called Sara. She told me about Ms de Castro.'

And that was when David took his first real look at the woman he thought of as his second mother – and saw that the normally pink-skinned Nora was now an ashen shade of grey.

'He's a monster, Nora.'

'But we will stop him, lad.'

'No, Nora, there is no "we",' he said, taking a sharp left onto Shore Road. 'As soon as we get to the inn, I am leaving you with McCall.'

'But you have to wait for back-up, David. Sara said Joe was only moments away and Sara and Arthur and

Miss Carmichael are already in Hyannis. The helicopter landed almost twenty minutes ago, so they can't be more than . . .'

'*Sara is coming here?*'

'Yes,' she hesitated, meeting his eye. 'I thought you knew. She went to see Miss Carmichael who helped arrange a State Police transport. Sara told her everything, and now she is on board and ready to issue a warrant for Doctor Logan's arrest.'

'*Shit*,' David said, banging his fist on the steering wheel as the outline of the picturesque Chatham Bars Inn became visible in the opaque wisps of fog.

'I don't understand,' said an obviously confused Nora. 'I thought that was what we wanted.'

'Yes, I mean *no*, I mean . . .' He caught his breath as he swung the car into the inn's circular gravel drive. 'I mean, I want that bastard behind bars, Nora, but not like this. Don't you see, the more people who are here the more targets he has to fire at. The man is a sharpshooter, for God's sake, and all this activity . . . he is bound to know we are here, which means we have lost our element of surprise.'

'But we don't even know where he is staying,' Nora argued, as David shoved open his driver's side door, and Nora unbuckled her seat belt to do the same.

'That is where his mother comes in, Nora. She wouldn't have come here without knowing where to find him.'

'You think she knows where he stores his guns?' she asked, trying to keep up with David as he bounded up the front steps.

'It's the only hope we've got.'

*

David pushed the nervous manager aside. It had taken him a good five minutes to persuade him to escort them to Deirdre McCall's room and now the tall, thin hotel executive was tapping on the door to the second-floor room like a timid little bird.

'Ms McCall,' he said, his voice barely above a whisper, until David moved in front of him and began banging on the door with his fist.

'Ms McCall, my name is David Cavanaugh and I am the attorney who represents your grandchildren. We believe your life is in danger and we have arranged for your protection. The police are on their way, Miss McCall, and . . .'

But nothing, not a sound – and when David pressed his ear against the door he could not detect any movement inside.

'Open it,' he said to the manager.

For once the man did not hesitate, simply put the golden key into the wide old-fashioned lock and turned.

They were in her room in seconds, the classic New England décor extending from the bedroom to the white-tiled bathroom beyond. Deirdre McCall had no luggage, merely an overnight bag with the bare essentials Tracey Scabo had left for her in that hospital room over two weeks ago. The bed had been slept in but the covers had been carefully replaced. The bathroom was empty bar a single toothbrush and tube of toothpaste left in a glass on the large oval sink by the window.

'Shit,' said David.

'Where is she?' asked Nora.

But David did not answer. He was already back in the bedroom, the eerie white light seeping through the balcony doors like moonlight through smoke. He began by lifting up McCall's things and scanning her room for anything that might tell him where her son might be. And then he saw it – the small envelope on the bedside table. It was a letter addressed to Jason Nagol, the postmark stamped in an era long gone. He grabbed the envelope and took two sheets of yellowed realty letterhead from within it, laying them flat on the bed.

'What is it, lad?' Nora asked, moving towards him.

'I have to go,' he said, folding the papers quickly and jamming them into his right breast shirt pocket. 'You need to stay here in case McCall returns,' he said, before heading towards the door.

Nora was shaking her head. 'No, David. You cannot do this alone.'

But he was not stopping.

'You know where he is, don't you?' she said, her voice quivering with fear.

And then, as if forgetting something important, he turned and moved back into the room before grabbing his beloved secretary quickly and holding her in a firm and loving embrace.

'I'm going to be okay, Nora,' he said and, after a pause, felt her give him the slightest of nods as her tears fell softly on his right shoulder.

'There is nothing I can say?' she asked quietly.

'No,' he replied.

She took a breath as she pulled back and placed her hands firmly on his shoulders, looking for all the world like a mother now sending her only son off to war. 'Be careful,' she said, perhaps knowing there was nothing else she could say.

And he kissed her gently on the cheek, before bounding out the door.

'Lieutenant Mannix, my name is Captain Mac Burns from the Chatham Police.' Joe took his hand as they both headed towards the curved front steps of the Chatham Bars Inn. The fog had slowed traffic to a standstill, which meant Joe's trip had taken longer than expected – and so he was grateful to see the local cops waiting for him when he and Frank arrived.

'You get your man down from Provincetown?'

During the drive south, Joe had had several discussions with the local cops, including asking them to identify the best shooter they had – and they had come up with a young rookie from Provincetown by the name of Kevin Molis who, according to Captain Burns, 'could shoot a flea off of a dog from a hundred yards away'.

'Officer Molis,' said Burns as he turned to a young man, one of several uniforms now coming up the stairs behind them.

'Yes, sir,' said the young policeman.

'This is Lieutenant Mannix from Boston.'

'It's nice to meet you, sir,' said the blue-eyed Molis, taking Joe's hand.

'Likewise,' said Joe, as they reached the wide front glass doors. 'Captain Burns here tells me you know a thing or two about hitting a target.'

'Yes, sir. My father was an artillery captain in the army, sir. I shot my first tin can at age three.'

'Good,' said Joe. 'Because the target I got in mind is slightly bigger than your average can of soup. I gather this fog is a problem,' he added, turning his head slightly to look back towards the ocean behind him.

'Not for me, sir,' returned Molis. 'I once shot two mountain lions and a cougar in a blizzard where visibility was close to zero. There's more to finding your target than actually seeing it, Lieutenant,' he added.

'Let's hope so,' said Joe, before turning towards the hotel once again and striding quickly into the lobby.

'Joe,' said Sara, rushing across the hotel lobby to meet him, the very sight of all these police easing her fears – just a little.

'How're you doing?' he asked, taking her hand softly before letting it go once again.

'I'm okay,' she managed. 'But we have a problem.'

'Where's your idiot fiancé?' he asked, as if reading her mind.

'He's gone,' piped in Nora, who, together with Arthur and Amanda Carmichael, was moving forward to join their little group. 'To find Doctor Logan.'

Sara read the frustration in Joe's eyes.

'It gets worse, Joe,' she said.

'How so?' he asked.

'Nora thinks he knows where Logan is.' She handed him the envelope. 'They found this in Deirdre McCall's room.'

Joe looked at the empty envelope, before meeting Sara's eye and nodding in understanding. He handed McKay the envelope and turned towards Officer Molis once again.

'What do you need, Lieutenant?' said Molis, obviously reading Mannix's stare.

'I need you to load up, Officer. It's time to get things done.'

'Lieutenant,' said Amanda Carmichael, falling into step beside Joe, who had moved back to address the police officers behind him. 'What are you planning?'

'I'm planning to deal with this situation, Miss Carmichael – to apprehend the asshole who murdered his wife.' He didn't mean to sound terse, but this woman's ambitions had been part of the problem from the get-go.

'Lieutenant,' she said again, this time grabbing his elbow and forcing him to face her. 'You have to be sure about this,' she said, her voice barely above a whisper, 'because if you aren't, this could be a major setback for the reputation of law enforcement in Massachusetts as a whole. Jeffrey Logan is a national institution, for God's sake.'

Joe couldn't believe what he was hearing. 'Jeffrey Logan *belongs* in a fucking institution, Miss Carmichael, and I couldn't give a crap if the masses think he is Christ reincarnated. Now you can either make the decision to be of use to us, or sit in that fucking corner, with a uniform by your side –' Joe pointed at some miniature Georgian furniture in the lobby's recess, '– until I decide I am ready to cut you loose.'

Joe waited, wondering if Carmichael was going to sit on the fence of procrastination for the sake of personal advancement, or jump off said fence to do her fucking job the way it was supposed to be done.

'Do you know where Logan is?' she asked after a pause.

And, gratefully, Joe sensed she was getting ready

to jump. 'There was an envelope left in the mother's room. Cavanaugh took its contents but the envelope is marked with the insignia of a local realtor.'

'And this realtor can track Logan down?'

'McKay is working on it,' he said.

Carmichael nodded.

'Cavanaugh has gone after him,' she said after a pause, and Joe could have sworn he detected a hint of trepidation in her eyes.

'Yes.'

'Is he armed?'

'He stole my gun.'

She nodded once again. 'Good,' she said, before releasing his arm and stepping back so that Joe might do his job. 'Good.'

David was on a family vacation at Sandy Hook when he first heard it, that paradoxical echo of peace and power. His father had put it to his ear. It was one of those large spiral conch shells that were all rough and barnacled on the outside but smooth and shiny within.

He heard that same sound now – the whoosh of the waves rolling onto the shore – but this time it was caused by the licking of the sea beyond the empty residence. Logan had left the door unlocked, as if he had been expecting visitors – which in effect, he had.

The cottage was a neatly arranged two-bedroom bungalow, tastefully decorated in what could only be described as Cape Cod chic. The beds were made and the kitchen clean but the fresh, nutty scent of coffee hung warm and inviting in the air. The shutters were closed as was the door that led to the garage, a high-security double lock making it impossible for David to seek out Katherine's car.

With Joe's .40 Glock by his side, David moved towards the back of the living room, to the white-washed bi-fold doors now covered with canvas roman blinds. He pulled on the cords, lifting the blinds to their extremities, revealing the white sandy beach, and every now and again, glimpses of the silver water, flat and heavy as if compressed by the low-lying cloud above it.

He continued out onto the deck – one of those distressed white oak numbers bordered by frameless glass. And that was when he looked left, back down the beach towards the Chatham Bars Inn, and saw the lone figure standing just beyond a blue and white striped beach canopy.

And despite the mist he knew that the man was looking directly at him. An assumption then confirmed as the man raised his right hand and waved.

'No Logan,' said the realtor, an elderly gentleman by the name of Boyce. 'And there is no Golan or Nagol either.'

'*Shit*,' said Joe, now cursing into his cell. He had been praying the realtor might find evidence of Logan having leased or purchased a property in Chatham in the same year as the postmark on Deidre McCall's envelope.

'Okay, Mr Boyce,' recovered Joe, now lifting his hands for quiet as the local cops rallied around him. 'I need you to think a little out of the box here. To play some with those letters – L.O.G.A.N. – like working out an anagram, do you see? If the letter was sent out in the year we discussed, it may have been giving some sort of confirmation of purchase or rental agreement in another name. Do you see?'

'Yes, I see,' said Boyce, who was obviously anxious to help. And Joe waited while the realtor flipped through what must have been some very old property documents, the rustling of paper now crackling clear and crisp down the line.

'Wait!' said Boyce after a moment. 'No, that won't work.'

'What won't work?' asked Joe, his heart skipping a beat.

'Well, there is something here, but the name has an apostrophe and that might not be what you are after.'

'What is it?' asked Joe, stealing a glance at Frank.

'There is a lovely seaside cottage on Shore Road. It was bought during the year in question at a very good price. These days those waterfront properties go for a small fortune, but back then you could pick one up for . . .'

'What's the name of the owner, Mr Boyce?' interrupted Joe.

'A Mr O'Glan,' said Boyce. 'But as I said, it has an apostrophe and . . .'

'And did this Mr O'Glan give a first name, Mr Boyce? And if he did, does it by any chance happen to start with the letter "J"?'

'Why yes, it does. The Christian name given here is Jeremy. Does that make any difference, Lieutenant?'

Joe allowed himself the slightest of smiles.

'I believe it does, Mr Boyce,' he said, knowing that at last they had found him.

*

'I suppose this is where I should ask, *what took you so long?*'

Jeffrey Logan was standing in the middle of the beach, his right hand holding a small silver pistol, his left cradling one of the most high-tech rifles David had ever seen.

David approached from his right, knowing that, despite the fog, the emptiness of this stretch of sand in August was no coincidence. Joe must be securing a perimeter, in the hope of finding Logan, and preventing his escape.

'You've been expecting me,' said David, lifting his own weapon – a gesture which resulted in Logan's face breaking into a smile.

'Seriously, David.' He laughed. 'You don't really think that pathetic piece of tin is any match for these two superior pieces of weaponry.' He lifted both his hands. 'Not that you could tell the difference. From what I know of you, my friend, you don't even have the balls to wear a wedding ring, let alone brandish a gun.'

David felt his finger slide slowly towards the trigger.

'Has Sara dropped that baby yet, by the way? Goodness me, the last time I saw her she really did look ready to pop. And you have been working her so hard, you slave driver! I mean, if there is anything wrong with that poor child when it finally sees the light of day . . .'

But David knew exactly what Logan was doing. 'Listen to you,' he said, 'preaching the gospel according to Jeffrey Logan as if I gave a fuck. Do you actually believe the crap that comes out of your mouth, Nagol?' he asked, and Jeffrey Logan flinched, just a little . . . 'Or is the endless flow of drivel simply a symptom of your Goddamned screwed-up psychosis.'

'*Drivel?*' said Logan, now starting to tense. 'That so-called *drivel* has influenced an entire generation of Americans.'

'Bullshit. You just repeated the obvious with an ingratiating smile on your face. You call yourself a relationship guru but the truth is, Golan –' David was mixing it up, '– you are just a social misfit incapable of connecting with anyone. You're a genetic mutant, Jeffrey, a biological mistake who should never have been born.'

There was silence, as Logan took a breath. 'Ah . . .' he said, nodding in feigned congratulation. 'I see now what you are trying to do. This is your way of drawing me out, of forcing me to act and end this thing once and for all. Is that what you want, Cavanaugh? Do you want me to shoot you, right here, right now – because if so, I am more than happy to oblige?'

'It's my way of telling you that you have finally met your match, Jeffrey – that my head is off limits, no matter what you say.'

'No, my friend,' Logan countered. 'I am afraid that you will never be off limits because you have no concept of how *not* to take things personally – just like Stephanie who . . .'

'Stephanie was ten times the human being you will ever be.'

'Stephanie was a whore,' replied Logan, his right arm raising slightly, his pistol cocked and ready to explode. 'I gave her everything and she did nothing but spit in my face.'

'You beat her until she was dead, you asshole. You tortured her and her two children every minute of every Goddamned day, and even *then* they still had the courage to stand up to you. You are nothing but a bully, Logan, and your wife, your children, she was . . . they *are* . . .'

And then David saw it – the tick above Jeffrey Logan's left eye. The man was beginning to flounder, David's 'truths' now hitting where it hurt.

'You want to know how many I have killed?' asked Logan, perhaps the only way he knew to recover. 'I mean, you have put so much work into trying to destroy me, I feel it is only fair that I pay you your due before I put a bullet through your head.'

'How many?' asked David, needing to draw him out.

'Six and a half,' he said. 'Counting the two homeless people and the small boy I picked off in the woods when I was barely a teenager myself. The little tike was on a hunting trip with his pappy who wrongly assumed it was he who accidentally popped his grandson and so . . . someone else took the credit for that.

'And then there was my father who I nabbed by slicing his tyre from a good hundred yards away – and my father-in-law who provided the perfect target for my new Heckler & Koch. And there was Katherine – well, you already knew about her; and my mother who, in all fairness to me, David, given the effort I have put into her, should in the very least count as a half.'

'You forgot to mention your wife,' said David, the mist now swelling around them, the air slick and cool and wet.

'See now,' he shook his head. 'That is the biggest

irony of all, my friend, because in this case at least, you give me too much credit.'

'You think you deserve admiration for murdering your wife?'

'*No* – and that is my point exactly, because as much as I wanted to end her pathetic excuse for an existence . . . somebody beat me to it.'

'This is ridiculous,' said Sara, rising from the edge of the bed in the still missing Deirdre McCall's room. 'There has to be some way we can help.'

'No, Sara,' said Nora. 'Joe was right. The best place for us right now is here in the safety of this room.'

Despite Sara's protests, a determined Joe had ordered Sara and Nora to retreat to Deirdre McCall's hotel suite. Arthur had been designated the role of helping Amanda Carmichael coordinate with the inn staff to round up the guests and send them to their allocated rooms as well, while Joe and his fellow cops had secured as much of the nearby coastline as possible, which was no easy task considering the growing thickness of the fog.

'God, it's hot in here,' Sara said, before walking to the bathroom to splash water on her face. 'I need some air, Nora,' she added, moving towards the balcony beyond.

'All right, dear,' said Nora, pushing back the door so that the two of them might move out onto the small patio.

'He's out there,' said Sara, her hands forming fists around the white-painted balustrade, the mist so dense it was like looking out the window of an aeroplane passing through thick cloud. 'He's out there alone with that psychopath and there is nothing I can do about it.'

'David's a smart man, Sara. He will work this out.'

'David is an idiot who thinks he can single-handedly save the world.'

'Which is why you fell in love with him in the first place,' Nora offered.

Sara nodded, the tears now falling freely down her face. 'I know, Nora. I know.'

'*Police!*' yelled Joe as he and his heavily armed team broke through Jeffrey Logan's front door. Their guns were up and their bulletproof vests heavy, their weapons sweeping from side to side, scanning every inch of the cottage for movement.

'*Clear!*' yelled an officer who had moved quickly into the bedrooms.

'*Clear!*' called a second who had taken the bathroom on the right.

The kitchen and living spaces were open, leaving no one anywhere to hide, so Joe lifted up two fingers, indicating he wanted the team to split, the first following Frank towards the door that led directly into the garage, while the second moved further into the house.

Frank smashed the lock with his gun barrel before moving quickly into the dark rectangular space – lifting his right pointer finger and twirling it clockwise so that the three officers accompanying him would surround the car. Frank tried the front passenger side first, his weapon at the ready, before the other uniforms tried the other three doors – a quick search revealing nothing but a woman's yellow cardigan and a matching floral umbrella.

Team two followed Joe into the living room proper and towards the open back patio doors, the strong smell of salt hitting their faces as the wind whipped briskly around them.

'We have Katherine's car,' said Frank, as he joined his boss near the terrace.

Joe nodded. 'Listen up, gentlemen, we need to pull this place apart. There is a gun cellar in here somewhere, and we won't be leaving 'til we find it.'

And then he and Frank moved out onto the deck.

'It's like pea soup out here,' said Frank.

But Joe was already lifting his hand, a gesture that started as a signal for Frank to stop, before transforming into a direction to turn his head to the right and look towards where he was pointing.

'What's that, Frank?' asked Joe, squinting into the light.

'What's what?' said Frank, the mist now moving in sheets.

'That,' said Joe, extending his arm a little further. 'There, a few hundred yards down the beach. It looks like . . .?'

'Two men,' said Frank, the images floating in and out of view like a TV screen with faulty reception. 'Jesus, Chief.'

'Molis!' called Joe, now moving into action. 'Officer Molis!'

'Yes, sir,' said the rookie who was now mere feet behind him.

Joe grabbed him by the shoulders, pivoting him around so that he might look in the direction of the people they *thought* they saw. And then he leaned in close as if willing the fog to move so that the sharp-shooting Molis could see them too.

'There!' said Joe. 'Just then, *did you see them*?'

'I saw them,' said Molis, already shouldering his rifle. 'You want me to take out the TV guy?'

'I want you to be a hundred per cent sure you don't hit the wrong fucking target.'

But Molis was already moving towards the glass, and lifting his rifle to fire.

'You're lying,' said David, taking another step forward.

'Well,' said Logan, his pistol still pointing squarely at David. 'I can understand why you would think that, given I have been known to spin a tale or two. But in this case, sadly, I speak nothing but the truth. I wanted to kill Stephanie but, as I have already explained, my two savvy offspring beat me to it.'

'That's a load of crap,' said David. 'Don't you understand, Logan? This is *it*. You have just admitted to six murders so . . .'

'Six and a half,' corrected Logan.

'It makes no difference,' countered David, the sweat now beading on his forehead. 'Whether or not you admit to killing your wife is irrelevant. You are going away for life, Logan. And no one will be happier about that than me.'

But Logan would have none of it, the man simply smirked and extended his right arm that inch further, while shouldering his rifle with his left, and aiming it inland, beyond the thick, grey haze.

'Do you want to know how they did it?' he asked, as if needing to see this through.

'I want you to stop fantasising and put down your weapons before I blow your fucking brains out.'

'See, there you go again, David. Your ability to allow your idealism to blind your view of reality is really quite extraordinary. It was all about choice, you see. My children weighed up the pros and cons and then decided on a course of action. Bad decision, as it turns out, but then I suppose they are paying for that now.'

'You are wasting your breath, Logan,' said David, shifting his feet. Despite himself, all this talk of the children was starting to get to him. He knew Logan was only playing mind games, but there was something about his assuredness that . . .

'Perhaps,' replied Logan, interrupting his thoughts. 'But I really would like to get back to the subject at hand. I was talking about choices, which is really quite appropriate given I am about to ask you to make one.'

David shifted yet again.

'Now, now, no need to jump the gun, David,' he said. 'No pun intended.'

Then Logan turned away from him, ever so slightly, to place his left eye on the rifle's circular viewfinder – his right arm still straight and steady, pointing directly at David's head.

'There,' he said. 'Do you see them?'

And despite the situation, David could not help but look.

'Wait,' said Logan. 'Wait, wait . . . There! See?'

And that was when David realised what Logan was aiming at – and the contents of his stomach rose in his throat.

'*No!*' he yelled, his right foot lunging.

'Hold it right there, David,' said Logan. 'One more step and I will kill them both. I must say it was very kind of them to present themselves as they have, like two lame ducks sitting stupidly on a levee. I am a reasonable man, David, and given I respect the fact that you have been my worthiest adversary to date, I am going to let you choose.'

'*Put the gun down*.'

'*No*,' yelled Logan, any trace of feigned conciliation now gone. '*You wanted to play this game, you fucking amateur, and now it is time to deal.* Who will you save, David – your beloved secretary or your pregnant fucking whore – the latter being the choice I obviously prefer, given I am guaranteed a two for one.'

It was as if time stood still, as every muscle in David's body seemed to tense, as every inch of his being focused on the power he held in his now sweating right hand. Without even thinking, he squeezed the trigger, the sound of gunfire – *bang, whoosh*, *bang*, *bang* – echoing across the endless bleak expanse.

And in the split second, just before he saw Jeffrey Logan's head explode, he noticed the fire spew from the end of Logan's rifle.

David dropped his weapon. And then he began to run.

PART THREE

83

The following morning

'David . . . David . . . wake up.'

He was drifting, stuck in that nowhere land between awake and asleep, where your conscious brain refuses to register your current location and situation. But then your senses kick in. Giving you little clues whether you wanted them or not – the soulless smell of antiseptic, the rhythmic beep of a machine, the vague sensation of fluorescent lighting, the cool air-conditioning on your skin.

'Lisa,' he said at last, his eyelids separating to see his younger sister standing above him.

'Hey, big bro,' she said with a smile. She was wearing her Mass General nurses' uniform, her plastic ID and stethoscope draped around her neck. 'You need to go home and get some real sleep. There is nothing you can do here now. I will call you if there's any change.'

'Hey,' said a new voice in the mix, and David turned to see his good friend Joe Mannix looking more than a little dishevelled at the hospital room door. 'How is she doing?' he asked, pointing at the sleeping figure in the bed.

'She's fine,' replied Lisa. 'We call it a false labour – in this case induced by stress,' she added, poking David in the shoulder.

'She hasn't had a contraction for the last six hours so at this stage we simply let her rest – which is exactly what this idiot should be doing,' she said, gesturing at her brother who was still slouched in the hospital room chair in front of her. 'Make him go home, Joe, at least for a little while.'

Joe nodded, moving into the room. 'You heard your sister.'

'I've been hearing her for thirty-six years, Joe,' said David with a half smile. 'It doesn't mean I have to do what she says.'

Lisa tousled David's hair in mock frustration.

'Seriously, David,' said Joe then. 'You really do need to take a load off.'

'Not until I hear the latest,' said David, now sitting up in his chair.

'Okay, I'll leave you to it,' said Lisa. 'But if you're not gone by the time I get back, I'll hunt you both down.'

And with that, Lisa was gone.

Jeffrey Logan was dead. He was in fact shot three times by three bullets from three different guns a split second apart – the actual bullet which slammed into his head first, was yet to be determined.

Nora Kelly was fine, the bullet from Logan's rifle merely grazing her left cheek. It was Nora's quick action that had saved Sara's life – given it was she who had spotted the spark of gunfire on the beach and pulled her surrogate daughter to safety.

Deirdre McCall had been arrested, so far the greatest injustice of it all. But Amanda Carmichael, after a long discussion with David and Joe late last night, had agreed that the District Attorney's Office would not push for jail time. She would in fact suggest that the elderly heroine had acted to prevent the likelihood of 'further serious casualties', and Carmichael planned to have her released as soon as was legally possible so that she might meet her two grandchildren.

'McCall was behind that cabana the entire time, Joe, just biding her time, waiting for an opportunity to shoot.'

'I guess she has waited a lifetime to deal with her son, David, so in the scheme of things . . .'

Deirdre McCall may have waited years to deal with her evil offspring, thought David then, but in the end she had undertaken the most selfless act any human being could carry out. She had killed the person she had given life to, so that others could live.

'So you think it was her bullet that hit Logan first?' asked David.

'Pretty sure. The Cape Cod ME said it appeared as if the initial impact came from about fifteen yards to the victim's left, which lines up with the cabana. So it appears to have been McCall's first, Molis' second, and your bullet . . .'

'And here I was thinking it was me who saved the day,' said David.

'Not a chance,' smiled Joe.

'That McCall is something else,' said David after a

pause. 'One minute she is in a hospital in Vegas, the next she is seeking out her son's gun cellar so she can put an end to his killing.'

Joe nodded. 'First she locates the house, and then she finds the cellar – which was not easy, by the way, considering it took our guys a good twenty minutes to see the tiniest of cracks between the floorboards. And then she pulls up the trap door, climbs down those stairs and chooses a weapon before loading it and . . .'

'That's a mother's determination for you,' said David, his eyes drifting across to Sara.

Joe nodded once again.

'What is it?' asked Joe after a time, perhaps reading the fresh look of recognition on David's face.

'I was just thinking,' replied David. 'We started off believing a son had killed his mother – and ended up with a mother killing her son.'

'That's some kind of justice,' said Joe.

'I guess so.'

Joe went on to explain that Malcolm Tyler's body had been exhumed late yesterday afternoon and that ME Gus Svenson would be undertaking the autopsy today. He also said that Las Vegas Detective Michael Lopez had called as soon as he heard the news – promising that David's statement regarding Logan's admissions had resulted in a fresh warrant for Damien Chi's arrest.

'The man killed seven people, David,' said Joe after a pause, and David felt his brow furrow. 'And sadly, part of me wishes the bastard was still alive so that we could drag him through the courts and put his famous ass in jail forever.'

But David was shaking his head. 'Not me,' he said. 'I got no problem with the way things went down, Joe.'

'Fair enough, my friend. Fair enough.'

David rose to his feet. 'I need to see the children,' he said.

'You need to get some rest.'

'There will be time for that later.'

'No, David,' said Joe, smiling as he pointed at Sara. 'Given the three months of sleepless nights you two have ahead of you, my guess is your time has run out.'

'Sounds nice,' smiled David.

'It is,' replied Joe.

David moved towards his friend to take his hand and pull him into an embrace, the two men saying nothing, knowing nothing needed to be said.

'You ever steal my gun again, I'll kill you,' said Joe at last.

'It was a one-off, Joe,' said David. 'Next time, I'll ask.'

It had come to him at midnight, not long after he had hung up from his good friend Tony Bishop. David had told no one of Logan's determination to blame his children for Stephanie's death, but the conversation remained with him, like a splinter in his side.

'Tony,' he had said, after he had given him a rundown on the day's events and Tony had spent the next five minutes asking a million questions as to David and Sara's welfare. 'There was one thing I wanted to ask you.'

'Ask away,' his friend had replied.

'The last time we saw Stephanie – back in February, at that St Valentine's Day ball – how did you think she looked?'

'I didn't see her at the ball, remember?' he had said. 'Missed her altogether which, to be honest, DC, I will never forgive myself for.' His friend had taken a breath.

'But I saw her in that video and Jesus, man, she looked terrible.'

David had said nothing, hoping his friend would go on.

'You know, weeks after her death, we had this meeting – me and Amanda, the insurance turd and Harrison. And Harrison said something about people often changing their wills and life insurance policies at the same time. He said nine times out of ten, people address those sorts of things across the board – wills, life insurance, health checks and so forth. And for some reason the health check thing stuck in my mind.

'And then I saw that video and, Jesus, DC, despite everything else I realised that Stephanie *did* have a health problem. Her husband was like a disease, slowly sapping her life away.'

Which was the truth, David knew . . . but perhaps not all of it.

'Gus, it's David,' he said, as he put his cell on speaker so that he could negotiate a left-hand turn out of the Mass General parking garage and onto Fruit Street.

'Hello!' said the Swedish-born ME, a genuine delight in his voice. 'Mannix tell me your situation. I am so glad you and Sara are all right.'

David knew that he meant it. 'Thanks, Gus,' he said. 'Listen, I know you guys are snowed under . . .'

'Yes, but not so much. The governor approved the

employment of two more examiners. My load has eased, just a little.'

'That's great news. I was wondering if you could check something for me.'

'I will conduct autopsy on Malcolm Tyler today and Katherine de Castro tomorrow.'

'Okay, thanks, but . . .' said David, not sure how to approach his question without raising Gus' suspicions. 'This is about Stephanie Tyler. You mentioned the last time we spoke, that Stephanie was an organ donor – and that her organs and tissues were harvested not long after her death.'

'That is correct.'

'And doesn't the New England Organ Bank send you some report to clarify this?' David was pretty sure this was the case. He had once worked on a previous case where such a report was used in evidence after a family disputed their deceased loved one's decision to be a donor.

'Yes,' said Gus. 'The NEOB give report on all organs and tissue given to organisations such as Lifenet for processing. They also explain what organs have been passed on for research to various approved research protocols.' Gus took a breath. 'Why, you need this?'

'Not me,' he lied, 'but the children. They want to donate some of their mother's fortune to the various transplant and research organisations.' Another lie. 'Do you think you could get someone to pull the report and leave it at reception? I'll race by and look at the list and leave it for you to re-file.'

'That would be fine. That is very kind of the children.'

'They are good kids, Gus,' he said, still hoping, that beyond all else, this was true.

Amanda Carmichael met him at her office door. 'Hi,' she said, extending her hand. 'Come on in.'

David moved into her office, the two of them standing somewhat awkwardly until she directed him to her sofa.

'The kids are here,' she said. 'I put them in the conference room until you arrived. I got my assistant to get them some sodas.'

And David saw the irony in her words – 'kids', 'sodas' – mere days before she was trying them for murder as adults in an adult court.

'How are they doing?' he asked.

'Pretty good under the circumstances,' she said, before adding, 'David, I am so sorry. It's just that the evidence pointed directly at the boy and . . .'

'It's okay.'

'No, no it's not. I should have listened to you, I should have listened to *myself* when my instincts told me Jeffrey Logan was . . .'

'Logan fooled a lot of people, Amanda.'

'Maybe so, but in my case I think I let it happen – for selfish reasons. Do you understand?'

'I understand you are doing the right thing by the kids by helping their grandmother,' he said.

Amanda smiled. 'Thanks.'

'How's Sara?' she asked after a pause.

'As of ten minutes ago she was still resting.' Moments after leaving the ME's office, David had called Lisa to check on Sara's status and his sister assured him she was still sound asleep. 'They call it a false labour. The pains stopped late last night and the baby seems to be doing fine so . . . all they recommend now is for her to rest and me to wait.'

'Not something you're good at.' She smiled.

'Never been my strong point.'

She smiled again. 'I have arranged for the children to go into foster care until their grandmother's situation is sorted out. With any luck she'll be free to take them before the week is out.'

'So maybe things have a way of working out after all,' he said, before they drifted into silence once again.

And then Amanda lifted her eyes, her bright blue orbs meeting his pale green ones. 'Listen, David, I . . .'

'It's okay,' he interrupted, knowing exactly what she was going to say. 'I think we were both scared of what we had gotten ourselves into, and the consequences it had for us, and the people that we loved.'

She nodded once again, perhaps deciding there was no more to be said. 'So we're good then?'

'We're good.' He smiled, before standing to take her hand. 'Thank you,' he said.

'What for?' she asked.

'For doing your job.'

'I went about it the long way, David.'

'That's okay – you got there in the end.'

J.T. Logan ran to him the minute he walked in the door – his long skinny arms reaching around David's middle, his face now buried in his chest. David held him tight, before looking up at his sister – her wavy hair free, her blue eyes moist, her face the spitting image of her mother's – and lifting his arm so that she might join them in their huddle, which she did, placing one arm around David, and the other across her brother's shoulders.

Moments later they sat down at the conference table, David on one side, the kids on the other. David took a breath before saying what he needed to say.

'When were you going to tell me?' he asked, Chelsea lifting her head sharply in response, J.T.'s deep brown eyes darting between Chelsea and David and back once again.

'Tell you what?' Chelsea asked.

David said nothing, merely pulled the New England Organ Bank report from his inside jacket pocket and placed it on the table in front of him.

'What's that?' she asked.

'It's an organ and body tissue transplantation and research report. The NEOB issues one for every donor and sends it to the ME's Office as part of their obligatory paperwork. This one lists the organs and tissue that were taken from your mom – her brain, liver, her spleen, her kidneys, sections of her lower intestine and so forth – and explains what happened to them post-removal.'

The kids said nothing.

'The Center for Liver Research and Diagnostics who were given your mom's liver rejected it for any productive research outright given it was in the final stages of cancer – a secondary cancer which, according to the report, had most likely started in her bowel.'

'I . . . ah . . .' began Chelsea.

'I know she was dying, Chelsea,' he said, wanting

her to know that there was no point in denying it. 'So now you need to tell me what happened, starting with . . . how long did she have?'

'She . . . two weeks, maybe a month,' Chelsea offered, this time without hesitation. 'She didn't find out until the cancer was well advanced.' She took a breath. 'The doctors said chemotherapy would most likely be a waste of time so she made the choice to set things straight so that we would be okay after she was no longer around to look after us.'

'So it was her idea,' said David. 'All of it.'

'No,' said J.T. 'It was Father's idea. It had *always* been Father's idea. It's just that Mom came up with the plan to beat him to it.'

'Your father did not know that your mother was dying?'

'No,' said Chelsea.

'So you told your mother of your father's plans and she took control of her own murder so that she might liberate you two from him.'

'Yes.'

'She committed suicide.'

'Yes.'

'With your help.'

'*Yes*,' said Chelsea. 'And despite how it all went down, we have no regrets,' she said, gripping her brother's hand on top of the table. 'She said it was the last thing she would ask of us and, given all that she had sacrificed on our behalf, it was the very least we could do.'

And then Chelsea Logan took another long, deep breath before starting, once again, at the beginning.

*

'He's here,' said Chelsea, after seeing her father's car turn into their narrow Beacon Hill street. She had been standing at the window for the past half hour; her father was running late.

Chelsea met her mother in the hallway, and Stephanie felt the nausea boil in her stomach as she took her daughter's hand.

'All right,' she said, praying that she would have the courage to see this through. 'We don't have much time so you must do exactly as we discussed.' She turned towards her son, crouching so that she might meet his eye.

'J.T., as soon as it is done you must remove the evidence and put it in the laundry and down the toilet like we discussed.' They had gone over the details a million times, but for some reason, she felt the need to voice them one more time. 'Then you have to come back here and wait in the hallway so you can play out the rest as part of your father's plan. This will not work unless you stick to his strategy, do you understand?'

But J.T. was sobbing, unable to respond.

'Please, my love,' she said, her own tears now streaming down her face. 'This is the only way. I love you both so much.' She grabbed for Chelsea's hand once again. 'I will always be here,' she said, her other hand now flat against her little boy's chest. 'In your heart, and he will be gone and you and your sister will be free and I will live on in you and your grandchildren and their grandchildren and . . .'

But then they heard the grinding of the automatic garage door, and she held them quickly and kissed them both before moving into the kitchen.

The rifle had been set up over an hour before. The

heavy red oak hat stand had been placed at the end of the table, her husband's long-sleeved T-shirt then stretched and pulled over the top. She had slotted the rifle through the right T-shirt arm, before tying it to the hat stand with the strongest string she could find – an extra length of twine looped around the trigger and draped lengthways, across the table, waiting for her to take her seat.

'Quickly now,' she told herself. 'There is no time, you have to move.'

She checked on her props – the wine and the Vanity Fair, *now placed equidistant on the table before her – and then she reached forward to grab the string so that she might pull, tightly, and force the trigger into compression.*

She took a breath, and then another, counting them down until she had the courage to choose the one that would be her last. Then she closed her eyes and said a prayer for her children, and a final one for herself, before grasping the string and . . .

Snap!!!!

Nothing.

The string broke! The STRING BROKE, and she had no choice but to call for her children.

'God, no,' she said, pushing back her chair and rising from the table and rushing into the hallway once again. 'J.T.,' she said, sadly, simply, because he was the closest to the kitchen door. 'Quickly. Chelsea,' she yelled towards the top of the stairs, 'stay exactly where you are.'

She grabbed J.T.'s hand and pulled him into the kitchen before getting on her knees and placing her hands on his cheeks and clasping them, hard – willing him to focus, forcing him to listen to what she had to say.

'J.T.,' she began. 'There is no time. Your father will walk

into this house at any minute. The string has broken. You need to get behind that hat stand and underneath that T-shirt. You need to place your finger on that trigger and you need to squeeze.'

'NO!' he yelled.

'YES! There is no other way.' She was sobbing. 'Please J.T. Do this for me. I cannot die knowing you are left with him. Please, my son. Please give me this gift. Allow me to end this the way I want to. Let me die so that you can live the way you and your sister deserve. I beg you, my love. Please, DO THIS FOR ME SO THAT I CAN DO IT FOR YOU.'

J.T. nodded, ever so slightly, as his mother pressed her lips firmly on his forehead and whispered, 'Make sure you close your eyes. I love you,' then moved back to the chair for the very last time.

And then a shaking J.T. manoeuvred himself underneath his father's T-shirt, and slotted his long skinny arm through the now tight right-arm hole. He placed his finger on the trigger, closed his eyes, and then he yelled, 'I LOVE YOU, MOM,' and then . . . and then . . . he fired.

'So you pulled that trigger?' asked David.

'Yes.'

'And flushed the string?'

'Yes.'

'And removed the T-shirt so you could take it to the laundry and make out that . . . that your father killed her and was trying to hide the evidence.'

'We used the toilet off the kitchen to flush the string,' said Chelsea. 'But we had to go down the hallway to reach the laundry, and by that stage Father had heard the shot and was already well inside the garage. So . . .'

'He met you in the hallway on the way to the laundry,' continued David. 'You lost time, after the string broke, which ruined your entire plan.'

'Yes.' Chelsea nodded. 'And the funny thing was, Father knew exactly what we had been up to. He didn't even need to go into the kitchen. He just took control. He told J.T. that unless he put on the T-shirt he would kill me. He wrapped his handkerchief around the rifle and held it to my head – and then he called 911.'

'And all this explains why your father's ears were intact and why yours, J.T., were not,' he said, looking at the boy. 'And why, given the gun was resting on the T-shirt that was still draped over the hat stand when it exploded, you had no recoil burns on your shoulder and . . .'

'Everything else was as we told you,' said Chelsea, as if imploring him to understand. 'Don't you see, David, my father's way . . . that is the way it *would* have been if we had not intervened. Father changed Mom's insurance, he drilled us on how it would all go down. It was just that in the end, Mom wanted it to happen on *her* terms – so that we would be free.'

'It was a stupid idea,' David said, the fruitlessness of it all adding to his frustration. 'Stephanie – she knew better, she should have come to me, she should have asked for my help.'

'But she *did* ask,' said Chelsea. 'She just waited until she was dead, for if she had approached you while she was still alive, my father might have found out . . . and then, she knew, it was me or J.T. who would have suffered.'

And then a memory came back to him – a conversation he had had with Joe Mannix many weeks ago. Joe had asked why a smart woman like Stephanie did not run – why, if she knew her husband was planning to kill her, she did nothing but sit there and wait for her moment to die.

But now David understood exactly why Stephanie had made that decision. It was not because Logan had sucked the life out of her, the cancer was doing that. On the contrary, if anything, it told him that Stephanie remained the fighter she always was. Logan simply fuelled her determination to use her own death for his demise – so that, in a manner of speaking, she could take him down with her, effectively setting her children free.

'And then your father confessed,' said David.

'Yes.'

'And everything . . .'

'. . . everything went wrong,' said J.T.

'Until now,' said Chelsea.

And then there was silence once again.

'You should have told me earlier,' said David.

'We tried to – at least, I tried to tell Sara.'

David recalled Sara's report of Chelsea's odd behaviour in their very first meeting together – her fixation with the hat stand and the concept of 'reaching' across the table.

'But I knew Father was listening so there was little that I could do. J.T. and I . . .' she paused '. . . we decided it was safest to stick to Mom's story. And then I was arrested and realised that nobody would believe us in any case. So we kept our mouths shut until we had the chance to meet with you together. And then . . . then I guess we left out some of the details, so that we could point the finger at my father, exactly where it belonged.'

David could think of nothing more to say.

'Please, David,' Chelsea began, her eyes searching his for some indication as to what he was going to do. 'I know we should have told you, but in the end we had nothing to cling to but the legacy our mother had given us. She wanted us to have the life she could not – and while we did not know her before she met our father, we always had the feeling she wanted us to live as she once lived, before the walls closed in around her.'

David was not sure what to say, and even if he wanted to, he had no time to respond, as a knock on the conference room door made them all jump, and Amanda Carmichael walked slowly into the room.

'I'm sorry,' she said, realising the children had been crying. 'I've interrupted.' And then, perhaps noticing the red in David's own eyes she continued: 'Is something wrong? I mean, if there is any other way I can help – if there is something else you want to run by me, I might be able to . . .'

David turned back to the children, their eyes now set on his. And in that moment he realised that the lies, the deception . . . they were the only tools these children had to bring their father to justice. They had stuck to their original premise to protect their mother's memory – and no matter what, David knew, he had no right to take that away from them.

'There's nothing, thanks, Amanda,' he said, scooping the New England Organ Bank report off the table. 'The kids are just glad this is over.'

An unsure Carmichael, her brow slightly furrowed, finally relaxed her face and nodded, as she stood aside for two other people to enter the room.

Nora Kelly entered first, her left cheek bandaged, but her bright smile wide.

'Hello, children,' she said, before nodding at David and returning her smile to the kids. 'I want you to both thank Miss Carmichael for making this possible.'

But their blank stares obviously told her that they weren't quite sure what she was referring to.

'Oh dear, I am sorry,' she said. 'I am not explaining myself very well. It's just that Miss Carmichael here arranged for you to have another visitor today, just a short visit, mind you, until things can be made more permanent.'

Then Nora stepped aside, to take the hand of another woman standing just beyond the door.

'Children,' said Nora. 'I would like you to meet your grandmother.'

And Deirdre McCall, without the jumpsuit and handcuffs David knew she was supposed to be wearing, moved nervously into the room.

The children stood, and did not hesitate before moving forward to embrace her. And as their grandmother's arms held them close, their three heads bent as one, J.T. Logan turned his neck ever so slightly to look at David once more to mouth a simple, 'thank you'.

David nodded, knowing that there was not now, nor ever would be, anything else to say.

EPILOGUE

Very early the following morning

Risks.

That was what everything came down to. Those you face and those you shun, those you embrace and those you avoid, those you accept and those you reject. And in the end, David figured, the number of risks you took was what made the difference between living and just existing, between walking the fence and bravely taking the plunge.

He was doing that now – taking another plunge. But this was not like the other gambles he had wagered. This risk – this huge, almighty venture that he and Sara were undertaking was, he knew, perhaps the greatest they would ever tackle in their whole, entire lives.

'Okay, Sara,' said Doctor Taylor. 'You can push now, the baby is almost here, in fact, as far as I can tell, it has its father's hair.'

'It's fair?' asked David.

'Yes,' said the doctor. 'But I was actually referring to its dishevelled style,' she added.

David squeezed a now exhausted Sara's hand and smiled.

'Oh, God,' she said, as she used every last ounce of energy to finally give birth to their child. And seconds later they heard its first cry and David watched in wonder as his child was lifted up and over so that it could be placed in its mother's arms. It was so small and vulnerable, but at the same time so loud and strong, and he almost felt humbled just to be in its presence, something so pure, so unaffected, so real.

'Please, Doctor,' said Sara through her own tears of joy, 'I want David to take the baby first. I want him to be the one to give it to me, so that it knows we are in this together.'

David took the tiny life in his own two hands – *his* child, *his* future, the greatest thing he had ever created, before moving to the woman he loved more than anything, and kissing her gently on the cheek.

'You haven't told me,' she said, as she reached out her arms.

'Told you what?' he asked.

And she could not help but smile.

'Oh God, I'm sorry,' he said, as he looked at his child once again. 'It's a girl,' he added, as if it was the most important piece of information he would ever impart. 'We have a daughter, and she is perfect and . . . Sara – it's a girl.'